"The M[...]
and "The Whisker
of Hercules"

TWO CLASSIC ADVENTURES OF

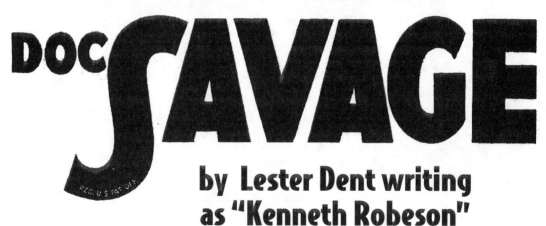

DOC **SAVAGE**

REG. U.S. PAT. OFF.

by Lester Dent writing
as "Kenneth Robeson"

Foreword by Gerry Conway

with new historical essays by Will Murray

Published by Sanctum Productions for
NOSTALGIA VENTURES, INC.
P.O. Box 231183; Encinitas, CA 92023-1183

This Nostalgia Ventures edition is an unabridged republication of the text and illustrations of two stories from *Doc Savage Magazine,* as originally published by Street & Smith Publications, Inc., N.Y.: *The Monsters* from the April 1934 issue, and *The Whisker of Hercules* from the April 1944 issue. This is a work of its time. Consequently, the text is reprinted intact in its original historical form, including occasional out-of-date ethnic and cultural stereotyping. Typographical errors have been tacitly corrected in this edition.

ISBN: 1-934943-06-1   13 Digit: 978-1-934943-06-9

First printing: June 2008

Series editor: Anthony Tollin
P.O. Box 761474
San Antonio, TX 78245-1474
sanctumotr@earthlink.net

Consulting editor: Will Murray

Copy editor: Joseph Wrzos

Proofreader: Carl Gafford

Cover restoration: Michael Piper

The editor gratefully acknowledge the contributions of Howard Wright, Jack Juka, Tom Stephens, John Gunnison and the Lester Dent Estate in the preparation of this volume, and William T. Stolz of the Western Historical Manuscript Collection of the University of Missouri at Columbia for research assistance with the Lester Dent Collection. *The Whisker of Hercules* restorations by Will Murray.

Nostalgia Ventures, Inc.
P.O. Box 231183; Encinitas, CA 92023-1183

Visit Doc Savage at www.nostalgiatown.com and www.shadowsanctum.com.

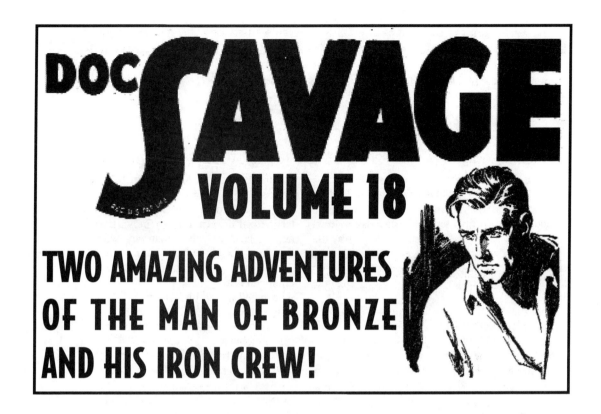

DOC SAVAGE
VOLUME 18
TWO AMAZING ADVENTURES OF THE MAN OF BRONZE AND HIS IRON CREW!

Thrilling Tales and Features

Cover painting by Walter Baumhofer

Back cover art by Emery Clarke, Walter Baumhofer and Modest Stein

THE NAME IS SAVAGE... DOC SAVAGE
by Gerry Conway

In 1964, I was twelve years old, and my favorite hero in the world was James Bond.

Wait, you say, I thought this was an introduction to a pair of Doc Savage novels. How'd James Bond get into it?

Allow me to explain.

By 1964, I'd been reading comic books for five or six years. I was a fan of Superman, Batman, the Justice League of America, The Flash, Green Lantern, and lately, the Fantastic Four. But by the time I was twelve years old, of course, I knew they weren't real, and that there was no chance on God's earth that I could ever have adventures like they did.

That didn't stop me from trying. When I was eight or nine years old, I suggested to my Dad that we dress up like Batman and Robin and fight crime; after all, we had a car that kinda looked like the Batmobile if you squinted real hard, and my Mom was pretty good with a sewing machine, and my Dad was really smart and strong. We could do it. All we needed was the outfits. My Dad, bless his heart, said he'd think about it. My Mom said she'd get started on the costumes just as soon as she found the time. I made plans for our crime-fighting career, but other things came up, and after a while, got enthused about something else. Building a spaceship on our apartment house roof, I think. Wonder whatever happened to that idea?

Anyway. By the time 1964 rolled around, I knew there wasn't much hope I'd ever be a superhero — but a *secret agent,* fighting spies like 007, now *there* was a dream with some real career possibilities. Like a lot of other boys (and girls too, I imagine), I jumped aboard the James Bond bandwagon. I bought James Bond toy guns, I bought a James Bond super-secret spy attaché case, I bought James Bond bubble gum cards, I went to James Bond movies, and I bought a James Bond record album containing themes from James Bond movies. I was all about the James Bond, all the time.

(Trust me, this *does* tie in with Doc Savage. Just give it time.)

*Any*way. By the fall of 1964, I was so immersed in James Bond, I'd burned my way through every tie-in product there was, till the only thing left for me to try was the original Ian Fleming novels.

And that's where I got stuck.

For a twelve-year-old, those Fleming novels were tough going. I mean, James Bond was in them, all right; so were Dr. No and Goldfinger; but there was also all this yucky talk about stuff like sex, and boring talk about stuff about food and drinking, and long, detailed, yawning descriptions

about places and people I just didn't care about, and the writing was so British and hard to follow, and there wasn't a cool car, and there was no giant laser, and, and, and...

The books were just... disappointing.

But that didn't stop me from going back to the drugstore paperback rack, hoping the next book I picked up would somehow capture the magic of the hero I'd seen on the movie screen. I kept hoping he'd be there, that guy who was larger than life, that guy who could do anything, whose world was full of fantastic adventures, who was equipped with amazing super-scientific gadgets, who faced incredible villains and triumphed over impossible odds...

I kept looking on the paperback rack for that guy, that hero.

And finally, I found him.

But his name wasn't James Bond.

His name was *Doc Savage.*

(See, told you there was a Doc connection. Told you. But wait, there's more!)

The first Doc Savage novel I saw was *The Man of Bronze,* tucked in the rack between a Signet edition of *Dr. No* and some dumb science fiction novel by a guy named Philip K. Dick. (Don't think my twelve-year-old mind didn't find *that* name hilarious, by the way; but I digress.) One look and I was riveted. Who was this amazing-looking guy with muscles and a torn-apart shirt? What's *he* all about? Let's see what the back of the book says...

Oh my God! Listen to this:

"To the world at large, Doc Savage is a strange, mysterious figure of glistening bronze skin and golden eyes. To his amazing co-adventurers — the five greatest brains ever assembled in one group — he is a man of superhuman strength and protean genius, whose life is dedicated to the destruction of evildoers. To his fans he is the greatest adventure hero of all time, whose fantastic exploits are unequaled for hair-raising thrills, breathtaking escapes and bloodcurdling excitement."

Oh my God!

And there's a picture of these five guys, Doc's amazing co-adventurers, and they look like real people! This picture on the back cover, it could be a photograph, or a picture from a movie! Are there movies about this guy? Is this Savage guy another James Bond?

No, Doc wasn't *another* James Bond...

He was *better* than James Bond.

I bought that book, brought it home, and started reading. And because I was still a James Bond fan, I played my album of James Bond movie themes, like I did when I tried reading the Fleming novels. (It helped put me in the mood, and made it easier to imagine the Bond in the books was the Bond from the movies, even though he wasn't, really.)

I read that entire first book, the entire *Man of Bronze,* in one long sitting, an entire Saturday, and I played my James Bond movie theme album over and over while I read, and when I was finished with that one, I ran out and bought the next, *The Thousand-Headed Man,* and read that, playing the James Bond themes over and over, and after that, I got the next book, *Meteor Menace,* and I read that one too, with the James Bond theme playing in the background, the music from *Goldfinger* and *From Russia With Love* and *Dr. No* gradually merging with images of Doc and Renny and Monk and Ham and Long Tom and Johnny and the lost land of Hidalgo and the red-fingered Mayans and the Thousand-Headed Man.

James Bama's 1965 cover for *The Monsters*

To this day, I can't hear the James Bond theme without picturing Doc and his five aides in a big flying boat on their way to South America.

Overnight, I went from James Bond fan to a fan of Doc Savage, and once you're a Doc fan, you're a fan for life.

Waiting six months for the next three Bantam Docs to come out was agony. I passed the time drawing a comic book version of *The Thousand-Headed Man.* (I was beginning to shift my interest in comics from reading and collecting them, to writing and drawing them. I'd already tried my hand recreating some of my favorite *Fantastic Four* stories. Trying to adapt a Doc novel was my first real attempt at creating a comic that wasn't a direct copy of some comic I'd already read.) I reread the first three books. I asked my Dad to take me to Manhattan so I could check out the 86th floor of the Empire State Building. (He said he'd think about it.) And I waited, and waited...

And then, there they were: *The Polar Treasure, The Lost Oasis,* and oh God, yes, it's too good to be true—*Brand of the Werewolf.*

I didn't just read those books. I *consumed* them. (Especially *Brand.* I mean, come on, *werewolves!* In a book! Oh my God!) And I waited, waited—

only two months this time, and then here it was, the Doc Savage story that fulfilled all my longing for adventures fantastic and inexplicable, for a villain with super-science on his side, for gadgets and an heroic battle between good and evil...

The Monsters.

One of the very stories you now hold in your hand.

Magic, sheer magic. That cover—the giant hand holding Doc in a grip of iron—and the story inside, they fulfilled everything I'd ever hoped to find in a James Bond novel, and never did.

It didn't get any better than this.

(Of course, it did get better: *The Land of Terror* came out two months later. Doc and dinosaurs! Beat that, 007! But if you've been following this line of reprints, you've already read that one. If you haven't, go out and buy it. Right now. It's not really a better story, all of the Docs are equally great in my mind, but hey, it's got dinosaurs. And Doc *fighting* dinosaurs. I mean, come on, how cool is that?)

A wiser man than I am once said, "The Golden Age of Science Fiction is thirteen." By that he meant, I suppose, that your sense of wonder, your willingness to suspend disbelief and let your jaw drop with uncritical astonishment, peaks right before puberty. I was lucky to discover Doc and his crew just as I reached that magical age. A few years earlier, I wouldn't have wanted to read an adventure story without pictures and word balloons; a few years later, I might've been too "sophisticated" to appreciate Lester Dent's wild-ass storytelling without sneering at its inherent silliness. But I found Doc at just the right age, when my sense of wonder and my need for a hero who was almost real enough to believe in were at their most potent. And I never would've found him if I hadn't been a fan of James Bond.

Told you I'd tie all of it together.

Gerry Conway has written comic books (The Amazing Spider-Man: *"The Death of Gwen Stacy,"* The Punisher), *science fiction novels* (Mindship), *movies* (Conan the Destroyer, Fire and Ice), *and television (*Law & Order: Criminal Intent). *He lives in Los Angeles with his wife and daughter.*

Never before had Doc Savage and his men fought against such overwhelming odds as they did against

THE MONSTERS

By KENNETH ROBESON

A Complete Book-length Novel

Chapter I
THE PINHEADS

ON the fifteenth of the month, Bruno Hen did the thing which was actually his first step toward disaster—a disaster that was to affect not only himself, but many others as well.

Bruno Hen sold his furs on this date.

Most of the pelts were muskrats, cunningly stolen from the trap lines of Bruno Hen's neighbors, the chief loser being big, honest, slow-witted Carl MacBride. The thefts were slyly executed, for Bruno Hen was as foxy a half-breed as the North Michigan woods held.

Ox-like Carl MacBride never suspected.

Not that Carl MacBride liked Bruno Hen. One

day big MacBride had come upon Bruno Hen killing a chicken for dinner. The breed had been choking the chicken to death and taking great glee in prolonging the fowl's death agonies. After that, Carl MacBride held a suspicion that no more cruel a breed than Bruno Hen ranged North Michigan.

The fur market was strong the day Bruno Hen sold. His pelts brought more than he had expected. So he decided to celebrate.

This decision was his second step toward disaster.

The Atlas Congress of Wonders was showing at Trapper Lake that day. The Atlas did not amount to much as a circus, being financially very much down at the heel. But it was the best Trapper Lake offered. So, by way of celebrating, Bruno Hen went to the circus.

That was his third step in the direction of disaster. The fourth pace, taken all unknowingly, was when he stopped in front of the freak side show.

"Ladies and gentlemen!" bawled the side show barker. "We have here a stupendous, marvelous, awesome, dumbfounding sight! We have here the three most amazing beings ever to come from darkest Africa! Look them over, good people. Try to make yourselves realize that these monstrosities are actually human. They are called the pinhead men. They are cannibal savages from darkest Africa!"

The Atlas Congress of Wonders was not above faking an occasional wild man or a cannibal, but it chanced that these pinheads were the genuine articles. They had been brought from Africa by a more affluent circus, which had then gone bankrupt.

Bruno Hen moved close to the platform to stare at the three pinheads. He had never seen such hideous humans.

The pinheads were squat, the tallest reaching barely to Bruno Hen's topmost vest button. They were nearly as broad as tall, and they were as black as human skin could practically be. They might have been oversize monkeys, shaven bare of hair, dyed black, and given a high polish.

The contour of their heads was especially haunting. Instead of being rounded in the fashion considered normal, the skulls sloped upward to a sharp point. The pin-pointed heads were also very small in proportion to the rest of their gnarled black bodies.

The pinheads had a trait of casting darting, animallike looks about them. At times they jumped up and down, after the fashion of chimpanzees. They emitted caterwauling noises—apparently their way of conversing with each other.

Trapper Lake citizens, looking on, probably thought this behavior was part of the circus act. They were mistaken.

The poor pinheads were beings almost devoid of mentality.

BRUNO HEN looked at the pinheads and grinned from ear to ear. The idea of human beings so handicapped by nature tickled him. He laughed out loud. That laugh was his fifth step toward disaster.

The pinheads stared at Bruno Hen, their attention drawn by the laugh. Bruno Hen's smile was derisive, but the pinheads did not have the intelligence to realize that. They thought the grin friendly. They smiled back, jumped up and down, and beat their chests with nubbins of fists. Back in the African bush, that was the way one showed heart-to-heart friendship.

Bruno Hen thundered another laugh. It was the same kind of a laugh Carl MacBride had heard when he had come upon the breed slowly throttling a chicken to satisfy a lust for cruelty.

The utter cruelty of that loud laugh caused the barker to end his spiel abruptly and stare at Bruno Hen. The barker ran his eyes up and down the breed's person.

In Bruno Hen he saw a bulky lout constructed on the lines of a brown bologna. Bruno Hen's clothing was frayed, greasy. It never had fitted properly. He wore high deerskin moccasins, obviously made by himself. He wore a dazzling-green hat and a blinding-yellow necktie, both new.

The barker was a pleasant-natured soul. He did not like Bruno Hen's laugh; it sent wintry chills along his spine. He decided to bullyrag Bruno Hen to persuade him to move on.

The barker sprang to one of the three pinheads, and made an elaborate pretense of listening to the unintelligible cackle the fellow was making.

"Crowd right up, folks!" he yelled. "An amazing thing has happened! These pinhead cannibals from darkest Africa claim they have just recognized a member of their tribe who was lost years ago!"

The barker leveled an arm at Bruno Hen. "The pinheads claim this man as their brother tribesman."

The crowd roared its laughter.

The pinheads hopped about, clucked and gobbled. They were just happy. But it looked as if they were agreeing with the barker. Actually, they couldn't understand a word he said.

Bruno Hen glowered. His fists made big knobs at his side.

A grinning pinhead leveled an arm at the breed and spouted gibberish.

The barker yelled, "The gentleman from Africa declares that anyone can tell this man is his brother by looking at that green hat and yellow necktie."

At this point, to the barker's relief, Bruno Hen stamped off. He yanked his green hat over his eyes and loosened his yellow necktie, as if it were too tight.

Bruno Hen's swarthy neck was purple and he was muttering under his breath. It was a tribute to his stupidity that he thought the pinheads had said what the barker declared they had. Accordingly, he was very angry with the pinheads.

Farther down the midway was the strong-man show. A fellow with remarkable muscles stood on the platform.

"We have one of the strongest men in the world!" the barker was claiming raucously. "Only ten cents, a dime, a tenth part of a dollar, to see him perform. I might even say this man is the strongest in the world. The only other man who might be his equal is Doc Savage. But, unfortunately, this Herculean gentleman and Doc Savage have never matched strength. We do not know who is actually the stronger."

Bruno Hen scowled blackly.

"You may never see Doc Savage, folks!" yelled the barker, "So step in and see one of the strongest men in the world!"

Bruno Hen tried to remember who Doc Savage was. He seemed to have heard the name before.

Soon the breed came to a show featuring a mental marvel, a fellow who claimed to be able to answer any question asked of him without consulting a reference book. The mental marvel was supposed to know all things—or so the barker was saying.

"The only living man who may possibly be a greater mental marvel than this individual, is Doc Savage!" extolled the barker.

Bruno Hen scratched his head, trying to remember.

"Doc Savage you may never meet, my good people," the barker howled. "So pay a dime and see the mental marvel who is almost his equal!"

Abruptly, Bruno Hen remembered who Doc Savage was. He was an almost legendary figure, a man of mystery, who was reputed to be a superman in strength and mental ability. Doc Savage resided in New York. He traveled to the ends of the earth, punishing wrongdoers and helping others out of trouble.

In Trapper Lake stores, Bruno Hen had heard traveling salesmen tell of Doc Savage's fabulous feats.

Little dreaming that Doc Savage—to whom amazing feats were commonplace events—was to play an important part in the future of Trapper Lake, Bruno Hen walked on. He did not give a hoot about the future of Trapper Lake, anyway.

WANDERING over the circus grounds, Bruno Hen soon found himself back among the tents and wagons which the performers used for living quarters.

He came to a stop; his porcine eyes glittered. He put a wide, fatuous grin on his face.

Coming toward him was a young woman with the most striking hair Bruno Hen could recall having seen—hair the exact shade of steel. The young woman had it drawn like a tight steel skullcap, with steellike knobs over her ears.

She wore boots, laced breeches, and a brilliant red jacket. The garments set off a shapely figure to great advantage. A shiny metal revolver was belted about her waist.

Bruno Hen was nothing if not bold. He prepared to accost the young woman.

The girl evidently knew the ways of such louts. She veered off and avoided him.

Not daunted, Bruno Hen followed her. He stopped, however, when he saw the young woman pick up a chair and calmly climb into a cage with several ferocious-looking maned beasts. These greeted her with ugly roars.

The steel-haired girl was a lion tamer.

Standing back, marveling that the lions did not devour her instantly, Bruno Hen watched the cage as it was hauled into the Big Top.

Inside the Big Top, the ringmaster was bellowing, "And now we are going to present that extravagant, unparalleled exhibition of human nerve—" He paused to get the proper drama. "Jean Morris, and her troop of bloodthirsty, untamed lions!"

Bruno Hen loitered about in hopes of getting another glimpse of the young woman with the amazing steel hair. But she did not appear. He concluded she must have left by another exit.

He got to thinking of the pinheads again, and his rage arose. He stalked off the circus grounds, bought some groceries in Trapper Lake and betook himself home.

Bruno Hen had no idea that he had laid almost the full foundation for future disaster.

BRUNO HEN'S cabin was located not far from the shore of Lake Superior. The structure was a patchwork of logs, cheap slab lumber and tar paper. It had one room. An open fireplace served for both warmth and cooking. There was a window, and plenty of cracks for ventilation.

Except for big, slow-witted Carl MacBride, who lived half a mile down the lake shore, there were no near neighbors, There was no telephone, and Bruno Hen took no newspaper.

Hence, when the Atlas Congress of Wonders went bankrupt in Trapper Lake after counting the proceeds of its last performance, Bruno Hen did not learn of the fact immediately.

The day following his experience at the circus, he expertly robbed a gill net set by Carl MacBride. He took only such fish as he wished to eat; but instead of leaving the others in the net, he removed them and tossed them aside. He was not doing the fish a kindness, for he knocked each finny specimen in the head before discarding it. There was a peculiar twist to Bruno Hen's brain which made him delight in cruelty.

The pretty circus lion tamer haunted his thoughts somewhat. Memory of her steel-hued hair especially stuck with him.

The next few days Bruno spent in overhauling his canoe, replacing a staved rib or two, and applying a coat of varnish. The fishing season was near. With the coming of summer, he usually traveled south to a district more inhabited, where he offered his services as a guide.

It was a week to the day after his visit to the circus when Bruno Hen took his next step toward disaster.

He was getting a late supper when he heard a noise. He was frying fish. Over the sputter of grease, he thought he heard a low moan.

With a quick gesture, he put out the light. Being of an evil nature himself, Bruno always expected the worst from others. His eyes became accustomed to the murk. Although there was no moon, the sky was cloudless and the stars furnished fitful luminance.

The breed eyed the window. The pane needed washing, but he could discern an object outside. His hair all but stood on end.

One frenzied leap took Bruno Hen across the cabin to his rifle. He snatched it down, then dashed outside.

The thing at the window had been a hideous apparition, yet vaguely familiar. A cold dew stood on the breed's skin as he squinted into the night.

"Hell!" he swore.

The odious specter at the window had been one of the pinhead cannibals.

ALL three of the grotesque little black fellows huddled near the window. They trembled after the manner of frightened animals.

Bruno Hen, seeing that they were very scared of him, felt more bold.

"What d'you want?" he demanded.

The answer was a hooting, clucking conglomeration of sounds. Bruno Hen could understand no word of it. He could not tell that the unfortunate pinheads, stranded when the circus went broke, were slowly starving. Unable to speak English, and lacking the intelligence to convey their needs by making signs, the pinheads were in a predicament.

Bruno Hen scowled at them, thinking of the mortification they had caused him at the circus.

"Get outa here!" he snarled.

The pinheads only waved their arms more vehemently and cackled louder. They were desperate for food. One kneeled, seeking to grasp Bruno Hen's knees in supplication.

Bruno Hen kicked the pinhead, sending the unfortunate fellow sprawling away.

Apparently pleased by the sound of his foot on human flesh, the breed launched another kick. He struck with his rifle barrel, with his fists.

The pinheads, weakened by lack of food, could evade only a few of the blows. Mauled and bleeding, they finally managed to drag themselves away.

"I'll do worse next time you show up!" Bruno Hen bawled after them.

The pinheads disappeared in the timber to the southward. The breed stood in the starlight until he could no longer hear sounds of their footsteps. Then, chuckling, he entered his cabin.

It was possibly ten minutes later that he heard faint but terrible human screams.

These came from the direction the pinheads had taken. They lasted only a moment, and ended with unpleasant abruptness.

"Probably two of 'em eatin' the third one," Bruno Hen snorted.

The breed did not know, but he had just taken his final step toward disaster.

Chapter II
TERROR

MONTHS passed.

Bruno Hen went southward during the fishing season. Pickings as a guide, much to his disgust, proved slender. Only two short engagements did he obtain in some ten months. Finally, there was a third job. This one promised to pay well.

Bruno Hen, however, made the mistake of trying to lift a fat wallet which his temporary employer carried in a hip pocket. Upon being discovered, he narrowly missed getting shot. To evade jail, he was forced to flee back to the timber fastnesses out of which he had come.

If stolid Carl MacBride was surprised at Bruno Hen's premature return, he said nothing about it. MacBride's fish traps had yielded a more abundant catch during the past weeks, but he had failed to attach the true significance to this.

If Carl MacBride was not surprised at Bruno Hen's early return, he *was* surprised when the breed paid him a visit a few nights later.

Something was wrong. MacBride could see that as he admitted the breed to his cabin. Bruno Hen's eyes rolled. He perspired freely, although the night was cool.

There was a noticeable bulge in one of his coat pockets.

"Did you hear anything a few minutes ago?" the breed asked bluntly.

Carl MacBride shook his head. He never used a word where a gesture would do. He had heard only the usual night sounds—insects and nocturnal birds.

Bruno Hen's next question was more surprising. "What happens when a man goes crazy?"

MacBride did not laugh. "Search me. He has funny ideas, I guess."

"He sees things, huh?"

"I reckon."

The visitor wiped his forehead with his palm, then swabbed the palm on his corduroy pants. Abruptly, he thrust a hand in his bulging coat pocket.

He brought out an enormous roll of greenbacks. "You're the only honest man I know, MacBride," he said. "Want you to do me a favor."

Carl MacBride was a great mountain of a man, reddened by many winds, and with eyes as blue as Lake Superior itself. He eyed the money placidly.

"Sure, I'll do you a favor," he rumbled. "But I ain't takin' pay for it."

Bruno Hen placed the money on a table.

"Take it," he directed. "If anything happens to me, use this kale to hire the best detective in the world."

Carl MacBride batted his lake-blue eyes.

"I want the detective to investigate whatever happens to me," Bruno Hen went on. "I want the best damn detective there is anywhere! Plenty of money here to pay his bill."

MacBride eyed the currency. There were many thousands of dollars in the bank roll. He knew it must be Bruno Hen's life savings.

"What's got into you?" MacBride rumbled. "This whole talk don't make sense."

Bruno Hen swallowed uneasily, squirming. A flush darkened his swarthy skin. He seemed on the point of answering.

"Maybe it don't amount to nothin', after all," he mumbled. "But if somethin' happens to me— hire the detective."

"I'll do that," MacBride agreed.

Bruno Hen took his departure, ignoring the slow questions which Carl MacBride asked. The breed carried a flashlight, and kept this blazing steadily as he made his way through the timber. He washed the beam about continuously, seeming to be in deathly fear of some habitant of the darkness.

From the door of his cabin, big Carl MacBride watched the retreating breed. He shook his ponderous head slowly.

"Somethin' is sure wrong with that guy," he grunted. He fingered the roll of money thoughtfully. "Bruno Hen kinda acts like he'd seen the devil."

With that last statement, Carl MacBride came far nearer the truth than he dreamed.

HAVING reached his shack, Bruno Hen locked himself in. He tore up parts of the floor and spiked the rough plank across the windows. Loading his rifle, he placed it on the table alongside a fresh box of cartridges. He charged both barrels of his shotgun, and arranged a little mound of shells. Loading his revolver, he belted it on.

He did not sleep at all that night; he scarcely sat down. Around and around the hut he paced nervously, stopping frequently to peer outside through the cracks.

There was a brilliant moon. In the surrounding timber there were no stirrings except for the undulating of tree boughs before a gentle breeze. Out of the far distance came sometimes the squawling uproar of fighting lynxes; a lonely wolf howled mournfully. The odor of pine came with the breeze.

This peace of the woodland night seemed to soothe Bruno Hen not at all.

Strangely, the breed did not leave his cabin at all the following day. Literally hundreds of times, he peered outside as if in deadly expectation. It was apparent that he had seen something—probably on the night before he visited Carl MacBride— which had frightened him. The more he thought of what he had seen, the more terrified he seemed to become.

Toward noon, he slept a little. He did not sleep that night. The following day, Carl MacBride came over.

"Wondered how you was comin'," MacBride said.

Bruno Hen peered out at his neighbor through his barred window. He did not invite MacBride in. In fact, he said nothing.

MacBride, big and slow moving, ambled around the shack. He noted that the place had been turned into a fortress.

"Afraid of somebody?" he asked.

The breed scowled. "You git! Tend to your own business."

Not taken back, MacBride grinned pleasantly. "I've got your money, if you want it back."

"Keep that money. If somethin' happens to me, you hire the best detective in the world, like I told you."

"I been readin' in a magazine about a feller that makes a business of helpin' other people out of trouble," MacBride offered. "Maybe he'd do."

"What's his name?"

"Doc Savage."

Bruno Hen recalled the flattering references which he had heard the circus side show barkers make to Doc Savage. A muscular Hercules and a mental marvel, they had termed Doc Savage.

"He'll do," growled the breed.

"O.K.," said MacBride. "But listen, Bruno, what's ailin' you?"

"Nothin'," snarled the breed. "You go 'way."

"You must be nuts," opined Carl MacBride, and took his departure.

By way of paying the good-natured giant back for that last crack, Bruno Hen left his cabin during the afternoon and raided one of MacBride's fish traps. He selected several choice walleyes, and turned the rest of the catch loose. The breed was thoughtful as he slunk back toward his cabin.

"I ought to have told MacBride about what I seen prowlin' around here the other night," he said slowly. "Hell! He would think I was crazy."

Reaching his shack, he fastened himself in securely. Exercise seemed to have lulled his fears somewhat.

He lay down and slept.

THE night was well along when Bruno Hen opened his eyes. He lay in a sort of drawn rigidity, listening to what had aroused him.

It was a strange wind, which seemed to be blowing outside. This came in puffs, regularly spaced.

The breed shivered from head to foot. The gusty sounds were too peculiar to be made by a natural wind.

Using extreme care to make no noise, Bruno got up. He gripped his rifle in one hand, his shotgun in the other. He crept to one of the timbered windows and crammed an eye to the crack.

What he saw caused him to shriek out in awful horror.

Jumping back, he lifted his rifle. It was high-powered, intended for bagging moose. He fired. The slug slapped through the planks as if they had been paper. Again the breed fired. He pumped jacketed lead through the wall until the magazine was empty.

Plugging in fresh cartridges, he continued his wild firing.

"It's worse'n it was before," he moaned, referring to the horror outside.

Over the whacking of the rifle and the breed's moaning there sounded a tremendous rending and tearing. The breed stared upward in ghastly terror.

Parts of the roof of his shack were being torn off. Stout boards split apart or snapped off. Rafters buckled under some cataclysmic force.

Still firing madly, Bruno retreated to the other side of the cabin.

With a final squawling of withdrawn nails, and a cracking of wood, a section of the roof came off. Something extended through the aperture.

The breed emitted one squawling shriek after another. He dashed from end to end of the cabin. He was like a trapped rabbit.

The breed's neighbor, Carl MacBride, unlike many big men, was a light sleeper. He heard the yelling and shooting coming from Bruno Hen's cabin. Leaping up, he yanked on his pacs, grasped a rifle and ran for the uproar.

Long before he reached the breed's cabin, MacBride heard Bruno Hen's shrieking die. Its termination was a piercing, bleating sound, remindful of a mouse which had been stepped upon.

Arriving at the shack, MacBride found an amazing sight. The structure itself was little more than a great shapeless wad of timber and planks.

Striking matches for light, he circled the spot. His gaze lighted upon a timber as thick as his leg, and he whistled softly in amazement; for some-thing snapped off that timber as if it were a match stick.

MacBride stood still, straining his ears. There was an occasional creak from the settling ruin of the cabin. From out on the lake he thought he heard faint splashing. This was very distant.

No other sound came. The bedlam at the cabin had been so awesome that the night birds, animals, and insects had been frightened into complete silence.

MacBride now dug into the cabin wreckage. He found a gory wad of a thing. He had to examine it for some seconds before he would believe it was the earthly remains of Bruno Hen.

Bruno Hen had been crushed to death in ghastly fashion!

Carl MacBride made a slow circle of the cabin and the vicinity, searching. Then he headed for his own cabin, running.

"This is a job for that Doc Savage!" he muttered.

Chapter III
PLANE ACQUAINTANCE

MODERN passenger planes are remarkably efficient creations. Not only are they capable of great speed, but the cabins are soundproofed until it is possible to conduct a conversation in ordinary tones. Pretty hostesses serve coffee and sandwiches.

Big Carl MacBride occupied a seat in one of these passenger ships, as it rushed toward New York. He tried to look nonchalant. He balanced a cup of coffee clumsily on one calloused palm and held a tiny sandwich between thumb and forefinger of his other hand. Between nibbles and sips, he eyed the surrounding clouds.

This was his first time in the air. From impressions gained in a life spent on the ground, he had supposed clouds were fairly solid things; but he was discovering they were really of a very wispy nature, with hardly more body than widely diffused cigarette smoke.

A fellow traveler interrupted the bulky woodsman's thoughts.

"I see you like to read back issues of magazines," the fellow remarked.

Carl MacBride turned his head. He saw a tall man with a freckled nose, reddish hair and a reddish mustache. The latter was an artistically waxed creation. The man was attired in a quiet business suit, and looked prosperous.

The fellow had been perusing a newspaper. This was folded carelessly, and an advertisement was uppermost. It was a strange sort of an ad. It consisted simply of large black type in the center of a white space:

BEWARE!
THE MONSTERS ARE COMING!

This somewhat unusual advertisement was not in line with Carl MacBride's gaze, however. He failed to see it.

The big woodsman had always associated freckles with friendly individuals. He smiled, and said: "Sure—if the magazine ain't too old, I enjoy it just as much as a late one."

"I notice you were reading about Doc Savage," said the freckled man.

"Yep."

"My name is Caldwell," the fellow traveler introduced himself. "Quite an interesting chap, this Doc Savage."

"Do you know him?" Carl MacBride asked eagerly.

"Oh, no, although I'd rather like to. I've read of his accomplishments. I guess almost everyone has heard of him."

"Yep. He's quite a detective, I reckon."

"Detective!" laughed Caldwell. "Doc Savage is not a detective."

Carl MacBride's jaw fell. He was shocked. The article in the magazine was all he knew of Doc Savage. He had judged Doc Savage to be a detective, for the story was one telling how Doc and a group of five assistants had ferreted out a gang of villains seeking to seize the nitrate industry of the South American country of Chile.

Believing Doc Savage to be a detective, MacBride was now on his way to ask him to investigate the death of Bruno Hen.

"Not a detective!" he gulped.

"Not exactly," smiled Caldwell. "He is more in the nature of what you would call a trouble-buster. He goes to the far corners of the earth, metes out justice to evildoers, and helps those in trouble."

Carl MacBride breathed a little bit easier. Doc Savage might be interested in Bruno Hen's death, after all.

"What do you know about Doc Savage?" MacBride asked. "This magazine story didn't tell very much."

"No one seems to know a great deal about Doc Savage," replied Caldwell. "It is general knowledge, however, that he is a man who has been trained from the cradle for his present purpose in life. The training was done scientifically by his father, who is now dead. As a result, Doc Savage is almost a superman, both in physical capabilities and in mentality."

"How do you mean—physical capabilities and mentality?" Carl MacBride asked vaguely, befuddled by the—to him—high-sounding phraseology.

"They say that Doc Savage has developed his muscles until he is the strongest man ever to live," Caldwell explained. "He has also studied intensively in every branch of science. He has become a mental marvel. In other words, he knows about everything."

The plane dipped sharply.

Caldwell looked over the side. "We're nearing New York City."

CARL MACBRIDE showed little interest in New York City, although he had never seen that impressive metropolis before.

"What else do you know about Doc Savage?" he asked eagerly.

"Well, not much more," Caldwell rejoined amiably. "Doc Savage has five men who help him. Each one of these is a world-famous expert in some line. One, according to what I've heard, is a chemist, another a lawyer, and a third is an electrical expert of ability. Of the other two, one is an engineer and the other a geologist."

"Sounds like some crew!" ejaculated the big woodsman.

Caldwell eyed Carl MacBride. "You seem rather interested in Doc Savage?"

"I am," MacBride grinned. "I'm on my way to see him."

Caldwell looked properly impressed at this, his brows rising in astonishment.

"Imagine!" he ejaculated. "Say, that is the most interesting thing I've heard in a long time."

Carl MacBride expanded before the flattering tones. He wanted to talk about the strange demise of Bruno Hen, anyway. He proceeded to do so.

He told the story in detail. Drawing a newspaper from his pocket, he exhibited it.

"I cut that from the Trapper Lake *Clarion*, as you can see by the name at the top of the sheet," he explained.

Caldwell read the clipping.

"It says here that a peculiar tornado dipped down and demolished Bruno Hen's cabin, killing the breed," he remarked.

"That newspaper feller done some tall guessin'," MacBride said confidentially. "My cabin ain't very far away from the breed's place. There weren't no daggone tornado. I'd have heard it. Anyway, the sky was as clear as crystal."

Caldwell returned the clipping. "And you are going to New York to get Doc Savage to investigate?"

"That's right. Bruno Hen gave me the money to do it. It's only fair that I should live up to the promise I made him."

"Quite true," Caldwell agreed; then broke off to watch a young woman who came down the aisle from the washroom.

Carl MacBride also eyed the girl. She was a striking vision. She had hair the exact hue of steel. Her traveling costume, while neat, was somewhat worn. MacBride's contact with pretty girls had been largely from their pictured faces in magazines. This young woman was as entrancing as any photo he could recall having seen.

The girl passed the two men without a glance. Her eyes were a steel color that about matched her hair. She took a seat forward.

A battered traveling bag reposed on the floor beside the girl's seat. Carl MacBride possessed eyesight an Indian would have envied. He read the writing on the tag appended to the young woman's bag:

JEAN MORRIS
THE WORLD'S PREMIER WOMAN
LION TAMER
THE ATLAS CONGRESS
OF WONDERS

"Atlas Congress of Wonders" had a line drawn through it. Immediately below the circus name was written: "New York City."

Carl MacBride scratched his head. He remembered that the Atlas Congress of Wonders was the circus which had gone broke in Trapper Lake many months before.

MacBride recalled one particular morsel of gossip. There had been three pinhead savages with the stranded circus. These had wandered off and mysteriously disappeared.

"There's the New York airport," said Caldwell, interrupting the woodsman's thoughts.

IN the excitement of disembarking, Carl MacBride lost track of his friendly traveling acquaintance, Caldwell.

Had he been able to watch Caldwell, he would have received a surprise. Caldwell scuttled around to the deserted side of the field operations office. Hidden there, he opened a large bag which was his only luggage.

He unearthed two large, blue automatics, and slung them in holsters under his armpits. Next came a hand grenade of the small, fluted type used in the world war. He pocketed this.

The bag yielded a banjo. The round body and the neckpiece of the musical instrument were in separate sections which clamped together. The banjo actually held an ingenious, silenced gun, which could be fired simply by plucking one of the banjo strings.

One who knew how could aim this unusual weapon with accuracy, without seeming to do so.

Working rapidly, Caldwell combed out his waxed mustache. He applied a chemical to it and smeared more of the same compound in his hair. Mustache and hair turned black. He drew a ragged coat from the bag and donned it. He sagged his shoulders as he walked.

A stooped musician with a stringy black mustache and black hair got in one of several cabs waiting nearby.

New York is a city harboring many curious people. The taxi driver thought little of it when his fare querulously commanded him to wait a few minutes before starting.

Not until Carl MacBride had clambered into a cab and rolled in the direction of the business district, did Caldwell permit his machine to move. Issuing terse orders, he contrived to follow the hulking woodsman without calling his driver's attention to what he was doing.

When they had traveled twenty or thirty blocks, Caldwell became sure of their destination. It was Doc Savage's office. He ordered his conveyance to halt while he entered a telephone booth located in a tobacco shop. He got a number.

Caldwell and the party he was calling recognized each other's voices. They exchanged no names.

"Exactly what we were afraid of is happening, boss," Caldwell informed the other. "This lunk of a backwoodser is on his way to see Doc Savage."

"You sure?" asked the voice at the other end of the wire. "We don't want to go to a lot of trouble taking care of him, unless it's necessary."

"It's necessary, all right, boss," said Caldwell. "I pumped the guy while we were on the plane. He never suspected a thing. Came right out and told me the whole story."

"He told you he was on his way to get Doc Savage to investigate what happened to Bruno Hen?"

"That's exactly what he told me."

The voice at the other end swore violently. "We've got to stop him before he gets to Doc Savage."

"I've got a grenade, my gat, and that silenced pistol-in-a-banjo contraption. I'll be able to stop him at Doc Savage's office."

"Nothing as reckless as that!" ordered the other. "Can you keep MacBride in sight and nail him somewhere en route?"

"He's headed straight for New York on the main road. Guess I can overhaul him."

"Do that. Get him on the road somewhere."

Caldwell, his deadly banjo tucked under an arm, dashed to his cab.

"Whoop it up, buddy!" he ordered the driver. "If you get me downtown fast enough, there's an extra twenty in it for you."

"Get the twenty ready," retorted the driver, and they were off.

Chapter IV
THE KILLER

CARL MACBRIDE had never before visited a

city of any consequence. So he stared with great interest as they approached the cluster of towering skyscrapers. The tremendous size of the structures caused a feeling of awe.

One building in particular reared like a great thorn of gray masonry and shining metal above the spiked tops of the other cloud-piercers. Not only was it among the tallest, but its simple, modernistic lines made it far the most impressive.

Carl MacBride made a mental note that, before he left New York City, he would go to the top of the towering, modernistic structure to have a look at the town.

It had not occurred to the big woodsman that he might have difficulty in locating Doc Savage. Up in his woods country, one had merely to walk into town and inquire for an individual and someone would be able to point him out. Everyone knew everybody else.

It occurred to Carl MacBride that he had better ask where Doc Savage resided.

"How do you find anybody in this town, partner?" he asked the taxi driver.

"Look in the phone book is one way," was the reply.

"Maybe you know the feller I want to find—his name is Doc Savage."

The taxi driver turned to eye his fare, and almost ran off the pavement. He straightened his machine out, then pointed ahead to the skyscraper which Carl MacBride had admired.

"Everybody knows that guy. He hangs out on the eighty-sixth floor of that building."

The fact that the driver knew the whereabouts of Doc Savage's headquarters did not impress Carl MacBride as much as it should have. In New York, the average individual knows only his business acquaintances and immediate friends.

"You got an appointment to see Doc Savage?" asked the driver, taking advantage of the obvious amiability of his fare to ask questions.

"No. Do I need one?"

It had not occurred to the lumbering woodsman that an appointment might be necessary. In the backwoods, a business appointment was a rarity. There was time for everything.

"I don't know Doc Savage personally," the taxi driver said. "I've seen him a time or two. He's a big shot, so you'd better get an appointment."

"How'll I go about doing that?"

"Phone him."

"Stop off somewhere," Carl MacBride commanded. "Guess I'll call him."

The cab pulled up in a filling station which displayed a public telephone booth sign.

A NEWSBOY loitering at the filling station in hopes of making a sale, ran out.

"Read the latest mystery advertisement about the coming of the monsters!" he shouted.

Curious, Carl MacBride bought a paper. The "mystery" ad was in black type in a square, white space. It read:

WARNING!
WATCH OUT FOR THE MONSTERS!

"What's this mean?" the woodsman asked.

"Nobody knows," replied the newsboy. "Newspapers all over the country been gettin' them advertisements in the mail, along with money to pay for their insertion. It may be a movie stunt—to get people talkin' about some picture that'll come out soon."

Carl MacBride frowned and tucked the paper in a pocket. He entered the booth and thumbed through the directory until he found Doc Savage's name.

The telephone was a dial type. He was unfamiliar with the dial device, and had some trouble with it. Eventually, however, he got his number.

The voice which came to his ears was one so profoundly impressive that he knew instinctively that the speaker must be Doc Savage. The tones were deep, vibrant with controlled power. MacBride had never before heard a telephone receiver reproduce with such distinctness.

"I want an appointment with you, Mr. Savage," said the woodsman. "It's something mighty important. My name is MacBride."

"You do not need an appointment," Doc informed him. "Feel perfectly free to see me at any time."

MacBride reflected that the driver had given him some bum advice.

"I'll be right up," he said.

"Is your business something you would care to discuss over the telephone?" Doc Savage asked.

MacBride was so impressed by the remarkable voice that he did not answer for a moment.

"I'd rather tell you in person," he said finally.

"Very well."

The telephone conversation terminated.

MacBride went to his cab. The machine moved toward the towering skyscraper which was Doc Savage's headquarters.

Big Carl MacBride did not know it, but this chance pause to telephone was instrumental in prolonging his life. Caldwell had passed without observing the big woodsman in the filling station phone booth. Even now, the murderous Caldwell was hugging his death-dealing banjo, and cursing.

"I've lost the big lunk somewhere," he gritted. "Well, hell! I'll have to catch him at Doc Savage's office, after all."

CARL MACBRIDE was even more impressed by the big skyscraper which housed Doc Savage's office, when he alighted before it. Head back, mouth open, MacBride peered upward. When he entered the lobby, the magnificence of the ornate place made him feel mouselike.

His amazement at sight of the great building accounted for the big man's failure to note a fellow with black hair and black mustache who carried a banjo and lurked in a corner of the lobby. MacBride lumbered into an elevator.

"Doc Savage's office," he said.

He was promptly rushed to the eighty-sixth floor. He found a door which bore, in very small bronze letters, the name:

CLARK SAVAGE, JR.

There was a button, but few persons had doorbells where Carl MacBride came from. He rapped the door with his knuckles in the good old-fashioned way.

The door opened.

The unusual voice over the telephone had partially prepared Carl MacBride for the sight of an unusual personage when he confronted Doc Savage. Even then, the bronze man was so far beyond expectations that MacBride gaped in amazement.

Doc Savage had evidently opened the door by some mechanical means. He stood, not near the panel, but some feet from it—in the middle of a great office. This was fitted with a costly inlaid table, an enormous safe, and a number of comfortable chairs.

That the bronze man possessed amazing physical strength was evident from the enormous tendons which bundled his neck and cabled his hands. He was a giant; but his proportions were symmetrical, and standing in the massively furnished office, he seemed little larger than an ordinary man.

The mighty bronze man's eyes held Carl MacBride's attention. They were strangely impressive, those eyes. They had the appearance of tiny pools of flake gold which eddied and whirled continuously.

The bronze of Doc Savage's hair was somewhat darker than the bronze of his skin. He was attired in quiet business garb.

"Doc Savage?" asked Carl MacBride, although he knew he was confronting the man he sought.

"Right," confirmed the remarkable man of bronze.

Carl MacBride took a step into the office.

An elevator door down the corridor opened. A man popped out. He had a black mustache, dark hair, and carried a banjo. He raised the banjo to the level of his eyes and gave one of the strings a forcible pluck.

DOC

There was a *chunging* sound—it might have been a man emitting one harsh cough. A tongue of flame leaped from an almost indistinguishable round hole in the side of the banjo.

Carl MacBride opened his mouth wide, and a crimson flood came out. His knees buckled. His hands clamped to the back of his neck, where a bullet from Caldwell's deadly silenced gun had clubbed a hole.

He slammed face down upon the floor. MacBride felt no pain from the impact, for he was dead.

Chapter V
THE CLIPPING

CALDWELL, the killer, was in a position where he could view Doc Savage's office. He saw the giant bronze man, got a most unnerving look at the weird golden eyes. He realized that Doc, having witnessed the killing, was a menace.

Caldwell darted his banjo weapon in Doc Savage's direction and plucked the trigger-string. The concealed gun lipped powder flame and slugs.

Caldwell's eyes threatened to jump from their sockets.

A weird thing had happened to his bullet. It had disintegrated in a grayish lead puff in mid-air, some feet inside the door.

He fired the hidden gun until it was empty. He wrenched out his two automatics and squeezed the weapons at the office door. They convulsed thunderously, and spouted empty cartridges.

To all of the bullets the same fantastic thing happened. They splashed into innumerable fragments in mid-air or became shapeless blobs which fell back to the floor.

Caldwell spun and fled. He dived into an elevator, menaced the attendant with his gun and forced an instant descent.

As the cage sank, Caldwell heard a fragment of weird sound. The note was not loud, yet it penetrated to the descending elevator with remarkable clarity. It seemed without definite source; it might have been a product of the movement of the very air itself past the sinking cage. It was not a whistle, nor did it seem quite the emanation of vocal chords. A mellow trilling which defied description, the sound trickled up and down the musical scale.

Caldwell, unable to define the note, dismissed it as a freakish trick played by his own ears.

He was wrong. The strange, undulating note was the sound of Doc Savage. It was the small unconscious thing which the bronze man did in moments of stress—when thinking, or surprised, or contemplating some unusual procedure.

AN onlooker, knowing Doc Savage, and cognizant of the mighty bronze man's abilities, would have expected pursuit of Caldwell. At Doc Savage's disposal here on the eighty-sixth floor, was a high-speed elevator capable of dropping the bronze man to the lobby level before Caldwell could arrive.

Doc did not pursue the slayer. Instead, he moved into a room adjoining the office. The walls of this chamber were banked with book shelves. Massive cases laden with ponderous tomes stood thickly on the floor. It was Doc Savage's library, and it held one of the most complete collections of scientific works in existence.

The bronze man seemed to be moving without hurry, but his speed was surprising.

Beyond the library was another vast room. This held glittering arrays of bottled chemicals, banks of test tubes, retorts and filtering devices. Electric furnaces and costly metal-working tools occupied the floor space.

In the center of the great workshop-laboratory Doc Savage halted. He stood before a paneled cabinet. A microphone dangled in front of this. Inset in the cabinet was a square panel that resembled frosted glass.

Doc spoke into the microphone. "Did you see what just happened in the outer office?"

From a loudspeaker, the grilled throat of which was almost unnoticeable on the side of the cabinet, the reply came. It was couched in a tiny, almost babylike voice.

"We did," said the small voice. "Ham and me both saw it. And we're off."

Doc Savage reached over and flicked a switch. Upon the panel of frosted glass a picture appeared. It depicted cold concrete floors, walls, and an array of parked automobiles. There was a door in this pictured room. Two men were just diving through it, making a wild departure from the place.

Doc switched off the televisor-phone with which he had communicated with those two men. He returned to the outer office. Here also, but concealed cleverly in the walls, was another televisor-phone. This one had transmitted an image of what had occurred in the office to the two men to whom Doc had spoken.

Doc Savage and his five men were accustomed to keep each other in view with these devices whenever convenient. Thus they could witness danger which might threaten each other.

They had many enemies.

In approaching the lifeless body of Carl MacBride, Doc circled widely to avoid the agency which had caused Caldwell's bullets to mushroom so mysteriously in mid-air.

It was nothing more mysterious than an upright sheet of clear bullet-proof glass.

Due to the fact that he had many enemies, it was Doc's custom to first greet strangers from behind this unnoticeable shield.

THE giant man of bronze closed his office door to avoid the notice of passersby in the corridor. Then he examined the body of the unfortunate Carl MacBride.

The first thing Doc brought to light was that the enormous roll of bills which Bruno Hen had given the big woodsman. He riffled through the money. In the act of doing this, his nostrils quivered slightly. He lifted the bundle of currency and gave it an olfactory test.

Doc Savage had a daily exercise routine of two hours which he had taken unfailingly from childhood. The exercises were scientifically designed to develop his every sense—touch, hearing, sight, the sense of smell, and taste. His faculties were far beyond those of an ordinary man.

Doc identified the odor easily, faint though it was. The scent of musk!

Continuing his examination, he brought out a newspaper clipping—the one Carl MacBride had shown his plane acquaintance, Caldwell. After noting that it was from a Trapper Lake, Michigan, paper, Doc read it:

TRAPPER LAKE MAN
VICTIM OF WEIRD TORNADO

Bruno Hen, trapper and fisherman residing near the lake shore five miles north of Trapper Lake, met death last night in what authorities have decided was a freak cyclone. Hen was found crushed to death in his demolished cabin by Carl MacBride, a neighbor.

MacBride, it is reported, heard sounds from the direction of Bruno Hen's cabin. Rushing to the spot, he found his neighbor dead in the wreckage of his home.

MacBride reported that he saw no evidences of a tornado, and that it was a moonlight night.

The coroner and the sheriff, however, point out that a tornado is the only explanation for the demolished condition in which the cabin was found.

The tornado apparently dipped suddenly upon the exact spot where the cabin stood. After annihilating the building, the twister tore up brush and smashed down small trees over a narrow path to the lake's edge. The storm evidently progressed out over Lake Superior without doing more damage.

Bruno Hen, it will be remembered, a few months ago sold the largest collection of muskrat pelts trapped in this vicinity in a long time.

After he finished reading, Doc Savage's fantastic trilling sound came into being. So low as to be scarcely audible, it existed for three or four seconds, then ebbed away.

Bruno Hen had sold muskrat pelts. The scent on the roll of bills was musk, such as would be put there by the pawing of hands which had skinned muskrats.

Doc Savage carried the bills into the laboratory and used a fingerprinting outfit upon them. He discovered a few of Carl MacBride's prints upon the bills, but the preponderance of handling had been by another set of fingers.

Having found musk odor on bills which Carl MacBride had hardly touched, and which were thick with the other fingerprints, Doc felt there was a likelihood that the money had originally been the property of Bruno Hen.

The giant bronze man returned to his search of the body.

The dated stub of an airways ticket showed that Carl MacBride had come to New York by plane that day.

DOC brought out the newspaper which Carl MacBride had purchased in the filling station. MacBride was a laborious reader, and in perusing the strange advertisement regarding the giants, had traced the words with a fingernail. The indentations were plainly discernible:

WARNING!
WATCH OUT FOR THE MONSTERS!

Doc Savage studied this with no little interest. Then he went to the library, and came back bearing a tray. This contained newspaper clippings.

One, from a Detroit paper, read:

BEWARE!
THE MONSTERS BRING DEATH
AND DESTRUCTION!

Another, from a Chicago paper, stated:

TERROR!
THAT IS WHAT THE MONSTERS BRING!

There were numerous others, all in like vein. In no case were the advertisements signed. They came from newspapers in Cleveland, St. Louis—every city of consequence in the country.

Doc Savage sorted over these thoughtfully. His fingers, sensitive and possessed of a dazzling speed, for all their superhuman strength, turned to the clipping concerning the weird death of Bruno Hen.

The giant man of bronze made it his business to keep tab on all strange circumstances. Thus did he sometimes see danger before it struck.

He had collected these "monster" clippings because their very nature was sinister. Doc had newspaper connections. Through them he had learned that no one actually knew what was behind the "monster" advertisements. It was no motion picture press agent's build-up.

The ads simply came in the mail, with money to pay for their insertion. And in each case, the ads had been mailed from Trapper Lake, Michigan.

Chapter VI
MYSTERY MANSE

IT was more than an hour later when the telephone buzzer whined and Doc Savage picked up the instrument.

The tiny childlike voice which had spoken to him from the televisor-phone in the laboratory came over the wire.

"At the junction of Hill Road and the Hudson Turnpike, in New Jersey," said the small tones.

"Be right out," Doc replied, and hung up.

The bronze man took his private high-speed elevator to the skyscraper basement. This lift was the product of his inventive genius, and operated at hair-lifting speed.

Stepping from the elevator, Doc entered his basement garage. This was the chamber with the array of parked cars which had appeared on the scanning screen of the televisor-phone.

For his immediate purpose, Doc chose a long, somberly colored roadster. This machine, as he wheeled it up to the street, showed by its acceleration that the hood housed a powerful engine. Wending through traffic, it attracted no attention, due to its quiet hue.

Not so the bronze man. Scarcely a glance rested upon him that did not become a stare, so striking was the picture he presented.

The roadster swept over George Washington Bridge, which connects Manhattan Island with New Jersey. When traffic thinned, the machine increased speed. It traveled just within the bounds of safety.

Several times, traffic policemen sprang into startled life as the car moaned past; but they subsided upon observing the occupant. The greenest rookie knew there was an imperative order out to extend to this man of bronze every possible cooperation.

Hill Road ran east and west, and the Hudson Turnpike was a north and south thoroughfare. The two intersected in a nest of filling stations and hot-dog stands.

Doc Savage pulled into a gasoline station at the intersection and ordered fuel.

A few yards distant, a crowd of excited children surrounded a man whose appearance was nothing if not startling. He came near bearing more resemblance to an ape than to a man. His furry hands dangled on beams of arms well below his knees. He had a little nubbin of a head. His hair grew back from his eyebrows. The huge simian fellow's face was likeable, although entirely homely.

This pleasantly ugly personage was amusing the kids by calmly folding pennies between a hairy thumb and forefinger. The feat of strength he performed without great exertion.

The gorilla of a man hardly glanced in Doc's direction.

He ceased performing for the amusement of the children and entered a large sedan which stood nearby. He drove westward along Hill Road.

Doc Savage, having paid for his tank of fuel, also rolled westward along Hill Road. He topped the first hill. In the valley beyond, the gorillalike man had stopped his car.

Doc came to a halt alongside the simian one. "Where's Ham, Monk?" he queried.

Monk grinned, showing a tremendous array of large white teeth. His head seemed to disappear entirely behind the grin; certainly, there did not seem to be room for much intelligence in his head.

His looks belied the truth, however. He was Lieutenant Colonel Andrew Blodgett Mayfair, whose ability as an industrial chemist had brought him worldwide fame and a fortune in money.

MONK was one of a group of five who had associated themselves with Doc Savage. These five men were all capable of commanding high monetary returns, had they chosen to exercise the professions at which they were skilled. But they loved adventure. Possessing ample wealth, they had thrown in with Doc Savage in his career of punishing evildoers in the far corners of the earth.

Monk pointed down Hill Road. "We trailed the killer to a kind of a funny-lookin' country estate. Ham's watchin' the place. We better go on afoot."

Doc switched off the roadster motor. So silently had it operated at idling speed that cessation of movement of the ammeter needle was all that showed the cylinders had ceased firing.

The two men strode along Hill Road, leaving the cars drawn into weeds beside the highway.

"We had the televisor from your office to the basement garage turned on while we were working on a car," Monk said. "We thought you might want us or something. It was lucky we did. We saw the killing, and got a good look at the guy who did it. We caught sight of him as he left the building."

Doc nodded. "I figured you would have the televisor-phone turned on."

Monk was puzzled. He scratched his knob of a head and eyed the giant bronze man curiously. "Wonder why that guy was killed," he offered.

"To shut his mouth, obviously," Doc Savage replied. "The killer may have been a hired slayer. That's why I allowed him to escape—so you fellows could trail him to the man who hired him, if any."

Monk nodded as he waddled along. His legs were so bowed that his gait was grotesque; he seemed momentarily on the verge of taking to all fours.

"Any idea what's behind it?"

"Remember the mysterious advertisements which have been appearing in newspapers recently?" Doc queried.

"You mean that 'Beware the Monsters!' stuff?"

"That's it. Those ads were mailed to newspapers all over the country. They were postmarked, everyone of them, as being mailed from Trapper Lake, Michigan."

MONK squinted his small eyes. He had known of the "monster" advertisements, but had not been aware that they had been mailed from Trapper Lake. Doc, he realized, had unearthed this fact in the course of his usual checking on things which might be of sinister nature.

"Why'd the murdered man want to see you, Doc?"

"Possibly concerning the mysterious death of a trapper named Bruno Hen, near Trapper Lake," Doc replied. "He had a clipping concerning the Bruno Hen death in his pocket."

"What about Bruno Hen's death?"

"He perished, according to the report of the local officers, in a mysterious tornado which struck on a moonlight night, and did nothing but demolish Bruno Hen's shack and tear a path to the nearby lake."

"Queer tornado!" Monk grunted.

"A neighbor claimed there was no tornado. His name was Carl MacBride—the man who was killed at our office door."

"Huh! If not a tornado, what did he claim it was?"

"The clipping didn't say."

Monk squinted ahead. His small eyes in repose were nearly invisible so deeply were they sunk in their pits of gristle.

Hill Road at this point was seldom traveled, due probably to the fact that its macadam surface was uncomfortably roughened by the weather. Untended brush made a wall on either side.

"That shyster lawyer, Ham, should be waiting along here somewhere," Monk declared, his small voice pitched even lower than usual.

The gentleman to whom Monk referred in such undignified terms promptly stepped out of the brush. He was Brigadier General Theodore Marley Brooks, one of the most astute lawyers ever to be graduated from Harvard.

"You homely missing link!" Ham whispered irately at Monk. "One of these days I'm going to skin you and make a red fur rug!"

Ham was slender, slim-waisted, quick-moving. His clothing was absolute sartorial perfection. He was a tailor's dream.

In his right hand Ham carried a black cane. Ham was rarely seen without this.

The unlovely Monk turned an innocent look on the enraged Ham.

"Always threatenin' me!" he complained in low tones. "What's on your mind now?"

Ham shook his cane in the air and turned purple. He was not, however, making undue noise with his dramatics.

"You left that infernal pig behind and had him follow me around!"

Monk seemed grieved.

"Habeas Corpus must be takin' a fancy to you," he groaned. "I never thought that pig would stoop so low as to associate with a shyster lawyer."

At this point, Habeas Corpus walked out of the brush.

A more astounding-looking specimen of the pig family than Habeas would be difficult to find. The pig was undersized, razor-backed. He had the legs of a dog and ears so large as to resemble wings.

Habeas eyed the dapper Ham, emitted a friendly grunt and ambled toward the lawyer. Ham launched a spiteful toe at the pig. In dodging this, Habeas displayed an agility as surprising as his appearance.

Habeas was Monk's pet. The homely chemist had trained the pig until the porker seemed to possess a near-human intelligence.

Doc, low-voiced, interrupted what amounted to a perpetual quarrel. "Where's the killer, Ham?" he asked.

"He went into a funny-looking place over the hill."

Doc noted the appellation, "funny-looking." Both Monk and Ham had used it.

"What do you mean—funny-looking?"

Ham, like many orators, had a habit of making gestures when he spoke. He gestured now, although his words were whispered.

"We're in the country," he said. "There's no reason for anybody having a high wall around his place. But there's one around this joint. It's at least forty feet high."

"Forty!"

"Every inch of that." Monk entered the conversation with his small voice. "I ask you, Doc—what does anyone want with a forty-foot wall out here in the country?"

"I walked around the place," Ham said, scowling at Habeas Corpus. "There's only one entrance. That's secured by the strongest steel gate I have ever seen."

Doc Savage did not comment on the somewhat startling revelations. He went forward.

Monk and Ham trailed him. They exchanged throat-cutting looks. Actually, either of them would have sacrificed his life for the safety of the other, should necessity for such an act materialize.

The pig, flopping big ears at Monk's heels, grunted contentedly.

"Put on the muffler, Habeas," Monk directed.

Obediently, the pig fell silent.

Chapter VII
THE ELECTRIFIED NET

AS Doc and his two aides topped the hill, the mysterious wall came into view.

"Some joint, eh?" Ham suggested.

The wall was so high as to conceal whatever lay behind it. A somber barrier of gray, it was altogether forbidding.

"Concrete," Ham offered softly.

They left the road. The brush was high; it grew thickly. They eased through the leafy maze with little sound, and came to the gate in the wall—the only gap, according to Monk and Ham.

This gate was notable for its size, being fully fifteen feet wide and equally as high.

Monk breathed, "Look at the size of the bars."

Monk possessed furry wrists almost twice as thick as those of an ordinary man. The gate bars were of a diameter about equal to his wrists. The gigantic gate was supported by a multiple array of ponderous hinges. Apparently, it opened and closed through the medium of machinery.

"They wouldn't need bars a fraction of that size to hold elephants," Ham said. He ran a finger thoughtfully up and down the glistening black length of his cane.

Doc Savage listened for a time, but detected no sound. He moved along the wall, eyes ranging its towering height. When he had circled the place completely, he had proven Monk and Ham's declaration that there was only one entrance.

The wall did not enclose much of an area.

Doc Savage withdrew with his two men to a point remote from the gate of giant bars.

From within his clothing the bronze man produced a collapsible metal grapple hook. To the shank of this was secured a long silk cord. He sprung the hook open, then tossed it upward expertly. The grapple fastened itself somewhere on the opposite side of the wall.

Doc mounted the thin cord with an amazing ease and speed.

Nearing the crest, he slackened his pace. From a pocket came a tiny periscopic device. This instrument he had put to frequent use in the past. Its barrel was little larger than a match; the average eye would fail to detect its projecting above the wall. Its tiny lenses were finely ground; its functioning was almost equal to that of a larger instrument.

Doc jutted the periscope above the wall, not showing himself.

What he saw brought forth the weird trilling note which was characteristic of the bronze man.

He swung atop the wall. Crouching there, he gestured to Monk and Ham, directing them to ascend the cord.

Monk grasped the thin thread. The hairy chemist had bent copper pennies quite easily for the amusement of the children. Great as was his strength, however, he could barely cope with the task of mounting the silk thread—a feat which Doc had accomplished with ease. Monk was perspiring prodigiously from the effort when he reached the top.

Monk had buttoned the pig, Habeas Corpus, inside his coat.

Ham struggled valiantly to mount the silk line. But his most Herculean efforts got him less than ten feet from the ground. His hands became sweated and he slipped back.

Doc made gestures indicating that the lawyer should tie the cord under his arms. This done, Doc hauled him upward.

The three men surveyed the enclosure.

"For the love of mud!" Monk gulped. "What kind of place is this, anyway?"

STRETCHED over the walled area was a huge,

Doc mounted the thin cord with an amazing ... speed.

crisscrossed net of copper cables. The cables were nearly three inches in thickness. Their mesh measured nearly a yard.

"I don't understand this!" Ham muttered. The lawyer had retained a grip on his cane as he was hauled up. Now he gave the cane handle a twist, and withdrew a long, slender blade of steel.

Ham's innocent-looking black stick was a sword cane.

"Notice that the cables are insulated from each other," Doc said.

These insulators were substantial affairs of a brown dielectric composition.

"The cables are built to carry a high-voltage electric current," Monk decided.

"Don't touch them," Doc warned. "They may be charged."

"What gets me, is the solidity of the construction," Ham mused.

From the gigantic net, they dropped their attention to what lay below.

Beneath the net stood a house of native stone. It was vast; undoubtedly old. Its state of repair was good. It was two stories in height, the rooftop almost reaching the thick cables.

"I'll bet that place has fifty or sixty rooms," Monk muttered, and held Habeas by an ear to keep him away from the insulated copper hawsers.

Untended shrubbery surrounded the house. It was carelessly crushed down at some points. Nowhere was there sign of life.

"We make swell targets up here," Ham said grimly.

The grapple had hooked on the wall lip. Dangling it by the silk cord, which was not a conductor of electricity, Doc used the hook to short-circuit two of the crisscrossing cables.

There was a crackle and a blue-hot spark. The big net was electrified!

"Enough of a current to kill a man, if you ask me!" Monk grunted.

"You fellows keep an eye on the place," Doc suggested.

Monk and Ham nodded. From their clothing they drew weapons which resembled slightly oversize automatic pistols. They were fitted with drum magazines, and the mechanism looked somewhat intricate.

These were superfiring machine guns perfected by Doc. Their rate of fire was so rapid that their roar was like the hoarse song of a gigantic bass fiddle. In addition, the slugs which they discharged did not produce fatal wounds, being "mercy bullets" charged with a drug which brought only unconsciousness.

Doc Savage calculated briefly, then sprang outward upon the spreading copper net. He went forward in a series of agile leaps, maintaining perfect balance.

His position was dangerous. Should he touch two of the metal hawsers simultaneously, death by electrocution would be almost certain. He was safe as long as he poised on only one conductor at a time, just as a bird can perch, unharmed, on a high tension power line.

Soon he was over the house roof. The net mesh was amply large to permit him to drop through. He did so, executing the move with a batlike quietness. The roof shingles were very old.

The bronze man listened for a time. His ears, attuned to the keenness of a wild animal's, detected vague stirrings. There was also an odor—a beasty odor.

Doc worked down the steep slope of the roof. From eaves to ground was an appalling drop. He took it with the casual ease of a great, tawny cat. Leaves fluttered slightly as he landed in the shrubbery.

Doc's two men still crouched on the wall, alert. Monk shook his small head, indicating he had seen no danger astir.

The shrubbery, unclipped for months, was over Doc's head at points.

From the wall crest, Monk howled, "Look—"

A rifle sounded from a window of the house.

To his remarkable vision, developed and kept sharp by scientific methods, Doc owed his life. He saw the rifle barrel even before Monk perceived it and started his yell of warning.

Doc saw the face behind the gun—the visage of the man who had killed Carl MacBride.

A split second before the gun discharged, Doc veered left. The bullet chopped shrilly at the space he had vacated. Seeming not to slacken his pace at all, the bronze man gained a sheltering corner of the house.

FROM the top of the wall came an abrupt, almost deafening moan. Monk and Ham had put their supermachine pistols in action.

The rifleman ducked from view so quickly, that he was unhit.

Monk and Ham hastily made the grappling hook fast and slid down the silk cord. They used care not to touch the charged copper cables. Monk had his pet pig under an arm.

Ham came up, sword cane unsheathed. Monk lumbered on his heels. The pig, Habeas, trailing Monk, was as excited as the simian chemist.

"We'd better get inside," Doc said crisply. "That fellow may try to use his rifle from another window."

The bronze man reached a window and gave the sash a rap with his palm. Glass fell with a brittle clanging. Doc crawled in through the opening.

Ham and Monk kept at his heels. The homely chemist grabbed Habeas by an ear and hoisted him inside.

The room in which they found themselves was large, apparently a smoking room. The chairs were upholstered in leather; the furniture was massive, dark. A thick layer of dust reposed over everything. Cigarette stubs were scattered about with great carelessness for the well-being of the furniture.

Not for a long time had the place received a cleaning.

Doc yanked open a door. It gave into a hallway. This, too, needed cleaning.

The men went down the hallway, making no attempt at silence, except when pausing to use their ears. But no sound did they hear; nor did they see anyone.

They came to the room from which the rifle had been fired. An empty, high-powered cartridge shell lay on the floor. It reeked of burned powder.

The rifleman had fled.

A scuffling sound led the trio toward the upstairs regions. They mounted stairs which were carpeted. From the carpet nap their feet knocked up little puffs of dust. It had been long uncleaned. At the top they found a corridor lined with many doors. Passages branched off from it.

"You'd think this place was a hotel," Monk breathed.

To their left a door opened. The bright metal snout of a pistol poked out.

A determined feminine voice said, "Don't move!"

Chapter VIII
THE EX-LION-TAMER

THE young woman was tall. A plain traveling frock set off the enticing curves of her form almost as effectively as would have an evening dress.

Her hair was her really striking feature. Young women with attractive figures were fairly common. Not so hair such as this. It was the shade of steel. And the young woman's eyes were as metallic as her hair.

Doc acted while her command still echoed. His hand drifted with blinding speed to Ham's sword cane. Surprise had slackened the dapper lawyer's clutch on the weapon. Doc swept it from his hand and flung it, hilt first.

The hilt hit the girl's gun hand. She squealed and dropped her gun, then sought to recover it.

Lunging, Doc scooped up the gun before she got it. His fingers banded the young woman's wrist, not tightly enough to inflict pain, but with a firmness which prevented her flight.

The girl threw back her head and shrieked.

There was splintering terror in her voice.

"I'll do it!" she wailed. "I'll do it!"

That she was genuinely frightened, Doc could tell by her trembling. Her firm muscles quivered under his clutch.

"Where's the fellow who shot at us?" he demanded.

The girl looked surprised. Her struggling ceased. "What—what—" She seemed bewildered. "You mean—you're not one of them?"

"Who are you?" Doc asked her.

The girl stared distrustfully. She seemed a bit more at ease when Doc released her wrists.

"My name is Jean Morris," she explained.

The name meant nothing to Doc. This was the first time he had heard it.

"I'm a circus lion-tamer by profession," Jean Morris elaborated. "My last job was with the Atlas Congress of Wonders. It went broke in Michigan."

"Not at Trapper Lake?" Doc asked sharply.

"How did you know?"

"Do you know a man named Carl MacBride?" Doc queried, instead of answering her.

The girl's burnished-steel head shook a negative. "No."

Monk now addressed Habeas Corpus. "Go hunt 'em, Habeas. Hunt 'em up!"

The pig trotted off.

The girl stared after the pig, surprised at the unlovely porker's prompt obedience.

"I got 'im trained until he's better'n a bloodhound," Monk grinned.

Doc entered the room from which the young woman had accosted them. It was a bedroom, bleakly furnished. The mattress was missing from the bed; there were no curtains at the windows. Long disuse was apparent everywhere.

Doc crossed to a window badly in need of washing. Looking out, he found he could keep an eye on the gate.

Monk stationed himself in the door, apparently waiting for the return of his pig, Habeas Corpus.

"How did you get here?" Doc asked the young woman.

Her eyes snapped. "In answer to an ad in a circus trade journal—an ad offering a job to anyone who could speak the language of the pinhead tribe of African natives."

"You speak it?"

"I do—a little. There were three pinheads with the Atlas Congress of Wonders. They were pitiful little fellows. They used to follow me around like three black dogs. I learned to speak some of their language."

Doc Savage's features indicated neither belief nor disbelief. He asked, "When did you come to New York?"

"Today, by plane. I had been directed by telegram."

She thrust her fingers into a tiny pocket in her frock and brought out a folded yellow paper. "Here it is"—handing it to Doc.

Doc accepted the wire, and read the contents.

J MORRIS
CARE OF GUIDE'S HOTEL
TRAPPER LAKE MICHIGAN
 JOB YOURS STOP CATCH PLANE IMME-
DIATELY FOR NEW YORK AND COME TO
MY HOME ON HILL ROAD NORTH OF CITY
      GRISWOLD ROCK

"Does Griswold Rock own this place?" asked Doc.

"A taxi driver told me he did," the girl replied.

Monk had been listening for the return of Habeas. Now he glanced at the girl.

"That name—Griswold Rock—sounds kinda familiar," he said.

"Griswold Rock is president and chief stock-holder of a small railroad which serves northern Michigan," Doc said. "He is well known."

"There are several men here," said the girl. "I don't think I saw Griswold Rock, though."

"You said there were three pinheads with the Atlas Congress of Wonders," Doc reminded the young woman. "What became of them?"

"They disappeared. They wandered into the country, and that was the last heard of them."

"How long ago?"

"Almost a year."

"Then the circus did not go broke recently?"

"Oh, no, it went on the rocks months ago. I have been working in Trapper Lake as a wait-ress."

With a slow gesture, Doc Savage indicated the high wall and the mysterious net of copper hawsers.

"Have you any idea about the meaning of all this?"

"No," the girl shuddered, "the place gives me the jitters."

"SOMETHING must've happened to Habeas Corpus," Monk groaned.

"You three stay here," Doc directed. Then he was gone down the stairway into the lower regions of the house.

Reaching the library, he glanced about. The furnishings, while old-fashioned, were not cheap. Condition here, as elsewhere in the house, indicated months of cleaning neglect.

The library was empty of life.

Doc crossed to a ponderous desk which was something of an antique. Letters littered the top of it. More letters, obviously containing advertising matter, had been flung upon the floor.

Doc ran through the epistles. All were addressed to the same individual: "Griswold Rock."

Doc read several missives. They pertained to routine operation of the railroad with which Griswold Rock was associated.

One thing was evident from the text of the missives. Griswold Rock had been operating the railroad from seclusion. It seemed that he had not visited the offices during recent months, but had handled all business by letter, telephone and tele-graph. Just why this somewhat peculiar condition should exist, the communications gave no hint.

Doc left the library and continued his hunt.

Monk's pet pig should have returned long ago. The fact that Habeas had not appeared was omi-nous.

Doc Savage examined a kitchen, a dining room, and a large pantry without finding anyone. He did, however, note an enormous food supply. This indicated some tremendous eaters were around.

Doc dropped to all fours and pressed an ear to the floor. The wood brought faint noises from somewhere in the house. But they were too vague to be located.

Glancing from a window, Doc noted ruts which seemed to be auto truck tracks, swinging from the great barred gate and terminating against one wing of the house. This particular wing was win-dowless, little more than a great wooden box.

The peculiarity of the construction was interesting.

Doc Savage worked in that direction. His inten-tion was to investigate the box of a room.

A door barred his progress. He tested it with his shoulder. Judging from its solidity, the panel must be armored on the other side with sheet steel.

There was no peering through the keyhole. It

MONK

was covered on the opposite side by a swinging shield. This refused to move when Doc probed it with a slender metal instrument which he extracted from a pocket case.

Doc worked at the lock with his metal probe. He threw the tumblers, but the door still resisted. It must be barred on the inside.

Doc moved to a window, lifted it, poked his head out and surveyed the surroundings. He was under no delusions. Death was aprowl somewhere in this fantastic place, for all of the quietness in the air.

Doc saw no one. He clambered outside and, circling, he examined the wing of the house which was like a great box. At the end he found ponderous doors, closed tightly. Nowhere was there a crack to permit inspection of whatever was inside.

Doc tried his giant muscles against the panels. The wood only groaned.

The sun was low. The huge copper net overhead made a barred shadow pattern on the concrete walls, and on the sides and roof of the house.

Inside the house, Habeas Corpus began squealing terribly.

Chapter IX
THE MAN OF FAT

DOC SAVAGE dived around the corner of the boxlike wing of the house and reached the open window through which he had come a few minutes before. He pitched himself quickly inside.

The pig was squealing somewhere in the basement regions.

Doc plunged through rooms, hunting the entrance to the cellar.

On the stairway which led down from the upper floors, Monk and Ham created racket. They were descending. Evidently they had left the girl behind; the sound of her feet was not mingling with theirs.

"Stay with the girl!" Doc yelled at them.

Monk and Ham came to a stop on the stairs. From behind them came a sudden awful sound. A board snapped with a tremendous noise. Planks broke, splintered. Nails pulled out of wood with shrieks like dying things.

The bedlam drowned the squealing of Habeas Corpus.

Monk and Ham wheeled back up the stairs, reached the top and pitched down the hall. Aghast, they skidded to a halt.

A fantastic thing was happening to the hall floor. It was heaving upward, forced by some unearthly power from beneath. Stringers were crashing apart, planks rending and tearing.

Beyond the point where the floor was upheaving they could see the steel-haired girl. Then the buckling of the floor blocked their view.

The hallway was dimly lighted. Dust was arising. These two factors joined to prevent Monk and Ham from ascertaining the cause of the fantastic destruction.

The Thing was smashing up from the boxlike part of the house which Doc Savage had sought to investigate.

Doc Savage joined Monk and Ham.

"It's something alive—a monster!" Monk gulped. "Hear it breathin'?"

The breath sounds were like great, windy rushes.

Doc produced a flashlight. It traced a beam like a white-hot thread. This spiked out at the boiling dust clouds, but could not penetrate deeply enough to show anything.

Behind them, in the lower regions, Habeas Corpus squealed monotonously.

Then the steel-haired girl cried out in an awful fear.

Monk and Ham held their tiny superfiring pistols. They did not dare use them blindly, for fear of hitting the girl. The slugs were not lethal, but one in an eye could do damage.

The clouds of dust, swirling in the glittering crystal rods of the flash beam, suddenly convulsed more violently. Wreckage, splinters and small planks flew toward them.

"Back!" Doc rapped. "It's coming for us!"

MONK and Ham found their arms grasped by Doc's powerful hands. They were all but carried down the stairs. They had moved none too quickly. The monster seemed to be trying to get to them.

It was evidently baffled by the dust, and by the strength of the timbers which composed the old house. It seemed to turn back.

The steel-haired girl, who had been briefly silent, began to shriek again. But her yelling suddenly decreased in loudness. It was as if she had been dropped, still screaming, into a bottle, and the bottle corked.

"The thing yanked her down into the lower story," Doc said grimly.

Monk wiped sweat off his simian features.

"I've seen a lot of unearthly things in my time!" he gulped. "But this takes the cake."

In the basement, Habeas Corpus still squealed.

"I'm gonna see what ails that pig!" Monk rapped, and plunged off.

Doc lunged toward a window. Before he reached it, a loud throbbing roar arose. This came from the boxlike room. It lifted to a great syncopation of power.

"A truck!" Ham yelled.

There was a clanking of machinery; the great door in the end of the house swung open.

A motor van lumbered out. The thing was long, the great closed box of a body rolling on a four-wheel truck at the rear. This body was of steel, and access was had by two doors at the rear. These were closed.

The van driver was the man with the dyed black hair and mustache—he who had killed Carl MacBride.

Ham flipped up his machine pistol. It bawled, ejector spraying empty cartridges. But the bullets only turned into chemical-and-lead smears on the windows of the van driver's cab.

"Bulletproof glass," Ham growled disgustedly.

Doc Savage plucked the little superfirer from Ham's clutch. The bronze man's fingers worked on the weapon, flipping the magazine drum off.

In the cartridge intake chute, Doc inserted several special shells which he extracted from a pocket.

The great van had evidently run over a buried trip device in the driveway. The gate of thick steel bars was opening.

Doc lifted the gun; his ability as a marksman was as accomplished as his other capacities. Then the gun blasted fire.

On the sides of the van appeared tiny, grayish puffs, as if snowballs had broken. Nothing else happened.

The van rolled through the great gate and was gone.

"Blast it!" yelled Ham.

HAM remembered that ejaculation for a long time, due to what immediately followed. For the floor seemed to sink several inches under their feet, then jump. The walls rocked. A terrific explosion all but shattered their eardrums.

Wreckage came spouting down the stairway which led to the second story. Walls cracked open like over-ripe fruit. The sides of the house split, to let out spurts of smoke and flame.

The roof over the boxlike room which had held the van spit in the middle and folded outward like a double lid.

Smoke, flame and debris, propelled by the blast, spurted up through the coarse net of copper cables.

Doc and Ham were catapulted the length of the room in which they stood.

Their eardrums, strained by the first concussion of the explosion, registered the crash, thump and bang of wreckage falling back to earth.

Doc Savage glanced through the shattered rectangle of a window. The explosion had practically annihilated the mysterious wing of the house which had harbored the big van.

Overhead, boards and lath had fallen back upon the coarse net of copper. Dust from the explosion whirled in a great pall.

"The girl!" Ham gulped. "She couldn't have lived through that explosion!"

The dust cloud, settling and rolling aside, partially dispersed. Flames appeared—fire sweeping the wreckage of the house wing. Scattered tongues became scarlet bundles. They licked at the wood, flared up and spread.

"The explosion scattered an incendiary compound," Doc rapped out.

The bronze giant and the slender lawyer flung out through the window and ran toward the fire. Waves of heat assailed them, searing as they drew closer. Extinguishing such a blaze was beyond all possibility.

They circled the inferno, eyes searching. They discerned several things of interest, the chief item being the amount of broken glass in and about the wreckage.

Countless test tubes and bottles seemed to have been smashed. Here and there lay pieces of shiny, intricate apparatus, all battered beyond recognition.

"There was a laboratory of some kind here," Ham hazarded.

Neither man mentioned the main fact—that there was no sign of the girl. Nor did they voice a hope both held that the girl had been carried away in the van.

Monk had not put in his appearance. He had been absent since before the blast, when he had started searching for Habeas Corpus.

"We gotta get him out," Ham wailed.

There was genuine concern in Ham's voice—a marked change from the sarcasm with which he addressed Monk when they were face to face.

THE two men reentered the house. They found, beyond a door which opened off the kitchen, a stairway leading to the cellar region. A loud, thumping noise drew them to the right.

The basement was filled with smoke. The fumes were blinding, irritating to the lungs. Sounds of the fire came to their ears, an increasing roar. Mingling with this was a shrill whine— an electric generator.

Then they sighted Monk. The ungainly chemist was pitching himself against a door—a panel which did not bulge in the slightest under his weight.

There was a small, square opening in the door, apparently for ventilation purposes. Through this came the mournful squeal of Habeas Corpus. Too, the generator whine emanated from here.

"I don't seem to be able to do a thing toward bustin' this down," Monk groaned.

Doc dabbed his flash beam through the hole in the door.

Inside, Habeas pranced about. It was a large, bare concrete chamber. It held a huge motor-generator set, obviously employed to charge the overhead net of copper cables with electricity.

Doc gave the head of the flash a twist. This caused the beam to widen, and illuminate the entire room more effectively.

"I'm a son-of-a-gun!" Monk exploded.

A man lay on his back in the middle of the floor, glassy eyes fixed on the ceiling. He reposed near the big motor-generator.

The man was short, very fat; his fat looked soft. His hands lay on the floor in lumps, like a semi-melted formation of butter. He was reposing face up, and his jowls hung down in buttery bags against his ears.

His business suit, while expensive, was wrinkled. His shirt was soiled. He wore no necktie. The man did not move, or even shut his wide-open eyes.

Doc thrust a hand in the door opening, and explored on the other side. "It's sheeted with steel," he explained.

The bronze man now examined the lock. It was of the key type, with the lock mechanism on the other side. Picking it would be slow work.

Two small bottles appeared in Doc's fingers. Using a match stick, he poked a pinch of powder from one of the bottles into the keyhole. He followed this with a bit of compound from the second bottle.

"Back!" he said sharply.

They retreated.

There was a brilliant flash and a whooping roar! Splinters and torn steel geysered from around the door lock. Chemical reaction of the two compounds which Doc had used, had caused the explosion.

Doc shoved the door open. Squealing delightedly, Habeas Corpus bounded for Monk.

The man on the floor was stirring. He groaned; his eyes closed, then opened again. He acted like one who had been asleep, and was awakened by the explosion.

Doc grasped the fat man's arm; it was very soft, as if he had clutched a partially deflated inner tube.

Picking the fat man up bodily, Doc carried him out of the room.

"Better get out of here," he called over his shoulder. "That fire is spreading fast."

Monk scooped up Habeas Corpus, and said, "I wonder how the pig got in there?"

Without replying, Doc Savage carried the fat man up the stairway and outdoors, Monk and Ham following him.

They ran toward the gate, which still gaped open.

With his sword cane, Ham pointed at the net of electrified cables above. Then he indicated the high, forbidding walls.

"If you ask me, this whole place is nothing but a gigantic cage!" he declared.

"What I was thinking, too," Monk rumbled. "I wish I could get my hands on this Griswold Rock, who owns the place. I'd find out what it's all about."

The man Doc was carrying squirmed feebly.

"I am Griswold Rock," he said.

Chapter X
THE PRISONER

THE bronze man and his two aides digested this surprising information as they ran through the gate.

Doc lowered the fat man. Then he left the spot, running. He vouchsafed no information as to where he was bound.

"I wonder what Doc's up to now?" Monk muttered.

"He put some special kind of bullets in my gun and shot at the departing truck," Ham offered. "I don't know what the idea was. But he may be working on that angle."

Doc Savage topped the hill, descended into the valley beyond, and reached the roadster. He had run a quarter of a mile at a speed a champion sprinter would have considered remarkable, yet his breathing was hardly hurried.

Built into the roadster was a radiophone transmitter and receiver. Doc switched this on.

"Renny!" he called.

Out of the radio loudspeaker came a roaring voice which might have been owned by a disturbed lion.

"On deck, Doc!"

"Where are you, Renny?"

"In your office. Just drifted in."

"Long Tom and Johnny there?"

"Sure. Right beside me."

The men named were the other three members of Doc's group. The bronze man issued rapid orders to the men.

"I want to locate a large van-bodied truck," he said. "It's painted red."

"There's only about a thousand red vans in New York," said the lion-voiced "Renny."

"Use the planes," Doc directed. "Fly over Hill Road, and over the Hudson Turnpike. Look for red vans, large ones. When you find them, size them up with ultraviolet light and fluoroscopic spectacles."

"I get you," said Renny.

Doc switched off the apparatus and returned to the spot where he had left Monk and Ham.

Great clouds of smoke were climbing above the high concrete wall. Doc found the pleasantly ugly chemist and the sword-cane-carrying lawyer eyeing plump Griswold Rock.

The fat man was holding his head. From time to time, his fingers explored in his hair.

"Has he talked?" Doc asked, indicating Griswold Rock.

Ham shook his head.

"They made me drink something," Griswold Rock muttered. "That was right after they saw you fellows on the wall. I no more than drank the stuff, then I passed out."

"Where were you when that happened?"

"Upstairs."

Monk nodded, as if a point had been clarified. "They carried you down to the basement, and Habeas Corpus followed. That explains how Habeas got locked up with you."

"I don't remember what happened," Griswold Rock mumbled.

Monk waved a hand at the concrete-walled enclosure, from which smoke poured as from a titanic chimney.

"Is that your place?" he asked.

The fat man nodded gloomily. "Yep. But it isn't like it used to be. They made me build the wall."

"Made you?" Ham asked.

"Exactly," said Griswold Rock. "I've been held a prisoner for almost a year. To preserve my life, I had to do what I was told."

"Who were your captors?"

"Pere Teston was the head of the gang."

"Pere Teston?"

"He's a former employee of my railroad," explained the fat man. "He worked in a Michigan division point. He was discharged because he failed to show much interest in his work."

GRISWOLD ROCK poked a soft arm angrily at concrete wall and the gate of metal bars.

"They made me transact all my business by letter or telegraph, and sometimes by telephone. One of them stood at my side with a gun," he grated.

"You don't know the purpose of the wall and the electrified net of copper cables?" Doc asked.

"No. They made me buy motor-generators to electrify the net. I don't know why."

"Ever see any kind of a monster around?"

"Monster!" muttered Griswold Rock. He shuddered. "Maybe that explains the sounds I occasionally heard."

"What sort of noises?"

"It's hard to describe them. Pere Teston kept me in a windowless room in the basement, but sometimes I could hear things walking about. Huge things!"

"Ever hear anything about advertisements in newspapers?"

Griswold Rock nodded vehemently. "Yes—I did. They were inserting ads in every paper in the country. I don't know what kind—or why."

"Was Pere Teston a slender man with freckles and a mustache?" Doc asked.

The plump railroad magnate shook his head violently.

"No. Pere Teston is a shriveled runt. The skin on his face is white, dead-looking. Once you see him, you'll never forget his skin!"

The fire had progressed rapidly. A house wall collapsed, slapping a great cloud of sparks above the concrete enclosure. In the distance a fire engine moaned. Someone had evidently telephoned an alarm to the nearest suburban station.

Doc Savage went to the gate. From the recesses of his clothing came an unbreakable tube. The powder this contained, he sprinkled upon the gate bars. Fingerprints became visible.

Doc Savage made no effort to photograph them. He merely studied them, fixing the whorls indelibly in his mind. Months could elapse before the bronze man glimpsed like prints, yet he would still recall their configuration, to such retentiveness had he attuned his memory.

Upon one particular set of prints, Doc bestowed a great deal of attention. Then he joined the others.

Griswold Rock was saying, "I am not a brave man. They kept me terrified."

"Didn't you make an effort to escape?" Monk queried.

The fat man nodded. "Oh, yes—several times. But I do not seem to be very ingenious. My attempts always failed. Only yesterday, I managed to get as far as the gate. I'd have gotten away, too, I believe, but the mechanical fastener defied me. I could not discover how it operated, although I fumbled all over the gate."

Doc Savage reached out abruptly and grasped Griswold Rock's fat wrist. He turned the hands palm up so as to inspect the fingertips. His experienced eye appraised the whorls and rings.

"You left your fingerprints on the gate," he said dryly.

Griswold Rock raised his eyebrows in surprise.

"I just found the prints," Doc explained. "We'd better clear out of here now. Hear that fire apparatus?"

Griswold Rock was eyeing Doc. He emitted a loud ejaculation.

"I know who you are!" he exclaimed. "You're Doc Savage, the fellow who has become so famous as a trouble-buster."

Doc waved the party in the direction of the car. Doc entered his roadster. Monk, Ham, and Griswold Rock and the pig got in the other car.

With its siren moaning, the fire engine approached on Hill Road.

Doc's party took the opposite direction. They got away without being seen, thereby avoiding the necessity of answering the questions of curious firemen.

NOR was the presence of Doc Savage ever connected with the mysterious walled mansion which the fire fighters found aflame. Never afterward in public did Doc mention the place. He told no one, outside of his five aides and the others immediately concerned, of what had occurred at the fantastic spot. He did not tell that he had discovered the enclosure to be a prison for the retention of some species of fantastic monster.

The monster angle, however, was unearthed by an aggressive newspaper reporter who turned up on the scene. This news hawk possessed an imagination. He was employed by a tabloid which was not averse to coloring its news with a little invention.

This journalist of wit, after studying the high concrete enclosure with its over-flung net of copper cables, played havoc with the speed laws in getting to the nearest telephone. The next edition of his paper appeared with tremendous black headlines.

LAIR OF MONSTERS FOUND!
MYSTERY MANSE GOES UP
IN FLAMES

The story below was vague as to detail, but it made interesting reading. It stated that the property was owned by a railroad man named Griswold Rock, and added further that Griswold Rock had not been in evidence at his New York club during recent months.

It suggested that the police conduct a search for Griswold Rock; and, climaxing the yarn, was a suggestion that the mysterious "monster" advertisements, which had been appearing in newspapers throughout the United States, were connected with the unusual establishment which had been found in flames.

It happened that this tabloid newspaper was noted for the scatter-brained quality of the reports it published, and as a consequence, its deductions were not taken seriously.

Some of the more sedate metropolitan journals dispatched reporters to the fire, and these later turned in stories which were carried on inside pages in small type.

To the very fact that the tabloid newspaper first connected the mystery mansion with the "monster" advertisements, could be attributed the small amount of real notice which the affair received. Nobody took the tabloid seriously.

Since the newspapers never connected the walled estate of Griswold Rock with the hideous menace of the monsters which was soon to cast its grisly spell over the cities of the United States, they remained blissfully unaware that, in turning up their noses at the flamboyant tabloid, they had passed up what might easily have been the front-page story of all time.

Furthermore, the tabloid itself failed to profit as much as it might have, for its reporter lacked the detective ability to follow up the possibilities which his imagination had suggested; or maybe the reporter did not believe what he wrote. He might merely have come uncannily near the truth in conjuring an interesting yarn out of his fertile brain.

At any rate, no one connected Doc Savage with the fire, least of all the fire fighters who arrived too late to witness the bronze's man departure. While they were playing the first streams from their chemical extinguishers on the blaze, Doc Savage rolled along the deserted road perhaps two miles distant.

Chapter XI
THE ULTRAVIOLET TRAIL

DOC SAVAGE switched on the radio telephone. There came immediately from the loudspeaker the sound of static and, intermingling with these cracklings, a many-throated drone.

The droning, sent from other transmitters, was the sound of plane motors.

"You fellows sighted anything?" Doc asked.

Out of the loudspeaker came a well-modulated, cultured voice. This belonged to "Johnny," who was known to his learned associates as William Harper Littlejohn. He had once been the head of the natural science research department of a famous university.

"No," said Johnny. "Not a sign of them yet."

Doc lifted his gaze. Flying low and to the southward, he could see a plane.

"Roll your bus, Johnny," he suggested.

The distant ship spun over slowly in the sky.

"O. K.," Doc said. "I've got you spotted."

The bronze man halted his roadster. Monk was driving the other machine. The pig, Habeas Corpus, was perched on his lap. He drew to a stop alongside Doc's car. The three men and the pig piled out.

For the benefit of Griswold Rock, and for his men, who had not heard the entire story, Doc Savage gave a brief synopsis of all that had occurred. While doing this, he spoke close to the microphone which fed the radio telephone transmitter, so that his men in the distant plane would get the story clearly.

Monk showed particular interest in the newspaper clipping concerning the death of the half-breed woodsman, Bruno Hen.

"Tornado—nothing!" he snorted. "I'll bet it was the monsters—whatever they are—that wrecked the cabin."

Griswold Rock shuddered violently. "The more I think of my last months, the more terrible they become," he moaned. "My captors forced me to sign so much stuff that they wouldn't let me read!"

Doc Savage studied Griswold Rock. The

plump fellow certainly had not taken much exercise recently. He was carrying some of the flabbiest fat the bronze man had ever seen.

"The Timberland is the name of your railroad, isn't it?" Doc asked.

Griswold Rock's fat jowls went through a convulsion which was evidently a nod. "That is right."

"And you direct the destinies of the railroad absolutely?"

"Yes. I am not only president, but I also own much of the stock—that is, providing I didn't sign it away with some of those papers they made me put my John Henry on without reading."

"Is the town of Trapper Lake on the Timberland Line?"

"We have a station there. Not a very profitable one."

THE sound of the plane became audible in the sky to the east; a moment later the ship appeared. The craft was of a type as yet rarely seen in the air lanes. Its shape bore faint resemblance to the popular autogyro.

Actually, it was a true gyro, another product of Doc Savage's fabulous inventive skill. In making a take-off, the ship was capable of rising vertically.

The ship became stationary less than fifty feet above their heads. The door of the closed cockpit opened; a hand appeared.

It was an enormous hand—fully a quart of bone and gristle encased in a skin which resembled rhinoceros hide. The owner of the big hand thrust his head out. He had a long, horselike face which bore an expression of utter gloom.

With his other hand, he threw a lever which turned the motor exhaust into a muffler. The engine assumed a surprising quietness.

"We ain't having any luck yet," he called. His voice resembled the roaring of a disturbed lion.

This was Renny—Colonel John Renwick. The engineering profession used his name in terms of highest respect. His engineering feats had given him a worldwide reputation and earned him a fortune.

Renny permitted himself only one form of amusement. When the opportunity offered, he liked to demonstrate his ability to knock the panel out of the strongest wooden door with one blow of his enormous fists.

"Long Tom is further west," Renny advised. "Guess you saw Johnny's bus."

He swung the gyro in the direction of the strange walled enclosure with its grille of copper cables. From this, great quantities of smoke still poured.

Renny circled the fire for a time. Then he returned, and hovered his craft in the air over Doc's head.

The big-fisted engineer had an ejaculation which he used at every opportunity. He employed it now.

"Holy cow!" he boomed. "That's the dangedest-lookin' place!"

Then he climbed his plane, and followed Hill Road into the distance.

Griswold Rock had been an interested observer. He now addressed Doc.

"I believe the tales I've heard of you were to the effect that you have five associates. Was that fellow with the enormous hands one of them?"

Doc nodded. "He's one of the greatest of engineers, when he chooses to work at it."

From the loudspeaker in Doc's roadster came the words which he had been awaiting.

"Here's the van, Doc," said a shrill voice.

GRISWOLD ROCK started violently. Evidently the ramifications of Doc's communication system were beyond his comprehension.

"Who was that?" he gulped.

Instead of replying, Doc started the roadster engine. The giant bronze man had a habit, somewhat disconcerting to those who did not know him well, of seeming not to hear questions which he did not wish to answer.

Had he chosen, he could have taken time to explain that the voice belonged to Major Thomas J. Roberts, an electrical wizard whose contributions to that science were among the greatest ever made.

The public knew little of "Long Tom" Roberts' work, for the reason that his discoveries were largely beyond the understanding of the average layman. Within fifty or sixty years, textbooks would no doubt state that Major Thomas J. Roberts had done important pioneering and discovery work along many lines.

"Where is the van, Long Tom?" Doc asked.

"It's going north on Hudson Turnpike."

"We'll see if we can overhaul it," Doc said grimly.

Griswold Rock grimaced and became quite pale. "Can't you—can't you let me out somewhere?"

Doc and the others eyed Griswold Rock curiously. Most men, when frightened, put up a front of exaggerated bravado to hide their fears. Not so this fat man. He was terrified, and not backward about asserting the fact.

"I'm an awful coward!" he wailed. "I'm especially scared of these devils."

"Do you want them punished?" Monk demanded.

"Of course I do! But I don't care about going after them myself."

Ham eyed his sword cane thoughtfully. Apparently he was wondering how a man with such a marked lack of physical courage had managed to become manager and major owner of a railroad. Big business men, with whom Ham had come in contact, had always been go-getters with plenty of courage.

"You go with us," Doc told Griswold Rock. "We'll keep you out of danger."

Often in the past, Monk and Ham had seen the remarkable voice of the bronze man work miracles. Never had it secured a more profound effect than now. Griswold Rock seemed to draw courage from the powerful tones.

"I feel as safe with you as anywhere," he said, and got into the roadster.

THE car hurtled forward in a fashion which caused Griswold Rock to utter a terrified choking sound and grasp the door. However, as he observed the expertness with which Doc guided the machine, his trepidation subsided. Within a mile, he was resting easily on the cushions, although seventies were dancing on the speedometer.

"Still got the van in sight?" Doc asked into the radio mike.

"I'm cruising above it," came Long Tom's radioed reply.

"Sure it's the right machine?"

"Positive. The fluoroscopic glasses show the presence of the chemical mixture you always use, Doc."

Griswold Rock wrinkled his plump brow at these words. "You put something on that van to identify it?"

"Shot bullets laden with a chemical concoction at it," Doc replied. "They splashed the chemicals on the sides and roof of the van."

The fat man waved his pursy hands. "For the life of me, I cannot comprehend how that could help you."

"To the naked eye the chemical mixture presents nothing extraordinary. In fact, it's hardly noticeable. But the stuff has the property of fluorescing, or glowing, when exposed to ultraviolet light. Ordinary vaseline, for instance, has a similar property. This stuff glows with a different color—a hue peculiar to itself."

"But you speak of fluoroscopic eyeglasses."

"The glowing marks are very small. Since it is now daylight, special eyepieces are needed to make the glow visible."

There came an interruption, a sound like metal knocking rapidly on wood. It emanated from the radio loudspeaker.

"Doc!" Long Tom's voice rapped excitedly from the instrument. "They've got a machine gun—"

The rapping grew louder, drowning out the electrical wizard's tones. Then, with an ominous abruptness, the racket ceased completely.

"That clatter sounded like a machine gun!" Griswold Rock wailed.

Doc Savage said nothing. He put weight on the gas accelerator. Larger and larger speedometer figures crawled past the dial marker.

For a time, Griswold Rock failed to note the new pace at which they were traveling. Then, chancing to look at the speedometer, he turned very white.

Chapter XII
THE TUNNEL

LONG TOM ROBERTS had studied the red van intently through binoculars, before dropping down close to it. He had searched particularly for possible loopholes, but had seen none.

Too late, he learned they had been covered by clever covers—caps disguised as the heads of rivets that held the van body together.

A procession of lead slugs, gnashing angrily at his left wing, was his first warning of disaster. The leaden stream made a quick march for the cockpit.

It was the hammer of these slugs which Doc Savage had heard over the radio.

Long Tom was not flying a gyro, but another of Doc Savage's ships—a rather nondescript-looking biplane. Doc used this type of craft when not wishing to attract attention by being seen in his distinctively-designed speed ship, or the gyro.

The crate heaved over on a wing tip as Long Tom trod the rudder and cornered the stick. It got away from the hungry lead.

He jerked a lever in the cockpit. On the cowl, hatches rolled back; a disappearing machine gun jumped into view. This was synchronized to fire through the prop.

Out of the van top, more bullets climbed. Every third or fourth slug seemed to be a tracer. The metallic threads waved like a deadly, windblown gray procession of raindrops.

Long Tom's gun fired from Bowden controls on the stick. He ringed the van in his sight; his hand clamped the Bowden trip. The gun on the cowl shook its iron back, and smoked.

Like cobweb spun by an invisible spider, Long Tom's tracers ran down through the late afternoon sunlight to the van. Against the steel van body, however, they only made splotches of chemical fire, or spattered into shapeless blobs.

Long Tom felt his ship jar under him. The stick waggled in his hand as bullets lashed at the control services. He jockeyed the stick madly to evade the fire.

His plane had never been intended for combat. It handled sluggishly. A procession of slugs beat against the engine. Their sound was like rapid hammer blows.

The engine stopped.

Long Tom booted the ship into a flat glide, then looked overside. What he saw made him grind his teeth.

The only field suitable for a landing was one near the road. To plant the plane anywhere else would mean an almost certain crackup, for all around were trees, rocks and abrupt hills.

Long Tom slowed the plane by fish-tailing. He three-pointed perfectly on the clearing. While the ship was still rolling, he dived out and ran for the nearest bush.

He had hardly taken a dozen leaps when a machine gun stuttered behind him. He saw hazy tracer lines near his head. Dust gushed on a hillside in front of him. A dozen feet to the left he saw a shallow ditch. Long Tom dived into it.

The machine gun stilled its noisy chatter.

"Take the guy alive if you can!" shouted a man.

TAKE him alive they did. The ditch was not deep enough to permit Long Tom to crawl away. It chanced that he was at the moment unarmed.

Four men ran up. They were unsavory fellows, men who had followed the path of crime so long that it was reflected in their voices and actions.

"Lamp the guy!" snorted one of the quartet. "He looks like a case for the hospital!"

This statement about Long Tom was caused by the electrical wizard's unhealthy appearance. Long Tom was slender and only fairly set up. He was very pale, as if no sunlight had reached him for a long time. His appearance, however, was deceptive. Few men were healthier than he.

The four men pointed machine guns at Long Tom. These weapons were an airplane type, firing full-sized cartridges. Recoil was taken care of by an elaborate bracing device, which each man wore harnessed about his middle.

Long Tom arose from the ditch. He was searched.

"Who are you?" asked one of the gang.

The electrical wizard ignored the query. A man lunged forward and gave him a painful kick.

"Maybe that'll give you a voice!" the fellow growled.

The last word was still rattling his vocal cords when Long Tom's fist collided with the point of his jaw. The blow had the sound of a loud handclap. The man's eyes rolled, showing the whites. He sagged to hands and knees and began shaking his head foolishly.

"I ought to snuff your wick!" one of the other men snarled, and jutted his rapid-firer at Long Tom.

"Keep your shirt on!" growled a red-necked thug. "We'll drag him along. The boss may want to juice him for information. The punk had some reason for taggin' us with the sky lizzie."

"I'm in favor of giving him a lead pasting, Hack," grumbled the bloodthirsty one.

"Dummy up!" said Hack. "The big shot may not want him rubbed."

They placed stout handcuffs on Long Tom's wrists and his ankles. Then hurried him over to the big red van.

A man stood beside the machine, dancing about in his impatience. He was tall and waspish, and had freckles and dark hair and a mustache.

Doc's story, coming to Long Tom over the radio, had included a description of this man. The fellow was the murderer of Carl MacBride, the electrical wizard realized.

"Why didn't you smear him?" he yelled, indicating Long Tom.

"We thought the big greezer might want to put the screws on him, Caldwell," said the florid-necked Hack.

Caldwell—he had evidently not troubled to give Carl MacBride a fake name on the plane—considered this.

"No good! Too risky. Croak 'im!"

The men lifted submachine guns. For an instant Long Tom stared death in the face.

"Wait!" Caldwell rapped. "We'll plant 'im in the truck. That's better."

The van cab was commodious. It accommodated Long Tom and the four men who had seized him. Caldwell clambered into the rear.

The engine started; the van swung into motion. It traveled swiftly, taking tremendous runs at the hills.

THE electrical wizard listened. The monster, whatever it was, which had broken through the floor of Griswold Rock's house, must be in the rear of the van. He hoped to ascertain, from some sound, what the thing might be.

He heard nothing in the nature of a clew.

Hunched down in the seat, Long Tom surveyed the heavens. Twice, he saw planes. They were too distant for him to tell whether they were Doc's ships.

The setting of the sun came about abruptly, due to the rising of a bank of clouds in the west simultaneous with the descent of the blazing orb.

"I don't think we're doin' the brainy thing!" said one of the men in the cab.

"Nobody asked you!" growled Hack.

"Maybe not. But I don't get the idea of finishin' off the thing in the truck. After all the trouble we've gone to—"

"Sh-h-h!" hissed Hack. "It might hear you. This one ain't workin' so good. You know that. So the boss has decided to get rid of it. We'll bring up others for the big push on New York. Damn it! We'll have to get another headquarters."

"I hope that explosion got the bronze guy!" growled another.

"Dummy up!" said Hack, scowling at Long Tom. "This guy's got his ears unpinned."

"O.K., O.K.," the other muttered. "What are we gonna do after we get rid of our load?"

"Light out for the Trapper Lake country," replied red-necked Hack.

NIGHT clamped down blackly. Long Tom kept accurate check on their progress, and their where-abouts. They followed the State highway for a time, then turned off. He could see the highway markers.

Long Tom made no attempt at a break. His captors kept eyes upon him all the time they were on the ferry. Hands remained in gun-bulged pockets. His slightest move would have meant sudden death.

The van rolled on—for hours, it seemed. The terrain became hilly. At almost every brook they stopped and added water to the radiator.

At last, the van halted. There was a stirring in the rear. Long Tom peered through the window.

Caldwell appeared from the after regions of the van. Ahead of him he propelled the steel-haired girl, Jean Morris.

Her wrists were handcuffed at her sides; adhesive tape crisscrossed her lips. She could only glare rage with her metallic eyes and make angry noises through her nostrils.

The pair were illuminated faintly by the back-glow of the van's headlights.

Caldwell stared at Long Tom. He spat disgustedly.

"Don't let this guy get away!" he warned. "He's probably been listening to you guys talk, and knows plenty."

"We ain't been talkin'," lied the red-necked Hack.

Long Tom kept his pale face expressionless. In his listening, he had garnered one really important morsel of information. This gang seemed to have a headquarters in the vicinity of Trapper Lake, Michigan.

"How do we dish it out to him?" asked Hack.

"Just tie him in the van cab," said Caldwell. "Two of you birds come along with me. The other two are enough to do the job."

"Sure," said Hack. "I know the spot. I was raised in this country. The place is right ahead. It'll work swell."

"It'd better," Caldwell said grimly.

The van rolled ahead, leaving Caldwell, the steel-haired girl, and the two thugs behind. The ponderous vehicle covered perhaps two hundred yards, then angled into a disused side road.

The headlights picked out a tunnellike hole which slanted down into the side of a hill. Some time in the past, an attempt at mining had been made here. The tunnel was rather large—big enough for the van to be driven in.

The mumble of the engine became terrific thunder as the van entered the bore.

For the first time, Long Tom detected the vibration of something of great size moving in the van rear. The monster was apparently disturbed by the roar of the engine.

"I hope the thing don't try to get out!" Hack muttered.

"The van will hold it," grunted the other.

Long Tom tested the handcuff links uneasily. He was stronger than nine out of ten run-of-the-street men. His muscles, however, were unequal to snapping the stout steel links.

"Gettin' uneasy, eh?" jeered Hack.

The fellow drew another set of handcuffs from his pocket. He grasped Long Tom's leg.

The electrical wizard kicked and pitched about violently.

The driver cursed. His attention was distracted; the van crashed into the tunnel wall and stopped.

Both men seized Long Tom. Clubbing him with pistols, straining, grunting, they managed to link his ankle manacles to the steering-post.

"Let's go!" snapped Hack.

They piled out of the cab.

Long Tom heard scraping sounds, then saw the reddish flicker of match-light. He leaned out. Although his feet were secured, he could see the two men. They were applying a match to a fuse which led into a large steel tool locker slung under the van body.

The fuse hissed, and spat sparks. The two men whirled and ran.

THE van motor had killed itself when the machine collided with the tunnel side, and inside the tunnel there was comparative silence, except for the noise of the running men. Somehow, to Long Tom, it was as if the receding steps were in actuality the departure of his own life-ghost.

He wrenched madly, fighting the handcuff links. The steel circlets scraped skin off his wrists and ankles, cut flesh, and rasped tendons. And they held him.

Back in the van interior, the monster stirred uneasily.

On the faint chance that he might arouse the thing and cause it to break free, and in some manner accomplish the saving of himself, Long Tom began to yell.

"Bust out!" he shrilled. "They're trying to kill us!"

There was a violent stir, a terrific impact inside the van; then great blows.

The thing realized something sinister was underway. Either it had understood Long Tom or had sensed the danger.

Long Tom peered out of the cab, stretching as far as the handcuff links would permit. The sparking fire had crawled along the fuse until it was lost to view inside the box.

The monster's struggles caused the van body to rock slightly on the springs.

Long Tom widened his mouth to yell again. The shout, however, never came. Instead, he sealed his lips and listened.

He had caught a sound, a sound so weird as to defy description. A fantastic trilling note—it might have been the plaintive cry of some exotic feathered thing lost in the umbrageous depths of the ancient mine.

It was the sound of Doc Savage.

"Doc!" Long Tom yelled.

The giant man of bronze came plunging down the declivitous mine tunnel, flashlight in hand. He moved the beam occasionally to avoid larger lumps of rock which had fallen from the roof of the abandoned diggings.

The bronze man wrenched at the underslung tool locker into which the fuse ran. It was of steel, heavily constructed like the rest of the van. Opening it was work for a key, or for a steel-cutting torch.

Inside the van the monster struggled futilely.

Doc Savage leaped to the rear. A huge padlock secured the doors, too strong to break! He whipped to the cab and grasped the stout handcuff chain which linked Long Tom to the steering column.

Long Tom had battled that chain futilely. His best efforts had not even elongated the links. The chain parted under Doc's fingers as if it were cheap, soldered watch linkage.

Long Tom was yanked out of the cab and borne toward the tunnel mouth at a dizzy speed.

Doc Savage's flashlight funneled white, and in the incandescence, stony outthrusts of the tunnel walls cast weird, squirming shadows.

Here and there lay lumps of coal which had disintegrated from long exposure to the air. Grayish shale floored the tunnel, this still bearing depressions left upon the removal of tramway ties. Through these, the van tracks rutted deeply.

Long Tom gnawed his lips. He was holding his breath, unaware of doing so. Would the explosion come before they got out?

It did not. Doc Savage dived through the entrance, and veered to the right. In his haste he made some noise. Rocks rolled; bushes whipped.

Drawn by these sounds, from a spot at least a hundred yards distant, a powerful hand-search-light protruded a white tongue. Doc and Long Tom were embedded in the glare. From behind the light, angry yells volleyed.

"Hell—it's the bronze guy!" Hack howled.

Two gun muzzles, lipping flame, became like winking red eyes above the white-hot mouth of the hand searchlight. The bullets passed Doc and Long Tom so closely that the ugly sound was not the conventional *zing*, but more like the snap of glass rods.

From the tunnel mouth came a great, whooping roar. The big hole spat shale, dust, and lumps of old coal.

It might have been the mouth of a gigantic cannon.

Chapter XIII
THE MICHIGAN CLEW

THE concussion of the explosive within the tunnel caused the earth to quake until Doc all but lost his balance, despite his tremendous agility.

Rubble was blown from the mouth of the tunnel with sufficient force to carry many yards; the stuff blasted in the direction of Hack and his companions.

As the hail of debris struck, the pair stopped shooting. Either a rock broke their light, or they switched it off, for its glitter vanished.

Doc Savage, with Long Tom's manacled frame across his tremendous shoulders, pitched through the night. The hill into which the tunnel penetrated was steep. There was danger of the explosion sliding its top down upon them.

The cataclysmic force of the detonation seemed to lift the entire hilltop. Great cracks split and gaped open. Trees upset. Rocks and soil spurted upward, as explosion-gas escaped through the rents.

The hilltop settled, causing great gushes of dust. The tunnel mouth closed completely. The reverberations of the blast whooped and thumped, like unseen giants fighting each other, until they weakened away into nothingness.

The monster within the van, whatever might be its nature, certainly had perished in that blast, buried under hundreds of tons of stone, shale and earth.

A more effective tomb would be hard to conceive.

Doc Savage lowered Long Tom. By way of proof that the bronze man's earlier feat of snapping the handcuff links was no freak, the linkage securing Long Tom's wrists and ankles now parted easily under Doc's great corded hands.

"How'd you get here, Doc?" Long Tom demanded.

"Renny picked me up in the gyro," Doc

explained. "Using the ultraviolet light, we managed to locate the van. We followed the thing, and lost sight of it when it went into the tunnel. I dropped down by parachute to see what had happened."

"The steel-haired girl was taken off the van a few hundred yards back," Long Tom offered.

With the ghostly abruptness as of a bronze specter, Doc Savage vanished into the night. He made directly for the spot from which the shots had been fired.

DUST rolled in choking waves. The cloud banks that had made the sunset so abrupt had gorged the sky with their sooty mass. Dust and clouds, combined, made the night very dark.

Far overhead, Doc could hear faint hissing noises. They might have been made by the wind. Actually, they were the sound of the silent motors which propelled Renny's gyro and the larger speed plane in which Johnny and the others rode. Johnny had landed and picked up Monk, Ham, and fat Griswold Rock.

Griswold Rock had not been enthusiastic about taking to the air, having admitted a fear of airplanes.

Doc Savage, using his fabulously sensitive ears and nostrils, ascertained that the gunmen had fled. He increased his speed. The fleeing pair had taken to the disused road which approached the mine mouth.

Doc, catching faint sounds of their flight, ran faster. His quarry had turned off the road into a very level field. Doc caught a faint tang of gasoline.

Out of his pocket came a small boxlike device. It was a radio transmitter-receiver, designed for an ultra degree in portability. He clicked the switches.

"Renny! Johnny!" he called.

"I'm on," Renny's thumping tones replied.

"Me, too," added Johnny's more scholastic voice.

"Toss out flares," Doc commanded. "I think these fellows have a plane waiting down here. There's a smell of gasoline in the air."

That this deduction was correct was quickly verified. A plane motor whooped into life out on the level field.

High overhead, almost against the black flanks of the clouds, a light appeared. Rivaling the sun in brightness, it bathed the earth in glittering white, causing every grass blade to stand out. It was the flare which Doc had ordered. It sank slowly, lowered by a small parachute. Its intensity seemed to increase as it eased down in the sky.

Doc caught sight of the plane. It was a low-wing cabin job, and it looked fast.

Caldwell himself was inside the glass enclosed cockpit, handling the controls.

GIVING his engine no time to warm up, Caldwell fed the cylinders gas. The low-winged ship picked up its tail and scudded across the field.

In the calcium dare, Doc Savage discerned a feminine face jammed to the cabin windows. The steel-haired Jean Morris apparently was still a prisoner.

The plane vaulted off.

Above, Renny's gyro and Johnny's speed ship came spiraling down to attack.

Doc, directing the affair by radio, commanded, "Watch it, you fellows! The girl is in their plane."

His warning was hardly necessary, however. Caldwell's plane climbed with astonishing speed. To the west, clouds hung very low. The craft made for these. As it banked, Doc caught a glimpse of the license numerals in the flare glitter. He made note of the number, fixing the figures in his retentive memory.

It dived into the vapor bank and was lost to sight before it could be overhauled.

"Holy cow!" came Renny's disgusted ejaculation from the gyro. "We haven't got a chance of trailing them through these clouds."

Renny's gyro and Johnny's faster bus swung in great circles, searching. Johnny even climbed the ship above the clouds, where there was moonlight. No trace did they discern of Caldwell's aerial conveyance.

It had made an escape.

Johnny tossed out another flare, banked down and leveled off. There was some bouncing to his landing, but considering the landing speed of his ship, it was expert.

Long Tom had joined Doc. He watched Johnny get out of the plane.

"Johnny sure looks like the advance agent for a famine," the electrical wizard remarked.

This described Johnny's appearance accurately. He was extremely tall, and thinner than it seemed possible for any man to be. Dangling by a ribbon from his left lapel was a monocle—actually a powerful magnifier.

Griswold Rock scrambled out of the plane after the gaunt Johnny. Rock's fatty face was white as dough, and was dripping perspiration. His hands trembled.

"I hate airplanes!" he wailed. "They always scare me."

So that only Doc could hear, Long Tom remarked, "Everything seems to scare that guy!"

Renny now dropped his gyro lightly upon the field. Alighting, he fanned a huge fist in the general direction of the sky.

"Holy cow!" he rumbled. "How're we going to trail 'em?"

"I can help out," Long Tom said shortly. "I

overheard them talking. They've got a hangout somewhere near Trapper Lake, Michigan. They were going to head for that spot."

Griswold Rock held up plump, soft hands in a gesture of incredulity.

"Surely you're not going to follow them!" he ejaculated. "Don't you see that they are too dangerous to monkey with?"

Big-fisted Renny answered this. "Cracking down on guys like them is what we do for a living."

GRISWOLD ROCK shuddered, and all of his fat jounced and shook.

"I'm a coward!" he wailed. "Don't count on me. I wish I could go to South America or some place until this is all over."

Doc Savage began outlining his intended course of action.

"Renny," he addressed the big-fisted engineer, "your knowledge of engineering includes dope on excavating methods. You probably know where machinery and men can be gotten in a hurry."

Renny nodded and looked gloomy. The gloomy expression was deceptive. The more somber Renny looked the more he was probably enjoying himself.

"You will start excavation on the closed mine tunnel," Doc told him. "Dig in and see what the monster was."

"O. K.," Renny said.

Doc Savage now addressed Ham, whose specialty was law. "You go over the records and recent legal papers of Mr. Rock's Timberland Line railway. See if you can unearth anything of value. Mr. Rock will want to know what kind of papers he has been forced to sign recently, anyway."

Fat Griswold Rock suddenly shook his fist violently at the sky where the plane of their enemies had lost itself. Color came into his flabby cheeks.

"You don't need to look for the chief villain!" he yelled. "It's that chemist, Pere Teston."

For the briefest moment it seemed that Doc Savage's weird trilling note was audible. His five men showed marked interest, for the sound indicated that the big bronze man had just heard something which he considered important.

"Chemist!" Doc repeated. "You neglected to state that he was a chemist."

"Did I?" Griswold Rock clucked regretfully. "I was excited. I suppose I left out that detail. It's not important, anyway. He was a half-baked chemist."

"Half-baked!"

"I mean he had crackpot ideas. He was a nut on scientific farming. He was always going around talking about increasing the efficiency of farm animals. He got so goofy about the idea that he was worthless to my railroad as an employee, so we fired him."

"Along just what lines did he hope to increase the efficiency of farm animals?" Doc asked pointedly.

"I don't know." The fat man shrugged. "I didn't pay much attention to that. He was just another employee. Now, though, I wish I'd kept my eye on him."

Doc asked several other questions. These merely developed the fact that Griswold Rock had no more information of importance to divulge.

"I don't want to go to Michigan with you!" said the fat man.

"We have no intention of forcing you into danger," Doc told him. "You can remain here in New York, if you prefer."

"The rest of us are going to Michigan?" Long Tom demanded.

"We are," Doc told him.

Chapter XIV
NORTHWARD

THE remainder of the night, and part of the following day, was filled with fast, if unexciting, movement.

Big-fisted Renny, calling on engineering acquaintances and contractors, assembled steam shovels, a fleet of dump trucks, and workmen. He began operations on the caved-in mine, scooping his way in to ascertain the nature of the monster which Caldwell's gang had buried.

"This job is apt to take some little time," he reported.

Ham, the legal expert, set to work on the papers of the Timberland Line, Griswold Rock's railroad. Although the little railway operated in Michigan, its main offices were in New York.

"I moved the headquarters down here," Griswold Rock explained. "I never did like northern Michigan. It gets too cold for me up there in the winter."

In his first few hours of searching, Ham unearthed several noteworthy morsels of information. First, Griswold Rock had signed numerous checks under duress. They were large checks— they totaled nearly a quarter of a million dollars. Furthermore, it was evident that Pere Teston had been the recipient of all of these sums. At least, his name was on the face of the checks, and on the back in endorsement.

Fat Griswold Rock did not seem greatly concerned over the huge inroad on his finances. Apparently he could stand monetary loss, but any threat of danger to his person drove him frantic.

"I got out of it lucky!" he said, and fingered his own fat bulges lovingly.

Another interesting detail turned up by Ham was the fact that the Timberland Line had recently bought tremendous quantities of food. This stuff ranged from some hundreds of sacks of flour, to several carloads of dressed beef. There were literally carloads of groceries.

"The purchase orders for that junk must have been among the papers I was forced to sign!" Griswold Rock declared. "This is the first time I've seen them. But they have my signature, all right."

Ham traced down these food supplies. He learned the material had been transferred to a barge in Lake Superior, near Trapper Lake. No one seemed to know what had happened after that. The barge had simply gone away late in the night, and had come back empty.

"Oh, gracious!" ejaculated Griswold Rock. "They've bought enough food for an army! What can it mean?"

"It means that this is something gigantic and carefully planned," Ham decided.

All of Griswold Rock's bulges shook as he shuddered.

"I have an awful feeling," he moaned. "It is that some gigantic, awful menace is hanging over us. I tell you these devils must contemplate something horrible. I've a notion to go to Europe until it's over."

"Suit yourself!" snapped Ham, somewhat disgusted by the fat man's manifestations of profound cowardice. "But before you sail, give me legal authorization to go through the records of your railroad up in Michigan. I want to do some more checking there."

"Very well," Griswold Rock agreed.

He signed an authorization which Ham drew up.

It was well past noon before Doc Savage took off in his largest speed plane for Michigan. With him went Ham, Monk, Johnny and Long Tom. Each man carried such mechanical devices and supplies as he believed he might need.

They left Renny behind, superintending the excavating of the buried monster.

"I'm going to Europe, or somewhere," said fat Griswold Rock, as he saw them off.

THE speed plane Doc was using for the Michigan trip, in addition to being his largest, was his newest. It was a gigantic thing, built to the bronze man's personally drawn specifications—a ship which had created a small furor in the aeronautical world. It was nearly a hundred miles an hour faster than anything approaching it in size.

The fast craft was volleying over the Trapper Lake region of northern Michigan when sunset approached.

Doc was handling the controls. He had not slept the previous night nor that morning. Moreover, the giant bronze man had that morning taken the two-hour routine of exercises which he never neglected.

The exercises consisted of muscular exertions, performed so strenuously that they spread a sheen of perspiration over his great frame. A series of sound waves above and below those audible to a normal ear, he had employed to attune his hearing. He tested an assortment of odors, this sharpening his olfactory organs.

He read pages of Braille printing—the writing of the blind which is a system of upraised dots on paper—to make his sense of touch more acute.

There were scores of other angles to his routine, all intended to develop mental and physical perfection. All of the exercises were scientific in nature, calculated to obtain the most pronounced results.

Despite the exercises, intensive activity, and lack of sleep, Doc Savage showed no signs of fatigue. His companions did not regard this as unusual. They had become accustomed to Doc's phenomenal powers.

The pig, Habeas Corpus, reposed on a coat in the aisle.

The air was cooler in these northern regions. Ham, carefully attired in tailored outdoor garb, felt the chill and glanced about in search of his topcoat.

He saw Habeas. His eyes popped. His neck became purple.

"Ow-w-w!" he shrieked. He made a pass at the pig with his cane.

Habeas sought shelter under Monk's seat. Ham tried to reach him, but was fended off by Monk's hairy hands. Ham promptly belted Monk over the head with his sword cane.

"You fuzzy baboon!" he gritted. "You put that pig up to eating a hole in my coat! He never chewed on things before!"

Monk looked at the overcoat on which Habeas had tried his teeth. It was a straw-colored garment, the latest in weave and cut. Monk lifted a scornful lip.

"If you'd wear clothes like other men wear, it wouldn't have happened!" he snorted. "Habeas must've thought that funny-lookin' thing was a new kind of fodder!"

Ham's swing with his sword cane missed as the plane heeled over on a wingtip, and he had to grab a seat to maintain his balance. Doc was circling Trapper Lake.

TRAPPER LAKE was considered something of a metropolis in this remote woods region. It boasted a population of nearly seven hundred. The largest building in town was the hotel, the Guide's House. The sign on the Guide's House stood up as the most prominent object in town.

The fact that many of the buildings were constructed of logs gave the town an aspect somewhat out of place in this modern age.

The Timberland Line railway depot was a squatty red structure.

No level ground suitable for a plane landing was discernible near town.

"We'll go on and land on the lake near Carl MacBride's cabin," Doc offered. "We'll be on the spot then, ready to look things over, when daylight comes."

Bony Johnny looked surprised. "How we going to find the cabin?"

"That shouldn't be hard," Doc told him. "The newspaper clipping gave its location in a general way."

From their altitude, the shore of Lake Superior was visible to the northward. Red lines, slanted across the lake by the setting sun, seemed to squirm with the undulations of the waves.

The few miles to the lake shore they covered in short order. Renny, peering over the side, slanted a quart of pointing knuckles.

"There it is," he rumbled.

He had discovered the wreck of Bruno Hen's cabin. Brush and timber resembled a moss growth around the demolished structure. The fragments of the shack itself were not unlike a bunch of crushed and broken matches.

Doc's plane was an amphibian, capable of alighting on water or land. The undercarriage wheels disappeared into wells.

The bronze man dropped the big ship expertly on the lake, then taxied inshore.

He did not beach the craft. Instead, he pressed a lever and a light grappling anchor was lowered mechanically. This caught and held on the bottom. Collapsible boats came out of a locker and were planted on the water. They paddled ashore.

A late-calling meadowlark made sound; a jaybird scolded them angrily. Along the lake, leaping fish made splashes. It was a peaceful scene.

They walked to the ruin of Bruno Hen's cabin.

HAM, leaning on his sword cane, studied the wreckage in the pale gray light which was all that remained of the day. The ruin had been yanked apart by curious individuals. These persons had tracked down whatever sign the surroundings might have held. In addition, there had been a heavy rain since the disaster.

"We'll wait for daylight to hunt clews," Doc decided.

They pitched their tents on a bit of high ground near the wreckage. While the others did the actual erecting of the shelters, Doc paddled out to the plane and made use of a powerful radio set which it held.

"Wonder what Doc's doing?" Long Tom pondered, battening down a tent stake with a dead branch.

The question was answered when Doc rejoined them.

"Caldwell's plane actually flew to this vicinity,"

Doc announced. "Checking with the airports between here and New York disclosed one which saw the ship during the night. The plane circled, but the pilot was evidently afraid to land. He went on."

"How'd they come to notice it?" gaunt Johnny asked curiously.

"There was an alarm out for a ship carrying the license numerals which that one bore."

The men showed surprise. They had not known that Doc had spread an alarm for Caldwell's ship.

"The license number should show who owned the craft," Johnny exclaimed.

"It was stolen a month ago from a commercial air transport company in southern Michigan," Doc replied. "A checkup revealed that."

"Another crime to be charged against Caldwell, or Pere Teston, or whoever is behind this," Johnny said thoughtfully.

Complete darkness arrived. This night, like the previous one in New York, was cloudy.

"Kinda feels like a storm," Monk remarked. The homely chemist was engaged in playfully upsetting Habeas Corpus with a toe. The pig seemed to like this.

While they were cooking supper, cottontail rabbits occasionally ventured into the zone of firelight, only to flee as someone moved or spoke. Owls hooted mournfully. Insects clattered high notes, and bullfrogs whooped in bass.

It was a peaceful scene. They settled for the night in pneumatic sleeping bags. All were tired; they soon dropped off to sleep.

Chapter XV
NIGHT TERROR

THUNDER was chuckling softly in the distance when Monk awakened, Doc's hand upon his shoulder. There was no lightning. Monk squirmed, peered into the inky void, and gulped. "Hey, what the—"

"Quiet!" Doc cautioned. "I think something's going to happen."

Monk bounced out of his bag, much to the disgust of Habeas, who had been asleep on the foot.

The pig grunted a few times in discontent, then with strange abruptness it became silent.

Monk fished out a match and thumbed it alight. He hid the tiny flame in his cupped palm, so that only a spear of light escaped and fell upon the pig.

Habeas was sniffing like a pointer. Coarse bristles along his back were on end. Monk listened, and could hear nothing. But the pig had detected the presence of something.

"Habeas has remarkably keen senses," Doc said softly. "The nearest of the things must be at least a mile away from us."

"What things?"

"Just a minute," Doc said, "I'll let you listen."

The bronze giant went to the other men and awakened them. All moved to one side, a few yards clear of the camp.

A strange-looking bit of apparatus stood here. Doc had evidently erected this after the others had gone to sleep. Long Tom, the electrical wizard, recognized it instantly.

"A supersensitive listening device!" he said.

The electrical expert did not trouble to explain further that the thing utilized sensitive parabolic pickup microphones and amplifiers of great power, similar to those employed in radio sets. He presumed that the others knew this.

Doc Savage flicked a switch which connected the loudspeaker to the amplifier output. The sensitivity of the listening device was at once apparent. An owl hooted in the distance, and the sound poured out of the loudspeaker in a great bawl. Habeas Corpus grunted. That, too, was magnified a thousand fold.

Suddenly there came from the loudspeaker noises foreign to the other night sounds. These were watery notes, a great splashing and gurgling. Then came tremendous hissing noises, as of a monster breath expelled.

Doc switched off the listener.

"Huh?" Monk gulped. "That sounds like some-

Collapsible boats came out of a locker and were ... paddled ashore.

thing wading along the edge of the lake."

"There's another of the things in the opposite direction," Doc advised. "As far as I can tell, there are only the two of them. They're approaching slowly."

After a brief interval, the bronze man switched on the listening device again. This time, the splashing sounds were louder, and it was evident that they came from both up and down the lake shore.

"Do you reckon they're huntin' us?" Monk asked uneasily.

"We'll wait," Doc said. "We won't use this listening device anymore, either. The things may hear the amplified sounds."

The men waited, listening so hard that they could almost hear the gurgle of blood in their own veins.

NO listening device was needed now. The noisy wading was becoming louder as the fantastic waders of the night approached.

"I hope they meet each other and fight it out," Long Tom said uneasily. "They sound as big as elephants."

This proved a futile hope. The gigantic things prowling along the lake shore apparently met. One of them emitted sound, a roar which terminated in a hacking and sputtering.

"For the love of Mike!" Monk breathed. "First time I ever heard a sound like that."

There came a loud clank. It was like a tin can being kicked, only infinitely louder. It was followed by another. Metal crumpled noisily; rivets shrieked; brace wires parted with loud dongings.

"Our plane!" Monk growled. "They're tearing it up!"

He started forward.

"Wait!" Doc admonished sharply. "Those things may be dangerous."

A tremendous splashing was accompanying the ruining of the plane. This came nearer, as if the monsters were pushing the plane to the beach.

"Ain't we gonna do something about this?" Long Tom asked indignantly.

"I planted a camera in the treetops, upon first hearing them," Doc explained. "The things are almost in position now to have their pictures taken."

From the ground beside the electrical listening device Doc picked a metallic-looking object, slightly smaller than a baseball. He threw this in the direction of the beach.

The thing detonated with a flash that stabbed at their eyeballs like hot flame. It was powerful flashlight powder which would expose the plate of the camera. He had been able to plant the camera with shutter open, thanks to the murk of the night.

At the flash, both monsters came crashing through underbrush and timber toward the camp.

"They must have located our place by the camp fire earlier in the night," Ham breathed grimly.

"Scatter!" Doc ordered. "These things show signs of intelligence. They're dangerous."

Stealthily, the men parted.

Doc Savage remained where he was, except that he moved a few feet to one side, stooped, and opened a bag. This was part of their equipment, all of which they had fortunately removed from the plane.

Out of the bag Doc took two metallic containers, each of perhaps a quart capacity. Balancing one of these in either hand, he waited. They were great tear-gas bombs.

He delayed throwing until convinced one of the monsters was within fifty feet. Then he hurled both gas bombs. They landed, bursting with loud *whups*.

Then Doc dodged wildly. Something came at him—something thrown. Whether by accident, or due to the fact that the monsters had heard some slight sound which Doc had made, the object was thrown accurately.

It hit Doc. It was such a blow as he had never before felt. He was propelled backward, crashed into a tree, bounced from it to a smaller sapling, and dropped. He lay perfectly still after he fell.

THE thrown thing had not struck Doc Savage squarely, however. A shift, executed almost as he felt the thrown object, had put him partially in the clear. He had an opportunity to tense his great muscles to absorb the shock.

He lay in the soft weeds and dead leaves for only a moment, then reared up. The monster was charging him.

Doc glided to the side, one hand exploring the blackness for saplings and trees, to avoid collision. With his other hand he felt for his flashlight. He found it—a shapeless mass of battered metal and squashed glass. It had come into contact with a tree and was useless.

The monster missed Doc and ploughed on through the brush, travelling blindly. Its coughing, hacking, sputtering and other hideous sounds indicated the effects of the tear gas.

It veered toward the lake, its companion following. With a great splashing, they fled into the night. They traveled with amazing speed, for their sounds were soon lost to the unaided ear.

Doc started toward the beach, desirous of getting to his camera. The plate should tell them the nature of the monsters. But he encountered the tear gas. The night breeze, which was very light, had not yet pushed the stuff out on the lake.

Rather than trouble to dig a gas mask out of

his duffle, Doc decided to wait until the breeze dispersed the vapor. That should not take many minutes.

His men came back to the camp.

"Have any of you got ideas about what the monsters were?" Doc asked them.

None had. It seemed nobody had a flashlight in his possession during the affair. This explained why no light had been shown.

Doc dug a flashlight from their luggage and swiveled the beam about. He was searching for the thing that had been thrown at him. It took only a few minutes to ferret out the object.

"*Whew-w-w!*" Monk breathed. "Did one of them throw *that?*"

That was one of the motors from the big speed plane. The thing weighed several hundred pounds, yet the monster had apparently thrown it without great difficulty.

Doc spattered the flash beam about.

"Look here!" yelled the bony Johnny. "Tracks the things made!"

The prints were tremendous, being roughly rectangular in shape, and sunken deeply in the soft earth.

"They're big as graves," Monk muttered.

This was an exaggeration, the prints measuring in no case more than two feet in length.

The amazing thing, however, was that they were without definite shape.

Doc Savage, examining them, noticed that the earth was pressed perfectly smooth where the weight of the monsters had borne down. There was no mark of hair or scales, nor were indentations of claws distinguishable.

"The prints don't give us much of an idea," Doc said. "Fortunately, we have the camera."

They spent several minutes inspecting the undergrowth, noting how saplings were crushed down, and even small trees bent aside and their limbs torn off.

"Those babies were really strong," Monk muttered.

The gas had dispersed by now.

"We should have a good flashlight photo of the things," Doc declared, and led the way toward the beach.

Once on the sandy strand, he stopped. He played his flashlight beam. For a moment, the fantastic trilling note which was part of this remarkable man of bronze became audible. It seemed to have a slightly disgusted quality.

"What is it, Doc?" Monk asked.

"The monsters smashed into the tree that held the camera," Doc advised. "Moreover, they seem to have been lucky enough to walk on the camera. There's hardly enough of it left to stuff a pipe."

Chapter XVI
THE SUICIDE SLAYING

THE storm on the horizon threatened with hollow thunder for the rest of the night, but did not materialize. Morning sun brought silence to the owls—they had not resumed their hooting for nearly an hour after the visit of the monsters. Meadowlarks, bobolinks, and thrushes greeted the dawn. The rays of the sun turned into glistening jewels the dew which dappled the leaves and grass.

Doc and his men inspected the plane. It lay in shallow water, close inshore. One wing was torn completely off; the other was bent upward for half its length. The stout metal fuselage was dented, crushed. One motor had been plucked bodily from its mount—evidently the motor which had been flung at Doc.

"They sure wrecked the bus!" Monk exploded.

Doc Savage went over the ship, seeking clews. But if there had been signs of any, the lake water had removed them.

He studied the size of the holes which had been beaten in the fuselage. They were nearly large enough to permit a man to crawl inside. The thin alloy metal had parted under the impact of great blows as if it had been paper.

"The things have an almost fantastic strength," Doc commented.

He gave his attention to the tracks which were imbedded in the beach sand and in the softer woodland loam.

"The prints seem to have been made with a substance as unyielding as steel," he declared. "A flesh-and-blood foot would show some change in configuration."

He went over the scene thoroughly. Deep in the tangled brush beyond the camp, whence had charged the monster which had flung the plane motor, Doc found a clew. It proved that their visitants of the night had not been metal robots of titanic proportions.

The clew was a crimson fluid. The red stuff was spilled over leaves, and across the grass for a short distance.

The monster had apparently snagged itself on a limb.

Doc Savage spent half the morning going over the vicinity. Satisfied at last that he was going to unearth nothing, he scrutinized the remains of Bruno Hen's cabin. He spent an hour at that job, but found nothing of value.

They visited Carl MacBride's cabin, and Doc went through MacBride's belongings. The inspection revealed that Carl MacBride had no near relatives.

"That's a relief!" muttered homely Monk, who

had entertained visions of the unpleasant task of informing someone close to Carl MacBride that the man was dead. Such jobs usually fell upon Monk.

Doc and his party went back to their camp site, packed their equipment in tump-line rigs, and set out to walk the five miles to Trapper Lake.

THEY covered half of the five miles, and came upon a grassy glade surrounded by a dense growth of conifers. The group were crossing this when Doc flung himself face downward.

"Drop!" he rapped.

The others had only time to sag their jaws in astonishment before a short, shrill whistle knifed at their eardrums.

Every man flattened; they knew that sound. It meant the passage of a high-powered rifle bullet. The grass was almost knee-high. Prone in it, the men could not be seen at a distance of more than fifty feet.

"Spread out, brothers," Doc directed. "He's liable to try random shots into the grass."

"How'd you locate him, Doc?" Monk called.

Not getting an answer, Monk angled over to find Doc, with the intention of putting the question again. But the bronze man was not to be found.

Doc, at the moment, was scores of yards away, He traveled swiftly, almost against the ground.

Another bullet made a loud buzzing sound through the grass.

Doc's discovery of the rifleman had been no accident. For the previous mile of their progress, the bronze man had noticed a marked lack of bird life. To his trained eye, this indicated someone was moving ahead of them and had frightened the feathered creatures away. Accordingly, he kept his eyes open.

He had sighted the bushwhacker's rifle as the fellow aimed.

The rifleman had a plain white handkerchief tied over his face.

Doc gained the edge of the clearing. Not until he was well into the conifers did he arise. A mighty Nemesis of bronze, he circled to flank the attacker.

He was unsuccessful. The rifle wielder, suspecting his shots had missed, had fled. He could be heard plunging through the brush.

Doc Savage, heading across to intercept the man, found his path barred by a great thicket of brambles. Large trees grew out of the thorny maze. Their branches almost interlocked in spots.

Scarcely slackening his running pace, the bronze man hurtled upward in a great leap. His hands clamped a low limb, and the momentum of his leap carried him over. With an acrobatic agility he landed atop the limb, maintaining a perfect balance.

He remained there so briefly, however, as to seem not to pause at all. He swung up and out, caught another limb, and repeated the process until he stood among the topmost branches.

He glided out on a bough and sprang into space. An onlooker, not knowing the tremendous quality of the bronze man's muscles, would have felt he was committing suicide. Doc's hands found the branch of another tree. He went on through the aerial lanes.

His progress involved Herculean exertion, but he was probably traveling as swiftly as the fleeing rifleman.

Beyond the brambles, Doc dropped to the earth. He was on his quarry's trail. His path led through tangled brush, through thickets of stunted evergreen.

They descended a sharp slope. A sluggish stream appeared, wide and shallow. At one point, a log had fallen across the water. The bushwhacker's trail led directly to the log.

Doc Savage reached the log and stopped.

The water beneath the log was only a few inches deep, and it overlay unpleasant-looking sand. This sand was riled, disturbed.

At one point, great bubbles were rising and bursting.

QUICKSAND! And the bubbles arising might mean someone had fallen in. Or it might mean that Doc's quarry had dropped a rock into the treacherous sand, in an effort to pull a trick.

Doc's eyes ranged the log. It was covered with a green moss. This was undisturbed. The bushwhacker had not walked across; and nowhere was the quicksand stream narrow enough to leap.

Doc gazed around. There were no limbs to which the fugitive might have sprung to hide his tracks.

The opposite bank of the stream was a wall of brush and small trees, and beyond lay thick timber. To gain refuge, the bushwhacker would have had to take wing.

The fellow was in the quicksand. No doubt of it!

From Doc's clothing came the silken cord and grappling hook which he so frequently found of use. He doubled the cord twice, and took a loop around the log.

Monk and the others came up. They were scratched; their clothing was torn. Ham's immaculate garb hung in tatters. They had evidently had a tough time with the brier thicket.

"Hey, Doc!" Long Tom yelled in horror. "You ain't gonna go into that stuff, I hope!"

Doc did not reply. He knotted the ends of the silk cords around a wrist and tied them securely, allowing just enough line to prevent his arm sinking below the surface.

The giant bronze man dropped into the quicksand. As he had expected, the stuff was very loose and liquid. This accounted for the quick disappearance of the bushwhacker.

Doc churned about. He had no trouble sinking in the stuff. The difficulties would come when he sought to extricate himself.

His feet soon found a yielding form. He worked at this, and got it clamped between his knees.

Then came the laborious job of hoisting himself. It was a terrific task, even for Doc's matchless strength. Very slowly—his rising was hardly perceptible to the eye—he lifted himself and his prize.

Great tendons, which were normally part of the symmetrical mold of his arms, stood out in tremendous fashion. His arms might have been corded with steel bars. Perspiration rivulets wriggled down his bronze skin, and mixed with water which covered the quicksand.

The sand made unlovely bubbling noises. Doc's men waited on the bank above. Monk had to be restrained from wading out into the quicksand, with the idea that he might be of some assistance.

At last, Doc lifted the bushwhacker free of the quicksand. He carried the fellow out and laid him on the bank. The man's handkerchief mask was gone now.

It was Caldwell, the slayer of Carl MacBride. A knife hilt stood out from his chest.

IN a dazed fashion, the gaunt Johnny fumbled with his monocle magnifier.

"The knife—this fellow was murdered!" he gasped. "Is he the same man who fired upon us?"

"The same," Doc replied.

"Weren't there any other tracks around?"

Instead of replying, Doc stood erect and ran across the log which spanned the quicksand. He entered the thick bushes on the opposite bank. There he found the explanation of the knife in Caldwell's heart.

Tracks! There was the print of a large foot encased in pac-type shoes. The maker of the print had stood for some time.

Doc followed the pac trail of Caldwell's killer. It was a short procedure. A hundred yards to the right, the quicksand brook joined a larger stream. The murderer had entered a canoe.

Doc worked up the stream, then down. He studied the fish, for the water was clear, trying to ascertain in which direction the finny denizens had been frightened to cover by the passage of the canoe. It was not this, but the absence of turtles from logs, that gave him his clew. The killer had gone downstream.

Doc set out in that direction.

A low *pop-pop-pop* came from ahead—an outboard motor.

Ten minutes later Doc gave it up. He could not hope to overhaul a canoe fitted with an outboard.

He rejoined his men. They had the contents of Caldwell's pockets spread out on the grass. These consisted of a penknife, cartridges for a rifle, a case of cigarettes, and a sheet of yellow paper which had evidently been torn from a grocery wrapper.

Three words were written on the paper:

THE DEATH MILL

"What in blazes do you reckon that means?" Monk demanded.

They left the body of Caldwell where it lay. As a death shroud, Monk and Ham contributed what the brier thicket had left of their coats.

It did not take them long to reach Trapper Lake.

"Not such a hot-lookin' town," Monk decided.

Changing the subject impolitely, Ham pondered aloud, "But why was Caldwell murdered?"

"Probably because we knew his identity," Doc replied.

"But he was masked when he shot at us."

"We saw his face when he killed Carl MacBride in New York," Doc reminded. "That made him a liability to his gang. He was a definite individual for whom we could hunt."

"Wonder if Pere Teston killed him," pale Long Tom muttered thoughtfully.

Doc did not reply.

They worked their way through the business section of Trapper Lake. This was spread along a single street.

Doc entered a general store. In slightly over a minute, he was outside again.

"You fellows wait here," he directed.

Ham waved his sword cane. "But what—"

He withheld the rest. Doc Savage had already vaulted a wooden fence and set out across lots.

In the general store, Doc had asked about a spot called The Death Mill. This place, it seemed, was an old grist mill on the outskirts of town. The ominous place had been deserted for years, it seemed, ever since the former owner had been caught in the grinding stone and crushed to death. Hence the name—The Death Mill.

Doc sighted the dilapidated structure. Mischievous boys had knocked planks off the walls; the roof had shed shingles, as if it had the mange.

Doc took to roadside brush as he drew near. He circled the mill warily, for he could hear sounds from within—nervous pacing.

A man came to the ramshackle door and stood looking out. It was fat Griswold Rock, who had vowed he was on his way to Europe when Doc had last seen him!

Chapter XVII
RENNY'S MYSTERY MISSION

DOC SAVAGE bobbed into view.

For a fat man, Griswold Rock moved suddenly. He jumped at least a foot in the air. He leaped backward, and his head, due to his own clumsiness, banged the ancient door jamb. He sank to his knees, half stunned.

He began to tremble. The trembling was an interesting phenomenon, for it made all of his fatty bulges seem to be filled with kicking frogs. It was almost a minute before he controlled himself.

"I'm so g-g-glad you've come," he stuttered.

Doc's bronze features exhibited no change of expression.

"Your t-t-telegram s-said you'd be here ab-bout this t-time," continued Griswold Rock, still stuttering.

"Telegram?"

"The one you sent me in New York. I g-got it just as I was ready to leave for Europe."

"I sent you no telegram!"

Griswold Rock had gotten to his feet. At the words, his knees buckled as if the tendons had been cut. In his distress, his fingers seemed to wriggle separately, like fat living strings.

"The t-telegram t-told me to come here and w-wait," he wailed. "It was s-signed with your name. Do you think it was a t-trap to m-murder me?"

Instead of answering, Doc Savage roved his gaze over the surroundings. The weeds were very tall, the brush rank; vines entwined to make a labyrinth. Somewhat scrawny-looking walnut trees thrust above the whole. It was a macabre place, suggesting rattling chains and ghostly cries.

"There are no tenanted dwellings nearby," Doc reminded.

Griswold Rock tied his hands into a fatty lump. "They decoyed me here. Maybe they planned to seize me again. Worse still, they might have intended to kill me."

Doc Savage entered the abandoned mill and moved through its moldy rooms. He even examined the cracked, long-disused grinding stones in which the former operator had met his death.

Dust was thick. That made it simple—for the bronze man's trained eyes—to ascertain that no one but Griswold Rock had visited the place recently.

"Where is the telegram which you received?" Doc asked.

"I took a room in the Guide's Hotel," explained Griswold Rock. "I left the wire there."

"Let's go have a look at it."

The backwoods nature of Trapper Lake was evident as they made their way through the streets. Wooden planks were evidently cheaper than concrete, and most of the sidewalks were composed of this material.

The residents were robust, friendly souls. Although Doc Savage and Griswold Rock were strangers, they received pleasant greetings.

The Guide's Hotel, in addition to being the largest building in town, was the newest. It was entirely of frame construction.

The two men went directly to a room on the second floor. Griswold Rock opened his suitcase.

"Oh, my!" he wailed. "It's gone! Somebody's taken the telegram!"

DOC SAVAGE left the room and descended the stairs. He found the hotel proprietor.

"Have you noticed anyone prowling around within the last few hours?" he asked.

"Within the last *two* hours," amended Griswold Rock, who had followed Doc. "I just arrived here two hours ago. I came most of the distance from New York by plane."

The Guide's Hotel proprietor was a grizzled man with humor in his eyes.

"'Sides you two," he declared, "only one stranger has been in this here building today."

"What did that one look like?" Doc asked.

"He was kinda tall, middlin' thin, and had one of them there movie mustaches. Just looking at it made me kinda want to reach out and jerk it off."

"Did the fellow have freckles?"

"Yes siree. Come to think of it, he did."

"Caldwell," said Doc.

"It's his description," Griswold Rock agreed. "Pere Teston is a wizened fellow, and no one would ever forget his weird, dead-looking face. So it wasn't Pere Teston."

Doc made no comment on this.

"They were afraid the telegram would be evidence against them," Griswold Rock continued after a brief interval. "Caldwell came and got it. I tell you I'm worried! They're after me and they're clever."

"Caldwell will not bother you," Doc advised.

Griswold Rock looked surprised. "But he is one of the gang."

"He is also dead." With a few terse words, Doc described the demise of Caldwell.

"Caldwell was stuck with a thrown knife as he reached the log," Doc finished. "He toppled into the quicksand. The murderer escaped. There was no clew to his identity."

"What about the killer's tracks?"

"They were made by extremely large pacs. The size indicated the killer was wearing them over his shoes."

"That sounds like Pere Teston!" Griswold Rock ejaculated. He shuddered. "That shriveled fiend has small feet."

Doc's four men arrived at the hotel. It was decided to make the hostelry their Trapper Lake headquarters.

Doc Savage inquired for a long distance telephone connection with New York City, and learned there were no phone wires out of town.

Doc set up his radio apparatus. Working through a station on Long Island, which transposed his words from the ether to land-line, he got in contact with Renny.

"How's the excavating going forward?" he asked.

"Better than expected," Renny reported. "Doubled the working crew this morning. I located a hydraulicking outfit such as they use for gold mining in the west, and we're using powerful streams of water to wash the hill away."

"Did you check up on the fingerprints found on the gate of Griswold Rock's estate?"

MONK and Ham exchanged glances which, for once, were surprised instead of mutually insulting looks. Here was an angle upon which they had not known Doc was working.

"I checked the prints," Renny reported. "The classifications were broadcast to leading police departments."

Renny paused at the other end to give an order to someone, probably an associate in the excavating work.

"Here's a strange thing about the fingerprints, Doc," he continued. "They were all of men who have escaped from prisons within the last few months."

"All from one particular prison?" Doc asked.

"No. Several different states. One bunch got out of the Jefferson City pen, in Missouri. Another broke out of the Oklahoma hoosegow at McAlester. All got outside aid in escaping."

"This may be significant," Doc remarked.

"Here's something else that may be, too," Renny reported. "The police have a record on Caldwell. His picture is in the rogue's gallery. He has served two prison terms."

"For what crimes?"

"He's a crook who makes a specialty of getting other criminals out of jail. He was caught doing this a couple of times. That's how he happened to go to the hoosegow."

"Anything else?" Doc asked.

"Nope."

The radio and land-line consultation ended with that.

Doc Savage turned to his friends. They eyed him expectantly. It was Doc's custom to assign his associates work which fell in their respective lines.

"Monk," Doc said, "you'll fix up chemical bombs. Make them strong enough to knock out an elephant. Use a gas which produces unconsciousness, rather than fatality."

Monk nodded. The job was up his alley.

Doc assigned work to Ham—the lawyer was to delve further into the records of the Timberland Line railroad, in an effort to see what he could find.

"If you wish, you can assist Ham in this matter," Doc told Griswold Rock.

The plump man trembled violently, but nodded.

"Very well," he groaned. "It seems I had best help you fellows, greatly as I am frightened. I will never feel at ease until this devil, Pere Teston, is brought to justice."

Johnny, the bony geologist, whose learning naturally included an understanding of earthquakes and the seismographic method used to study them, was to plant sensitive listening devices in the earth. Long Tom, the electrical wizard, was to assist in this.

"The idea is to trace the direction which the footsteps of these prowling monsters take," Doc explained.

THE remainder of the afternoon was spent in following Doc Savage's suggestions.

The homely Monk possessed a remarkably compact portable chemical laboratory which he always took upon expeditions of this sort. Long Tom, the electrical wizard, likewise carried an assortment of devices. The two experts utilized their equipment to carry out Doc's suggestions.

Doc Savage spent some time working with devices which he himself had brought. During this interval, he secluded himself in a room of the Guide's Hotel.

When the bronze man appeared, some time later, he was placing in a pocket objects which resembled ordinary .410 gauge shotgun shells.

Ham and Griswold Rock returned to the hotel near nightfall.

"I talked to conductors on some of the Timberland Line passenger trains," Ham reported. "They gave me some interesting dope. It seems that they have noted some very tough-looking passengers on their trains during recent months. These fellows are obviously criminals. All of them got off at Trapper Lake."

Ham paused; he could not resist an urge for dramatics.

"These tough-looking fellows were always in the company of a certain man!"

"Don't beat around the bush!" growled Monk, who was listening. "Who was the guy?"

"Caldwell!"

Griswold Rock wrung his fat hands in fright. "I cannot understand this. Caldwell has been extricating criminals from prisons and bringing them to this vicinity. Why?"

That was the mystery.

It was deepened somewhat by information which Doc Savage secured by radio, later in the day. A fresh crop of "Beware the Monsters!" advertisements had appeared in newspapers all over the country. These had been mailed from Trapper Lake.

Doc consulted the Trapper Lake postmaster. The latter was reluctant to speak at first, but Doc produced credentials signed by the highest of government officials. The postmaster turned into a fountain of information.

Yes, he had noted a man mailing many letters to newspapers all over the United States. Yes, he could describe the man.

He described Caldwell.

Monk, having completed his chemical bombs, did some prowling about town. The homely chemist was an excellent mixer. When he returned to Guide's Hotel he had some information.

"Caldwell seems to have pulled one of his jail deliveries right here in Trapper Lake," he declared. "The local calaboose was broken into about a year ago. A fellow called Nubby Bronson was taken out. The man suspected of engineering the jail delivery answers the description of Caldwell."

"Who was Nubby Bronson?" Doc asked.

"A local bad man," Monk explained. "The fellow had served several short prison terms for petty crimes."

"Was he in for a serious offense when the jail delivery took place?"

"That's the strange part. He was serving thirty days for stealing traps. The jailer said he seemed satisfied with his lot. They were surprised when the break took place."

Doc Savage considered this for a time.

"The inference is that Nubby Bronson did not want to get out of jail bad enough to hire his own delivery?" he queried at last.

"That's the idea," Monk agreed.

Griswold Rock gestured astonishment with his fat hands. "But why should Caldwell break into jail to free a man who did not particularly want to escape?"

If Doc knew the answer to that question, he gave no indication of the fact. He maintained silence.

THE Guide's Hotel, they discovered, set an excellent table. Strangely enough, it was the thinnest man in the party—skeletonlike Johnny—who was the heaviest consumer of food.

"I wonder where the stuff he eats goes to," pondered homely Monk when Johnny, having eaten prodigiously, arose from the table looking, if anything, thinner than before.

Ham scowled at the pleasantly ugly chemist.

"One doesn't have to wonder where your grub goes to. It's converted into hair."

Later, Doc employed his radio transmitter to obtain a connection with New York City. He sought to locate Renny.

"Mr. Renwick left New York by plane about an hour ago," reported one of the big-fisted engineer's associates.

"Left the city!"

"That is correct."

"Why?"

"The excavators uncovered some object late this afternoon," the man in New York explained.

"What was it?"

"No one but Mr. Renwick knows. It was he who found the thing. He ordered all work to cease, and finished the digging personally. He wrapped his discovery in canvas and carried it away. I believe he took it with him in his plane."

"In which direction did he head?"

"There was something said about northern Michigan, I believe."

Doc Savage broke the connection.

"Renny found something important," he informed the others. "He is rushing it up here by plane."

"Then we should hear from him before morning," Monk declared.

Chapter XVIII
THE TERROR THAT SWAM

ALTHOUGH there were no long distance telephone lines, Trapper Lake itself boasted a local phone service. Rooms in the Guide's Hotel were fitted with instruments.

It was slightly past midnight when the bell in Doc's room snarled. The bronze man scooped up the receiver.

"They've attacked Renny!" yelled a shrill voice.

"Who is this?" Doc countered.

The voice was one he had never heard before. The words sounded as if sawed out by a high-pitched violin string.

"Renny is fighting a mob in a patch of woods about a mile north of town," continued the shrill voice.

"Who are you?"

"Renny says he must have been unlucky. He landed right among the gang. I'm calling from the edge of town."

"Are you going to identify yourself or not?" Doc demanded grimly.

"I live in a cabin close to where Renny's having his fight," said the informant excitedly. "He gave me fifty dollars to come and call you."

Doc Savage started to ask questions. A click denoted the receiver had been deposited on the hook at the other end.

"Ham—watch Griswold Rock," Doc ordered.

The fat railroad man had retired to his room, but he now appeared in the door.

"That is very kind of you," he said earnestly. "I would be terrified if one of you gentlemen was not nearby for protection."

"Long Tom—Johnny," Doc asked. "Have you got your seismograph devices all set?"

"Sure."

Homely Monk had been listening. A slow grin overspread his features as he saw that he was to accompany Doc.

"Get your chemical bombs," Doc directed. "Better leave the pig."

Down the street, Doc and Monk found Trapper Lake asleep. Street lamps—they were electric bulbs which dangled from wires spanning the thoroughfares—had been extinguished long ago. A light burned in the depot of the Timberland Line railroad.

The town had only one cab. Finding it at this hour was out of the question. Doc and Monk headed north, running. Monk, considering his short, bowed legs, was capable of surprising speed.

They were nearing the edge of town when sounds of shot came rapping to their ears.

"Rifles!" Monk ejaculated. "The fight!"

A bullfiddle of a moan suddenly drowned the other gun noises.

"It's Renny!" Monk howled. "That noise was made by one of our machine pistols!"

A MOMENT later, Monk found himself running alone. The homely chemist had thought he was running fast, but Doc had left him behind so suddenly that it seemed to Monk that he had turned around and traveled backward.

Until this moment, Doc had been skeptical of the phone call. It was the sort of thing by which a trap would be sprung. But hearing the moan of the supermachine gun had alarmed him more than a little. The weapons were not public property—Doc manufactured them himself; the only ones in existence were those in possession of his men.

For some distance, Doc followed the rutty roadway. This sloped downward and became more rugged, the wilderness on either side more impenetrable.

More rifle shots sounded, and the superfirer blared hoarsely. The sounds came from the left.

Doc veered over. He was forced to go slowly, for the darkness was intense.

He could hear Monk come thumping up. The homely chemist was trying for speed rather than quietness. His approach was anything but silent.

From far down the road—from a point which Monk had passed—a whistle shrilled. It was a blaring whistle of the sort used by policemen. Doc Savage jerked to a halt and listened.

"Monk!" he yelled. "Duck under cover somewhere. Stay quiet."

The bronze man's great voice reached the homely chemist and halted him. Most convenient shelter was the ditch beside the road. Monk flopped into it.

He listened. There was only the fluttering of leaves as they were moved by the night breeze. Monk jammed an ear to the ground. Borne by the earth came thudding noises which might have been gigantic footsteps.

The thumpings approached. Then there was loud breathing—tremendous breathing, such as they had heard the night before on the lake shore.

Doc's powerful voice crashed, "The gas bombs, Monk!"

Monk clawed at a pocket and brought out a gas mask of very compact construction—merely a nose clip and a mouthpiece. From the latter, a tube led to a breath-purifier which was not as large as Monk's hand.

Doc, Monk knew, would be donning a similar mask.

The gorillalike chemist stood erect, preparatory to hurling his gas bomb. But he never threw it.

A rasping, metallic voice thundered out. In volume, it was gigantic.

"They've got gas!" it said. "Don't take chances. Beat it! Get Griswold Rock!"

The metallic nature of the huge voice indicated it was issuing from a loudspeaker. And it was the voice of the red-necked thug, Hack.

Obeying the order, the monster wheeled and charged off in the direction of town. It was followed by another, then a third, and a fourth. Monk's hair all but stood on end as he listened to the thunder of Gargantuan footsteps.

But he was not too unnerved to whip out his flashlight and spray it after the monsters. The things were beyond thick brush. He saw nothing to give a clew to their nature.

OVER where Doc Savage was positioned there sounded a sharp report, and powder flame spurted. Doc was shooting.

Running, Monk joined Doc. He found the bronze man with an ordinary .410-gauge shotgun-pistol. As Monk arrived, Doc again fired at the sound of the fleeing monsters.

The big bronze man was charging the weapon with the special cartridges which he had manufactured during the afternoon.

Doc Savage fired his over-sized pistol twice more from where he stood. Then he ran to the road and sent more of his special bullets down it.

"It was a trick to decoy us out of town," he said grimly. "They've gotten one of our machine guns, somehow."

"D'you reckon they got the weapon off Renny?" Monk asked uneasily.

Doc did not answer this, for it was not the bronze man's habit to hazard guesses. He headed in the direction of town, running swiftly, Monk lumbering along behind.

They had covered scarcely a hundred yards when sudden, scalding white light washed over them. The beam came from some distance down the road.

Doc slammed against Monk. Together, they spun into the ditch.

Machine gun lead moaned and ripped along the road. The volleying metal scooped clods and kicked dust into the ditch. The mingled buzz of ricocheting slugs was like the droning of oversized bees.

"This must be the guy who gave the command with the loudspeaker," Monk hazarded.

The homely chemist was tugging to get his superfiring machine pistol from its holster.

"I was afraid this lead-sprayer wouldn't stop the big babies," he growled. "I'm sure gonna use it on this cookie, though."

He reared up on his knees. His gun howled, and the light promptly went out.

"Got him!" Monk exclaimed, his usually small voice boisterous and gleeful. He ran toward the machine gunner.

But he had not gotten the fellow. That slight error would have cost him his life, had Doc not seized his leg and yanked him down. As Monk sprawled prone, a fresh storm of machine-gun slugs swept the road.

"Didn't you notice how steady the light was?" Doc inquired. "The fellow laid it on something."

While the machine-gun slugs were gnashing at the opposite side of the road, Doc Savage lifted for a quick look. He could not detect the muzzle flame of the weapon.

"The gun must have a flame-digester on the muzzle," he said. "Otherwise, we could spot it."

The bronze man quitted the roadside ditch. Working to the right, he reached a mass of vegetation. He worked through this with a quietness little short of uncanny. In developing his ability to move silently, Doc Savage had studied the ways of the masters of stealth—the hunting carnivora of the jungles.

He listened, hoping to locate his foe.

But it was another sound which caught his attention. Shrieks! Excited cries! Shots, the crashing of timber and the squall of a fire siren! The uproar came from the direction of Trapper Lake.

The monsters had fallen upon the town.

Chapter XIX
THE MONSTERS RAID

THE machine gunner menacing Doc Savage could be heard running. He was making in the direction of Trapper Lake.

Doc plunged in pursuit.

The fleeing gunner turned off the road. There came a squeak of automobile springs, the metallic clank of a slamming door. An engine moaned and headlights came on. The car dived into the road and scooted away.

Doc Savage sprinted. Given a break, he might have overhauled the machine before it gathered too much speed. But the driver suddenly sprayed machine-gun bullets over his back trail, on the random chance that he might score a hit. In addition, Monk started shooting from down the road.

To avoid being caught in the cross fire, Doc Savage was forced to retreat. The car's headlights were lost in the windings of the road.

Monk came lumbering up.

"Blast it!" he growled. "If there had been some kind of a target to shoot at, I'd have bagged him."

Falling silent, the homely chemist listened to the uproar from Trapper Lake. Women were screaming now. Pistols whacked; shotguns made cannonlike bangings. Men howled and cursed. Wood splintered, and large things upset with jangling noises.

Doc and Monk headed toward town.

After a time, they were conscious that, from the sky, beginning in the infinite distance and growing louder, had come a drone.

"A plane!" Monk ejaculated. "That'll be Renny!"

Doc Savage drew his flashlight and pointed it at the plane sound. His thumb tapped the button, and the lens spouted long and short bursts of light—the telegraphic code.

A flashlight eye blinked answer from the plane.

"It's Renny!" Monk grunted. "He seems to be flying the gyro."

With his light, Doc directed Renny to land on the road.

"We'll tackle this mess in Trapper Lake from the air," he advised Monk.

The windmill ship spun down and hovered overhead. Hood lamps under the wings spread a glare which illuminated the road. Then it landed.

Renny thrust his somber features into view. He cut the exhaust into the muffler cans, and the motor became silent enough to permit conversation.

"Got any flares?" Doc cabled to him.

"Nope," Renny rumbled. "I unloaded all extra equipment to lighten this crate so it'd fly faster."

Doc and Monk piled into the gyro cabin. The ship, while not large, would lift Doc and his five men. Doc took the controls.

"You just got in?" he demanded, as he guided the gyro into the air.

"Just got here," Renny agreed.

"Was a supermachine gun stolen from you in New York?" Doc asked.

"Yeah—how'd you guess it?" Renny boomed, surprise in his great voice. "I left the thing in the car while I was supervising the excavating. Someone lifted it."

"They were watching you!" Monk ejaculated. "Whoever stole the gun probably came on by plane."

"What did the digging in New York yield?" Doc asked.

"The dangedest thing!" Renny rumbled. "I'll show it to you now."

THE big-fisted engineer twisted and dropped an enormous hand to a canvas-swathed package reposing on the floorboards in the rear of the cabin of the plane. He began unwrapping it.

"Huh!" Monk muttered. "The darn thing, whatever it is, is almost as big as a suitcase!"

"Get ready to have your hair stand on end," Renny boomed.

He flung back the last thickness of canvas.

Monk stared. His small eyes all but jumped from their gristle-walled pits. His oversize mouth opened as much as was possible.

"Whe-ew!" he exclaimed.

Up until that moment, Renny had possessed the biggest hand Monk had ever seen. Renny's paws were tremendous.

Yet, compared to this monster hand which had been swathed in canvas, Renny's was as the hand of a baby alongside that of a man. It was natural in shape, but unearthly in its hugeness.

Renny himself whistled in awe as he once more looked at it.

"Holy cow!" he boomed. "The guy who owned that must have weighed a ton."

The bronze countenance of Doc Savage exhibited no marked change as he inspected the titanic relic. It was as if he had expected something of the sort.

"Is this the only part of the monster you uncovered?" he asked.

"No," Renny said. "The rest of the body was there—the fragments of it, that is. The thing was instantly killed in the explosion."

"For the love of mud!" Monk's tiny voice was wisplike. "So this hand belonged to the baby who reared up through the floor of Griswold Rock's house."

Doc Savage dropped the gyro down toward Trapper Lake. Their discussion, and Renny's exhibition of the colossal hand, had taken only a moment.

At two or three points in Trapper Lake, houses were burning. These scattered flickering red light over the rest of the town. The crimson-swathed scene was starkly fantastic.

The giants—they were monster men—had already raided the Guide's Hotel.

They were now retreating. In order that their heads might not project above the housetops they were bending almost double. They were like hideous men in a toy town.

"Holy cow!" Renny boomed. "Never thought I'd see a thing like this!"

"The big babies are wearin' armor!" Monk breathed.

Monk had hardly spoken when they were witness to a potent demonstration of the effectiveness of the shiny steel plates which banded the giants' chests, heads, and legs—even their feet.

A Trapper Lake citizen leaped out of his cabin. He held a rifle. Taking deliberate aim, he fired.

The bullet merely tilted a helmet over on the ear of a giant. This particular giant was a big black fellow. His head, judging from the shape of his helmet, came to a conelike point, instead of being rounded.

"Remember the three pinhead savages from the circus?" Monk yelled. "That must be one of them!"

After adjusting his helmet, the pinhead giant charged the woodsman who had fired.

The rifleman ducked into his cabin, ran through it, popped out of the front door and scuttled into the concealment of high weed.

The pinhead thought the rifle wielder was still in the cabin. The black monster thrust a head in the door, then tried to get inside. Twisting, squirming, he barely managed to make it. But he apparently had difficulty moving around the interior.

The roof burst open and his tremendous shoulders and head appeared. He wrenched his arms free. He tore rafters out bodily and threw them away, great scabs of shingles still attached. Finally he extricated himself from the ruined house.

"They're tremendously strong, even for their size," Monk breathed. "Dumb, too, or he wouldn't waste his strength bustin' out through a roof like that."

The pinhead followed his fellow giants out of town.

DOC SAVAGE tooled the gyro after the monster men. He kept fairly high and switched on the brilliant landing lights. These illuminated the giants.

The monsters were running down the road which led to the lake shore. They came to a wooden bridge. Three of them stepped upon the plank at once. The timbers gave way, precipitating them into the creek below. There was a great splashing as they extricated themselves.

Doc Savage advanced the gyro accelerator. The ship did not have a conventional propeller. Its speed was regulated by the inclination of rudder-like vanes affixed to the tips of the rotating wings. Advancing the accelerator set these vanes to digging into the air at a greater angle.

Doc had discovered that the giants were following a car. The top of the machine bore a cluster of four large loudspeakers.

"That's the guy who tried for us with the machine gun!'" Monk declared.

Doc sent the windmill plane toward the fleeing car. They were close to it when a man stuck his head out of the rear door.

It was Griswold Rock. The fat man flailed about with his pudgy fists; he drove fierce blows back into the car at a target which could not be seen. He made imploring gestures with his arms, as if pleading for help, then was yanked back out of sight into the car.

A man swung out, clinging to the running board of the automobile. He held an aircraft-type machine gun harnessed to a belt about his waist. With one hand he elevated the weapon. Its muzzle flamed red fire.

The bullet stream—a reddish thread of tracer—missed the gyro by fully a hundred feet, then sought the target in wild sweeps. The bouncing car was not a foundation conductive to marksmanship.

"I'll fix that cookie!" Monk gritted, and leaned out with his superfirer.

Monk's gun hooted, and the man on the car sagged. Monk was a remarkable shot when he could see his target. Mercy bullets from his rapid-firer had stricken the gunner with instant unconsciousness.

Hands inside the car caught the senseless man, however, and hauled him inside.

"Now, if I can pot the driver through the top of the machine!" Monk chortled.

He never had a chance to try this. Doc suddenly whipped the gyro away from the spot.

"Hey!" Monk yelled. "We may be able to bag—"

Doc merely pointed at the fuel gauge.

"I made it here non-stop from New York!" Renny groaned. "Fuel is about gone."

"We'd best get far enough away that the giants won't see us when we make a landing," Doc offered.

The engine died, fuel gone, as the bronze man was bringing the ship down some miles to the north. He had picked a spot near the lake shore.

"What a break!" Monk groaned.

Chapter XX
THE WINGED PERIL

DOC SAVAGE had selected an emergency landing spot near the lake shore for a specific purpose. He dug binoculars out of the cockpit duffle pocket, then quitted the windmill plane.

He ran for the beach. Here, as along most of this wilderness shore, there was timber. Doc sought a large tree. He did not use his flashlight, but felt about in the black night with his hands.

Finding a towering pine, he mounted. Monk and Renny, puzzled, clambered up after him.

The monsters, from the direction they had taken, should have reached the lake shore perhaps two miles away to the westward. Doc focused his binoculars in that direction.

"What's the idea?" Renny asked.

Doc passed the binoculars to him. "Take a look."

Renny did so. In the jet night he could not see the giants. But he did discern tiny spots which glowed with an unearthly purple luminance.

"Say, what's them light patches?" he demanded.

"A chemical compound akin to phosphorus," Doc explained. "The stuff begins to glow after it is exposed to the air half an hour or so."

Monk, astride a limb below, emitted a knowing snow. "The dope was in the shotgun slugs you plugged at the giants!"

"It was," Doc admitted.

The bronze man fell to watching the luminous spots which marked the position of the monsters. The glowing patches moved out into the lake and became stationary.

The great loudspeaker voice of Hack, thundering out, carried over the two miles with surprising volume.

"Bring the speed boats!" Hack called.

A moment later, in answer to the red-necked man's behest, marine engines sputtered into life. Boats had been waiting out in the lake. They sped for the shore.

"Three of them!" Monk decided, after counting the craft.

The giants went aboard the speed boats, and the craft headed out into the lake.

The glowing spots on the giants seemed to grow larger, although the monsters were being carried away.

"They're trying to rub the shiny stuff off," Renny thumped. "Their efforts just spread the dope."

Doc Savage got careful bearings on the direction taken by the launch.

Distance finally swallowed the glowing smears on the giants.

DOC and his two men moved down the lake shore to the point where the boats had been boarded.

They found the car with the loudspeaker equipment. It was parked near the shore, deserted.

Later, Doc traced the license number of the vehicle. The machine had been purchased in Detroit a few weeks before by a man giving his name as Pere Teston, but who answered the description of the slain Caldwell.

On its side the car bore the advertising of a political party which was now campaigning. It developed that the car had no connection with the political organization, however.

"They put the sign on it so the loudspeaker wouldn't attract suspicion," decided big-fisted Renny.

The men returned to Trapper Lake.

The town was in an uproar. Women still screamed, sobbed and had hysterics. Men galloped about, wild-eyed, their persons bristling with weapons. Almost everyone was barefooted, having been routed out of bed. A number of old fashioned male nightgowns were to be seen.

Despite the noise and turmoil, not a great amount of damage had been done by the giants. The house into which the pinhead monster had crawled was a wreck. A number of fences had been torn down; gardens were trampled. The door of the Guide's Hotel had been demolished. Shapeless tracks of the big, armored feet were thick.

"One of the infernal giants just butted the door down and climbed in," reported the dapper Ham.

He indicated the hotel door with his sword cane. "I made a pass at the brute. Then retreat looked good, so I jumped from the handiest window."

"They came after Griswold Rock!" declared Long Tom.

Doc and his men scattered, and devoted themselves to attending to the injured.

The giants had seized four Trapper Lake men in the course of their raid. Using only their leviathan hands, they had crushed every vestige of life from these victims. The bones of the unfortunates had been broken, limbs wrenched from their bodies, their skulls crushed.

"I saw one of the men get killed!" wailed a Trapper Lake citizen. "A giant just picked him up, took his head in both hands, and mashed it like you and me would bust an egg."

HAVING stayed awake the rest of the night, Trapper Lake looked around in the morning and saw something like fifty newspaper men. While there were no long distance telephone lines out of town, telegraph wires paralleled the Timberland Line railroad, and wires had conveyed news to the outside world of the visit of the giants.

The press took fire. Almost half the passengers on the next train were newspaper reporters, and the other half newspaper cameramen.

More correspondents came by plane. A blimp flew up from Detroit, carrying the reporters and cameramen of a tabloid newspaper.

It dawned on newspapers in every large city in the United States that here was the explanation of the strange "Beware the Monsters!" advertisements which they had been publishing.

A tri-motored speed plane came in with the sound cameras of a newsreel concern. Two enterprising journalists brought their own radio stations and operators.

Before noon, Trapper Lake stood on the front pages of every newspaper in the country in two-inch black type, or larger. Pictures were telephoned. Maps were drawn with X marking the spot where Trapper Lake stood.

Some enterprising city editors, unable to get pictures, had their artists draw giants. Exaggerated stories were flying around, so the artists drew their giants tossing houses around.

The giants grew in size with every repetition of the tale. Trapper Lake had its share of tall story tellers, and these fellows outdid themselves. The giants became bigger and bigger.

Word got out that Doc Savage was on the scene. A wild rush to interview the bronze man ensued. A New York newspaper wired its reporter, promising him a year's vacation in Europe, all expenses paid, if he could get a first-person story from Doc.

The reporter hunted like a wild man, but failed to earn the year in Europe.

Doc Savage, being possessed of a hearty disapproval of seeing his name in public print, had withdrawn to the seclusion of a clearing some miles from town. Here he and his men discussed and consulted with each other.

They had done some sleuthing before the newspaper locust swarm had arrived.

"I checked on the fingerprints of the giant's hand which Renny dug up," Long Tom said.

He mopped perspiration off his pale brow. "You remember that bird, Nubby Bronson, who was taken from the Trapper Lake jail?"

"Sure," Monk grunted.

"The fingerprints of that big hand and Nubby Bronson's prints were the same in design."

"Well, I'm a son-of-a-gun!" cried bony Johnny. "They grabbed Nubby Bronson out of jail and made him into a giant!"

Ham, his sword cane tucked under an arm, came up. He had been working with the portable radio.

"I've broadcast a description of those giants, as you directed," he told Doc. "They answer the description of the criminals whom Caldwell got out of jails all over the country."

"We know now why Caldwell was collecting them," said Monk. "He was gathering them for

Pere Teston to make into giants."

With that, Monk scratched the winglike ears of his pig, Habeas Corpus.

The dapper Ham scowled at the pleasantly ugly chemist and his equally homely pet.

"The pattern must have been mislaid the day you two were made!" he snorted.

Monk sighed, as if he had stood about as many jibes as he could bear.

The pig, Habeas Corpus, was looking intently at Ham, as if he resented the dapper lawyer's words. The pig opened his mouth.

The thing which happened then always drove Ham into a screaming rage. The pig seemed to speak distinct words:

"I'm gettin' dang tired of the stuff this funny-faced lawyer calls humor."

Ham purpled very indignantly. He gripped his sword cane.

"Dramatics!" sneered the voice from the pig. "Ain't he a funny-lookin' snipe in them rags?"

Ham was particularly touchy on the subject of his clothing. He still wore the garb which had been ruined in the bramble thicket, although it was far from his liking. He slashed suddenly with his sword cane.

Monk dodged wildly to get clear.

Monk had learned ventriloquism solely for the purpose of having Habeas Corpus express scathing opinions of Ham. The business of the talking pig, although ridiculous to watch, invariably filled Ham with rage.

The conversation reverted to the giants.

"But for what purpose did Pere Teston make the big fellows?" Renny pondered.

THE world got the answer to that question that afternoon.

To the mayors of four great cities, the mail brought letters. The cities were Detroit, Cleveland, New York, and Chicago. The letters bore Trapper Lake postmarks.

They had been mailed during the visit of the giants!

The four mayors had read the newspapers, so they knew what had happened in Trapper Lake. They could not fail to know it—the news was in scareheads all over the front pages.

The four mayors opened the letters with curiosity. All four got the shock of their lives.

The Detroit mayor received his missive first. It read:

YOUR HONOR:

Have you read the "monster" advertisements in the newspapers recently? Those were part of my campaign. Possibly you have read of the episode at Trapper Lake last night. If not, I advise you to do so.

My giants visited Trapper Lake for a reason other than the seizure of Griswold Rock, although the latter was necessary. I wanted the world—particularly Detroit, Cleveland, New York, Chicago—to realize the power of my giants.

You will consult with leading bankers of your city, advising them to assemble five million dollars. The sum is to be in small, unmarked bills.

Tomorrow you will receive a letter of instruction about getting the money into my hands. That letter has been posted.

If my terms are not complied with, my giants will visit your city. They will not be in a pleasant mood. They will kill people, and wreak incalculable damage.

One giant will be designated to hunt you out personally.

You may think machine guns and gas will be effective against my giants. Do not be fooled. They wear bulletproof armor, and they have special gas masks.

I trust you will not make the mistake of thinking this is a crank's letter.

PERE TESTON

After reading that, the Detroit mayor tilted back in his chair and had a good laugh.

Then he sent out for the late newspapers and reread the Trapper Lake story. When he finished, he was not laughing. The story had made detailed reference to the crushed condition of the Trapper Lake victims. The mayor called several leading bank presidents and showed them the letter.

"What is the police force for?" asked the bankers.

So the mayor called the police chief, and the chief, in turn, had his men oil their machine guns and break out fresh gas bombs. Radio squad cars were set to prowling roads around the city. Police boats covered the lake front.

In Cleveland, New York, and Chicago, the reaction was about the same, except that in New York City, naval destroyers quietly took up positions around Manhattan Island. They knew Doc Savage's reputation in New York, knew his name had been in the past associated with the combating of perils before which police departments were helpless. If Doc Savage was involved in the matter of the giants, the thing was no laughing affair.

Newspapers ate up this newest development. Sheets that had red ink ran it in their biggest headlines. Here was *the* newspaper story of the year.

Pere Teston was investigated, and the facts unearthed added to the general excitement.

It was found that Pere Teston was a man who had dabbled in chemical experiments since childhood. But he had not made chemistry his profession—it had been a hobby.

Pere Teston, railroad men who had known him revealed, had for years maintained that it was possible to develop compounds to increase the size of living beings. The friends had laughed; they thought this was just another crazy idea.

That day, several of Pere Teston's former acquaintances collected large sums of money for telling their story to the newspapermen. Pere Teston, these men declared, had talked much of developing giant cows, who would give great quantities of milk. He had spoken of huge draft horses, which would be a boon to the farmer.

No one could recall his having spoken of an army of giant men to terrorize the world.

"Probably he thought of that later," said one man who had known Pere Teston.

"When did he disappear?" asked a reporter.

"A year or two ago, maybe," was the reply.

The truth was that no one seemed to be just certain when Pere Teston had dropped from sight.

Before nightfall, almost five hundred more planes were enroute for Trapper Lake, bearing correspondents and photographers.

BEFORE nightfall, too, Doc Savage and his men took off on a prowl of their own. Doc entertained an idea.

"Everything points to these giants having their headquarters somewhere in the lake," he pointed out. "Their food supplies, brought in on the Timberland Line, were transferred to barges on the lake."

"But where can their hangout be?" pondered big-fisted Renny.

"We got a line on their retreat last night," Doc said.

The gyro fuel tanks were filled to the slosh-over point with fuel smuggled out of Trapper Lake. They headed out into the lake.

Half an hour's flying put them over an island. It was covered with brush and rock, and certainly harbored no giants. Doc continued onward.

The previous night had been cloudy, extremely dark. This one promised to be gloriously moonlit. They flew high, dropping down when they sighted islands.

An hour passed; another. The fuel was holding out well. The gyro, thanks to its hovering ability, enabled them to scrutinize closely such islands as they viewed.

A half dozen specks of rock and soil they sighted without discerning a sign of the giants.

Another and somewhat larger island appeared.

Ham eyed his watch. "Ten o'clock and all's well," he stated.

He was wrong. Up from the isle ahead a plane came boring.

When it was still some three hundred yards away, machine-gun muzzles flamed like tiny red eyes from its cowl. Tracer bullets, climbing past Doc's gyro, might have been red sparks.

The attacking ship was a low-wing bus, very fast.

"That's the crate in which Caldwell and his gang hopped from New York!" Long Tom yelled.

Doc climbed the gyro, jockeying to one side, then the other, avoiding the machine-gun slugs. As the attacking ship slid past, Doc heaved the gyro over on its side and flicked the landing-light switch.

The illumination disclosed a face in the control cockpit of the other plane. It was the steel-haired girl—the ex-lion tamer, Jean Morris.

Chapter XXI
THE SWIMMING GIANTS

LIKE a thing frightened by the glare of the landing lights, the other plane scudded away. It banked and came back. Again the cowl-mounted rapid-firers opened red eyes.

Doc Savage hung the gyro motionless in the night sky and watched the thread of tracer bullets warily, prepared to maneuver the gyro clear if it came too close.

The sight of the steel-haired girl in the other plane had kept Doc from driving bullets into the engine of the enemy ship while the pilot was blinded by the floodlight.

"The hussy," Monk complained. "Who'd have thought this of her?"

"You were making calf eyes at her in New York," Ham snorted.

Monk grinned sheepishly. "I'd probably do it again, too. She's a looker."

The tracer bullets drew too near. Doc dropped the gyro straight down. The move was so abrupt that the men grabbed at their chairs.

Tracers ran strings of phosphorus fire through the space they had vacated.

"What are we gonna do about this?" Monk pondered.

Doc sank the gyro rapidly. The other ship followed them down in a tight spiral. Doc flattened some fifty feet above the lake surface. Advancing the accelerator, he streaked along above the lake.

It looked as if he had generously helped himself to suicide, for the other plane swooped down upon their tail, its two cowl guns lipping flame.

The lake surface was fairly calm, and the small geysers knocked up by the bullets were visible ahead of Doc's windmill. The tracers, as they ricocheted, seemed to be sparks bouncing from the water.

Doc waltzed the gyro right, then left. The other ship, attempting to follow these maneuvers with its sight rings, merely succeeded in firing wide of the target.

Renny used his enormous hands to mop perspiration off his forehead. He knew the danger they were in. Even Doc's consummate skill could not avoid the pursuing bullets for long.

Abruptly, for no visible reason, the plane behind gave up the attack. It wobbled off to one side, careening in the sky.

The pilot seemed to control his craft with the greatest difficulty. Trying to fishtail to reduce speed, the ship nearly went into a spin. Then it sought to land.

"Bet the gal don't know what happened to her," Monk howled gleefully.

IF the steel-haired girl was mystified, she was not the only one. The dapper Ham was also puzzled.

"What *did* happen?"

Monk slapped his bulging chest with a furry fist. "Give *me* credit for that."

"I didn't see you do anything," Ham sneered.

Doc climbed the gyro ... avoiding the machine-gun slugs.

"Doc turned the stuff loose, of course," Monk admitted. "But I mixed it before we took the air. It's gas. The stuff is in a tank in the back of the bus. Doc simply pulled a valve cord and released some of it. In the moonlight, our steel-haired lady friend didn't notice it."

Ham glanced at the other ship. "You can have the credit!"

"Huh?"

"The gas doesn't seem to have worked!"

To their astonishment, they saw that the other craft had straightened out and was climbing into the air.

"The glass enclosed cabin of the crate!" Doc said. "Just enough of the gas got in to cause temporary dizziness."

The bronze man hurled the gyro toward the other ship. His metallic features were expressionless. He reached a corded hand back into the cabin.

"Your rapid-firer," he requested of Long Tom.

The slender, unhealthy-looking electrical wizard passed over his compact little supermachine pistol.

"Every third slug in the ammo drum is a tracer," he vouchsafed.

The other ship, instead of turning back to give battle, was flying a straight course not far above the water.

"Givin' her head a chance to clear!" Renny boomed.

Conversation was possible inside the gyro because of the unusual efficiency of the silencer on the engine. The rotating wings had also been designed to create a minimum of wind-whistle.

Doc Savage drove after the other ship. It was flying slowly; he overhauled it rapidly.

"This is gonna be simple, after all," Monk said optimistically.

The fight had drifted through the sky until they were now hardly more than a mile from the island which they had intended to investigate.

The isle seemed to be nothing more than an expanse of rock, spotted here and there with stunted, wind-twisted trees. There were many large boulders on it.

Doc Savage opened the cabin window. Air rushed in, together with the loud hiss of the silenced motor. He aimed with his machine pistol.

But before he could fire, a tiny rip appeared in the fuselage of the other plane. This had apparently been made by a knife or an ax.

The muzzle of a machine gun poked through the opening, its snout slavering flame. The shooting was more accurate than previously.

Clattering, gnashing, lead chopped at the underside of the gyro. Long rips opened in the fuselage.

Monk's pig, Habeas, squealed in alarm.

Doc juggled the controls with a dazzling speed to get away from the deadly leaden hail eating at the fuselage. He succeeded; then the lead storm found them again.

This time, the slugs snapped in the region of the gas tank. They chattered with an appalling noise.

Again Doc maneuvered clear.

"Holy cow!" Renny thundered. "That last burst opened the fuel tank!"

An instant later, colorless gasoline washed over the floorboards. It reeked in the cabin.

The other pilot had been more fortunate than he knew. The fuel tank of the gyro was coated thickly with a fire-proofing and extinguishing compound—it was practically impossible for it to be fired by incendiary bullets. A burst must have struck, opening a leak through the spongy protective coating.

A stark grimness had settled on the faces of Doc's men. The sky brawl had progressed to a point where chivalry had somewhat lost its appeal.

The gyro flung in alongside the enemy ship. They made a discovery which was nothing if not interesting.

"Hey!" Monk howled. "The girl ain't flying that bus!"

THE steel-haired girl was lashed in one of the bucket seats in the pilot's cockpit. They could see that now, because she was pitching about madly, and apparently was on the point of freeing herself.

"I knew she was all right," Monk chortled.

The actual pilot of the other plane was a squat fellow in a tan blazer. Due to the shadows inside the plane, they could not tell much about him.

"He ducked out of sight and flew blind whenever he was close to us!" Monk decided, his usually small voice a great yell. "That's why we couldn't see him!"

The other pilot discovered that the girl had loosened her bindings. He flung himself toward her. Using the machine gun, he clubbed at the girl.

The young woman threw herself from under the descending weapon, then clutched its fluted barrel with both hands.

Pitching about in the fight that followed, one or the other disturbed the controls. The plane reeled over on a wing tip, motor bawling.

The squat pilot saw his danger. He released the steel-haired girl. Wildly, he battled the controls. But there was insufficient time.

The girl took one look at the water, then covered her head with her hands to break the force of the crash.

A wing tip knifed the water first. The wing crumpled. The plane hit the water and jumped end over end. The other wing left the fuselage as if sliced off by an invisible razor. The battered hulk wallowed a few yards and came to a stop. It began to sink.

Doc Savage drove the gyro toward the wreck. The windmill plane could land with equal facility on earth or water. Doc, however, did not intend to land. He hovered over the wrecked and sinking plane, the water some ten feet below. He turned the controls over to big-fisted Renny.

"See what you can do about that gasoline leak!" he directed. Then, head-first, he pitched overboard.

Doc struck the water cleanly, with a minimum of splash. His powerful frame curved expertly an instant after the moment of impact, and the result was a perfect shallow dive. He seemed scarcely to wet his back.

Doc stroked to the wreck. A hole gaped in the fuselage. He grasped the edge of this, hauled himself up and glanced into the cabin.

LONG TOM

The body of the pilot was being tumbled about by the water that poured into the cabin. There was a crease nearly three inches deep across the top of his skull, where he had smashed against a strut.

A few feet from the dead flier, the steel-haired girl paddled feebly. She was dazed, but seemed otherwise not seriously damaged.

DOC SAVAGE reached into the sinking plane and hauled the girl out. He was none too soon, for the stricken craft, weighted by its engine, sank. The whirl drew Doc and his burden beneath the surface. Powerful stroking on the bronze man's part brought them up again.

Bubbles the size of water buckets arose from the sinking plane and, bursting, made plopping noises.

Doc glanced upward, then around. The gyro was on the lake surface! It had settled there during the momentary space when the bronze man was under water.

"You'll sink!" Doc shouted warningly. "Those bullets all but tore the bottom out of the fuselage!"

"The gas is gone—leaked out!" Renny boomed. "We couldn't plug that hole. It was in an inaccessible position."

The men in the gyro were bringing out collapsible canvas boats. They tossed these into the water, then flung articles of equipment into the little shells.

The gyro settled, rocking a little. Doc's men voiced no more words; the business of transferring their paraphernalia to the boats was too urgent.

Monk moved Habeas Corpus from the stricken plane.

They completed the shift with only fragments of seconds to spare, and clambered hastily into the folding boats, barely escaping from under the great wings of the gyro as it went down.

Doc Savage paddled to the nearest folding boat. He lifted the steel-haired girl in; then, careful not to upset the shell, clambered aboard himself.

The steel-haired girl, recovered now, stared at Doc in the moonlight. She spoke, and her voice was calm for all of the ripping excitement of the last few minutes.

"They tied me in the cockpit," she said. "They wanted you to think I was your attacker."

"We guessed that," Monk put in, anxious to get the favor of the entrancing young woman.

Doc seemed about to ask the steel-haired girl questions, but withheld them. He leveled an arm.

"Our trouble seems to be just starting!"

The pig, Habeas, reared up from his position near Monk's feet. He looked toward the island. His tremendous ears shot straight in the air. He emitted a procession of staccato, excited grunts. Then he ducked below the gunwales of the boat, as if to shut out the sight.

In the direction of the island, three gigantic human heads projected above the lake surface. Huge black arms appeared and disappeared in measured swimming strokes.

"They're coming after us!" the girl shrilled.

CLIPPED to the light metal frame of the collapsible boats were telescoping oars. The men hastily freed these and began to paddle.

"One consolation," said bony Johnny, "is that those freaks can't swim as fast as we can row."

They paddled briskly. All six were men of more than average muscular development. The steel-haired girl, insisting on wielding a paddle, exhibited strength somewhat beyond the ordinary. The swimming pinhead giants dropped farther back.

"They're not wearing their armor," Ham remarked. "If they come close, we'll see how bullets affect 'em!"

Without interrupting his paddling, Doc addressed the steel-haired girl.

"The gang wanted you to teach them the pinhead language so they could issue commands to those three black fellows, didn't they?"

She nodded. "Yes. They made me repeat numerous commands until they understood how to issue them. I found out why they were so anxious to be able to give them orders. It seems that the blacks hated Bruno Hen. He had done them some injury. One night they escaped and murdered him. They wouldn't have done this, had their chief ordered them not to do so."

"Why was the giant murdered in the New York mine tunnel?" Doc questioned. "Or did you hear of it?"

"I heard," said the girl. "That particular giant had been stubborn about taking orders from Pere Teston. They were afraid of him."

"Pere Teston!" Doc asked sharply.

"He is the chief," the girl explained. "I did not see him. But his name was mentioned numerous times."

"What about Griswold Rock?"

"He's on the island somewhere. I didn't see him."

Monk put in, "What I fail to understand is why they seized Griswold Rock the second time?"

"I don't know why they grabbed him," the girl replied.

"Do you know any of their plans?" Doc asked.

"Only that Pere Teston intends to send his giants against Detroit tomorrow night."

To their ears came the mutter of a motor boat. It was a fast craft; it appeared a moment later, scudding around the end of the island. It veered to one side in order to keep clear of any bullets they might launch, and circled to get ahead of them.

"Holy cow!" Renny groaned. "That thing is making sixty an hour, at least."

The motor boat was soon ahead. A tripod, mounted on its bow cowling, supported a machine gun. This went into action, sending a ribbon of lead across the lake surface.

Doc's men tried returning the fire with their small supermachine pistols. The range of the other weapon, however, was too great. They were driven to back water, their own bullets falling short.

The swimming pinheads speedily overhauled them.

Chapter XXII
THE AWFUL ISLE

RENNY, with his huge, rocklike hands, was the most skilled marksman of the party, excepting only Doc. He lifted his supermachine gun and fired. The bullets traced a foamy line across the water, a line that sought and found one of the swimming pinheads.

The giant made a great gobbling sound of anger and dived beneath the surface. He came up some yards nearer.

From the speed boat came a tremendous voice—words launched by a loudspeaker of the high-powered type sometimes mounted on the underside of airplanes used in delivering advertising talks from the sky.

It was the voice of red-necked Hack.

"Everybody come out here and help!" Hack called.

Answering the summons, more giants appeared on the island. They might have been hideous genii, conjured by the rubbing of a magic lamp, for they sprang up from what had seemed a bleak, boulder-strewn hump of rock. Amid a great splashing, they swam to aid the three black, gigantic pinheads.

"It's only a question of time till they nail us!" Renny said glumly.

The speed boat darted toward their little collapsible shells, and its machine gun tossed salvos of sound over the lake surface. The bullets were carefully aimed. They herded Doc and his party toward the swimming monsters.

Long Tom, on his knees in one of the little shells, opened a light metal case. In this were racked objects which resembled metal cannisters holding movie film. These were ammo drums for the supermachine pistols.

"Some of these are explosive bullets," the electrical wizard announced.

The others had known this. Doc carried all types of cartridges—mercy slugs, tracers, incendiary bullets, armor piercers, and explosives.

Renny clipped a drum of explosive ammo into his weapon. He aimed carefully, after latching his gun into single-fire position, and fired once.

There was a flash, a loud report, and the giant who was Renny's target bawled loudly. The explosive slug had opened a gaping pit in his shoulder.

Hack's coarse voice came from the loudspeaker on the speed boat. "Don't kill the bronze man, or any of those with him!" it commanded.

Then the florid-necked Hack repeated the command in the hooting, gobbling dialect of the pinheads.

Doc's men swapped glances in the moonlight. Their features held blank surprise.

"Didja hear that?" Monk exclaimed. "Apparently they don't want to kill us."

"It may be a trick to get us to surrender!" the girl said wildly.

Doc Savage selected a container of equipment and opened it. He removed several of the compact devices called "lungs" by divers. These consisted of clips to close the nostrils, and mouthpieces—the latter with attached hoses which led to chemical breath purifiers.

Doc and the others donned these lungs. The bronze man himself showed the steel-haired girl how the contrivance functioned.

The pig, Habeas Corpus, watched these preparations with a beady-eyed intentness. His near-human intelligence was exhibited when he began squealing plaintively.

"Blast it!" Monk groaned. "We're gonna have to let 'im take care of himself."

"Can he swim?" Ham asked.

The dapper lawyer sounded anxious. Considering the desire he had expressed on innumerable occasions to slaughter Habeas, his present concern was surprising.

"He's a swell swimmer," Monk grunted.

The homely chemist lifted Habeas by the scruff of the neck and pointed at the island.

"We'll meet you there, buddy," he said optimistically.

The pig plunged overboard and began swimming for the rocky protuberance.

Doc and the others slid into the water. Each carried a case of equipment, these serving as weights. They sank beneath the surface.

Doc switched on his flashlight when he touched the lake bottom. The flash was waterproof. The others gathered about the light. As soon as they were together, they linked hands in a living chain. Doc switched off the light. He did not want the giants, swimming above, to spot the glow.

They moved along the lake bottom toward the island.

DOC SAVAGE wore upon his right wrist a small, highly accurate watch. This was made entirely of non-magnetic metal; and slung on a jeweled bearing between the crystal and the hands was a compass needle. This was luminous; and since the watch case was waterproof, it could be used underwater.

The water pressure was not especially disagreeable, the depth being scarcely more than twenty feet. Moonlight made a faint silvery haze overhead. Waves suffused this with undulating shadows. On the bottom, where they walked, it was very dark.

That water transmits sound more effectively than the air was demonstrated by the distinctness with which they could hear the slopping noises the swimming giants were making.

Distinct also was the throb of the speed boat's motor. This latter sound drew closer.

Unexpectedly there came a terrific concussion. Invisible fingers seemed to ram into the ears of Doc and his aides and press against the drums until the agony was intolerable. Their bodies felt the shock, a distinct impact from head to foot.

Doc Savage knew what had happened. Their enemies had explosives in the speed boat. They were dropping the stuff into the lake.

The first explosion, terrifying as were its effects, had occurred some distance away. Other detonations, occurring nearer, would bring crushing death.

Doc Savage dropped the case of apparatus which he was using for weight, and stroked to the surface. His five men and the girl followed.

"Tough," he said grimly when they were all afloat. "But to stay down there would have been suicide."

MOUTHING tremendous sounds, the giants converged upon their quarry. The manner of the monsters was ferocious. They seemed possessed of a killer lust.

The huge loudspeaker on the speed boat blasted metallic words.

"Do not harm them," Hack thundered. "We'll hold 'em until we hear from the chief."

Low-voiced, Doc addressed his five aides and the girl.

"Take it easy. We haven't a chance. They really mean that stuff about not harming us."

A moment later, one of the swimming giants reached Doc Savage. The monster chanced to be one of the pinheads.

Doc Savage, who towered in stature when beside ordinary mortals, was dwarfed by the grotesque proportions of the pinhead. A monster hand clamped upon Doc's arm. Desirous of ascertaining what strength the giants possessed, Doc struggled.

The result was astounding. For all of his fabulous muscular ability, he might have been a child opposing a mature man. Not wishing to anger the pinhead monstrosity unnecessarily, Doc permitted himself to be towed shoreward.

The girl, Monk, Ham, and the others were captured in like fashion and dragged toward the island.

Habeas Corpus had circled wide of the giants in swimming toward the island. A tiny funnel of wake, barely distinguishable in the moonlight, marked his position. He reached shore and disappeared among the rocks, much to Monk's relief.

THE stony isle, when they reached it, furnished a surprise. Its height had been deceptive in the moonlight, as had its formation. Viewed from above, it had seemed covered with boulders.

The largest of these huge rocks thrust up from the water near shore.

Closer inspection developed that the protuberances were, in many cases, camouflaged buildings.

In landing, the prisoners were towed close enough to these to observe details of their construction. Metal girders composed the framework. Over these were stretched stout-woven wires, the netting of which formed foundations for a canvas covering, cleverly painted and veined to resemble stone. The structures were unexpectedly large.

Each held a plane. These craft were large, trimotored amphibians.

A light was turned on in one hangar, permitting a man to resume work tuning a plane motor. This job must have been interrupted by the approach of Doc's gyro. Thanks to the light, and the fact that the cabin door of one of the planes was open, Doc's party got a glimpse of the ship's interior.

Wicker seats, usually a fitting of a plane's cabin, were missing.

"Seats taken out," Monk muttered.

"Holy cow!" Renny rumbled. "These planes are equipped to carry a giant apiece!"

Monk surveyed their gigantic captors, as if calculating the weight of the fellows. He nodded his bullet of a head as if satisfied.

"Yep," he said, small-voiced. "One of them would make a dang good load for a plane, but they could be hauled."

"Dummy up, big hairy," growled the ruddy-necked Hack, getting out of the speed boat which bore the machine gun and the loudspeakers.

"I been wondering how you was gonna move your big partners around," Monk told him amiably.

"Dummy up, I said," Hack gritted.

Long Tom surveyed their captors—those who were of normal size.

"Some of these are the birds who grabbed me near New York," he offered. "You know—in that van."

Hack yanked an automatic from an armpit holster. He waved it meaningly to enforce his command for silence.

Four men of normal size appeared. These fellows were tough-looking customers, swaggering and belligerent.

Doc Savage, studying them, said nothing; but he glanced at Renny.

The big-fisted engineer nodded.

The nod informed Doc that all of their captors—the thugs of normal size, as well as the giants—were convicts taken from the prisons of the United States by the ill-starred Caldwell.

Doc and the others were dragged inland. There was another captive on the island. They discovered this a moment later.

This prisoner, Doc and the others did not glimpse fully. Hack and another thug went ahead and removed this mysterious captive from under what seemed to be a great, flat-topped rock.

Black shadows lay among the great boulders. The pair moving the mystery captive kept in these, either by chance or through design, which accounted for Doc's not being able to identify the bound form which they bore.

"It's Griswold Rock!" guessed big-fisted Renny.

Doc, the girl and the five men were dragged toward the spot from which the other prisoner had been taken.

What had seemed to be a huge flat rock proved to be a camouflaged shed. It was of no inconsid-

erable size. This roofed and concealed a deep pit. The depression might have been a grave, except that it was considerably larger.

Doc and the others were searched to make sure they carried no weapons. The steel-haired girl's frock, being wet from her immersion in the lake, clung to her shapely figure in such fashion as to make it obvious that she carried no weapons.

All of them were forced to slide down a rope into the shed-covered pit. The depth was surprising.

They explored the stone floor and walls of the prison. The rock was smooth, offering not the slightest fingerhold. There was no fitting of any kind in the well-like pit.

"Holy cow!" Renny groaned. "We're sunk!"

"YOU said it, Big-fists," growled Hack's voice from the top.

Renny glared upward. It was very dark in the depths, and little lighter above, thanks to the shed.

"O. K., O. K.," Renny grumbled. "But your big scheme ain't gonna work, fellah. The people in those cities, Detroit, for instance, ain't gonna kick in with such huge sums of money."

"So you think," jeered the man above. "Listen, guy, them 'Beware the Monsters!' newspaper advertisements had the public stirred up and curious. They furnished just the foundation we wanted. They showed the public that this giant business ain't no two-bit scheme!"

"If you think they'll lay down and give up their money, you're crazy!" Renny shot back at him.

"They may not, at first," agreed Hack ominously. "But tomorrow night, we're gonna haul a load of the big boys down to Detroit. They'll wear armor that's proof against anything less than artillery, and they'll wear gas masks. What they will do to Detroit will be plenty. The other towns will kick in after that."

"Planes will bomb the giants!"

"Oh, yeah? Not when the giants carry off the mayor and some others for hostages."

"What do the giants stand to make out of the whole thing?" Renny asked curiously. "What good will money do them? They're just monstrosities. They can't enjoy themselves. They can't even talk coherently."

"After this is all over, they'll be returned to normal size," Hack retorted triumphantly.

"Can Pere Teston make them little again?"

"You said it, Big-fists!"

Doc Savage now entered the conversation, inquiring, "Are the giants taking part in this devilish scheme because they are under the impression they can be returned to normal size?"

"They don't think—they know!" Hack growled.

Hack now gave orders for two giants to station themselves nearby and watch the covered pit.

"Have any of the giants been returned to normal size?" Doc Savage called.

"It can be done all right!" yelled Hack. "Pere Teston did it with monkeys and guinea pigs. He even did it with a cow."

"But has he returned a *man* to normal size?" Doc persisted.

"Hell, no!" Hack snarled. "There ain't been no need of it yet."

"Are you sure that the animals, once reduced in size, enjoyed a normal span of life?" Doc questioned.

"What d'you mean, bronze guy?"

"I mean that the shrinkage in size probably brought on almost immediate death," Doc said quietly.

This seemed to be somewhat of a shock to the man above. There was silence. He swore softly.

"Hell, you're just tryin' to worry 'em! You know they're listenin'."

Hack now withdrew.

"Was that a bluff, Doc?" Renny asked. "Can't they be returned to normal size?"

Doc Savage vouchsafed no reply. Instead, he made a silent round of the pit, assembling his five men.

Chapter XXIII
ESCAPE AND CAPTURE

DOC'S aides were puzzled at first, not realizing his purpose in gathering them together. Then they comprehended; and without Doc issuing orders, they went into action.

Renny braced his head and arms against the stone side of the pit. With an agility befitting his apish build, Monk bounded upon Renny's shoulders and balanced there. Johnny topped Monk. Soon they had formed a human pyramid, reaching almost to the top of the pit.

Up this living ladder Doc Savage clambered. Upright on the shoulders of Long Tom, who was the lightest, he could reach the rim. He peered out.

In the moonlight beyond the camouflaged shed he distinguished the two guardian giants. One was to the north. The other stood at the south. All around the shed, the rocky isle was smooth. Chances of crossing this without being observed seemed *nihil*.

Over toward the other side of the island there was talk and laughter—some of the mirth being expressed in thunderous howling noises. This was evidently the only type of laughter permitted to the afflicted giants' vocal cords. Doc's dire prediction that they could not be returned to normal size apparently had not been taken seriously.

Making no noise, Doc Savage clambered over the pit rim.

It was then that he caught a faint stir in the darkness inside the shed. He poised, listening, thinking perhaps that it might be Hack. But it was not.

The pig, Habeas Corpus, nosed against Doc, making another faint stir as he did so. The homely shote had managed to reach the shed without being seen by the giants.

Doc grasped the pig. Through the medium of signs and a gentle shove, he made the intelligent porker understand that he was to run away from the shed.

The pig galloped off.

The giants saw him. So unusual was the appearance of the pig that their attention was gripped.

The running porker held their attention only a moment. But that was long enough for Doc to move, unobserved, from the shed to the sheltering maze of boulders.

A bronze phantom who blended with the tawny hue of the rocks and melted entirely into the shadows, Doc Savage made directly for the edge of the island. The huge camouflaged hangars jutted up darkly. He waded past them, on out into the lake.

Scarcely a splash marked his entrance into the water. He filled his capacious lungs with air and submerged.

Doc was capable of swimming a tremendous distance underwater. He had acquired the ability to do this in the manner that he learned all things—by studying the methods of the masters. The fine points of underwater work he had picked up from the skilled divers of the South Seas.

Coming to the surface at long intervals, projecting only his nostrils to replenish his air supply, Doc stroked into the lake.

He reached the point where his aides, the steel-haired girl, and himself had been forced to drop the containers of equipment which they had employed to hold themselves on the lake bottom.

The bronze man had made careful note of the location of the spot at the time of their capture by the giants. He had done this unobtrusively, and it had passed without being observed.

DOC SAVAGE chanced lifting his eyes above the surface. By aligning several of the larger boulders on the island, he located the spot where the equipment lay.

So accurate were his calculations that he found the cases on his third dive.

His sensitive hands explored a container. He was familiar with the boxes, having constructed them himself. This was not the case he wanted. He searched over the black depths of the lake bed until he found others. Not until he had identified the fourth container by touch, did he seem satisfied.

With the rather heavy box cradled under an arm, he stroked for the surface.

The return to the isle, swimming underwater for the most part, was by no means easy, the weight of the case being a tremendous handicap.

Realizing there might be watchmen near the hangars, Doc left the water at the opposite side of the island. He did not waste time resting, once ashore. The effort of the return swim, great as it had been, had tapped only slightly his fabulous reservoir of vitality.

Carrying the metal case of equipment which he had retrieved from the lake, he crept inland.

Toward the other end of the island, there was still noisy talk and coarse laughter. Doc Savage approached the spot. To no phantom in the stories of mythology was ever attributed greater stealth.

The mirth sounds were emanating from a large, camouflaged shack which was evidently a bunkhouse. After ascertaining the nature of this structure, Doc did not approach too closely. He did not wish to risk discovery.

He began a foot-by-foot search of the island.

Near the boathouse he found a hidden building of some size. This seemed to be a laboratory. Shelves of rough, temporary construction held a surprising array of chemicals.

Doc examined the compounds, noting particularly their nature. For light in viewing the container labels, he employed matches from a box which he found near a Bunsen burner. He kept the tiny flame carefully cupped in his palms.

He found books on chemical treatises. The fly-leaves of these bore the scrawled name of Pere Teston. There were also notebooks in the same handwriting.

The notebooks contained data on experiments at increasing animal growth. The cases described were apparently Pere Teston's earlier efforts. There was data on the abnormal growth of a cow. Pere Teston seemed to consider this of great importance. He had written:

"It will be noted that the milk-producing capacity of the bovine kept pace with the expansion in bone and tissue. This means that my process of size increase will result in the creation of more efficient farm animals.

"Particularly do I hope to be able to center the effects of my compound to certain organs of the animal in further experiments. This would achieve, for instance, cattle with enormous milk-producing capacities."

There were more notes of this nature. One set had to do with the growing of an enormous draft horse.

In these earlier experiments, dating back several years, Pere Teston had apparently entertained no idea of creating giant men to be used in terrorizing cities.

Doc found no data covering work over the last few months.

DOC SAVAGE left the laboratory and continued his search of the island. He entered several buildings, only to leave at once. They were store rooms, holding immense quantities of food for the giants' sustenance.

Near the south end of the island, Doc Savage came upon a small, shedlike structure of metal and camouflage-daubed canvas.

Cross-legged before this, so huge and ugly as to give the appearance of a grotesque, oriental idol, sat one of the giants. He seemed to be on guard. The fellow held a large pipe.

The giant poured tobacco into the over-sized bowl. His big, clumsy fingers had trouble with matches. Several broke; the night breeze blew others out.

The giant was fully occupied with his smoking difficulties.

Doc Savage circled and drifted, wraithlike, toward the shed. In negotiating one narrow stretch of rock, he was completely exposed to the gaze of the colossus. Crossing this, Doc chose an instant when the giant was carefully striking a match.

Unseen, the bronze man reached the shed.

The metal sides of this were open, the canvas cover having been rolled up for ventilation. This sheathing could be lowered if necessary, making the shed seem from the air—or from a distance of a few yards on the island—nothing more interesting than an angular rock.

Doc Savage eased inside, curious to learn what the giant was guarding.

That mystery was soon clarified.

A man reposed on the rocky shed floor. Darkness was complete where he lay, so black as to seem solidified. Doc Savage found the fellow only by touch, and through use of his sensitive olfactory organs.

Doc's bronze fingers explored, their skilled touch conveying impressions of almost visual clarity. He got the height of the prisoner, his probable weight. He found stout handcuffs on wrists and ankles.

The man lay perfectly motionless; none of his muscles stirred. Yet he was definitely alive.

Doc applied pressure on certain nerve centers, testing the reaction of muscles to pain. Doc's knowledge of drugs, their effects and their symptoms, was profound. He came to the conclusion that the captor's limbs were under the influence of injections of some local anaesthetic—some substance in the nature of the novocaine which dentists use.

Doc Savage examined the man's ankles again. The chain of the manacles encircled the steel framework of the camouflaged shed. Doc tested the links. They were very strong.

The bronze man began removing his shirt, it being his intention to wrap the cloth around the manacles to muffle the inevitable snap as he broke them.

Then the giant guard, probably with the idea of getting out of the wind to light his big pipe, entered the shed.

Doc Savage was under no delusions. The match flame was certain to reveal his presence. He left the strange captive and crept out silently on the opposite side.

For several minutes he loitered nearby. But the giant showed no sign of leaving the shed.

DOC SAVAGE continued his search. He found more huts. All were cleverly constructed to escape detection from the air. At last he located one of which he seemed to have been seeking.

This structure was obviously the headquarters. It held maps. These were marked with red lines to indicate the intended course of attack upon Detroit and other cities. There was also a large safe in the place.

Here, when he was upon the island, the mastermind of the giants obviously made his headquarters.

Doc Savage still carried the case of equipment which he had rescued from the lake. Opening it, he removed certain small boxes and coils of wire. He concealed a tiny disc of a device overhead, where it was unlikely to be observed. The insulated wires leading from this were so thin as to be unnoticeable to the eye. Doc carried these down a metal girder to a boxlike container of his apparatus, which he buried under the dry sand floor.

This done, Doc left the hut.

At the other end of the island stood the log structure in which the giants were quartered. Doc approached it cautiously.

At a concealed point only a few yards from this bunkhouse he planted more of his apparatus, hiding it in such a fashion that it was practically certain to escape detection.

Then he returned to the pit where his companions were imprisoned. The pig, Habeas Corpus, was not in sight.

Doc studied the giant guards intently. Then the bronze man's throat muscles tensed in a peculiar fashion. From the boulder some distance away came a voice—a voice resembling that of the florid Hack.

"Come over here a minute, you two big guys!" it directed.

The giants hesitated. They glanced at the shed.

"Hurry up!" rapped the voice from the rocks.

The giants were sure it was Hack's voice. They lumbered toward the sound. They had not taken a dozen steps when the voice came again.

"Never mind," it said, "I thought I heard a speed boat out on the lake. But it was just a frog croaking."

The giants returned to their position. Not overly-bright fellows, neither realized they had been tricked.

Doc Savage was an excellent ventriloquist and a master of voice imitation. Throwing tones which were very like those of Hack, he had decoyed the giants, getting their attention.

While the giants had looked away, Doc had crossed to the roofed-over pit. Here he found Habeas inside the shed. He tucked the pig under his arm and dropped into the pit.

Doc's five men all but held their breaths, waiting for their bronze chief to explain what he had been doing. No explanation, however, was forthcoming.

Two or three times, the men imagined they heard faint whisperings. These they dismissed as being gentle sounds made by grains of sand swept into the pit by the night breeze.

They failed to realize that Doc had drawn the steel-haired girl aside or that he was speaking to her in a wisp of a whisper.

Chapter XXIV
MASTER OF THE GIANTS

HACK, the thug with the neck which seemed perpetually flushed, appeared at the top of the pit half an hour later. He was excited; his electric hand lantern blazed light downward with an angry suddenness.

"What's been goin' on here?" he rapped.

Doc Savage did not look upward. His manner was tranquil. He ignored Hack's question.

"You, big bronze guy—I asked you a question," Hack grated.

"Yeah?" said homely Monk.

"Don't get funny. I'm talkin' to your boss. What's been goin' on here?"

Doc Savage seemed to consider, as if debating what could possibly be meant by the inquiry.

"We've been talking," he replied. "And we're getting a bit hungry, too. Suppose you produce some food."

"I'll produce some trouble," Hack promised harshly. "The big fellows say they heard my voice around here a while ago. I wasn't here. What did they hear?"

"Can the giants talk?" Doc asked. "From the sounds they have made in the past, I presumed their vocal cords were affected by the size-increasing process."

"They can't talk, but they can write out their words. What've you birds been up to?"

Doc glanced at his fellow prisoners and asked, "What have we?"

"Search me." Renny popped his huge fists together, and the impact made a rocky sound.

"You're givin' me a run-around!" Hack rasped.

Then Hack discovered Habeas Corpus. The sight of the pig brought a cry of angry surprise. He leaned over to see better, with the result that he nearly fell into the pit.

"Where'd that peewee edition of a hog come from?" he demanded, when he had recovered his balance.

Monk held Habeas up. He spread the shote's enormous ears, and asked, "D'you see these ears?"

Hack only snarled.

Monk, homely face serious, explained, "Habeas is a very special kind of a pig. You'd be surprised at what he can do. He uses his ears for wings. He can fly like a bat. He flew down here."

Hack made a choking sound of wrath.

"Habeas can talk, too," Monk added. "Listen."

He held the pig higher. Words seemed to come from the freakish porker's mouth.

"Say, Hack, when do we eat?" asked the voice.

Hack maintained a dumbfounded silence for a long minute. Then the explanation dawned on him.

"A ventriloquist!" he barked. Laughing heartily, he extinguished his light. "That explains the voice they heard."

In a loud tone, Hack yelled for four additional giants. These arrived, their heavy footfalls plainly audible to the prisoners in the pit.

After ordering the newcomers to assist in guarding the captives, Hack took his departure.

"Fat chance we've got of getting away, now," Renny groaned.

Monk moved close to Doc, and asked, "Did I do right—havin' the pig talk to him?"

"You could not have done better," Doc replied.

THE hours which followed seemed interminably long. Monk prowled around the pit walls like a caged gorilla. Habeas grunted at his heels.

"The sun must've forgotten to come up," Monk complained.

Later, the homely chemist was surprised to find Doc sleeping in the center of the pit. Reassured by the calmness with which the bronze man was taking their incarceration, Monk also tried to slumber. Failing even to keep his eyes shut, however, he gave it up.

He started a whispered consultation with the others by asking, "I wonder what Doc found while he was outside?"

"Why don't you ask him?" inquired the steel-haired girl.

"No use."

"Why not?"

"Doc's ways are kinda strange to those who don't know him," Monk explained. "If he don't want to give information, he won't."

"But you haven't asked him what he found," Jean Morris retorted.

"The five of us know Doc as well as anybody knows him. We can tell when he's got things to say, and when he hasn't. When he kept silent after returning, that was the tip-off. Right now, he's not talking."

"Humph!" sniffed Jean Morris.

To kill time, Monk managed to pry several small fragments of rock from the pit bottom. He pegged these up at the giants.

The monsters retaliated by showering down great handfuls of fine sand. The choking cloud produced great discomfort.

"Let them alone," advised Doc, who had been awakened by the sand. "They have the upper hand now."

Jean Morris decided to try her hand at persuading Doc to talk.

"What did you find outside?" she asked. "And what did you do?"

"That will be cleared up when the time comes," Doc answered.

And this was all the information the steel-haired girl received, although she put several more questions to the bronze man.

Disgusted, she flounced to the other side of the pit and tried to get some sleep.

Dawn came after what seemed an age. It gorged the top of the pit with reddish light. The depths remained gloomy.

Doc Savage approached Jean Morris where she sat apart from the others, and said something which the rest did not catch.

The young woman was apparently piqued by Doc's refusal to answer her questions. Her voice was waspish.

"I remember every word you told me last night," she said, "but you might inform me of what you found outside."

"Not so loud," Doc admonished, and left her.

The bronze man's aides exchanged surprised glances. This was their first hint that Doc and the steel-haired girl had held a consultation.

"We heard whispers right after Doc got back," Monk said thoughtfully. "He was talking to her then."

The five men eyed Doc. Curiosity was consuming them, and their expressions showed it.

"Listen, Doc," Monk said hopefully, "what's the idea of keepin' us in the dark?"

"Psychology," Doc replied.

"Huh?"

"If you fellows were told how our trouble here will work out—if it goes according to my expectations—your hopes would rise. You might get the idea you were almost out of the mess."

"And would that make us mad!" Monk snorted.

"On the contrary, it would make you highly elated."

"Spill it, Doc! After a night in this hole we need a pick-up."

"If the scheme goes wrong, you're going to be very disappointed," Doc remonstrated casually. "You will feel much worse than you would if you had known nothing of it. To save you that letdown is the reason I did not tell you."

"Well, we're all stirred up now," Monk grinned.

Doc studied them. He apparently concluded the purpose of his keeping silent had been defeated.

"All right, I'll tell you," he said.

But he never did.

PLANE noise came through the morning air. It started with a faint drone, like that of a mosquito, and loudened with surprising rapidity. It stopped the discussion and gripped their attention.

"Sounds like a fast bus," Renny offered, and eyed his huge fists in the dusk of the pit bottom.

The plane swooped overhead, so low that its propeller blast fluttered the canvas shed covering. Fine sand was blown into the pit.

"It must be a friend of theirs," Monk grunted. "I don't hear any sounds of excitement."

"It's the boss!" came Hack's excited yell from somewhere on the island.

Once more, the plane crashed its exhaust stacks past overhead. Then, with noisy backfiring, it landed. Motor boat engines sputtered and howled. They were evidently towing the plane into a camouflaged hangar.

The giants on guard at the pit made coughing and gobbling sounds at each other. Delight was distinguishable in the uncouth noises.

"They seem glad to see the big shot," said Long Tom.

"And no wonder," Ham snapped. "He's the guy who knows how to return them to normal size. If something would happen to him, they'd be in a fine pickle."

The arrival of the plane had completely occupied the attention of Doc's five men, so the bronze man was given no opportunity to explain his plans for their escape.

Amid many glad cries from the giants, men approached the pit. Hack's raucous tones became audible. He was explaining things to his chief.

"We've got the whole Savage gang," he said. "They're in the pit. We disarmed them. They're helpless."

"Then why in hell didn't you rub them out at once?"

The master villain spoke these last words—there was no doubt of it. Utter arrogance crackled in the voice. The tones were hollowly froglike.

"Pere Teston!" Monk breathed.

"It doesn't sound like a natural voice!" gasped Jean Morris.

"Too hollow," Monk agreed.

Doc Savage spoke. "The mastermind seems to be speaking into a tube to disguise his voice. Using a gas pipe, or perhaps a cardboard mailing tube."

Hack's harsh tone said, "We kept 'em alive, boss, thinkin' you might want to talk to 'em."

"They can tell me nothing of importance," snarled the master of the giants.

"They might know how Detroit is fixin' to receive us," Hack whined. He sounded servile, ingratiating. This was a marked change from his usual overbearing manner.

The master villain laughed harshly into the tube which he was using to disguise his voice.

"It makes no difference what Detroit does!"

Hack wailed, "But if they use airplanes and bombs on us—"

"We're not attacking Detroit tonight," retorted the ruler of the giants. "Instead, we'll give Chicago a surprise."

"Chicago—instead of Detroit?" Hack gulped.

"HACK, my friend, you are very dumb at times," said the cavernous voice. "You do not think that the few giants we have here, even with their armor, would stand any chance in attacking a city prepared to receive them."

"They're mighty big—"

"Size is not of supreme importance these days, my friend. It is brains which count. Bombs and modern machine guns would make short work of our giants."

"Then what are we gonna do?" Hack groaned.

"Do not sound so disappointed," chuckled the hollow tones. "My plan is based on psychology. If you had read the newspapers today, you would understand. The size of our giants has been exaggerated. Our earlier newspaper advertisements helped."

"I don't get you."

"The imaginative American public actually thinks we have monster men a hundred feet high. We will make our little foray upon Chicago, first bombing the light plant so that the city will be in darkness. The giants will smash windows, and catch a few people and break their necks. In the darkness few will see the big fellows. After that, rumor will have the giants infinitely larger than they are."

Hack seemed to be digesting his chief's words. "You think we can scare them towns into coughing up five million apiece?"

"We can certainly try," chuckled the hollow voice.

"But if we don't—"

"Then there are many other crimes our giants can commit, my friend. As you know, the compound which made them large also made them very hard to kill. Wounds which will overcome an ordinary man will not even faze these fellows."

"You're right, at that," Hack agreed.

Chapter XXV
DEATH MAGNIFIED

NOTHING was said for some moments. The giants made hootings and cluckings of a happy nature. The big fellows apparently had not relished attacking a city ready to receive them. The assault on unprepared Chicago was more appealing.

In the pit there was stark silence. Renny perspired, and blocked and unblocked his enormous fists. Monk, homely face grim, absently scratched Habeas Corpus behind the ears. The steel-haired girl was rigid, pale. The giant man of bronze alone was devoid of emotion.

They all knew that death crouched outside the pit.

Hack asked his chief, "But how're we gonna get the giants down to Chicago?"

"The planes," he was reminded. "Each is capable of carrying a giant. We'll land them at the lakefront, close to where the Century of Progress was held. From there, they can work into the heart of Chicago."

"Swell idea," Hack agreed.

"Dispose of the prisoners," snapped the master of the giants.

"How?" Hack asked.

"Use a machine gun. Then have the giants fill the pit with rocks."

Hack loudly directed a human monster to bring him a rapid-firer. This was done. There were clickings, as a fully loaded ammo drum was jacked into the mechanism. Hack appeared on the pit rim.

He was going to do the wholesale murdering himself.

Steel-haired Jean Morris moaned and covered her eyes with her hands. Monk made an animal snarling noise, and crouched as if to leap up at the killer.

Doc Savage rested his strange, flake-gold eyes on Hack.

"I left this pit for a time last night," he said.

"You can't kid me!" Hack sneered. "You're lyin'!"

"The giants heard your voice from the rocks," Doc reminded him. "The voice was thrown by ventriloquism, as you guessed, but its purpose was to cause them to look away, so that they would not observe my return."

This startled Hack. He blinked.

The master of the giants had heard the words. His voice rattled from the hollow tube he was using for a disguise.

"What's this, Hack?"

"He's kidding us," Hack growled.

"I was never more serious," Doc assured them.

"The giants heard a voice all right," Hack advised his chief. Then the scarlet-necked thug glared down into the pit. "What'd you do when you was outside, bronze guy?"

"When you learn that, it will be too late to help yourself," Doc informed him without expression.

"Whatya mean?"

"Disaster will have overtaken you."

The steel-haired girl suddenly removed her hands from her eyes.

"I know what Doc Savage did!" she screamed. "It's something that will destroy all of you. Take me out of here, turn me loose and I'll tell you what it is!"

"You hussy!" Renny thundered, and reached hands for the girl.

"GET back, you big-fisted hooligan!" Hack gritted from the pit top.

The command was hardly necessary. Renny had already dropped his arms. It had been his intention to clap a palm over the girl's lips and shut off her words. But it was now too late.

The hollow voice of the leader of the giants joined the discussion. The master villain, however, did not show himself.

"Take the girl out," he commanded. "We'll hear what she has to say. We can't run any risks."

"You've got to turn me loose in return for what I have to tell you," Jean Morris wailed. "You've got to promise that!"

"It's a promise," boomed the czar of the giants.

A rope dangled down into the pit like a bronze snake. Hack menaced Doc and his men with the machine gun, keeping them away from the hemp strand. The girl knotted the rope under her arms and was hauled up.

Doc Savage watched her as she reached the top of the pit. When the girl saw the master-sinister of the giants, she started violently and her hands made a fluttering gesture. "Oh—it's—" she began.

"Shut up!" warned the man's sepulchral voice.

The girl obediently controlled her surprise. Then she said, "What I've got to tell you is in confidence. Have you a place where we can talk in private?"

There was a pause, while the leader of the giants considered. "I've got a shack I use for headquarters. That'll do," he said.

He and the girl moved away, and their footsteps were soon lost to the ear.

There was something bordering on agony in the looks which Doc's five men exchanged. The perfidity of the young woman had been a bitter shock.

"I thought there was more to her than that!" Monk groaned, "After all we've done for her! Imagine her givin' us the double-cross!"

"We haven't done so much for her," Renny retorted gloomily. "She couldn't be much worse off than she was down here in the pit."

Long Tom, somewhat more pallid than usual, asked Doc curiously, "Did you really tell her what preparations you have made?"

"I talked to her last night," Doc replied.

Monk groaned and sat down on the pit floor.

Comparative silence fell over the men. The six giants remained on guard at the pit. Hack was also present, his machine gun ready in his hand.

The minutes seemed much longer than usual. When voices suddenly reached them, no more than five minutes had elapsed, although it seemed infinitely longer.

The steel-haired girl and the master of the giants were speaking. The voices obviously came from a mechanical loudspeaker, for they were metallic, although not loud. The leader of the giants was not disguising his tones now—and they had a familiar ring!

Doc's men registered astonishment. There was something about the voice of the mastermind that tickled their memories. Monk opened his cavernous mouth, as if to speak the name the voice brought to mind.

But the import of the words which they overheard caused him to keep silent.

APPARENTLY the conversation was occurring in the headquarters shack, although the loudspeakers were relaying it from the opposite end of the island.

"What did Doc Savage do last night?" the master of the giants asked.

"He arranged for the giants to learn something," Jean Morris retorted.

"Learn what?"

"The truth about a point on which you had deceived them."

"You're not talking sense!"

"Oh, yes, I am! Savage arranged for the giants to learn that they cannot be returned to normal size."

"Hell! How'd he find that out?"

"He went through your laboratory. He learned the method by which the size of these men had been increased. He has a vast knowledge of chemistry, and realized instantly that you had been lying to the giants. They cannot be returned to normal size and remain alive for any length of time."

The master of the giants swore violently, bitterly.

"It's a good thing I talked to you, sister," he snarled finally. "If them big boys found out they can't be reduced, they'd turn on me. How was it arranged for 'em to find out the truth?"

From the pit bottom, Doc Savage and his aides were watching Hack. The thug's features had become slack, astounded, as he listened to the words relayed by the loudspeaker. These words were not loud enough to reach back to the hut where the girl was being questioned.

The giants on guard had fallen silent. Theirs was a grim, ominous quiet. They had heard every word that had been said.

The widest of grins suddenly overspread Monk's homely face. He turned to Doc. "How'd you do it?"

"There's a sensitive microphone planted in the headquarters shack," Doc explained. "It is connected to my portable radiophone transmitter. There's a receiver and a loudspeaker hidden near the bunkhouse occupied by the giants. It's that loudspeaker you're listening to now."

"You concealed the apparatus last night!" Monk grunted.

"Right."

In his delight Monk bounced up and down, ape fashion.

"I see it!" he howled. "The girl didn't double-cross us. She decoyed the mastermind to his headquarters and got 'im to spill the truth!"

OUTSIDE the pit things began to happen. The giants made hoarse, violent sounds of rage. It had dawned on them that they were doomed to spend their natural lives as the monstrosities which they now were.

Hack backed from the pit rim with his machine gun. He must have decided to take sides with the giants. Possibly their nearness and their rage influenced this decision.

"The big shot has been lyin' to us," he yelled. "What're we gonna do about it?"

His answer was a thunder of gigantic footsteps as the monsters charged for the headquarters shack.

"Wait!" Hack yelled, and ran after them. "My machine gun may come in handy."

From other sections of the island howls of the giants arose. Although none of these unearthly sounds were words, their portent was clear. The giants had turned upon their master.

"Make a pyramid," Doc directed.

His men whipped into movement. Renny took up a crouching position against the pit walls, and Monk sprang atop his shoulders, then the others mounted. As he had done the night before, Doc Savage clambered up this living pyramid to the pit rim and hauled himself outside.

The monster men were converging on the headquarters shack. Some of them had picked up boulders almost as large as washtubs to use as missiles, and these seemed as light as pebbles in their hands. One huge fellow wrenched the covering off a camouflaged shack and tore out a section of iron framework as if it were of thin lath construction. Waving this, he charged with the others.

From the headquarters a machine gun clattered. The master of the giants was using it, and his slugs pommeled one of the oncoming monsters.

The big fellow shook under the impact, but kept coming. The vitality of the Gargantuan man-thing was astounding. Not until the slugs battered his head almost out of shape did he sink, sprawling.

Doc Savage glanced about. Nearby lay the rope with which the girl had been hauled from the pit. The bronze man scooped this up and tossed the end down to his companions. They climbed it.

Within some thirty seconds all five stood at his side, Monk carrying the excited Habeas by a leg.

Chapter XXVI
PERE TESTON'S END

DOC SAVAGE and his men made no move to join the fray. They merely looked on. In a fashion, this climax was reminiscent of others which they had witnessed Their policy was never to take human life directly, no matter how great the provocation, but their enemies had a surprisingly regular habit of coming to an untimely end as a result of their own machinations. And their foes were meeting such a fate now.

The master of the giants was a sly devil. He had evidently taken precautions against the possibility that his big fellows might turn upon him. He had plenty of weapons handy. Another giant collapsed before the withering storm of machine-gun lead.

Hack opened up with his rapid-firer. In doing so he made a fatal mistake, for he neglected to shelter himself sufficiently.

Hack's late chief returned the fire. Hack suddenly dropped his machine gun. He stood very straight and stiff and turned slowly, while a crimson flood began seeping from his body, as if it were sieved with many holes. His final collapse was abrupt, and marked the complete departure of life.

"Let's get out of range," Doc directed. "Over to the end of the island will do."

They worked across the rocky surface of the isle, pausing frequently to watch the progress of the fight. They saw that the steel-haired girl had escaped from the headquarters shack, and was retreating furtively. Her course took her toward the same headland for which Doc and his men were making.

The master of the giants—he was far from being their master now—had not noticed her departure. He was too busy dealing with his erstwhile monster followers.

"Got your eye on the girl?" Doc demanded of his men.

"Sure," Monk grunted. "The way she's going, she'll join us at the end of the island."

"Keep her with you," Doc directed. Then the bronze man dropped back.

Monk also halted. He stared anxiously after Doc, then called. "Hey, what—"

Ham grasped the homely chemist's arm. "You're holding up our stroll, you missing link. Come on."

They sprinted toward the farthermost end of the island.

DOUBLED low among the rocks, at times moving on all fours, Doc Savage made himself as inconspicuous as possible. He watched the giants closely, in order to avoid coming too near them.

Doc was making for the shack where he had found the strangely immobile prisoner—the poor unfortunate who was under the effect of the drug.

The bronze man could now see the shack among the boulders. He circled warily, apparently oblivious to the fighting off to his right.

The monster man guarding the hut had not quitted his post. The big fellow was bouncing about in impatience and making rage sounds.

The giant paced away uncertainly, as if to join the fight. Coming to a pause, he lumbered around and glared at the hut. He gibbered more wrath.

It was obvious that the stupid fellow considered the helpless man inside responsible for the unpleasant things which had befallen him. Emitting a roar, the monster charged the shack. He crashed in the covering with his fist and began tearing the framework apart.

Doc Savage pitched from cover. Swooping as he ran, he scooped up two flinty, elongated pebbles, each nearly the size of a man's fist. He held one of these in either hand; they were his only weapons.

The monster was on the point of forcing entry to the hut.

Doc yelled. The man-monstrosity wheeled, attention attracted. He perceived that Doc was going to attack. He hurriedly scrambled out of the hole he had opened in the hut wall.

Doc did not pause in his rush. It seemed that he intended to come to grips with the huge fellow. The monster opened enormous hands, spread his arms to receive the bronze man.

Giant among ordinary men though Doc was, he seemed diminutive alongside his huge foe.

What occurred next surprised the monster. Doc folded down, almost against the ground. The monster's hands clutched empty air.

There came two loud cracking noises. The man-thing squawled in agony. With the stones gripped in his fists, Doc had struck each of the fellow's kneecaps a hard blow.

The bronze man sprang clear. He dropped his rocks and shoveled up handfuls of the fine sand underfoot.

The man-giant had grasped his kneecaps and was wailing like a small boy who had fallen down.

Doc rushed him again.

The monster straightened, bellowing, to meet him.

Doc flung his fine sand into the big one's eyes.

The gritty particles blinded the monster. It weaved in aimless circles, howling, swinging random blows that encountered nothing.

Doc Savage darted into the hut. He scooped up the drugged man who lay there and bore him out. Carrying the unfortunate, Doc ran to join his companions.

THE fight between the giants and their late chief was rapidly approaching its gory end.

The master of the giants, keeping undercover, had not shown himself to Doc and the others. They had not, as yet, identified the fellow by sight.

The chief villain now began hurling small metal cannisters out of his retreat. These burst with slightly more noise than bad eggs, and spewed a lemon-colored vapor. This fog spread rapidly. It swathed the giants in a citrus mantle. The monsters began to scream and stagger in agony.

Renny and the others, nearing the opposite side of the island, could see the affair.

"Poison gas!" Renny rumbled.

There was a breeze across the isle. This swept such of the gas as fell short directly toward the monster men. Two of them turned to flee, but were too late. The lemon-hued cloud descended upon them.

"Whe-ew!" breathed Renny. "The breeze is a lucky break for us."

Not until much later did Renny realize that it was foresight against just such a contingency which had moved Doc to direct them toward the side of the island where the wind would sweep the gas away before it could reach his companions.

It became apparent that all of the attacking party—giants and normal men alike—were certain to be smitten by the poison vapor.

The men of ordinary size dropped almost instantly after encountering the fumes. The giants, with their infinitely greater vitality, survived some moments after the stuff swept over them.

A strange vengeance befell the master of the giants. The fellow had, no doubt, seized the three black pinhead savages against their will, and by feeding them his sinister concoction by force, had turned them into giants.

It was this seizure of the pinheads, indirectly, which had put Doc Savage on the fantastic trail, for the pinheads had escaped from the island to wreak vengeance upon the man who had mistreated them—Bruno Hen. The beating Bruno Hen had administered to the little black fellows, when they came pleading for food, had later been the cause of his own death.

And it was the three monster black pinheads who now wrought justice upon the czar of the giants. They, alone, did not swerve when the poison gas hit them. Probably they did not know what the stuff was, did not realize they were doomed, for all of their great size.

The three of them fell upon the headquarters shack. There was reenacted much the same drama which must have marked the demise of Bruno Hen. The monster pinheads beat at the sides of the shack. They flung themselves headlong and crashed in its walls.

Disappearing inside, groping in the wreckage, they sought the man who had made them the hideous things they were. An awful screeching arose as their enormous hands found their quarry, mangled and tore.

They hauled the lifeless body from the shattered shack and tossed it away as if it were an unclean thing. The body fell at some distance, and the pinheads started after it, as if to wreak further vengeance. But the gas was having its effect.

They began to claw at their chests. They pawed at their great mouths. They sank to their knees. After swaying there for a moment they toppled over, one at a time.

These three black monsters were the last of all the giants to die.

DOC SAVAGE joined his five men. Over one shoulder he carried the figure of the man he had rescued.

The steel-haired girl had joined the group. They all stared at Doc's burden. They noted the wizened, extremely pallid countenance of it.

The homely Monk scratched in the reddish bristles which furred the nape of his neck.

"This fellow answers the description of Pere Teston," he muttered.

"No doubt we will find he *is* Pere Teston," Doc replied.

It was some fifteen minutes before Doc's surmise was verified. There was still danger from the gas cloud which covered the other end of the island. While waiting for the wind to sweep it out over the lake, Doc Savage swam to the spot where they had dropped their equipment.

He dived until he found the box he desired. He brought it ashore. The container held medical supplies, restoratives, stimulants.

Using these, Doc revived Pere Teston. Before long the man could speak coherently.

"You *are* Pere Teston?" Doc questioned.

The wizened man nodded. "They have been holding me here for months—a prisoner."

"Why?"

"My chemical compound!" Pere Teston wailed. "I only intended to develop super farm animals. But they used it on men. They kept me here, made me mix the stuff."

Doc gestured toward the other side of the island. "How did the master of the giants first find out about your compound?"

Pere Teston grimaced and shuddered. "I went to him, hoping he would supply money to finance my experiments."

Doc straightened. He moistened a finger and held it up to judge the strength of the breeze.

"The gas has been swept away by now," he decided. "We could go over and take a look at the fellow who was behind all this."

Monk and the others ran ahead, anxious to be first to view the features of the master villain.

The steel-haired girl lingered behind. She kept her eyes on Doc. "You have guessed who he is?"

Doc Savage nodded. "When the giants made their raid on Trapper Lake, it was clear who he was. The fellow wanted to get away to supervise personally the raid of his monster men. So he had his giants come and get him."

Monk reached the spot where the czar of the giants lay. His loud ejaculation as he glimpsed the lifeless features carried distinctly.

"Griswold Rock!" he squawked. "Griswold Rock was the guy behind all this!"

THE group, which had gone to the body of Griswold Rock, came back. Their return was slow, for they angled right and left, inspecting the gigantic hulks of the men-monsters and the bodies of the thugs of normal size.

"The gang is all done for," Monk told Doc, when he had reached the bronze man.

Monk's words, in a sense, marked the end of the menace of the monsters.

It also signified the beginning of what, to the rest of the world, became a profound mystery. Doc and his men never told of the isle or of what had happened there.

Steel-haired Jean Morris, given her chance by a motion-picture company, on Doc's recommendation, became within a few months a star of some magnitude. She never told of the isle, either. It was something she wanted to forget.

Nor did Pere Teston talk. He followed a suggestion which Doc Savage made. Questioning him, Doc learned that Pere Teston was actually a man of great mental ability. The bronze man placed a considerable sum of money at Pere Teston's disposal for use in making scientific experiments. But Pere Teston's future work had nothing to do with increasing the size of men or animals.

"I'll never touch that stuff again," Pere Teston declared.

Pere Teston's gratitude to Doc Savage was profound. Many times he expressed his feelings.

"Anything I can do to repay you," he said earnestly. "Anything."

"Forget it," Doc advised. "Your payment will be your useful scientific work in the future."

Doc and his men buried the giants there on the island. They broke up the camouflaged shacks and disposed of them in the lake. The laboratory, with its bottles of chemical compounds, they also cast into the water.

One bottle alone did Doc Savage salvage. This held the growth compound which Pere Teston had developed. Later, Doc tested the stuff.

If the size of domestic animals could be increased to the benefit of farmers, he intended to place this elixir in the proper hands. He made, however, a surprising discovery—living things, after their size was increased, lived, as a rule, less than two years. From a practical standpoint, Pere Teston's concoction was relatively valueless.

Long before the completion of those experiments, however, a strange call came to Doc Savage. It came out of the northland, from the bleak, frozen wastes of the Canadian snow country. And it was a summons destined to plunge Doc Savage into a mad battle for one of the most fabulous treasures ever to exist.

Not gold or jewels, this treasure—nothing to glitter, or to be turned into rich ornaments. Yet its value was beyond price, and its quest brought down upon Doc Savage one of the most grisly menaces ever to stalk the northland.

The Mystery On the Snow the natives called the terror. Perhaps no better description could be found, for it was mysterious, hideous, uncanny. It struck repeatedly at Doc Savage and his five aides with an unseen horror which none fathomed.

And in the meantime, the world was wondering what had happened to the monsters who had raided Trapper Lake.

THE END

INTERMISSION by Will Murray

The Doc Savage novels selected for this volume are among the most unusual in the entire series. Published exactly a decade apart, they share a common origin.

The Monsters was written during that period when Lester Dent was struggling with the nervous collapse that caused him to temporarily shelve *Fear Cay*. The collapse was triggered by an apparent hallucination wherein Dent found himself talking to two characters he was writing about.

Perhaps that unnerving situation explains the nightmarish quality of *The Monsters,* arguably one of the most famous of Doc Savage novels.

When Dent put the unfinished *Fear Cay* aside, he had his next Doc outline in hand and approved. So no precious writing time was lost. He simply went on to *The Monsters,* while he simultaneously moved from Jackson Heights, Long Island to midtown Manhattan within easy walking distance of Central Park.

The origins of *The Monsters* are fairly easy to deduce. RKO's *King Kong* had broken boxoffice records earlier that year, lodging the terrifying proto-giant ape firmly in the public consciousness.

Since Kong ultimately fell from his perch atop Doc Savage's Empire State Building headquarters, Doc fans—perhaps even Lester Dent himself—might have speculated about a clash between the Man of Bronze and the Eighth Wonder of the World.

The scientific discovery of a pituitary growth hormone in 1933 supplied the motive power for the plot. Dr. Herbert Mclean Evans, professor of biology at the University of California's Institute of Experimental Biology at Berkeley, made medical history when he injected growth hormones extracted from the pituitary gland into test animals, resulting in dramatic growth. His earliest experiments produced unusually large rats. By 1935, a more perfected extract led to dachshunds of unnatural size and weight. Dr. Evans was also known as the discoverer of Vitamin E.

More tellingly, perhaps, Lester Dent was a fan of the tall tales circulating around the mythic lumberjack Paul Bunyan and his gigantic blue ox, Babe. A fantasy figure who emerged from campfire yarns told around lumber camps in the area of Wisconsin, Minnesota and Michigan, Paul Bunyan was said to be so big and brawny that he could capture a blizzard in a bag and shatter windows with his laugh. His size has never been correctly estimated, but legend has it the Grand Canyon was created when he dragged his mighty axe across that part of the United States. Mount Hood is said to have been built when Bunyan

piled boulders atop his campfire to extinguish it.

Stories of Paul Bunyan were at their height when Lester Dent was growing up. They first appeared in a 1906 newspaper, then proliferated in books and magazines over the following decade, growing in the retelling. Bunyan was that era's Captain Marvel. No doubt some of the mythic touches Dent applied to the Man of Bronze were inspired by the tall tale embellishments woven about the impossible lumberjack.

Dent wrote *The Monsters* in November, 1933. Nanovic requested revisions. His reasons are unknown, but since most of these changes were calculated to reduce the size and power of Doc's gigantic foes, perhaps he felt Dent had strained the bounds of credibility.

Unfortunately, these changes resulted in several inconsistencies. The Monsters fluctuate in size over the course of the story. After careful consideration, we've restored the altered scenes, and so have restored the original power and ferocity of Doc's most fearsome foes. This includes returning to Lester Dent's original objective for the Monsters' ultimate rampage, Chicago. When he shrank the Monsters, Nanovic ordered their objective scaled down to a more modest Milwaukee.

Not all of Nanovic's alterations impacted the "mountainous giants," as Dent dubbed them in his outline. Chapter XXVI is entitled "Pere Teston's End." But the hapless inventor of the monster-making serum actually survives the climax. What happened here was that Dent actually wrote a different denouement. It unfolded like this.

First, a climactic scene was cut and replaced by a different line of action, wherein Doc takes on one of the monsters to save Pere Teston.

Here is the original outcome. It follows the line that originally read: "He was too busy dealing with his monster erstwhile followers."

> One of the giants was somewhat behind the others. This one had been guarding the shack where Doc had found the strangely immobile prisoner—the poor unfortunate who was under the effects of the drug. This monster came to a stop. He seemed to deliberate, then lumbered back to the shack which he had been watching. He crashed in the covering, tore the steel frame-work apart and shoved inside.
>
> A moment later he reappeared. He was gripping the unfortunate, drugged captive. He raised the fellow high above his head and crashed him to the rock. He jumped upon the body. He seized a stone and battered. Then he ran to join his fellows.
>
> "Who was the victim?" Monk asked hoarsely. "I didn't get a look at him."
>
> "Neither did I," Renny muttered. "But it

couldn't be anybody but Griswold Rock."

"Well, he's finished now," Monk said soberly. "Poor cuss. Afraid of his shadow, but friendly enough."

Doc Savage and his aides joined the steel-haired girl.

"It worked," she said in a strained voice.

They sheltered themselves among the rocks and watched the hideous debacle to its gory end.

Then, the Big Reveal:

Doc Savage allowed some ten minutes for the breeze to sweep the gas cloud away over the lake before he judged it safe to advance. He and his aides came first to the drugged prisoner who had been slain by one of the giants.

"Holy cow!" exploded Renny, after one look at the victim's face.

The dead man was slender, and wrinkled. There was a striking peculiarity about his features. They were a corpse-like gray in color. Even in life, this individual must have had a face which resembled that of a dead man.

"Pere Teston!" Monk ejaculated.

Ham waved his arms. He was lost without his sword cane. "Then Pere Teston wasn't bossing the giants!"

"Pere Teston never intended that his compounds to increase physical growth should be used as they were," Doc Savage offered. "Teston's discovery was seized by another."

"You mean—"

"Pere Teston only intended to develop super farm animals. I found his notes in the laboratory here. He must have taken his secret to another man, perhaps to get money to finance his experiments. And the other man seized Pere Teston, and turned this compound to his own use."

Monk and the others ran ahead, anxious to view the features of the master villain.

The steel-haired girl lingered behind. She kept her eyes on Doc. The metallic orbs held admiration. "You have guessed who he is?"

Doc Savage nodded slightly. "When the giants made their raid on Trapper Lake, it was clear..." etc., etc.

The above text replaced the discovery of the surviving Pere Teston, and came directly after the sentence, "These three black monsters were the last of all the giants to die."

Dent simply forgot to change the chapter title to square with the new reality.

There is one other modification Lester Dent made to *The Monsters*. When preparing the outline, he included this interesting wrinkle for Chapter IV (then called "The Big Monkey"), wherein Doc and company first infiltrate Griswold Rock's county home:

"Doc, Monk and Ham invade the place. Topping

the wall, they are set upon by a giant gorilla of a species Doc has never before encountered. Doc whips the thing."

Later, the outline explains that Pere Teston first experimented with his accelerating compound "on a small monkey, increasing its size to that of an ape—the animal which Doc battled in N.Y."

I for one regret that Doc Savage never did tackle that Dentian version of King Kong. That surely would have been a classic battle.

The Monsters was not only a hit with *Doc Savage* readers, but it was often copied. A 1934 Popular Publications' *Doc Savage* knockoff, *The Secret Six,* copied it via Robert J. Hogan's *The Murder Monsters.*

Several years later, it inspired the story in *Batman* #1, wherein criminal scientist Hugo Strange created gigantic Frankenstein-like creatures which ran amok in Gotham City.

This particular story created a backlash when Batman machine-gunned the man-monsters from his Batplane. After that, editorial edicts proclaimed that, like Doc Savage, Batman would never again carry a firearm.

Even in the Doc Savage series, the theme was revisited. Laurence Donovan threw genetic giants into 1937's *He Could Stop the World*. They were hillbillies, not circus freaks.

Of course, the idea can be traced back to H. G. Wells' seminal 1904 novel, *The Food of the Gods,* wherein two scientists develop a chemical accelerator that induces fantastic growth in animals, insects and children—the latter of whom ultimately reach 40 feet in height. By 1933, this premise had become a staple of the science fiction pulps.

The nightmarish *Monsters* returned to haunt Lester Dent in 1943, when John Nanovic began assembling the contents of the first *Doc Savage Annual,* slated for publication that November. Nanovic asked Dent for his opinion on which three Doc stories should be considered. Dent's reply is unknown, but ultimately Nanovic selected *The Man of Bronze* and its sequel, *The Golden Peril.* Reader requests probably drove those choices.

The third novel chosen was *The Monsters.* Was this a result of Dent's input? No one can say.

Unfortunately, the wartime paper shortage killed the *Doc Savage Annual* before it could be published.

But John Nanovic didn't quite give up on the idea. If he couldn't reprint *The Monsters,* maybe he could induce Lester Dent to write a new version of that unforgettable tale. It would not be the first time they revisited a successful theme. Editorial thinking had it that most pulp magazine readers moved on every three years or so. An old plot given fresh treatment was just as good as a new one—or so they believed.

A similar discovery in 1943 fueled *The Whisker of Hercules.*

By this time, Lester Dent was comfortably living in La Plata, Missouri, and got into New York City only once or twice a year. In the absence of their frequent plotting sessions, editor Nanovic often sent plot springboards and other reference through the mail to Missouri.

One day in June, Dent received in the mail a newspaper clipping reporting the creation of synthetic Biotin by four scientists, Stanton A. Harris, Douglas E. Wolf, Ralph Monzingo, and Karl Folkers. A B vitamin, Biotin, was first discovered in 1936, and helps regulate growth in mammals.

Attached was this springboard:

DOC SAVAGE PLOT

Using this vitamin as a basis, crooked scientist—or crook who finds out what scientist is doing—builds up huge creatures—men he has captured or talked into going along on his experiments; men over whom he has some hold.

With these huge creatures he begins a reign of terror either over a section of the country he wishes to control, or over certain individuals he seeks to have revenge on. (Revenge might be a better theme than gain here.)

Doc and his gang get in on it, solve the secret—and find some fault in the process at present, but hold it for future development for society.

This is exactly the premise of *The Monsters.* No doubt Dent recognized it. For the outline he turned into Nanovic completely dispensed with giants—Dent no doubt realized that they would

be tough to bring off in the compressed Doc stories he was writing in 1943.

The Whisker of Hercules is probably as much a response to the comic book superheroes then dominating the newsstands as it was Nanovic's springboard. The character of Marvin Western, described as "The Most-developed Man in the World," was clearly inspired by a man whose muscle-building ads ran for decades in countless pulp magazines and comic books, Charles Atlas, "The World's Most Perfectly Developed Man." (Real name: Angelo Siciliano.) His Dynamic-Tension system of isometric exercises strongly resembles the regimen Doc Savage used to build his own powerful physique. Perhaps that is were it came from.

Dent mailed in the manuscript and received from John Nanovic a request for a quick rewrite to help disguise the true villain, whom the astute editor thought was obvious from the moment he entered the story. Dent was working on those changes when another letter came in, announcing that after more than a decade, John L. Nanovic had left Street & Smith due to an editorial staff consolidation. The first and greatest of the *Doc Savage* editors had left the fiction field forever.

Nanovic's replacement was Charles Moran, who helped edit Street & Smith's successful comic book line—something Nanovic steadfastly refused to do—as well as *The Wizard* and various Street & Smith sports pulps. Moran would soon institute sweeping changes in tone and style to *Doc Savage,* forever changing the series.

In fact, he put *The Whisker of Hercules* on the shelf for a few issues while he worked with Dent to retool. With Street & Smith's paper allotments cut to the bone, Doc Savage was about to shrink to digest size, and the novels would follow suit. For this edition we've restored deleted scenes, original chapter titles and footnotes Moran cut to make this story fit the reduced space—totaling some 1500 additional words.

The Whisker of Hercules ran in the April 1944 *Doc Savage*—exactly a decade to the month after its inspiration, *The Monsters,* which was dated April 1934. It may not be a coincidence that this novel too was set in a Great Lakes state—although Dent was vague on *Whisker*'s exact locale. Somewhere in Indiana, or Cedar Lake, Iowa is the best bet.

This was the final Doc Savage novel to include all five of Doc Savage's crew. And because Charles Moran dictated that Doc Savage abandon his trademark gadgets, *The Whisker of Hercules* rings them out of the series until nearly the end.

In short, this is the last classic Doc Savage novel. So enjoy it for that reason, if no other. •

THE WHISKER OF HERCULES

by Kenneth Robeson

How did the statue of an ancient god bring death and destruction to those who crossed Doc Savage and his friends?

*From the dim reaches of the past comes not the whisper...
but the whisker of Hercules... plunging Doc Savage and
his aides into the wildest, most mysterious maelstrom yet!
And a pretty girl keeps asking, "But was Hercules real?"*

Chapter I
WAS THERE A HERCULES?

THE heavy-faced man took a .22-caliber rifle out of the golf bag. And then the younger man, without saying anything or asking anything, hit the heavy-faced man. The young man hit the other first with his fist. Then he got a flashlight out of the dashboard compartment of the car and let the heavy-faced man have it again. Twice. The flashlight lens broke.

The driver of the car kept turning a scared face to look. But he continued driving.

The three men in the machine—the driver and the two who had fought—were silent for a while. That is, there were no words. The young man who had done the hitting had asthma badly, and it was worse when he was excited. He wheezed. The heavy-faced man who had been hit had fallen over on the seat cushion. He was not unconscious. He was merely lying still, trying to figure what he should do.

"She is my sister, damn you!" The young man rattled a little with his wheezing.

"Charley, I—"

"You were going to shoot her!"

"Charley, you're crazy!" The man with the heavy face was scared. "What gave you such an idea?"

"You got that gun out."

"I was only going to look at it, Charley."

"Sure, sure! I saw you look at it before we started out." He stared at the other. "I ought to fix you." He hefted the flashlight. "I ought to brain you."

The young man's facial expression, his wheezing, his gray hard grip on the flashlight which made his hand tendons show up like bone, were frightening things to the other.

"No, Charley, no! Listen, I only just bought that rifle and I was going to look—"

The young man made a cutting gesture as if the flashlight was a sword.

"You get this through your head!" he said. "If anybody touches Lee, if anybody lays a finger on her, I'll smear the lot of you."

He looked violently at the heavy-faced man, and glanced as violently at the driver.

He repeated: "I'll smear you, so help me! You and all the others. And that goes for the boss, too!"

There was more silence.

The car moved slowly, trailing a taxicab which was now about two blocks ahead. The cab was black, and no different from a passenger car except for a TAXI sign on each door and in front above the windshield. But across the back of the machine was a yellow banner advertising the Cedar County War Bond Drive. And this conspicuous banner made the cab easily followed.

Bitterness was around the young man's mouth. "This asthma may have kept me out of the army," he gave each of the other two a fierce look, "but it won't keep me from messing you up plenty if anything happens to Lee."

"The trouble is," said the driver, "she knows that story about Hercules."

"Yeah," said the heavy-faced man. "And it's plain as the nose on your face she's going to do something about it."

"She don't get hurt."

"Sure, Charley. She don't get hurt. Sure."

The heavy-faced man was vehement with his assurances. It occurred to him, as he felt tenderly of the spots where the flashlight had hit him, that he might have been too emphatic, so that it would arouse Charley's conviction that he was lying. Which he was. He thought: *We've got to kill her, even if she is Charley's sister. She doesn't know what that wild tale about Hercules means, but she can't be allowed to carry the story around. She has to be killed. Maybe we can do it as an accident, to fool Charley.* His thoughts kept prowling in that vein.

SHE was a long, dark girl who had a perpetually pleasant face. The unvarying agreeableness of her facial expression was unusual, and nice. The makeup of her features somehow kept them from looking sour even when—as she was doing now—she frowned or looked grimly worried.

"Taxi."

The driver turned his head. "Yes, Miss."

"Is that car behind following us?"

"Which car?"

"The sedan. The gray one."

After a while, the car driver became troubled. "I think it is, Miss."

The girl compressed her lips. She leaned forward. "Driver, my name is Lee Mayland. I live at 134 Highland Drive. I am a photographer by profession. That is, I worked for Mr. Leeds of the Hillside Studio until Mr. Leeds turned the business over to me to run and went off to war."

The driver was more troubled. "Why you telling me that?"

"The police might be asking you for the information. Also make a note of the license number of that car following us. The police might ask that, too."

"What's going on here?"

"I think I'm getting into some serious trouble."

"Shall I call a cop, Miss?"

"No."

The driver was silent a moment. His voice was suspicious, unfriendly, as he demanded, "Why not call a cop?"

The girl did not answer immediately.

"I would have to tell them a story about Hercules," she said. "A story they wouldn't believe."

The cab driver thought it over, then did what a life of hard knocks had taught him was the prudent thing to do. He pulled up to the curb, reached over, unlocked the cab door and threw it open. "I don't know what this is. I don't want any part of it. This is as far as I haul you."

"But—"

"Sorry, Miss. Get out!"

LEE MAYLAND paid the cabby and said, "Thanks, anyway," without resentment to the driver. The driver flushed and was sheepish, then he drove away.

There was a neighborhood drugstore near. The girl stood in the doorway and saw the car which had been trailing her go past. As nearly as she could tell, there was only the driver in the machine, but other men might have been out of sight, ducked down in the rear seat. The car went on and vanished along the curving boulevard. Lee was a little astonished, not sure now that the car had been trailing her.

She pinched her handbag thoughtfully with her fingers.

Anyway, she thought, I've learned not to talk too much to cab drivers. They seem to be fellows who look out for themselves.

She went into the drugstore, after glancing at the TELEPHONES sign.

She put a ten-dollar bill in front of the cashier. "All of it in quarters and dimes."

She took the change to the telephone and dialed long distance.

"I want to talk to a man named Doc Savage, in New York City," she said. "I think he is also known as Clark Savage, Jr. I'll hold the wire."

It was not long before the operator said, "I have Doc Savage in New York. Deposit one dollar seventy-five cents, please."

Lee poked coins into the slots. "Hello."

"Savage speaking," said a voice over the telephone.

Lee felt easier. The voice had a quality—later she was surprised at how quickly the voice reassured her—of firmness and amiable sureness that was reassuring. Lee perceived this impression from the voice immediately; there was no period of warming up. It was as if she was immediately acquainted with the other.

"I am Lee Mayland, speaking from Cedar County, from Center Lake. You do not know me, Mr. Savage. I am calling you because I once met a man who spoke very highly of you. The man was named Lieutenant Colonel Andrew Blodgett Mayfair, but I think the first thing he said was to call him Monk Mayfair."

"Monk Mayfair is one of my associates."

"Yes, I know. Mr. Mayfair said that if I was ever in trouble, to call on him for assistance."

"Mr. Mayfair is here. Do you wish to speak to him?"

"No."

"Why not?"

"Mr. Mayfair seemed to be very susceptible to even a moderately attractive young woman."

The voice of Doc Savage, which had been without particular expression in spite of its warmly friendly quality, now had an unmistakable sly amusement.

"I see your point," he said. "You have something which you wish judged on its merits, without your appearance being an influence."

"Yes."

"What is it?"

"First, tell me this: Mr. Mayfair said your profession was an unusual one. He said your business was simply helping people who got into unusual trouble."

"He used the word unusual?"

"Yes."

"It is not the exact word. But it is something near the right one. It will do for the time being. You have some unusual trouble?"

"I'll say I have!" Lee Mayland said fervently. "It is such a screwball thing that I'm afraid to tell the police. Because I've heard they sometimes send people—people who have a story like this one of mine—to a psychopathic hospital for examination. And I . . . well, I've got another reason for not going to the police. Don't misunderstand me—I'm not a crook."

"This sounds interesting, but not very definite."

Lee took a deep breath. "If you want something definite—who was Hercules?"

"HERCULES?"

"Yes. H-e-r-c-u-l-e-s." She spelled it out.

"What about him?"

"Who was he?"

"Quite a figure in ancient mythology. He performed superhuman tasks which were forced on him by an enemy. Providing that is the Hercules you mean."

"That's the one I mean."

"What about him?"

Lee asked grimly, "Did he ever exist?"

"Hercules was a figure of mythology."

"What does that mean?"

"It means he probably didn't exist in the form in which we know of him now."

"Did he exist at all?" The girl's question was serious and pointed.

"Perhaps. It is hard to tell about mythology."

Lee turned her head to look about the drugstore uneasily.

She said, "I guess I sound silly. But this is so serious it has me just about crazy. If I come to New York, could I see you immediately?"

"You think you need help?"

"I certainly do!"

Doc Savage said, "There is a plane out of Center Lake for New York at two o'clock. Could you make that?"

"Yes. But what about a priority?"

"Is this important?"

"Very."

"We will see that you get a priority."

"Oh, thank you!" Lee said fervently.

"You sound," said Doc Savage quietly, "as if you are scared."

"As a matter of fact, I am. I think my life may be in danger."

"Who from?"

Lee Mayland hesitated.

"I don't know," she said.

After the conversation ended, Lee sat staring uneasily at the telephone. The way she had hesitated, she realized, must have told Doc Savage that she was lying when she said she didn't know from whom she was in danger. She regretted the lie. She should have told the truth.

THE three men in the sedan—Charley, the man he had clubbed, and the car driver—had parked one street over, in the middle of the block.

Another car, occupied by a single man, pulled up and parked behind them. The man came to them. He was a small young man with yellow hair.

"I got a break," he said. "I saw her get out of the cab, so I parked in a hurry and went into the drugstore ahead of her. There were two telephone booths. She went in one. I was already in the other. Boy, was I lucky!"

"Who did Lee call?" Charley asked.

"Somebody named Doc Savage, in New York."

The car driver bolted up in his seat. He paled and kept losing color until he had a pallid blue hue.

"Blazes!" he said. "Oh, damn!"

Charley and the small man with the yellow hair stared at him. Charley asked, "What's wrong?"

"Haven't you heard of this Doc Savage?" the driver asked.

Charley shrugged. "I've heard Lee mention the name. I think she met a guy named Monk Mayfair, who works for Savage or something, and who made a play for Lee."

The man licked his lips. "And you didn't say anything about it?"

"Why should I?"

The man started to speak, but did not. Then he got out of the car, pulling at the knot of his necktie. His face was not healthy. He leaned weakly against the car, sagged down and sat on the running board. "Somebody—got—a drink?" His voice was thick.

"What the heck?" Charley got out of the car. "What's wrong, Spencer?"

The man put his face in his hands. "I'm sick."

The small yellow-haired man laughed. "I suppose hearing about this Savage made you sick?"

"That's right." The other spoke through his fingers. "You dumb fool! Wait until you hear the kind of man he is."

The small man lost his mirth.

Charley said, "Get in the back seat, Spencer. I'll drive. We'll get you to a doctor."

"Never mind the doctor," Spencer muttered. "I'll get over it." He waved a hand. "I've been scared before. Let me alone."

The heavy-faced man—the one whom Charley had earlier struck with the flashlight—asked a question. "What did the girl tell this Doc Savage? You hear?"

"Asked him if there had ever been such a fellow as Hercules."

"What answer did she get?"

"Evasive, I gathered."

"What else did she say?"

"That she was coming to New York by plane. I think Savage is going to get her a plane seat priority on the two o'clock plane. She gave Savage a general idea the thing was big, without telling him anything."

Charley groaned. "If Lee didn't talk freely, it means she suspects I'm in on it."

"Sure, she suspects you are," the yellow-haired man said violently. "Why the devil do you think she got to prying around in this in the first place?"

The heavy-faced man swore. "We've got to stop her."

Charley faced him grimly. "I won't have Lee hurt!"

The small man took off his hat and ran fingers through his yellow hair. "You giving orders, kid?"

Charley looked frightened. But he said again, "I won't have Lee hurt!"

"This goes to the boss, you know." The small man looked at him coldly. "He'll do the deciding."

Charley seized on that eagerly. "Let's go to him. Maybe he will have an idea what to do to stop Lee."

They got rolling.

The heavy-faced man sat sullenly in the corner of the seat. He touched his bruises where the flashlight had hit him, and scowled at Charley.

"Your sis is a slick chick," he said. "But considering what she's mixed up in, I wouldn't give much for her chances."

Chapter II
THE LIAR AT THE AIRPORT

LEE MAYLAND found another cab which took her to the airport. She did no wild talking to the driver. She was less frightened, now.

She told the reservation clerk, "I am Lee Mayland. I wish—"

"Yes, Miss Mayland," the clerk said. "Your reservation is for the two-o'clock plane."

"You have it already!" Lee was astonished.

"The priority notice just came through from New York. Is there anything else we can do for you, Miss Mayland?"

Lee glanced at the clock. It was only a little after eleven. Nearly three hours until plane departure.

"Thank you, no," she said.

She stood for a moment, lost in thought. Then she went out and caught a bus which went to the midtown section. Lee got out in front of the public library.

She told the librarian, "I want you to help me, because I haven't much time. Between now and one o'clock, I want to learn all I can about Hercules."

"Hercules?" The library attendant was surprised.

"You know, the old-time Hercules. The one in mythology."

"Yes, of course. I'll help you with the index."

THE reservations clerk at the airport was named Warner, and he was proud of his job. The army had missed him, not because he was physically disabled, but because he had a wife and baby, and also because he was an essential airline employee. Airline employees were being deferred as essential workers, for much the same reason as railroad men. Warner, however, had done one thing of which he was ashamed; when his number came up in the draft, he had asked for deferment, citing his work, and his request had been granted.

The exact truth was that he was neither a courageous nor patriotic young man, and he was afraid of going to war.

When a small young man with very yellow hair walked up to the reservations window at the airport and said, "Hello, Floppy!" Warner jumped violently. And not happily.

"Cornsilk!" he gasped.

The yellow-haired man laughed. "Nobody has called me Cornsilk in ten years. Not since I was a kid."

Warner moved his hands about uncomfortably. "Hah, hah, it's the same with me. I haven't heard that nickname, Floppy, for ten years myself."

The other grinned. "Not since we robbed that warehouse on Grant Street, eh?"

Warner didn't jump at that. He sagged. His mouth moved unsurely, finally forming itself into a round hole of pain.

"Remember that, Floppy?"

Warner said hoarsely, "Shut up! That was the only bad thing I ever—"

"Sure, sure, you were always pure as driven snow." The yellow-haired man grinned at him. "No guts, that was your trouble. Remember how you went to pieces on the warehouse job? You sure lived up to the nickname, Floppy, that night."

Warner held to the shelf inside the grill with both hands. "You want something, don't you?"

"That's right."

"What?"

The small man glanced around cautiously. He lowered his voice. "There's a girl. Lee Mayland. She has a plane passage to New York. Cancel it."

"Then you'll let me alone?" Warner asked eagerly.

"Sure, Floppy. Nobody will ever know about you and that warehouse deal. Too bad there is still proof that you did that warehouse job, incidentally. Too bad, but you needn't worry about it, as long as you've got friends."

Warner was frightened.

"All right, all right, I'll cancel—" He stopped, swallowed, said, "You say Lee Mayland?"

"That's right."

"But I—I can't cancel that. It came from New York. A man named Doc Savage, who owns a big slice of this airline. And more than that, the army has put out orders to cooperate with Savage fully."

The small man looked at the other unpleasantly. "Remember Put Williams? He's in State, serving a life stretch. He wants me to help him get out, and he'd jump at the chance to rat on you about that warehouse thing if I gave him the word."

Warner thought it over. He looked ill.

"Maybe I can give her reservation to a soldier, and claim I thought I was doing my patriotic duty," he muttered. "But the soldier would have to have a good story. I don't know of one."

The small yellow-haired man grinned.

"I know where I can get a soldier suit, Floppy. So start making out that cancellation."

BY half past one, Lee Mayland had dug a confusing amount of fact about Hercules out of the public library.

She had written down a portion of a statement which she found in the encyclopedia. This was:

> *Probably a real man, a chieftain of Tiryns in Mycenaean times and vassal to Argos, lies behind the very complicated mythology of Heracles (Hercules).*

She found this statement, or one similarly worded but meaning the same thing, in five different reference volumes. She seemed to consider this important, and was somewhat frightened by the fact.

She managed to find a taxicab which took her to the airport, and she reached the reservation window about fifteen minutes before departure time.

Warner, looking more than somewhat sick, said, "I am sorry but your plane reservation has been given to an army officer with an urgent priority."

Lee stared at him blankly. "But I thought I had passage assured."

"I know. These are war times. This soldier had a higher priority than yours, Miss Mayland."

"What am I going to do?"

"I am afraid we cannot help you, Miss Mayland. There are no more plane reservations available. I would suggest a train."

There was much nervousness in the way the girl's fingers were biting at her purse. And not a bit of happiness in her voice.

She said, "This is important. It is a frightfully vital matter."

Warner—he was a young man who thought little of himself—shook his head in bogus regret.

"I am awfully sorry," he said.

"Isn't there any way I might get a plane ticket?"

"It isn't the ticket. It's the space reservation you need. But I'll tell you what. You might hang around. Someone, at the last minute, might cancel out. It happens occasionally."

Lee Mayland seized on this eagerly. "I'll wait around. If there is a cancellation, give it to me. You will, won't you?"

"If there is a cancellation, you get it."

"Please! I just have to get to New York."

Warner twisted his mouth in shapes which he hoped meant sympathy, but meant shame and fear, only the girl did not notice because she had too many troubles of her own.

Lee Mayland noticed the small man with the very yellow hair as she turned away from the reservations window. He was standing close. Close enough to overhear.

"Pardon me," he said.

The girl thought that he was asking pardon because they had almost bumped together. She walked on. The yellow-haired man followed her and said, "Pardon me," again. And he added "I couldn't help overhearing that your reservation has been canceled. Perhaps I can help."

Lee Mayland stopped and looked him up and down. He was a man she couldn't tell much about.

"Rogers," he said. "My name is Rogers. Private flier. I have a plane."

"You have a plane!"

He nodded. "Here is the situation: I am making a flight to New York this afternoon. I have room for a passenger."

The relief that came into the girl's voice made it shake. "Oh, I see what you mean by helping me."

The small yellow-haired man registered embarrassment. "The truth is that I came over here hoping to find somebody who wanted to fly to New York. Somebody who would pay the regular passenger line fare, but pay it to me instead. I need the money."

"How long would it take you to get me to New York?"

"We can get in about an hour after the time of the airliner you would have taken."

Lee put out her hand. "It's a deal."

They shook.

Lee went back to the reservations window to turn back her ticket and get the money. She handed Warner her ticket, told him what she wanted. Warner became pale, and slid down out of sight, falling on the floor. He had fainted.

The yellow-haired man grinned. He wiped off the grin when Lee looked at him.

"Poor fellow," he said. "The heat must have gotten him."

It was not hot.

Lee was puzzled. "He seemed to look at someone behind us, and grow terribly scared."

"Nonsense," the yellow-haired man said.

But Lee turned and looked for anyone that Warner might have seen, anyone who might have frightened him.

There were only two men in that part of the waiting room, and they were devoting their attention to each other. They seemed to be quarreling. One was a very lean, dapper man with a large mobile orator's mouth. He wore an afternoon outfit, possibly the first afternoon outfit that had been seen in this town. The second man was a very large fellow with a long, sad face, and a pair of large hands. Neither of his hands, made into a fist, would have gone into a quart pail.

Lee said, "Do you suppose he would look at those two men and faint?"

The yellow-haired man, who thought he knew why Warner had fainted, smiled.

"Could be," he said "Maybe they're bill collectors. Let's get going."

There was another incident before they left the waiting room. Lee met her brother, Charles Mayland.

Charles Mayland pretended surprise. "Lee! What are you doing here? What on earth?"

He didn't sound genuine.

The girl did not fool around with evasion.

"You can't stop me," she said. "You can't do it."

Then she added, "You are my brother, Charley, which is all the more reason for my going ahead with it."

Charley had expected something like that. He took a flat package out of his pocket, a package the length and width of a legal-size envelope, and not much thicker.

He shoved this packet into his sister's hands.

"Take a look at that before you bite anybody," he said.

The girl said nothing more. She kept the package, wheeled, and walked outside behind the yellow-haired man.

The yellow-haired man wanted to leave the airport at once, but the girl had other ideas.

The man said, "I don't keep my plane at Municipal. It's too expensive."

"Wait," the girl said. "I want to make a telephone call."

LEE MAYLAND got Doc Savage's headquarters in New York on the telephone, but not Doc Savage.

The voice she got told her, "Doc isn't here, nor can he be gotten hold of at once. This is Long Tom Roberts, his associate. Or rather, one of Doc's five associates."

Lee was cautious. "I am sorry. This is a private matter with Doc Savage."

"You are Lee Mayland, calling from Center Lake. You have something mysterious troubling you. You are supposed to be headed for New York by plane, because Doc got you a plane priority." Long Tom Roberts, having given her this information about herself, tried to think of something else. "Oh, yes, you are interested in Hercules."

"How did you learn all that?"

"Doc Savage isn't just Doc himself. We're an organization, of which I am one."

"Oh."

"If you have something on your mind, you might as well tell me," Long Tom said.

"I am in trouble," Lee confessed.

"So we gathered."

"I mean—it's suddenly a lot worse."

"Tell me about it."

Lee said, "My plane passage was canceled. I think there was something phony about it. The man at the reservations window looked at two other men and fainted."

"What did these two men the reservations clerk saw look like?"

Lee described the pair—the dapper man and the man with the sad face and big fists—with good detail and accuracy.

She added, "A man, a small man with yellow hair, has appeared and offered to fly me to New York in his private plane. I do not know the man. Somehow I do not think he is all right. I do not know what to do."

Long Tom Roberts asked, "Are the two men, the well-dressed one and the one with the big fists, still around there?"

"Yes."

"Go along with the yellow-haired man."

"You think that is wise?"

"Quite wise," Long Tom said.

Lee said, "I hope you're right," and hung up.

THE yellow-haired man had a car waiting outside. "As I said, I don't keep my plane here, because it is too expensive," he explained.

They drove away in the car, a small coupé. Lee held the packet which her brother had handed her, held it in her lap, handling it, pressing it with her fingers. She seemed to be pondering whether to open it now, and she didn't.

The yellow-haired man began to talk complainingly. He grumbled about the cost of airplanes, the restrictions on flying because of the war, and the high rent of hangars, high cost of overhauls. He moaned about the tanglefoot of red tape which a man had to go through to do any civilian flying.

The girl knew—after half an hour—that all the talk was to keep her from noticing where they were going.

"You can cut it out," she said.

"Cut out what?"

"I know we're not heading for another flying field," Lee said.

The man glanced at her, with admiration for her courage. "You're a steady chick."

Lee eyed him. "You're trying to tell me I have nerve?"

"Yes."

"Well, you're wrong. I was scared stiff until it dawned on me that you were one of Doc Savage's aides."

The idea that he was being accused of being one of Doc Savage's aides hit the man slowly, as if he had a dose of poison.

"Eh?" he said.

"I talked to Savage in New York at eleven o'clock," Lee said. "A fast plane could get here in a little more than two hours. That gave you plenty of time."

What she was accusing him of being got hold of the man, and he forgot about the car. The machine eased off the road slowly, took the ditch, knocked a cloud of dust off the bank, and leaped back onto the road. The man kept it on the road.

"So Savage told you he was sending somebody to meet you," he said, as if he hadn't noticed what had happened to the car.

"No."

"But—"

"However, it was logical. And it was clever of him." Lee leaned back. "It was exactly what I expected of a man of his repute."

The man swallowed. "Well give me feathers and call me a bird!"

Lee smiled "So you can just stop pretending you're not a Doc Savage man."

"Don't worry, I will."

They drove seven or eight miles farther into a hilly country. They crossed two gurgling, leaping streams and passed a filling station which was closed. They saw no one and passed no buildings after the station.

The man pointed. "Look. Look up there."

When the girl turned her head, he landed a fist against her temple hard enough to make her unconscious.

A hundred yards farther, he turned off on a side road that was two tracks through brush, and shortly pulled up before a cabin. Four men came out of the cabin.

The four men were dressed as bird hunters, but their khaki and shotguns did not make them look like bird hunters.

They didn't seem to be at ease.

The yellow-haired man said, "You know a funny one? She thought I was a Doc Savage helper."

This didn't put anybody any more at ease.

The yellow-haired man alighted. "Get her out. Take her inside."

They took her inside.

"Two of you go down by the road and watch," said the yellow-haired man.

The two men he designated went outside. They were not giving any cheers.

"I don't like that Savage stuff," one said

"Me either," agreed the other. "Maybe we better just keep going."

"We might think about just that," said the first.

They stepped into the brush. Hands came out of the leaves and took them by their necks. There was some threshing around in the bushes, but not much.

Chapter III
THE VIOLENT MYSTERY

FOUR of the hands which had seized the pair belonged to the two men—the fashion plate and the owner of the fists—who had been in the airport waiting rooms. Another pair of hands belonged to Doc Savage.

Doc Savage worked on the seized pair. He did an operation, or manipulation, on their necks, using only the tips of his fingers and pressure. What he did made the men unconscious very quickly.*

Doc Savage was a man of unusual size with very bronzed skin. His hair was a bronze slightly darker than his skin, and his eyes were like pools of flake gold, pools always stirred and in movement. His other facial features were firm, regular enough to be pleasant without being pretty.

The enormous physical strength of the man was indicated by the way the tendons played in the backs of his hands—they were like rippling bars—and the hawsers of sinew which sprang out occasionally in his neck when he turned his head. His strength was shown also by the flowing way he moved, his lightness.

Doc Savage was a man with many unusual qualities, and most of these unique abilities or traits were the result of his being placed in the hands of scientists when he was a small child, and kept in their training until manhood. Many scientists had helped in his training. All of them had been well-chosen, intelligent men, with possibly here and there a crackpot who had done no harm.

The bronze man's first training had been aimed at developing his body, on the theory that a sturdy durable building was needed to house delicate efficient machinery. His training in physical culture had never ended. Every day—and very few days had he missed—Doc took two hours of exercises calcuated to develop various of his physical faculties. Hearing, sight, mental agility, olfactory senses—everything—got attention in the exercise routine.

*This method of producing unconsciousness, which is quite feasible, is often used by Doc. The details of the method are not given because, if the manipulator is not skilled, it is dangerous. Cases of death have resulted from inexperienced hands doing the job, sometimes wrongly called "hypnosis."—AUTHOR.

Four of the hands which had seized the pair belonged to the two men. Another pair of hands belonged to Doc Savage.

The result was that the bronze man was actually a physical marvel.

The well-dressed man was Ham Brooks. Brigadier General Theodore Marley Brooks, the eminent lawyer.

The owner of the fists was Renny Renwick. Colonel John Renwick, noted civil and industrial engineer.

Both belonged to a group of five associates who worked with Doc Savage.

Renny Renwick had a deep rumbling voice which, when he tried to whisper, sounded somewhat like a couple of paving stones rubbed together.

He whispered, "What now? Go in and take them?"

"Might as well," Doc Savage said quietly. "But first, we will give these two to Monk to keep."

Doc Savage picked up both senseless prisoners, without seeming aware that it was a feat of strength, and carried them through the brush about a hundred yards, coming out on a small clearing where a car stood.

The one man in the car complained, "Blazes, is the excitement over?" after looking at the two unconscious men.

Renny told him, "These two just strayed into the brush, Monk."

Monk got out of the car. "Good. I'll go get the rest of them."

Doc Savage waved him back into the car. "You stay here, Monk. Watch these two."

"The two don't need watching."

"The girl knows you by sight, Monk," Doc said. "That might just possibly be inconvenient."

"You are trying to keep me from the fun," Monk complained.

Monk Mayfair barely pushed five feet for height. He wasn't equally as wide, but looked it. All of him seemed to be made out of beef and gristle and short red hair like shingle nails. His build was remarkable enough, but the homeliness of his face was really astonishing.

"Come on," he pleaded. "Don't make me miss this shindig."

Dapper Ham Brooks laughed at him.

"What're you snickering at, you shyster?" Monk demanded.

"I know you," Ham told him. "It's the girl and not the fight that interests you."

BEFORE they left the car, Doc Savage indicated the two prisoners and told Monk, "If you can revive one of them, try some questions on him."

Monk said sulkily, "I suppose I ask him what it's all about?"

"That would be a good place to begin. All we know is that a girl named Lee Mayland tele-phoned to New York in a frightened voice. The frightened voice—and the fact that she was willing to spend thirty dollars or so on a plane ticket to get to us in a hurry—was so interesting we thought of flying out here in a hurry to meet her. So we did, and we found that her plane priority had been mysteriously canceled, and that a yellow-haired man was making her a proposition to fly her to New York in his plane. About thirty seconds checking with the Civil Aeronautics setup showed that no clearance had been given a private plane to fly to New York. So we trailed along to see what was happening."

Monk nodded. "I'll keep that in mind."

Doc Savage moved away with Renny and Ham.

Monk called, "I think I'll ask about Hercules, too."

Doc said nothing. They worked through the brush, which was thick. The ground was damp.

The big-fisted Renny rumbled in a puzzled way, "Hercules? Holy cow!"

"What about Hercules?" Ham asked.

"Nothing, except it just keeps coming into my mind."

No one said anything more until the cabin came in sight.

Renny blocked out his big fists. "Do we walk right in and mingle socially?"

Doc Savage indicated a small gadget which he had brought along from the car. This was a listening device on the order of electrical hard-of-hearing gadgets, except that it was more complex and several thousand times as sensitive.

"Wait here awhile," the bronze man advised.

He went forward to the cabin. Weeds and brush were thick enough to readily hide him. Vines had grown up the side of the cabin and partially covered one of the windows. He got under that window, and cautiously fixed the tiny pickup microphone—it was fitted with a vacuum suction cup—to the pane. After the amplifier tubes warmed up, he could hear most of what went on in the house. Ugly things were being said.

The yellow-haired man's voice: "There isn't any need of this, kid. There really isn't. You won't look well without fingernails."

Doc Savage had not heard the yellow-haired man's voice, but he felt this one belonged to the fellow. Doc had read the man's lips from a distance at the airport, and he judged the fellow's voice would be about like this. When you were an expert lipreader, you could tell somewhere near what the voice would sound like.

The girl: "I tell you, I only made two phone calls to Savage. You heard the first one, apparently."

"What about the second?"

"I've told you all that was said."

"Yes, and you confuse me not a little," the yellow haired man said. "You say Savage told you to come ahead with me?"

"Mr. Savage didn't. One of his associates named Long Tom Roberts told me to do that."

"Why?"

The girl's voice was weary. "I wish I knew."

"So do I. It bothers me. It makes me think you're telling one big lie after another."

The girl was silent.

The yellow-haired man complained, "You went to the library. You read up on Hercules."

"Naturally," agreed the girl. "And that proves I don't know as much as you claim I know. I was trying to find out what was what."

"No, it proves you know too much. You might as well admit it, and admit you told Savage everything."

"You brought me out here because you are afraid I had told Doc Savage enough to get you in trouble?"

"That's right. I wanted to find out."

"I didn't."

The man's voice, which had been ugly all along, grew more nasty.

He said, "Hand me those needle-nosed pliers, Chet. She doesn't care much for her fingernails, apparently."

There did not seem to be much point in hanging around outside any longer. Doc Savage stood up and beckoned to Ham and Renny.

THE association between Doc Savage and his five assistants was a peculiar one. It was not the relationship of employer and employees. As a matter of fact, no salaries were paid by the bronze man, and there was no formal understanding about who gave orders and who obeyed them.

The affair was a group of men interested in the same thing, which was excitement. That was the explanation of their association. The explanation might be childish; sometimes they thought it was. But they considered it sensible because it seemed sensible to them. And they did like excitement.

Monk's disappointment, a few minutes ago, when they left him behind, had been genuine. He had really resented missing the fight, although the girl had been a consideration, too. Monk had an eye for a girl.

Monk's liking for a fight was shared by the others. Monk was just a little more outspoken about it. Even Doc Savage, who did not admit of any lust for bouncing enemies around, was not noted for avoiding a fuss.

So Doc Savage, Renny Renwick and Ham Brooks went at the cabin with considerable anticipation.

They got along fine at first.

Renny had two small canvas sacks, open at the top. He handed Doc one.

"Monk gave me these," Renny explained. "He wants them tried out. You know what they are?"

Doc knew what they were.

"Put them through the windows," he said. "You go right. I'll take left."

Ham took the back door. There was a large flowering bush beside the door, and he got in that.

Doc Savage and Renny Renwick circled the cabin, running. The canvas sacks contained articles which resembled condensed milk cans. Every time they came to a window, they hurled one or more cans inside.

They met near the front door.

Renny, chuckling about the cans, said, "I guess Monk gets tired of being shot at."

Men were running around in the house. One opened the front door, saw Doc and Renny, popped his eyes, dodged back and slammed the door.

The man yelled frantically that there were visitors.

Doc Savage lifted his voice. Doc could put remarkable volume into a yell, and he did so now.

"Don't shoot in that gas!" he shouted. "The stuff in the cans is gas. A shot will set if off. It will burn you to death!"

Renny muttered, "It won't burn them to death unless Monk made a miscue when he mixed the stuff."

Doc, correcting himself, yelled, "A shot will fire the gas and it will burn you badly."

Evidently they didn't believe this inside the house. Because there was a shot. Following this— Doc and Renny could see the glow through a window—there was evidently quite a fire. There was then agonized screaming from one man.

Renny, in a great rumbling voice, said, "You see what happens!"

They gave those inside a few seconds to think over what they were up against. Then they went in.

THE gas was a typical Doc Savage gadget, but it was unusual. It was so unique that there was little likelihood of the men inside accepting it immediately as a fact. Nor did they.

Doc hit the door with a foot, planting his weight near the lock. The panel flopped inward when the lock tore out and the lock, with splinters, fell to the floor.

A gun roared. There was flame. It was orange, and seemed to burn like a cloud around the muzzle of the man's revolver. The flame did not spread over the room, but burned only within a short distance, not more than six feet, of the gun muzzle.

Monk, as a chemist, would have been pleased. He had spent a lot of time hammering his brains together trying to figure out a gas which would be made inflammable by the addition of the burned gunpowder gasses which came from a gun muzzle when it was discharged. The gas, to serve its purpose, had to be made inflammable instantaneously, so that the muzzle flame of the gun would also set it afire.

It seemed to be working very well, the gas burning only over the area, and possibly a couple of feet more, where the muzzle gas from the gun spread.

Renny roared, "Don't shoot, you fools! You want to be burned to death!"

There was no more shooting.

The yellow-haired man came out of the other room—the cabin seemed to have two rooms—holding a short hunting rifle by the barrel. He saw Doc Savage. He threw the rifle at Doc, who dodged it.

The yellow-haired man turned and ran, having thrown the gun.

There were two men in the room. Neither was badly burned. But they were temporarily blinded, hands to their faces.

Renny punched one lightly in the stomach with a forefinger. The man jerked his hands away from his scorched face. Renny whacked him on the jaw. Then Renny repeated the performance on the other.

Doc Savage followed the yellow-haired man. The latter, aided by another man, tried to take up a stand in the adjacent room.

They got the door shut. Doc pushed against the door. It was solid. He could tell, from sounds and on the other side, that they were wedging something against the door. A table, probably.

Doc doubled a fist, started to smash the door panel, but changed his mind. He had a surgeon's regard for his hands. Surgery was his specialty. He didn't want to smash his hands.

Renny came over, looking sad the way he did when he was pleased with everything, doubled a fist, and easily knocked a panel off. When he hit the door panel with his fist, it was as if he had used a sixteen-pound sledge.

Doc reached in, jerked the table loose, shoved the door open. They went in, Renny bellowing, "If you shoot, you'll get burned to death!"

The yellow-haired man and the other man didn't shoot. The yellow-haired man made for the back door. He went through it, and Ham speared him.

Ham used his favorite weapon, a sword cane. It was tipped with a chemical mixture which, administered hypodermically by a prick of the sword, caused quick unconsciousness. The yellow-haired man ran about twenty yards from the back door before he went down.

That left one man.

He had wide shoulders, a thin-lipped cut of a mouth, a crooked nose.

THEY noticed the black hair and black moustache of the man who faced them. Later they had good reason to remember these.

The moustache was a waxed one with pointed horns. It was intensely black. Also unusually black was the man's hair. The hair, oiled, was disarrayed.

The girl was tied across a table. A rope was fastened to her ankles and ran under the table and was tied to her neck. Her hands were free. There were burned matches on the floor and blisters on the girl's hands and face which the matches had made when they had been burned. On the floor was a pair of pliers with thin snouts.

The man with the black moustache and hair had a long knife with a thin double-edged blade. He sidled at them, cutting and jabbing at the air.

He knew how to use the knife. Doc and Renny avoided him warily.

"I'll cut your gizzards out!" the man said.

Ham Brooks laughed as he came in through the back door.

"You can start on mine," Ham said.

The black-haired, black-moustached man looked at Ham's sword cane. The blade was three times as long as his own knife.

He drew back to throw the knife at Ham, and threw it at Doc Savage instead. The knife certainly should have pinned Doc. But the bronze man, twisting and jerking his stomach back, managed to let the blade pass. The illusion, because of the speed with which the bronze man dodged, was a little as if the knife had gone through his middle.

There was a glassy crash and a wooden splintering. The knife-thrower had jumped through the window feet first.

Ham, chasing him, tried to lean through the window and spear the fellow with his sword cane while the man was floundering on the ground outside. He did not succeed, and the man ran.

Doc, Renny, Ham, all looked at the window, at the jagged glass still clinging to the sash. They decided not to jump through. Then ran out through the door instead.

The black-haired, black-moustached man sprinted for the woods. He pulled a revolver out of each hip pocket and threw bullets at them.

"We might accidentally have bad luck and he'd hit us," Renny said, and stepped behind a tree.

Doc and Ham found other trees.

Shouting for Monk's benefit, Doc said, "One of them is loose in the woods! Be careful!"

No answer came from Monk. But they knew he had heard.

They waited—Doc, Renny and Ham—for the escaped man to make some sound. He had stopped running, and was not causing any noise.

Ham said, "We may have to bushwhack around after him for hours. Renny and I will get Monk. The three of us will start playing Indian, Doc, if you want to clean up inside and talk to the girl."

It was a good idea.

Doc wanted to hear the girl's story.

THE girl was choking a little from the rope when Doc turned her loose. She rolled off the table and would have fallen heavily on the floor if he had not caught her. She sat on the floor, feeling her neck.

"In the other room!" she said thickly. "I thought I heard one of them move!"

It was possible that one of the two men in the first room had revived. Doc went into the room and found they hadn't. He stripped off their belts and belted their wrists together at their backs. He tied their ankles with their shirts. The whole job was makeshift, but would hold them for awhile in case they did revive.

The girl was burning some papers when he went back into the rear room.

When she saw him, she grabbed a sheet of brown wrapping paper and shoved it down in the flames.

"No! No!" the girl cried, when Doc went over to put out the fire.

He slapped out some of the flame, blew out part of it, picked up parts of the paper and extinguished it with his fingers.

The girl gasped, "Please!" She tried to get the bits of paper away by pushing with a hand.

But there was no writing on any of the intact paper. He examined some of the charred bits, and saw that there had been writing on them. Whatever was on the paper and meant anything had burned.

"What was it?" he asked the girl.

She shook her head. Then she said, "Nothing." Her hands moved about nervously. "It's none of your business."

"My name is Savage. You talked to me on the telephone."

"I know."

"You wanted to see me. You said you had trouble."

"Yes," she said. "But I was mistaken."

"Mistaken?"

"I really didn't need to see you."

"There was really no trouble after all?"

She nodded eagerly. "No trouble. It was just imagination."

He indicated the thin-snouted pliers. "There is no trouble, but they were going to pick off your fingernails."

She did not say anything more. She put her face in her hands, not sobbing, holding her hands against her face with the fingertips digging at her cheeks.

Outdoors, Renny Renwick let out a bellow that contained pain and astonishment.

Monk Mayfair came in the cabin door. He was excited. "Doc, there's something weird out here!" he said.

Doc Savage looked at Monk sharply, feeling that there was more emotion of shock—awe, fear, disbelief, amazement, wonder—in Monk's voice than he had ever heard there before. Monk had a hair-on-end sound.

Chapter IV
THE MAN WHO AGED

MONK led the way outside. They went a rod or two into the brush, and found Renny Renwick sitting on the ground. Renny was groaning as he worked with his left arm, which was out of shape.

"What happened?" Doc asked.

Renny shook his head and moaned.

Doc sank to his knees and worked with Renny's arm. The arm was out of joint, not broken. Doc prepared to get it back in place.

Monk pointed at the air overhead. "When I saw him, he was up there."

There was only one tree near. Doc nodded at this. "You mean he was in the tree? Did he fall out, or get knocked out?"

"No, no, not the tree." Monk seemed uncomfortable about what he was saying. "He was up in the air. Just flying through the air."

"In the air?"

"About fifteen feet off the ground. I guess he jammed the arm when he hit the ground."

Doc Savage's expression was peculiar. He got Renny's arm in position, said, "This will make you think the earth is coming to an end," and set the arm back in joint. Renny's mouth made a wide, fishlike, gaping movement that was without sound, and gave no other sign of pain. Except that sweat suddenly greased his face.

"When you can talk," Doc told him, "you might tell us how you got up in the air."

Renny breathed heavily, made a sound that might have been an opera singer conditioning his throat, and felt of his arm.

"I was thrown up there," he said.

"By what?"

"A man."

Doc Savage examined Renny's bulk, more than

A gun roared. There was flame. It was orange, and seemed to burn like a cloud around the muzzle of the man's revolver. The flame did not spread.

two hundred pounds of it, considerably more. Throwing Renny fifteen feet in the air was a little hard to take.

"Holy cow! I know it's improbable." Renny shook his head, added in a foolish voice, "I saw the guy. He stood there in front of me. I mean—he was there all of a sudden. One minute he wasn't there. The next, he was. And the next, I was flying through the air. There wasn't any awareness—at least I don't remember any—of his actually taking hold of me and throwing me."

Monk, not believing, said, "You're dazed, Renny. Take it easy."

"I'm not that dazed. I'm telling you how it happened. It was all in one flash, like lightning hits." Renny suddenly paused and stripped up his shirt sleeves. "There! Look! I knew something was making my arms hurt."

They looked at the hand-prints on Renny's arms. The outline of the hands, palms and fingers, were crushed into the skin and flesh, one on either of his arms.

"Holy cow!" Renny said, himself amazed at the prints.

Monk glanced at Doc Savage. Monk's large mouth was round with astonishment.

"Whoever was talking about Hercules wasn't kidding," Monk said.

THE girl screamed then.

They ran to the cabin.

The two unconscious men were gone. The yellow-haired man, who had been lying senseless outside the cabin, was gone.

Standing in the middle of the cabin front room, her eyes distended, her hands making pointing gestures, the girl said, "He didn't come in! He couldn't have come into the cabin! He was just *there!*"

"Who was?" Doc asked.

The girl looked as if she was going to pass out. "His face was horrible!"

Monk took the girl's arm. "Miss Mayland—Lee Mayland, you remember me, don't you? Monk Mayfair."

She nodded. "Yes, you're Mr. Mayfair."

Monk had a small, squeaky voice which he did well at making soothing. "Now get hold of yourself. Just be calm, and tell us what happened to those men we had overpowered."

"I don't know." The girl shuddered. "He must have made them disappear."

"Who made them disappear?"

"The man. The man who appeared so strangely."

"Get hold of yourself. Don't be hysterical," Monk urged.

Renny's big voice rumbled. "She's not being hysterical. Miss Mayland, was this man short and wide with a black moustache and black hair."

She nodded.

"Then it's the same guy," Renny said triumphantly. "The same one who threw me around."

Monk waved his arms. "What are you talking about, you two? That guy—black hair and black moustache—is the same bird who jumped out of the window. The one we were hunting outside."

"That's right."

"Then what is this stuff you're giving us about appearances and disappearances and such abracadabra?"

The girl, in a more rational voice, said, "Let me tell you what happened."

A loud metallic crash sounded and Monk yelled, "They've wrecked our car!"

Doc asked, "Where is Ham?"

"At the car." Monk headed for the door. "I persuaded him to watch the other two prisoners while I saw some action."

THE car was a wreck. It lay against a tree a few yards from where it had been standing before. It had hit the tree with enough force that the tree trunk was driven into the top—had caved the top in and smashed the steering column down to the floorboards—and the frame was bent, one wheel jammed out of shape.

Ham Brooks was standing looking at the car. There was no sign of physical damage on Ham, but he was staring fixedly at the car. He seemed too preoccupied to be in any way aware of their arrival, too occupied with staring.

Doc, Renny and Monk walked around the car, looking over the ground and in the bushes, not finding the two prisoners. They inspected the car interior. No prisoners.

Monk, by now indignant at the loss of all their captives, walked over to Ham. He kicked Ham, not too hard, in the pants.

"You blasted shyster!" Monk said. "You stand there dreaming and let them both get away."

Ham jumped. It was as if he had been awakened from a trance.

He said, "What?"

"What the heck knocked our car into that tree?" Monk demanded.

"I don't know," Ham said.

Monk said, "Don't give us a dopey answer like that." Monk then wheeled and examined the ground around the car again. He inspected the grass, the low bushes, searching for tire tracks and not finding any. Monk's expression grew strained. "Doc, what the blazes! I thought they must have bumped our car with a machine of their own. But there are no car tracks here. That is, nothing but what our car made. What happened?"

"I don't know," Ham said again.

"Where were you when it happened?" Monk asked him.

"Standing here." Ham pointed at a spot about fifteen feet away, the point where the car had been before it was wrecked. "The man was standing there."

Monk snorted unbelievingly. "I suppose it was a wide short man with black hair and black moustache."

Ham nodded. "Only his hair and moustache were more gray than black."

The girl said. "That's the same man."

"Hercules again," Monk said. He sounded disgusted, but more awed with fright and disbelief than disgust.

TWENTY minutes later Doc Savage finished a complete search of the vicinity, a search which ended when he found some remarkable footprints leading off through the woods. He went back to where the others waited at the wrecked car.

Monk and the others stared at him as he joined them. Because the big bronze man was making a small, weird sound which he made only in moments of intense mental excitement.

The sound, a low and exotic trilling, was not loud, and had no tune, although it was definitely of musical quality. The trilling was one of the bronze man's peculiar characteristics. He made the sound unconsciously, without being aware that he was making it, and only when he was excited.

"Miss Mayland, would you explain exactly what happened in the house," he said.

"Gladly," the girl said.

She had been waiting in the cabin for them, she said. Frightened. The presence of the unconscious men, two in the cabin and the yellow-haired man outside, had worried her. She was afraid they would revive, and did not know what to do if they did.

The appearance of the short wide man with the dark moustache and hair had been unexpected, silent, completely without explanation. She would swear he had not come through the doors or windows, because she would have seen him. She had glanced at another part of the room, and when she looked again, he was there.

Seeing the man had frightened her, and she had whirled and picked up the only weapon of defense she had noticed handy. A chair. When she turned with the chair, the wide dark man—or apparition—was gone. So were the two prisoners. That was the way it had happened, she said, and she knew it sounded silly, implausible.

"But it's the truth," she insisted.

Doc said, "Now go back and tell us why you called me and wanted our help."

She shook her head and was thin-lipped with stubbornness.

"That was a mistake," she said.

Doc looked at her thoughtfully for a while. He turned to Ham.

"Ham, just what did you see when the car was wrecked?" he asked.

Ham told a sheepish, but firm, story. It had about the same unbelievable note as the girl's tale, differing only in the detail that Ham had not seen the short wide man until after the car had hit the tree.

Ham had been standing a few feet from the car, watching the woods and listening for sounds, and wondering what had happened at the cabin. He had wanted to go to the cabin to find out, but had not dared leave the two prisoners, who were showing signs of reviving. There had been a loud crash. Ham had whirled. The short wide man—very gray of moustache and hair, not black—was standing there. Ham looked sheepish, pausing at this point in his story.

"I got the impression," he said, "that the man had thrown the car against the tree."

Monk's eyes popped a little. The story became too much for him, and he laughed foolishly.

"You've blown your top!" he said.

"I must have," Ham admitted.

Doc asked, "Where did this gray-haired, gray-mustached man go?"

Ham made a defeated gesture with both hands. "I grabbed for my machine pistol. To do that, I had to drop my sword cane, and the pistol got tangled in the holster—just for a second—and when I got it out and looked up, he was gone."

Monk snapped his fingers. "Like that, eh?"

"Like that," Ham agreed.

"Hercules," Monk said.

A small whimpering sound pulled their attention to the girl. Her eyes were shut tightly. Her face was drained. Monk sprang and caught her as she sagged. She had passed out.

Monk looked down at her, then at the others.

"When I mentioned Hercules, she fainted," he said.

"COME with me," Doc Savage said. "This is something you fellows might find interesting. At least, you can try to explain it."

The spot to which Doc led them was nearly two hundred yards into the woods. Here there was low ground, low grass, dampness and the odor of the woods. The earth was soft enough to take tracks.

Doc indicated a footprint.

Farther on—thirty feet—he pointed out another footprint.

A single track in each case. One a right foot, the other a left.

Farther on, about thirty feet again, there was another right-foot track.

The bronze man's face was expressionless as he said, "He seems to have been traveling."

The others looked blank and foolish. The bird life, which had been frightened by the earlier noise, had lost its fear and was making the usual bird cries. Far away, in the late afternoon sky, thunder thumped softly. The clouds, if any, must be close to the horizon, since the trees kept them from being seen.

Monk's voice was hoarse with excited disbelief. "Tracks at least thirty feet apart."

Renny Renwick had an idea. He jumped up and came down on one foot on the soft earth. Then he examined the track he had made. The track was not as deep as the other tracks which were thirty feet apart.

"Holy cow!" Renny moistened his lips. "The guy who made these was heavy."

Ham said, "Maybe he was carrying all our prisoners in his arms." Then Ham giggled foolishly.

A MAN with a horribly aged face and snow-white hair and snow-white moustache was lying beside the log off which he had tumbled when he died.

They found him after they had gone about three miles, laboriously trailing the widely spaced footprints through the woods. The following of the trail had been slow work. Doc Savage had done most of it.

They saw the body and went to it and found the man was dead.

"Stand where you are," Doc said.

The bronze man walked about fifty feet, then began searching the ground. He searched a circle completely around the log.

"Four men, carrying a fifth," he said. "They went on together."

Ham said, "The guy I pinked with my sword cane, the yellow-haired man, wouldn't have snapped out of it yet."

"Five men!" Monk was excited enough to yell without realizing he was yelling. "But we followed only one here!"

Doc Savage, his voice quiet, said, "There is no sign of how the five men got here. No tracks where they came. Only tracks where they left."

Renny Renwick was staring at the body in fascination. "Doc."

"Yes?"

Renny pointed at the dead man. "It's incredi-ble, but this must be the father, or grandfather, of the short man with the black hair and the black moustache who jumped out of the cabin window."

Doc glanced at Ham. "What about it, Ham?"

Ham seemed dazed. He closed his eyes tightly, as if trying to squeeze reasonable common sense into his brain.

"This looks like the man who—well—the car." He closed his eyes again. "Only he looks fifty years older."

Doc Savage turned to Renny. "You remember, back at the cabin, the short wide man with the black moustache and black hair had a knife."

Renny nodded. "He dropped the knife before he went through the window."

"Will you go back and get the knife, so we can check it for fingerprints."

Renny went away. It took him about an hour to get the knife.

In the meantime, Monk and Ham had followed the trail of the men who had left the spot carrying a fifth man. They found that the trail was plain, that even they could follow it.

Renny came with the knife, bringing cigarettes he had found in the cabin. They used cigarette ash to make fingerprint powder.

Doc compared the knife-handle prints with the prints of the dead man.

"Same man," he said.

"But the white hair and moustache—the age on his face!" Ham blurted.

THEY took the body with them. Renny had brought along a blanket from the cabin, and they made a sling out of that.

They did not talk much, probably because they were too busy thinking.

Monk dropped back, asked Ham, "Why is Doc taking the body along?"

"I don't know."

"Been easier to cover it and leave it. That is what he ordinarily would have done."

"Sure."

Monk said peevishly, "You're always bragging about that legal intellect of yours. Why don't you know something once in a while when it's important?"

Ham sneered at him halfheartedly and said nothing.

Soon there was a road, and near the road a farmhouse. On the farmhouse porch sat an unhappy, slightly damaged farmer. His wife was washing and iodining a cut on his scalp.

"Five fellows came along here awhile ago," explained the farmer indignantly. "They knocked me around some, and stole my car. Headed for town."

Chapter V
THE BODY OF HERCULES

CENTER LAKE, before gas rationing, had been a resort center. The resort business had frittered out. Center Lake had a railroad, airline, highways, bus lines—but the scenic section was not close to town. It was the surrounding hills and lakes, and with gas rationing, summer visitors couldn't get there. There was some defense work. But as a whole, times were tough. Doc and his party had no trouble getting accommodations at an elaborate tourist camp on the edge of town.

It was dark when they checked in. They put the body in one of the cabins without anyone noticing.

"At the airport this afternoon," Doc told the girl, "you talked to a young man."

The girl had gotten herself organized well enough to be sassy. "I talk to men frequently," she said.

The bronze man was not disturbed. "This one came up and handed you a packet wrapped in brown paper."

"Did he?"

"Apparently it was the packet you burned at the cabin."

She made an elaborate business of pushing her hair around with her fingers. Doc did not ask her any more questions.

He called Renny outside. The night was warm, and the lack of a breeze made it seem hot.

Renny said, "She didn't talk very freely about the young guy, did she?"

"She seems to wish she had not called us into this."

Renny nodded. "You did not mention that we already know the young guy was her brother."

"There was no point. Such a fact might be a club to knock her off balance and scare the truth out of her, but it would not work now. She is feeling too composed."

Renny chuckled in the darkness. "Reckon she'd be composed if she knew Johnny was trailing her brother."

Johnny was William Harper Littlejohn, archaeologist and geologist. He belonged to their group, Johnny and his big words.

Doc had called Renny outside to ask him to go to the police.

"We have not exactly followed the law in carrying the body around," Doc explained. "So you had better be frank with the police, and ask them to check on us. Have the police chief telephone New York at our expense and to talk to someone there—Commissioner Boyer would be a good man—to find out the truth about us. Boyer should straighten out matters so we will have no trouble."

"Anything else?"

"Try to find out what has happened to Johnny."

"He's trailing the girl's brother."

"Yes, but we should have had a radio report from him by now."

RENNY left, and Doc Savage worked the radio for a while in an unsuccessful attempt to raise Johnny Littlejohn. The radio was compact, transmitter and receiver and batteries all in less space than the usual portable broadcast receiver. There was not a whisper from Johnny.

Ham Brooks had gone to the airport for a half a dozen metal cases in which they carried their equipment. He returned.

Monk watched which equipment case Doc selected. He followed Doc into the room where the body lay.

"Yeah, that's what I figured," Monk said.

"What did you figure?" Doc was opening the case.

Monk pointed at the body. "In the cabin, that guy was young and husky and his hair and moustache were jet-black. When the girl saw him, he was still older. When Ham saw him, he was still older. When we found him, he was dead and an old, old man."

"Apparently."

"You don't think there is any doubt? The fingerprints on the knife indicated it was the same guy."

"Apparently."

"What," asked Monk, "do you think he died of?"

Doc glanced at the body. "It would be curious if we found he died from the infirmities of old age."

Monk winced.

"Don't rib me, Doc. I'm afraid that is what we will find. It scares me."

Doc said, "All the external signs point to death from the complications of old age."

"I hope not," Monk said, taking a look at the corpse and shivering. "If that's so, I'm liable to take to the weeds. The way I was brought up, people don't grow old that fast. I don't know whether I'm superstitious or what. But I hate to have what I think are truths, things I've always believed in, upset like this is going to upset 'em."

Doc was laying out instruments. "Is this going to disturb you?"

"I don't think it's going to soothe me," Monk admitted.

"Why not go in the other room and talk to the girl?"

Monk grinned faintly. "Thanks. Only she doesn't seem to want to talk to us."

"She just thinks she doesn't, probably."

"She doesn't act that way."

"Ask her about Hercules."

"Sure," Monk agreed. "Maybe she will talk about a nice reasonable topic like Hercules." He went into the other room. Doc heard the girl tell Monk that she preferred her own company, and heard Monk ask her if Hercules was the old-timer with all the wives, or was that Solomon?

Then Doc glanced at the window and saw that the yellow-haired man was standing outside, raising the window preparatory to coming inside.

A FEW seconds later, Doc Savage was having the same feelings which Renny, the girl and Ham must have had earlier in the evening.

The yellow-haired man pushed up the window, climbed in, crossed to the body, picked up the body, carried it to the window, climbed out with it, and went away.

While the yellow-haired man was in the room, Doc made three moves. None of the motions were crowned with the least success.

First, Doc tried to intercept the yellow-haired man. He was too late.

Second, Doc sought to close with the fellow while he was picking up the body. Too late again.

Third, Doc endeavored to clutch the yellow-haired man en route to the window with the body, or at least block the fellow's departure with the burden. Also too late.

The thing was so manifestly impossible that Doc Savage laughed. No humor was in the laugh. The sound of mirth—it was disturbingly a cackle—did more to disturb the bronze man than anything which had happened to him recently. There was no reason for the laugh, and the fact that he had laughed seemed touched with insanity.

He leaned out of the window. Yellow-haired man and burden were gone.

Monk, bursting in from the other room, yelled, "What went wrong?"

Doc looked at his own hands, which he opened and closed.

"Gas," he said. "They must be using some kind of gas which slows up a man's faculties."

Monk did not understand. He pointed at where the body had been. "Where's Hercules?"

Doc asked, "Did you hear the window go up?"

"Yes."

"You heard my laugh?"

"Sure."

"How long between them?"

"Between the window rising and the laugh—they were right together. Not over a second or two between them."

That was about as long as it had seemed to Doc Savage. He looked at Monk incredulously. He did not say anything.

THE head of the Center Lake police department was Chief Alexander Carey. He was a large quiet man whose hair had receded. He was no hick, even if he did smoke a corncob pipe.

"We thought there was a body," he said.

Doc admitted there had been. "A man came in and got it." He described the yellow-haired man.

Chief Carey shook his head, saying he didn't recognize the yellow-haired man from the description. "So he just walked in and packed off the body. I suppose we can charge him with armed robbery."

"He was not armed—did not show any guns."

The chief took the cob pipe out of his teeth. "Just came in and took it?"

"Yes."

"What were you doing?"

"Trying to stop it. He moved too fast for me."

"Which way'd he go?"

"He moved too fast for me to tell."

Chief Carey whistled. He glanced at one of his men. The man was grinning a grin of disbelief.

"Well, well, this is quite a story," Chief Carey said. "A man throws your car against a tree. He heaves one of your men twenty feet in the air. He carries off five of your prisoners, stepping thirty feet at a time. Now another one walks in and carries off the body of the first one before you can do anything about it. Is that what we're to believe?"

Renny Renwick said, "That's right, except that I was thrown about fifteen feet in the air, not twenty."

"Fifteen feet, not twenty." Chief Carey looked as if he was disgusted with himself for not being sensible enough to laugh at the story.

Doc Savage described the other men which they had captured—and lost—at the cabin in the woods. He located the cabin accurately.

He said, "Those men seized Miss Mayland here. You can charge them with kidnapping."

The girl stepped forward.

"No," she said. "You can't do that. I went with them willingly."

"You knew them?" Chief Carey asked.

She had an answer all ready. "No, I didn't know them. I have been wanting to buy a cabin in the mountains. They said this cabin was for sale, and I rode out with them to look it over. That's all there is to what happened."

Before he left, Police Chief Carey made a little speech for Doc Savage's benefit.

He said: "I had heard of you before, of course. I had heard that you were always involved in cases that were unusual. Tonight I talked to a New York police commissioner at Mr. Renwick's suggestion, and he said that anything you touched would be unusual. So I was expecting something unusual. Looks like I got it."

He left with that.

"We didn't make such a sensible impression," Ham Brooks said.

"We're not making a sensible impression on ourselves," Monk told him. "What do you expect?"

Renny Renwick was looking at the girl thoughtfully. "So you went with them willingly. And they were going to pick off your fingernails with pliers. But they were just pals."

She said nothing.

Renny added, "And you faint when you hear about Hercules."

She winced at that. But she said nothing.

BY midnight, it was in all their minds that something unpleasant had happened to Johnny Littlejohn, the other member of their party, who had started trailing Lee Mayland's brother at the airport.

The fact that Johnny had not reported by radio in all these hours was a bad sign. His orders had been to report each hour on the hour as nearly as possible.

Renny, who was not susceptible to a shapely ankle, said, "I'm having trouble keeping my hands off that girl's neck. She knows what this is about."

"She's scared," Monk defended. "She's got what she considers good reasons for keeping quiet."

"How do you know?"

"She's an honest girl," Monk said virtuously.

"All pretty faces look honest to you," Renny rumbled.

Ham added, "And the prettier the more honest, to Monk."

"That's a lie. Anyway, you guys ain't got no romance."

Renny said, "I've got a notion to turn her over my knee. You know what she's doing? Waiting for a chance to give us the slip."

Doc Savage looked at Renny thoughtfully. "Renny, could you get her shoes?"

Renny nodded. "You mean deceitfully, or otherwise?"

"Deceitfully. Tell her we are making casts of all our shoe prints so that the police will have an easier time identifying the footprints around that cabin in the woods."

Renny got up and went in the other room, where the girl was sitting tensely by a window, holding on her lap a magazine which she was not reading. She didn't believe Renny's excuse for taking her shoes.

"You're just taking my shoes so I can't escape!" she snapped.

"Holy cow!" Renny said. "Who said anything about escaping? If you want to leave, go ahead. Go wandering around loose and get your fingernails picked off."

She gave up the shoes.

Doc Savage, making sure the girl was not around to witness the operation, pried a heel off one of her shoes. He had to find the proprietor of the tourist place and borrow a brace and bit to drill a hole in the shoe heel. The heel was wood, leather-covered.

Monk snorted when he saw the capsule—a plastic capsule full of mechanism of electrical nature—which Doc was embedding in the shoe heel.

"That thing is a joke," Monk said. "Long Tom Roberts stubbed his toe when he made it. The things never did work worth a hoot. If she gets more than half a mile away from us, blooey! We lose her."

"Have you a better idea?"

Monk hadn't.

Doc finished concealing the tiny radio transmitter. Monk was correct about the thing. It was not in any sense a true radio transmitter, but it did generate a signal which was easy to locate with a direction-finder, although of very low power.

Renny returned the shoes to Lee Mayland. The girl was slightly courteous. "Do you men mind my staying here tonight?" she asked.

"We can stand it if you can," Renny said.

She was too sweet.

Renny told Doc later, "She's fixing to set her sail."

It was about two-thirty in the quiet and somewhat cooler morning when the girl pushed the screen out of her window and crawled out after it.

Chapter VI
THE WESTERN MAN

WITHOUT the gadget at which Monk had sneered, they would have lost the girl. Or she would have lost them. She pulled a very neat trick.

Her hat was an important part of the trick. It was a pert hat with a distinctive bow effect on top. It had a definite silhouette.

She went into a house, and when the light came on in one of the rooms, they could see her—the hat distinctive—in a chair. She remained there, rocking.

But Doc had the radio direction-finder turned on. He noticed the signal getting fainter, and shifting direction.

"Better see who is in the house," he said.

**The front door was a massive double affair on which was carved the
figure of an over-muscled giant …**

The young woman who answered the door said she was Iris Smith. Yes, she was a friend of Lee Mayland. No, she didn't know why Lee had asked her to sit in the rocking chair with the light on for half an hour. But Lee had asked her to do that, and Lee had obviously felt it was very important, so she had done so. No, that was all she knew.

Monk looked sheepish.

"You and your honest lady faces!" Ham told him.

Doc said, "Come on. She is almost out of range."

They took up the trail again. The sky in the east had a faint reddish cast that would soon turn into daylight.

In the outlying, and swanky, residential district to which the girl led them, they could distinguish the prosperous shapes of the houses.

When the girl went into the grounds of an estate more pretentious than the others, Renny muttered, "Ah, we're coming into the sphere of prosperity."

Unless they followed the path, there was a low stone wall which had to be climbed.

The radio receiver—the direction-finder—was a versatile instrument. By changing a circuit switch provided, it was convertible into a balanced bridge type of locator which—using another switch—could locate either nearby metal, or wires carrying current.

Doc explored the top of the stone wall with the apparatus, which registered the presence of a wire carrying a mild current.

"Capacity alarm," he explained. "Wire around the inside of the wall, just below the top, apparently."

"That means the gate will be alarm-wired too," Monk said.

Doc said, "Renny, you have the best dog-calling voice. Wait about five minutes, then pretend you think your dog jumped the wall. Lean over the wall when you call the dog."

Renny chuckled. "Lean over far enough to set off the alarm, eh?"

"Yes. Then you can watch the outside for us."

Renny gave them five minutes to get set, then began shouting for his dog.

"Here, here, Foxy! Come back here!" he yelled.

He talked to the imaginary Foxy in no uncertain terms. He leaned over the wall near the gate, and called angrily for the dog.

A wide-hipped narrow-shouldered man came out of the darkness carrying a white cloth draped over his arm. The white cloth looked like a folded sheet.

"What's going on here?" the man asked roughly.

"My dog," Renny explained. "I think he jumped over your wall."

"You're waking up everybody. Get the hell out of here."

"Nuts to you, sonny," Renny said, and yelled loudly, "Foxy! Here, Foxy! Here, Foxy!"

The man came closer. He carried a gun.

"This is a fine time of the morning to be walking your dog," he said.

"I work the night shift," Renny said. "Don't fool with me, brother. I haven't had any sleep tonight." He called the dog loudly.

"Go away," said the man. "You want me to call an officer?"

Renny became indignant. "You snob-noses that live in these big houses! Think you own the world!" He wheeled and walked off.

He reasoned that Doc and the others had made it by now.

DOC SAVAGE, Monk and Ham approached a large house made of gray stone and brick painted white.

"Psst! Come here," hissed Monk, who was ranging to one side. "Look at this thing. What is it?"

He meant a statue which stood in the shade—the moon shade, which was quite black—of a tall tree. The statue was a man-figure about twenty feet high.

"It scared an inch off my height when I saw it," Monk said. "I thought it was a real giant. That's what comes from all this Hercules stuff."

Doc Savage went over to the base of the statue, felt around with his fingers and located an inscription. He masked his flashlight beam carefully and showed just enough light to illuminate the name of the statue.

Monk said, "Hercules!"

They stood there wondering what a twenty-foot statue of Hercules was doing in the front yard of a house in Center Lake. But none of them said anything, probably because they did not have anything to say.

They walked to the house after Doc Savage said, "We might as well go right in. There is something about walking right in on a liar that discourages him."

"Bet it won't discourage that girl," Ham said.

The front door was a massive double affair on which was carved the figure of an over-muscled giant doing something or other—apparently standing with hands outspread to block entry.

"Hercules again," Monk muttered.

The door was unlocked. They pushed it back and went in.

Monk yelled loudly, "The place is under arrest!"

Ham sneered and said, "You arrest a house, of course."

A medium-sized elderly man came through a door into the large hall in which they stood. He looked worried. "What is it?" he asked. "What is wrong?"

Monk, in a mood to be sarcastic, said, "Please announce us to Miss Lee Mayland."

"Mayland?" The man shook his head. "I know no one by that name."

"Then," said Monk, "announce us to the girl who just got here."

The man blinked at them. "No girl came," he said.

"You don't know Lee Mayland?"

"No, sir."

"Do you know me?" Monk asked.

"No, sir."

Monk said, "Take a close look at me, and decide what you see."

The other was growing more puzzled. "I don't know you."

"Maybe not," Monk said, "but you should recognize in me a fellow who is liable to take an arm off you and slap you with it if you don't trot that girl right out."

From deep in the house somewhere came a man's voice crying, "Help! Help! Help, whoever you are! Get the police!"

It was a strange voice, but a woman's voice which they recognized joined in the crying, "Help! Help!"

Monk said grimly, "Well, I guess we stop talking and do something."

The woman's voice belonged to Lee Mayland. It was filled to the brim with terror and appeal.

The medium-sized elderly man to whom they had been talking lunged to the right to a tall ornamental hall cabinet. His hands went behind the cabinet and came out with a short repeating shotgun.

He fired the shotgun, putting the shot charge in Monk's chest between vest top button and belt buckle.

AT the shot, action swept through the house. They could hear feet pounding, and shouting. The noise was louder than Monk's moaning.

Monk had closed both arms over his middle and tilted forward, but he remained on his feet. He stood there swaying, arms over his chest, head drawn down and almost buried in his arms, making sounds of shock and agony.

Doc Savage reached the barrel of the shotgun and forced it upward. The gun discharged, and dug an ornate plaster design out of the ceiling, the plaster bits showering down.

The man did not fight Doc for the shotgun. The fellow let go, wheeled, went backward through the door. He slammed the door, got it shut, and they heard the lock clatter as it was fastened.

Then the man yelled, "Watch it, everybody! That's Doc Savage out there! Savage and at least two of his men!"

Doc Savage began hitting the door with a shoulder.

On the other side of the door, another voice, farther away said, "Why don't we clear out of here?"

"Good idea," said the man who had just escaped. "Get the word around."

Ham Brooks was saying anxiously, "Monk, Monk! Are you badly hurt?"

"Ugh—arg!" Monk said, gurgling.

Ham, driven to a frenzied rage by Monk's having been hurt, yelled, "I'll cover the back door!" He dashed outside.

Doc burst down the door he had been hitting with his shoulder. Beyond was a room which was empty, then another room occupied by two people—the girl Lee Mayland and a remarkable athlete of a man—who were tied to chairs. The two prisoners looked at Doc Savage with relief.

"The back door," the man said. "See if you can head them off!"

Doc went on through the house. It was a complex house, and not built according to the sensible plans which architects usually follow, so he got lost once, almost lost again, and heard shooting outdoors before he found the back door. Doc piled outside.

"Be careful!" Ham blurted from nearby. "They almost shot my ears off!"

"They got away?" Doc asked.

"Yes. They came out of the house as if somebody had dropped a match into a gasoline barrel."

"What direction?"

The question was answered by a flurry of shots, ten or a dozen, and a loud explosive expression of rage from Renny Renwick.

A car engine made a racket and left the neighborhood.

Renny Renwick, galloping up, said, "Holy cow! I've seen some scared and fast-traveling guys in my time, but those took the prize."

Ham asked, "They get away?"

"All of them." Renny nodded.

DOC went back into the house. Monk Mayfair was sitting on the floor. He had his shirt open, and was angrily removing his bullet-proof vest to inspect his midriff. "I think I've got some broken ribs, Doc," he said.

"It looked to me like the shot hit you in the stomach, not the ribs," Ham told him.

"Then I've got a ruptured spleen," Monk declared.

"You keep your spleen emptied on me all the time," Ham assured him. "So it couldn't be serious."

The girl was still tied to a chair.

The man—the stranger—was in the act of breaking loose. He was tied to a large, extremely stout chair, and the strands which held him were quarter-inch rope. Yet he broke loose without much trouble.

The stranger, Doc and the others realized, was really an extraordinary physical specimen. The fellow was a silver-haired man, wide shouldered, long-limbed, lean to gauntness, and with muscles which looked like bundles of steel wire covered with a good grade of buckskin.

The exhibition—and it was an exhibition—as he broke loose from the chair was remarkable. Ham's eyes popped. Monk even forgot his own trouble to watch. It wasn't often that you could see a man, using muscular strength alone, snap quarter-inch rope as if it was wrapping string.

The athlete stood up and shook off pieces of rope and fragments of chair.

"Poor Miss Mayland!" he exclaimed, going to the girl. "What a shameful thing to happen."

Doc helped him turn the girl loose. When that was done, and the girl was rubbing her wrists— she hadn't said anything as yet—the athlete extended his hand to Doc Savage, saying, "Western is my name. Marvin Western. You are Doc Savage, aren't you?"

Doc nodded.

Western said, "Do you mind if we see how my two servants are faring? I think they were locked in a closet in the rear."

Doc Savage followed Marvin Western, and they found and released two men. One was a medium-sized elderly man, and the other was younger. Both looked scared. The closet was small, and they were disheveled.

"They threatened to kill us!" wailed the older man.

Renny Renwick charged in from outdoors.

"That guard," Renny reported, "got away with the others. I tried to stop him when the shooting began, but he lit out like a scared cat."

Monk thought of something. He went to the front door, held it so the light would fall on the mighty muscular figure carved on the panels, and examined the figure. He compared it with the silver-haired athlete.

"Hey, this is you-—not Hercules," Monk said.

The man nodded.

Monk looked puzzled. "How come?"

"Why, this is my house. Why shouldn't my likeness be on the front door."

"Ain't it a little unusual?" Monk asked, baffled.

"I don't see why. Men put their names on their office buildings. They put their pictures on their business stationary. They print their pictures on the merchandise which they market."

Monk said, "Put some sense with that."

"Apparently," said the silver-haired man in an offended tone, "you haven't heard of me."

"Apparently."

"I am Marvin Western. Marvin the Mighty," he said, as if he was telling a great deal.

Monk gave Marvin Western a dumb stare.

Marvin Western caught Doc Savage's eye, beckoning. The bronze man, together with Monk and Ham, followed Western out on the front terrace. Renny Renwick and the two servants remained inside with Lee Mayland.

"I wanted to talk to you," Western said, "without that girl overhearing."

"Eh?" said Monk. "You suspect the girl?"

Western nodded. "You know what I think about that girl? I think she's a very sly baggage. I think she's masterminding this thing. I think she has started something, something that has turned out to be a great deal more than she thought it would be, and now she is trying to play innocent, and at the same time keep on directing the thing."

Doc Savage said, "But she called us into the affair."

"Of course! She had to."

"Why?"

"Because I was going to call you if she didn't," Western said grimly. "And I told her so. So she called you. What else could she do?"

Monk was displeased by the accusation against Lee Mayland. He scowled at Western. "Suppose you tell us who you are and what you know."

WESTERN was a professional strong man. He claimed, he explained, the title of Best-Developed Man In The World. There was actually such a title, but he did not hold it officially, having been flim-flammed out of it by favoritism in the one contest held in recent years. Since he considered the contest an unfair one—he was rather violent when he told Doc and the others about this—he believed himself justified in ignoring the results and claiming the title.

The others got the impression he probably sold strength-through-exercise courses by advertising in the magazines. This proved wrong. Marvin Western didn't sell anything, exactly. He was a professional athlete who did not compete, sell pamphlets, or pictures. He had no correspondence course. But nevertheless he was a professional.

He was the head of a cult of physical culture. Mental and Moral Strength Through Physical Fortitude, he explained, was the name of the organization. It had branches in a number of cities, and his only income—he made a point of this rather proudly—was from gifts freely given by people who believed in what he taught.

The story was quite believable. The man had a great deal of personal magnetism, and he was so obviously a remarkable physical specimen that it was understandable that he could impress people. He was quite a showman.

The statue in the yard, he explained, was really a giant reproduction of himself. So was the carving on the front door. They would find, he reminded them, other examples of his self-expression throughout the house.

When he finished, he was more calm, and speaking in the deep melodious voice of a man who did considerable lecturing.

"Now," Doc Savage said, "What about Lee Mayland?"

"Why, she is a friend of mine," said Western. "She and her brother belong to my group."

"You call your cult a group?"

"Cult is a word I do not like," said Western sharply. "It implies charlatanry."

"What else about Miss Mayland?" Doc persisted.

"She came to me for help."

"Just now?"

"Yesterday."

"What time yesterday?"

"Early yesterday morning."

"And you helped her?"

Western shook his head, the long silver hair falling over his eyes. "I am sorry to say I did not. I thought she was a victim of undue imagination after listening to her story, and I advised her to forget the whole thing. Perhaps I was in error."

"You believe she isn't innocent?" Doc asked.

Western nodded vehemently. "Yes. I want you to keep in mind that she is guilty while we talk to her. You will notice, I am sure, that she acts like a guilty person."

Renny Renwick said, "As much as I'd like to hear the rest of this, I think I'd better go outside and keep lookout. Those fellows might come back."

RENNY went outside.

The others went in to confront Lee Mayland. The young woman was sitting in a chair, hands tied together in a knot. She was pale, and chewing a lower lip.

"I have been telling Mr. Savage who I am," Marvin Western explained to the girl. "I have told them something of my work in physical culture. I thought it better if they knew who I am. I was hoping they had heard of me before, but apparently they have not."

"What was Miss Mayland's story?" Doc asked.

"She had better tell you that herself." Western turned his personality and melodious voice on the girl. "Tell them."

She said she wouldn't. She said it twice.

"That isn't wise," the athlete assured her. "This man is Doc Savage, who has an international reputation for helping people out of unusual trouble. You can trust him fully, as fully as you were willing to trust me, I assure you."

She said she wouldn't.

Western said, "Then I am going to give him the story myself."

The girl was silent.

The athlete then told the story, using his melodious voice to make parts of it—the parts in which he appeared, or where his judgment and good qualities were exposed—rather dramatic.

He had known the girl, Lee Mayland, for a long time. A year or two, anyway. He had known her brother, Charles Mayland, an equal time or somewhat longer. So it was natural that Lee Mayland should come to him for advice which required action and involved a danger.

What the girl had actually told him on her first visit was that her brother, Charles, was in a mess. In trouble. She had not specified the exact nature of Charley's difficulty. But she suspected Taft Davis of getting Charley in the mess.

Taft Davis was a small, dapper, quick-moving, quick-talking man with yellow hair. He had been a boxer, welter class, and a wrestler—the type of a job called a musclehead in the lingo—with carnivals and circuses.

At one time, up until about two weeks ago, Taft Davis had been a hanger-on around Marvin Western and the physical culture class. But two weeks ago, Western had expelled Taft Davis from the society. There had been no definite reason for the expulsion. Taft Davis, in the opinion of Western, had just not been sufficiently sincere, and for that reason had been asked not to hang around any longer.

The girl hadn't explained what Taft Davis had done that had gotten brother Charley into a mess.

That there was danger involved, and a need for action, was something Western had gathered from the girl's voice and manner rather than from what she said. He made a point of being sure they understood this.

He smiled at them at this point, saying the next was rather silly, in his estimation.

The girl had wanted to know about Hercules.

Western knew something about Hercules.

"Being a strong man myself, I have naturally been interested in the strong men of the past," he pointed out.

HERCULES, the silver-haired man explained to Doc Savage and the others, was the latinized form of the Greek name of Heracles. Heracles was a notorious Greek hero, but whether or not he had actually ever lived—the girl had been most concerned about this point, Western said—was a question of some uncertainty.

Western explained that he was inclined to believe that Hercules had been a real man, although the legend of his birth—sired by Zeus with Alcmene, wife of Amphitryon of Tiryns, when Zeus took the shape of Amphitryon—was fantastic by modern standards. However, such supernatural twisting of facts pertaining to birth was not unusual in those days, so it probably meant no more than the stories which, in these days, attribute to this or that world leader a background of illegitimacy. It was just talk, in other words.

The same tone of legendary exaggeration must be subtracted from the rest of the tale of Heracles, if one wanted the approximate truth. For example the snakes which Hera sent to kill Heracles in his cradle—and Heracles' dispatching of the snakes—this should be denuded of its fantastic side, and accepted merely as a very young fellow killing some snakes, then it became reasonable enough.

The other feats of Hercules—the seizing of the Lion of Nemea, the Hydra of Lerna, capture of the stag of Arcadia, capture of the boar of Erymanthus—these and other feats had a touch of realism. In fact, of the so-called Twelve Labors of Dodekathlos, there were only two—the bringing of the apples of the Hesperides, and the fetching up of Cerberus from the Lower World—that were downright fantastic, and some spinner of tales might just have added these for the touch of the supernatural.

"To make the story short," said Marvin Western, "I am inclined to believe that the legends were the exaggerated stories of the life of a real man. But the real Heracles must have been a wonder."

Western now looked apologetic, and said, "All this talk about Hercules is not as senseless and aimless as it might seem."

"We were interested, all right," Ham told him. "There has been some reference to Hercules before."

Western nodded.

"Exactly," he said. "I now want Miss Mayland to tell us both about Hercules' whiskers."

Doc was watching the girl, and he saw her wince. She clenched her hands and looked at them.

Monk was intrigued.

"Whisker?" He stroked his chin. "You mean likes grows on your chin?"

"So I presumed," said Western. "As a matter of fact, Miss Mayland did not state what she specifically meant."

Monk eyed the girl. "What did you mean?"

WHEN it became evident that the girl was not going to speak, Western said, "On her first visit to me, Miss Mayland said something about Hercules' whiskers. She said it as if it was important, as if it meant a great deal. Then she became abruptly silent. That was all she said."

Ham looked at the girl. "What about it?"

She shook her head slightly, said nothing.

Western tried pleading.

"Miss Mayland, this is a terrible affair, apparently," he said. "And you have involved me by coming to see me. I do not know why you came. I do not know anything about the mess. But I want to know. I have a reputation with my—my followers—and I want this thing straightened out at once. I am not knowingly implicated in this thing, and I want people to know it."

There was fright in her eyes as she stared at them. Enough fright to make all of them feel uncomfortable. But she was silent.

Monk shook his head slowly. The girl, he was deciding reluctantly, looked remarkably guilty.

Marvin Western spread his hands palms up.

"I feel so foolish," he said. "This childish talk about the whiskers on somebody named Hercules who lived thousands of years ago. It is such an idiotic—"

Renny Renwick came in from the outside, to announce, "Johnny is on the radio. He wants you, Doc. Wants to talk to you."

Chapter VII
FLIGHT BY DAY

WILLIAM HARPER LITTLEJOHN knew most of the big words that other people didn't know, and liked to use them. He said, "I'll be superamalgamated. An intransmutably predestinative enigma."

Then he realized he was talking to Doc, and dropped the jawbreakers. He never—for what reason was not quite clear—used the words on Doc, although he plagued everybody else with them.

In normal English, Johnny said, "I began to think the girl's brother was something in perpetual motion. Believe it or not, he has been moving, and I have been following, ever since he left the airport."

Doc asked, "Where did Charles Mayland go?"

"He walked," Johnny explained. "He walked the streets, he walked in the park, and he walked in the country. If you ask me, he is a boy trying to get away from his conscience."

"Did he meet anyone?"

"Not until half an hour ago, when the kid went to a spot on the lake—it's a rowboat—where he met some other men."

"Is a yellow-haired man one of the others?"

"Yes."

Doc got the description of the rowboat and the part of the lake where it lay from Johnny, who said, "They're just drifting along the lake shore. It looks as if they're waiting for someone else, before they go wherever they're going."

"What about Hercules?"

"Eh?"

"Heard any references to Hercules, or seen anything which reminded you of him?"

"This Hercules you're talking about is the same as the ancient Greek named Hercules?"

"Yes."

"This is the first I've seen or heard of him. What do I do about this rowboat full of guys?"

"Give me twenty minutes," Doc said, "to get out there."

THE girl was pale and desperate.

Doc Savage, glancing at her, said, "You really should talk, Miss Mayland. We have your brother and his friends cornered."

She lifted out of her chair, hands to her lips. Her cry of horror was wordless.

Doc asked, "What is it all about?"

She stared with a wordless what-can-I-do-now apprehension. But she did not speak.

Renny beckoned Doc aside, to say, so that the girl could not hear him, "Western might be right about her, Doc. She kind of acts to me like a girl who had started out masterminding something—you can see she's clever—and what she started has gotten a lot bigger and more terrible than she expected."

Doc said, "The idea of her brother being involved is what is frightening her."

"Sure. But she isn't losing her head. And some of that emotion she's showing may be acting."

"Renny," Doc said, "you stay here. Keep an eye on her. Western says he wants to cooperate. Have him help you." He turned to the athlete, and asked, "That all right with you?"

Marvin Western said, "She is welcome to stay here," when Doc Savage glanced at him. Western then added, "Anything I can do to help you gentlemen, I will willingly do. I feel I owe atonement for the bad reception they gave you."

Monk felt of his stomach and muttered reception being a mild word for it.

Doc Savage went outside with Monk and Ham. The dawn reddened the clouds which packed the sky. They did not seem to be rain clouds.

TWO blocks south and a block east, Doc Savage stopped the car, a machine they had rented during the night, and told Monk and Ham, "We are not going to leave Renny and the girl alone in that house."

"Yeah, I was wondering about that," Monk said.

"You and Ham watch the grounds. Do not show yourselves unless you have to. But keep an eye on the place."

Monk and Ham got out. They were disappointed. "I might be able to help with that rowboat matter," Monk suggested.

"Blast you, you've had your action for the night when you got shot in the stomach," Ham said. "If anybody goes with Doc, it'll be me."

"Both of you watch Western's house," Doc said.

When he left Monk and Ham, they were quarreling.

The quarrel, which began mildly, and progressed to what a stranger would have mistaken for the verge of fisticuffs, lasted while Monk and Ham were walking back to the Western estate.

The squabble made them feel better. It let a certain amount of steam out of their systems.

"You know something?" Ham asked.

"Listen, if you're leading up to a wise crack about my intelligence—"

"I'm not—although plenty could be said about it," Ham told him. "I just wanted to mention a feeling I've got about this whole thing."

"What kind of a feeling have you got?"

Ham said thoughtfully, "Somehow I begin to get a sensation of size, of magnitude, of consequence. For a while I was more or less in a whirl because of the goofiness of the thing—Renny getting thrown fifteen feet in the air, the car dashed against a tree, something incredible and apparently human carrying off five men, and that body. And the aging of that fellow at the cabin, the way he became an old, old man in a couple of hours. But the whole thing, I've got a feeling, will tie in together. And when it does—we've got a golly-whoppus on our hands, I bet you."

Monk had the same opinion, but disliking to agree with Ham, he was silent.

There was plenty of light from the early morning sun as they took positions where they could watch the Western mansion. The grounds went to wide stretches of lawn instead of shrubbery, so it was easy to position themselves where it was impossible for anyone to come or go without their noticing. A rabbit could not go from house to street, or street to house, without them seeing it.

They would have sworn to this.

There was one other thing that touched up the situation so that what happened later was even less believable.

Both Monk and Ham personally saw everyone in the house. They came out on a balcony, and had breakfast.

They were Renny, Lee Mayland, Marvin Western, the lackey who had shotgunned Monk, the lackey who had talked with Renny over the stone wall—with the latter doing the serving.

They finished breakfast and went inside. Lee Mayland was yawning.

Thirty minutes later, Renny came flying out of the front door and circled the house at a tearing run.

Monk and Ham immediately ended their concealed watching and scrambled over the stone wall and ran to the house.

Renny saw them and yelled, "You two been watching the place?"

Monk and Ham admitted this.

"Then which way'd they go?" Renny shouted.

"Who?"

"Everybody."

"What the dickens happened?" Monk demanded.

Renny pointed at the top of his head. "I've got a knot there like an apple. I heard Western yell out, 'Watch the infernal girl! She's got a—' And I didn't find out what she had, because she hit me—it must have been her—a clip on the noggin. I was out a minute or two, and when I got up, everybody seemed to have scrammed."

"Which way did they go?"

"Holy cow! Didn't you see them leave the house?"

Monk said, "They must have left on Ham's side of the house."

Ham shook his head. "Not my side. They probably took Monk's side, and Monk was asleep."

"Who was asleep?" Monk yelled.

"Oh, don't deny it. You didn't get any sleep last night, and you were probably napping—" The expression on Monk's face halted Ham. Ham stared at Monk uneasily. "You *were* asleep, weren't you?"

"I wasn't even drowsy."

"Nobody left?"

"Nobody."

"Not on my side, either," Ham said. "They must still be in the house."

Nobody was in the house. The house was big, not as impressive by daylight as it had been at night. The manifestations of Western's ego scattered about the place—there was more than the statue of Western in the front yard and the muscular carving of Western on the front door—gave a cheap carnival touch.

The girl, Western, the two men, had mysteriously disappeared.

Chapter VIII
THE CRY OF DEATH

UNTIL ten years ago, there had been no lake at Center Lake. The big dam on the Cedar River had been completed, and the resulting lake had been a scenic as well as an economic addition to the town and to Cedar County.

In the vicinity of the dam, the lake was not picturesque. But about three miles back the hills began—the natives called them mountains for the benefit of the summer vacationists who'd been plentiful before gasoline rationing—and the lake was as scenic as any. The hills were steep enough to pass as mountains. And, for some distance along the south shore of the lake, there were sheer cliffs which had been called the Cedar Palisades. They made an impressive sight to anyone boating on the lake. A path led down the face of one of these precipices to a houseboat which was tied to a pine tree growing out of a stone ledge which formed a natural dock.

When a tin can was tossed off the cliff top and came clattering down to land in the water a few yards from the houseboat, a man on the houseboat porch was considerably concerned. He sat there tense, one hand on the fishing reel which was hanging over the back of his chair. There was a revolver in the creel.

Another man with the same frightened expression on his face as the first put his head out of the deckhouse. "What was that?"

"Somebody tossed something. That can there." He pointed. "Over in the water."

The other glanced up at the cliff, then at the can. "Get it, you mutt!"

The lookout got a long cane fishing pole off the houseboat roof and worked along the face of the cliff trying to reach the can. He fell in, making a splash. Three more men had come out of the houseboat interior. When the man fell in, all of them laughed.

The lid was fastened on the can with adhesive tape, they discovered, to keep water from reaching the handwriting covered paper inside.

They gathered around the paper.

One laughed. "Lucky Charley isn't here. He might recognize his sister's handwriting."

They read farther.

"Hey, from the boss!" one said, surprised.

"What the hell did you think?"

Halfway through the missive they turned as one man to stare at the other side of the lake.

The rowboat was loitering along the distant shore, about a hundred feet from the beach.

The guard dripped water on the deck. "Bless me, you reckon Savage is there watching that rowboat already?"

... the lake water was clean and clear, so the mud that welled up to their knees and rose in low rolling masses like something alive was frightening.

A yellow-haired man came out of the house-boat cabin. He looked weak, ill. His hair was not as yellow as it had been, for now it was streaked somewhat with gray. There were more lines, lines of age, on his face than there had been.

He asked, "What's this?" weakly.

"The boss heaved a note down the cliff, Davis," one told him. "It's got bad news."

"Why didn't he come himself? Why the hell the note?"

The man gestured, in a cautious fashion as if he was afraid of someone seeing him, at the rowboat on the other side of the lake.

"Savage is probably over there watching the rowboat," he said in a frightened voice. "Savage and one of his helpers named Johnny Littlejohn. The boss didn't want to be seen."

The yellow-haired man became more ill-looking. "Where'd you get that?"

THEY had gotten it out of the note, they told him, whereupon he seized the missive and read it. The beginning surprised him, the middle alarmed him, but the end made him lick his lips.

"It could work." He examined all of them. "You fellows all read this?"

They had.

"You game to follow instructions?"

They were agreeable, one muttered, "If it gets rid of Savage, I'm ready for anything. That guy is beginning to get my goat in not a small way."

They went into the houseboat cabin. The place was sketchily furnished with odds and ends of house furniture. None of the fittings were boat stuff, so that the effect of the whole was landlubbery.

The yellow-haired man, gesturing, said, "Get the diving gear."

The diving equipment was not true diving stuff, but escape "lungs" of the type kept on sub-marines. Evidently they had been stolen from a naval supply depot, or possibly from a plant man-ufacturing them for the government, because they were still in the factory cartons.

"How we going to know these'll work?" asked someone who was apprehensive.

"Oh, they'll work, all right. They were tested at the factory."

A man took a mirror off the cabin wall.

"Ready to signal the rowboat?" he asked.

"Might as well. Better wait a minute, until we get better organized."

They were worrying about their belongings, money and watches and such, which the water might damage. Someone hit on the bright idea of getting some small fruits jars out of the galley and sealing the perishable stuff inside, then pushing the jars inside their shirts.

The yellow-haired man took the note which had been heaved down the cliff in the tin can and tossed it on the table, open so that anyone could read it.

"What is Charley going to think when he reads that note and finds out his sister is behind the whole thing?" a man asked uneasily.

The yellow-haired man called Charley an unpleasant name.

"Charley needs his feet kicked out from under him," he said.

"He's likely to blow his top."

"Let him."

A man took the mirror on deck, where he moved it about in the sun. Although the other shore of the lake, close to the rowboat, was three-quarters of a mile away, he could see the darting bit of reflected sunlight which the mirror threw on the shore.

He got the mirror reflection on the rowboat. Another man flapped his coat in front of the mir-ror, turning it into a crude heliograph.

They evidently did not know code, because they merely made four short flashes, then repeated them.

The rowboat began to approach the houseboat.

JOHNNY LITTLEJOHN watched the rowboat go into motion, and permitted himself a large word to express his relief. "Supermalagorgeous," he said.

Johnny was a very long man who was remark-ably thin and bony. His clothes fit him the way clothes fit very thin men, as if they were hung on a pole. The monocle which he habitually wore attached to his left lapel was a relic of the past when he'd really had a bad eye. Doc had repaired the eye, and Johnny still wore the monocle, but with a magnifying lens.

Doc said, "It is heading for the houseboat. They got that sun signal from the houseboat."

Pocketing his binoculars, Johnny said, "Let's go," and as they ran through the trees, "Wonder why the rowboat hung around there so long?"

Doc Savage said, "Lookouts, possibly," and slowed his stride so that Johnny could keep up. "From where the rowboat was lying, they could watch both ends of the lake." He ducked under a branch, added as Johnny almost chinned himself on the bough, "Where the rowboat was lying is also the only place from which they could see the highway in both directions. Ideal lookout spot."

Johnny running was a grotesque figure, but he covered ground. "It was worrying me," he said. "Thought it funny they were waiting there."

In order to reach the houseboat traveling on land, they had to go about four times the distance which the rowboat need travel. The rowboat beat them. But not by much. The occupants were climbing on the houseboat.

Johnny slowed down to ask, "What do we do now?"

"Get aboard," Doc said. "Or at least get alongside and put a listening-mike aboard."

IN the houseboat, the yellow-haired man, who now had gray in his hair, distributed diving lungs to the newcomers from the rowboat.

He also kept an eye on Charles Mayland, watched the young man's curiosity lead him to take a look at the note on the table, upon which the yellow-haired man drew a revolver.

"Don't start anything," he told Mayland. "It's time you found out."

Pointing at the note, horror a huskiness in his voice, Mayland said, "That—is Lee—it can't be! I don't believe it!"

"We don't give a damn what you think. What are you going to do about it?"

Young Mayland put his hands over his face and said thickly, speaking in such a way that you thought only of how he meant it, not how melodramatic were the words, "I wish I could die."

Somebody laughed.

"You can die now, if you want to," the yellow-haired man said, and threw a diving lung at Mayland.

The apparatus hit Mayland's chest and fell to the floor.

Mayland stared at the diving lung dully, seemingly without awareness or any kind of decision, until the others had their lungs donned. Then he bent slowly, and picked it up. He was pale. His asthma rattled in his throat and chest. He put on the lung.

"Out we go," the yellow-haired man said.

They had a special hatch for escaping from the houseboat. The hatch was a well affair in the floor—the bottom of the hull—of the boat. Like a fish well, it extended up above waterline, and had a lid. By opening the lid, a man could drop down, leaving the boat without his departure being seen from the outside.

The escape hatch was of newer construction than the rest of the boat. It had been installed recently. A box, built at the same time as the hatch, obviously held window-weights attached to cords made into the shape of harness to hold the men on the bottom of the lake while they walked away.

"How deep is it?"

"Twenty feet."

"That's pretty deep."

"It won't hurt you. It will feel kind of black and scary down there for a minute." The yellow-

haired man got a rope and they all took hold of this. "Hang onto the rope," he said. "We will stay under the boat for two or three minutes until the bubbles get out of our clothing. Then follow me."

He showed them an illuminated compass on his wrist.

"There's a wire down there that we can follow where we're going," he told them. "But if we get lost, I've still got the compass."

They began going through the hatch.

It was dark on the bottom. And cold, bitterly cold. They had supposed the lake bottom would be clean and hard because the lake water was clean and clear, so the mud that welled up to their knees and rose in low rolling masses like something alive was frightening.

But the fear of Doc Savage was greater than any other fear, and they lined out and got going.

They had the troubles natural to men inexperienced underwater. The lungs did not seem to deliver enough oxygen, and some of them got to gulping, which made it worse. And two of them lost their sash weights, thereafter having a devil of a time, only able to stay down by clinging to the rope to which they all were holding.

THEY walked, it seemed to them, for miles. The distance was actually no more than a quarter of a mile. Now and then they felt the wire which their leader, the yellow-haired man, was following.

When they came out, it was in a narrow gully which cut its way into the lake. They sank into the gully while still underwater, then turned and followed it. Those who knew where they were going, knew this was near the end, pushed eagerly against the others.

The sunlight blinded them. They tore off the lungs, and hung to the stone sides of the gully, to roughness of the stones and to bushes, gasping.

The yellow-haired man was all in. He was very sick and messy for a while.

"Help me," he gasped. "Help me up where I can see the houseboat."

They aided him to climb a short distance. He watched the houseboat.

"I don't see Savage on board!" he said hoarsely. He was afraid now.

He reached out and pulled some vines aside, uncovering a set of three storage batteries and a coil from which wires led away in the direction of the houseboat and the cliff which almost overhung it.

"Watch," he gasped. "Watch for Savage. I'm dizzy as hell. I can hardly see."

All of them strained their eyes. One had brought binoculars, but these were water-filled, useless.

Then one chanced to swing his gaze across the

lake, and said, "Look over there!" and, "Isn't that one of them?" while he pointed.

Some of them watched Johnny, and the others watched the houseboat.

Soon Renny appeared and waved both arms feverishly while he stood facing the houseboat. After nothing happened, he shaped his hands in a funnel at his mouth to send his fabulous voice booming across the lake.

Mixed up with the echoes from the cliff, they could hear Renny's, "Hey, Doc! Hey, Doc, on the houseboat!" quite understandably.

From the houseboat: "What do you want, Renny?"

Doc's voice. But it was unnatural and muffled, as if the bronze man was inside the boat.

The yellow-haired man's curse was as much a sigh of relief as profanity.

"I guess that Savage is on the houseboat," he said. The yellow-haired man cursed again. He grasped a switch attached to batteries and coil and closed it with a fierce jab.

His, "Now let's get the hell away!" was mixed with the rumbling roar that rose up and became the greatest of sounds, and the quaking of the earth.

Chapter IX
MONK THE MIGHTY

THE blast, sight and sound of it only, drove Renny Renwick back several paces on the opposite shore of the lake. When he stumbled, sat down, he remained sitting.

They could not tell how, twenty seconds after the explosion, exactly how much of the cliff had come down. There was too much dust. Rock dust and earth dust, smoke from the explosive, black and yellow and brown, billowed out over the lake surface, chasing a tidal wave that gathered itself and gushed in a foaming crest that for a while barely kept abreast of the smoke, then drew ahead, rushing and twisting and piling over itself.

Monk—he spoke very calmly now, but in a few seconds he became almost hysterical—said, "The boat was mined, too. It blew up at the same time as the cliff."

"T.N.T.," Renny said. "I know what T.N.T. sounds like and looks like." His voice was tiny, unnatural.

There was no sound now, except an occasional grinding as a rock slid, and the gobbling of echoes of the blast, dying away like summer thunder among the hills.

"Doc and Johnny were aboard," Ham said. "We saw them go aboard. We didn't see them leave. So they were aboard."

The tidal wave took some time to cross the lake, and horror was still holding them there when the wave came rushing up on the bank with a wet grunt, falling to pieces in a watery sheet.

Renny rushed for the water.

Monk and Ham each got him by an arm and stopped him.

"What you think you're going to do?" asked Monk.

"We've got to get over there. I'm going to swim." Renny tried to reach the water, not struggling with them, just straining toward the lake.

Monk said, "Here, here, cut in your brains! It's three quarters of a mile. Suppose they want to shoot you? Swimming, you'd make a fine target."

Renny shook his head with eyes pinched shut, then said, "Yes, sure," as he wheeled and ran for the dam crossing.

BY mid-afternoon about a hundred men, including four divers rushed by plane from Chicago and Cleveland, had brought up a few fragments of the houseboat and the news that the rest of the wreckage, together with whoever had been on the craft, were buried under the twenty feet of lake water and stone, plus an additional thirty feet or so of stone which the blast had tossed down from the face of the cliff.

Monk and Ham and Renny made arrangements for keeping the workmen on the job and paying for it.

"I can't bear to stick around here any longer," Monk said, which was the way the others felt, too.

The Cedar County sheriff, a tall man who chewed tobacco and looked rural, but talked like an English diplomat, showed them the blasting batteries and coil. They had seen these before, but he showed it to them again, and said he had something else.

"Diving lungs like submarine men have," he explained, indicating a small pile of the gadgets. "They seem to have been heaved into the water here. My men have been bringing them up one after the other."

"That would explain why Doc thought they were on the boat," Monk admitted.

"Another thing," said the sheriff—his name was Calvin Stout. "We trailed the chaps up the road. There's a kind of a shed on the road. They've been keeping two cars there, a farm kid up the road says. He thought they were just summer sports. They've been around about a week."

"The kid describe any of them?"

"Some of them. Some of the descriptions match the ones you gave us of the chaps who took Miss Mayland to the cabin in the woods."

"Maybe that will help."

Ham Brooks asked the sheriff, "Any trace of Marvin Western?"

"No, and I'm worried about that," the officer said. "Western is one of our leading citizens. Done a lot of good for this town."

"What about the girl, Lee Mayland?"

"Not a sign so far." The sheriff frowned. "You know, if Lee is furnishing the wits for this, she can give us some trouble. She's smart. I remember she was sort of a genius in school, and the way she's got out in the world since then—well, she's nobody's fool."

Ham gave the sheriff a bit of information. "Western seemed to feel that she had started something, and it turned out blacker than she thought, but that she was going through with it come hell or high water."

"Could be. That's like a woman. And Lee isn't no ordinary woman."

Ham asked, "But you have a dragnet out for her, and men trying to save Western?"

"You bet we have." The sheriff looked at them over a cigarette he was making. "What do you fellows think is behind this?"

"If we told you," Ham said gloomily, "you would think we had been taking an opium pipe to bed with us."

"I probably would," the sheriff admitted. "I talked to Chief of Police Carey about it. He gave me quite a dance about a man who could throw another man fifteen feet in the air, toss a car into a tree, carry five men off piggyback while taking thirty feet at a step, and packing off a body before Doc Savage could do a thing about it although Savage was in the same room at the time." The sheriff held a match to the cigarette he had made. "That was really a wild and hairy tale. Any truth to it?"

"It's all truth, whether you believe it or not," Ham assured him.

"Well, I'm damned," the sheriff said, and went off shaking his head.

Monk and Ham walked toward the road where they would find a police car willing to take them into town.

"We should have told him there's something called the Whisker of Hercules," Ham said grimly. "Then he would have been about half as confused as we are."

They caught a ride into town in a State Patrol car.

THE tourist establishment was quiet. "We've got to get some sleep," Ham pointed out. "Maybe after four or five hours the police will have dug up a clue of some kind." And Monk and Renny agreed with him.

Remembering the explosion trap into which Doc Savage had stumbled, they split up in three different cottages for sleeping.

Ham Brooks sat on the bed in the north cabin for a while eyeing his damaged sword cane, then temporarily mending the sheath with bicycle tape, making what he considered a messy job of it. Then he lay back on the bed without undressing, something he would never have done in a state of mind anywhere near normal. He contemplated the ceiling for a while, then said, "Blast it, my nerves must be going. I'm seeing things."

He sprang on to the floor, goggling at the attic-hatch which was over the bed.

"Get down out of there!" he ordered.

The man looking down through the hatch—Marvin Western—asked, "Is it safe?"

"Sure," Ham said. "What on earth are you doing up there? The sheriff and everybody is hunting you. We thought they might have killed you."

"They were going to, I'm afraid," Western said. "Is—is that she-devil around, by any chance?"

"Who?"

"Lee Mayland. We made a big mistake about that girl." Western grimaced uncomfortably. "I hate to sound unmanly, and cowardly. But, and I say this frankly, I have become more terrified of that girl than I would be of a cobra."

"She isn't around," Ham told him. "Come down before I ram this sword up through the ceiling!"

Western climbed down out of his attic hideout saying, "I thought maybe she had thrown in with you again with that innocent story of a brother in trouble."

Ham said, "Wait a minute," on his way to the door, where he called: "Monk! Renny!" And both Monk and Renny arrived in a hurry, Monk wearing nothing but his socks and a sheet.

Renny took several unbelieving looks at Western, then rumbled, "Holy cow! Good, good! Where did you catch him?"

Western struck a dignified pose, bulging his great chest impressively.

"I have been hiding in the attic, waiting for you to return," he told them.

Snorting, gathering his sheet about him toga fashion, Monk said, "Listen, strong boy, your story had better be convincing."

Western, after a moment, said, "You're not taking the right attitude."

"We're not taking the arms and legs off you yet. You're lucky," Monk stated.

"I'm not afraid of you." Western sounded afraid.

Monk, who wanted physical action too much to be reasonable, said, "You will be afraid, if I take hold of you."

Western made some muscles gather under his skin like live rabbits. "I can break every bone in your carcass."

"If I was a carcass, you might," Monk admitted. "Don't overrate yourself, you muscle-bound wonder."

Ham, a lawyer and more inclined to be diplomatic than the others, put in, "This is not getting us anywhere. Calm down, Western. Monk, you chimpanzee, cut it out."

"I wish I hadn't come here to see you." Western said. "I expected a better reception. I have become a very scared man."

Monk grimaced. "A great big hunk of muscle like that, scared!"

Ham told Monk, "It's your girl friend, Lee. She seems to be sprouting horns we hadn't expected."

Monk said uncomfortably, "Well, I—uh—she was mighty nice looking."

"This isn't the first time their looks have fooled you," Ham said.

Western was stretching. "Cramped up there, lying in the attic, I became stiff," he explained.

Western glanced apprehensively at the door. "The girl is at the bottom of it," he added. "I am sorry, but that is now certain. To do her justice, I think she isn't at ease in her mind, but I also think her feeling is desperation rather than one of repentence." He looked at them grimly, "It hurts me—hurts me to say such a thing about a woman—but I don't feel the least pity toward her."

"She must have thrown a scare into you,"Monk said.

"She did. I admit it." Western shuddered. "That girl is a consummate actress, and a creature of consummate nerve. She isn't scared. That was an act."

Ham took over the questioning by asking, "Just why *did* you come?"

Western said, "First, you're probably wondering why I left my house. I didn't—not willingly. That girl held us up at the point of a gun. I don't know where she got the gun. She forced myself and my two employees out of the house. Against our wills, I assure you."

"With Monk and Ham watching the house, and me in the house," Renny said. "How'd she do that?"

"She simply hid us in—ah—a secret room where I take my exercises. You thought we had gone. After you departed, she took us away."

The man stopped and consulted his watch.

"Go on," Monk requested.

Western shook his head. "I want to show you something. I think we had better hurry." He looked at them appealingly. "I know I have not told you enough to satisfy you that I am an honest man.

But, due to the urgency of the situation, will you come with me?"

Renny rumbled, "We're as urgent as any situation," and turned to the door saying, "Wait until I get my hat, and Monk gets his pants."

Monk and Ham felt the same way, a little desperate. The situation looked strange, but they didn't care.

MARVIN WESTERN guided them to an old touring car and peered anxiously at the gasoline gauge, muttering something about the injustice of his only having an A card.

Getting the car rolling, he said, "This is an amazing thing I intend to show you."

Monk was suspicious enough to be unfriendly. "Pick up the story where you left it—where the girl took you out of your own house."

"Myself and my two employees. Not myself alone."

"All right, start there."

"She took us on foot some distance to where a truck waited," Western said, unruffled. "The truck was one of those van types with a large enclosed body. It was standing in some thick bushes, and I escaped, simply dashing away from them. They pursued me with fervor, naturally. So I did what they did not expect, doubling back and entering the truck, where I concealed myself under some large quilts or padded blankets of the type used to protect furniture when in transit. I take it this was a furniture moving van. Failing to find me, they came back, entered the truck and drove to the spot where I am taking you."

This was so interesting it had Monk, Ham and Renny on the edge of the cushions.

"At their destination, they stopped the truck and everyone unloaded," Western continued. "After tarrying for a while in the truck, I crept to the rear and looked out."

He glanced at them, apparently to see if they were approving of his courage and ability, his sagaciousness.

Then he continued, "I then saw that the truck was in a large brick building, while everyone had gone up a flight of wooden stairs. So I also ascended the stairs, using caution, whereupon I saw the most remarkable sight."

He paused long enough for them to wish to the devil that he would go on, but did not quite give them time to start asking questions.

"I watched for some time, learning that they intended to leave in a body, and would be gone for twelve hours or so, whereupon I withdrew, left the building, went to my home, got my car, and began hunting you. I previously had learned—Mr. Renwick, here, told me this morning at breakfast at my home—that you were quartered at the tourist place. So I concealed myself in one of the cabins, and was still there when you found me."

Monk blurted, "Wait a minute! Is that the story?"

"It is."

"Didn't you say something about a remarkable sight?"

"Yes."

"We're a little curious about it."

Western sighed. "I know. Yes indeed, but I am not going to make you think I am crazy by telling you about it. I am going to show you, let you see for yourselves."

"Now that's a fine stunt to pull," Monk said grimly.

Western glanced at them, said, "Remember Hercules."

"Eh?"

"Just remember Hercules, and you will be somewhat prepared for what you will see."

MONK, Ham and Renny had time to put no more than a dozen questions—unanswered—before Marvin Western wheeled the car to the curb and pointed.

They examined a large red brick eyesore, three stories, with the windows boarded shut on the first floor and scattered panes of glass broken out on the second and third floors.

"That it?" Monk asked.

"There is a rear door," Western explained. "Perhaps we had better use that. I will drive around on the back street."

By back street he meant a littered cavity of an alley which smelled of nothing recent. They left their car far back between two buildings where it was not very noticable.

Western walked straight for the grimy back door of the place, with Monk and Ham and Renny walking behind him.

Monk stooped without breaking his stride and picked something off the ground, a small round rock. He used the rock, which was not quite as large as a baseball, to hit Marvin Western behind the ear.

"What'd you do that for?" Ham demanded.

"A pixyish streak in me, I guess," Monk said. He contemplated the old building. "I just thought he might be rushing us in there."

Renny sank to a knee and examined Western, who was unconscious. "Well, it's a wonder you didn't crack his skull," Renny said. "Someday you are going to kill somebody, picking up rocks and hitting them."

Monk grinned. "You want to continue the lecture, or go in and see what awaits us?"

Renny indicated Western. "You've got to carry him."

"That's right," Ham said. "You beaned him. You carry him."

Monk indignantly tried to vote them down, failed, and shouldered the unconscious man.

They passed up the door of the old building. Down the alley fifty yards or so they found another door into another building with a dark, stinking interior. Prowling around in this, they located stairs, then a ladder, and a hatch which put them out on a second-story roof.

From the roof, all they had to do was pick a few panes of glass silently from a window, and the way was clear into the old building which was supposed to house something so strange and unbelievable—according to Western—that a man's sanity would be doubted if he told about it.

Something to do with Hercules.

Chapter X
A MIGHTY MONK

THEY climbed through the window, then lifted Marvin Western inside, took off their shoes, and went to a door where they found themselves face to face with a large blue-eyed man. This man was one who had been at the cabin in the woods. He came through the door unsuspecting and happy.

Everyone was about equally astonished. But Monk and Ham and Renny got over it the quicker. Monk grabbed the man's mouth. Renny grabbed his throat. Ham used the end of his sheathed sword cane like a billiard cue and tapped the fellow senseless. They lowered the victim to the floor, and began breathing again.

With the lips only, Ham said, "So the place was empty, eh?" He went over, bridged his sword cane against Marvin Western's head, and insured Western remaining unconscious for a while longer.

Monk finished taking five guns—pistols and revolvers—out of the victim's clothing. He added a sheath knife and a pocket knife, both able to take a life.

"Commando," Monk said, also with his lips only.

"A scared crook, more likely," Ham said, the same way.

Doubled so low and stepping so lightly that it would have been funny at another time, they eased through the door by which the heavily armed man had entered. There was another door. They passed through. Then they fell over each other retreating.

"Holy cow!" Renny whispered.

"With exclamation points!" Ham agreed. "There must be twenty of them."

Monk crept back to the door and counted, reporting, "Only fifteen."

From the roof, all they had to do was pick a few panes of glass silently from a window, and the way was clear into the old building …

"The girl there?"

"Yes. Back in the corner, where it's dark, sitting in a chair."

"Anybody else we know?"

"All the gang who were at the cabin in the woods, plus those in the rowboat, plus Marvin Western's two employees, as he called them, who were at Western's house this morning."

"Some collection," Renny muttered.

"The jackpot," Ham agreed. "What do we do now?"

Monk said, "If you guys want to play detective, I think we can crawl into a spot where we can hear what they're saying to each other. And, if a fight does start, we won't be much worse off than we would be anywhere else."

"With fifteen of them, I can think of lots better places to be," Ham said. "But okay. Let's see if we can hear why they're all here for a pow-wow."

As Monk had predicted, they were able to get to a spot where they could get the general sense of what was being said in the gabfest.

THE yellow-haired man, Taft Davis, looking ill and quarrelsome and older and much more gray-haired, had the floor and was saying, "—not getting us anywhere. Your arguments don't hold water because you don't know what you're talking about. I've told you, and that should settle—"

A man interrupted with, "But Taft, you look older than this morning. You're still aging. Hell, look in a mirror and see—"

"I've looked in a mirror." The yellow-haired man pushed all arguments away by waving a hand. "I don't feel any worse."

"But—"

"Look, Frank, here's why it hit me so hard," Davis explained patiently. "The idea of going up against Savage at the tourist camp scared me, but the boss said we had to have Staicu's body because Doc Savage, by doing an autopsy and analyzing, might have found out the truth. As I say, I was scared, so I took a little too much of it. I wanted plenty of effect. I overdid it. I got more than I needed. That's why it aged me about twenty years."

The men sat around staring at him. They seemed to have something ahead of them about which they were not very happy.

"How much," asked one of them, "will this job age us, do you figure?"

"Five years, about," said the yellow-haired man. He gave all the impression of trying to sound more positive than he was.

"Does that mean five years off our lives?"

"It might mean a little off. Maybe not five years. But what's five years stacked up against

what we're after?"

"Five years is eighteen hundred twenty-five days," said a mathematician.

"Don't start being funny."

"If it's funny to you, go ahead and laugh," said the figurer. "It's a hell of a long time to me."

The yellow-haired man fell back on logic. "It's five years you don't *live,* so you haven't lost it. Look at it this way, you fellows! Lots of times you've pulled a caper when getting caught meant a stretch, and more than one of you have served time. That was time out of your lives that didn't pass easy because every day was a day in jail. This is time that is easy because you don't live it."

That seemed to satisfy them.

THE yellow-haired man now got down to business by hauling a photographic slide projector out of a box together with slides. What he had was better than a map. It was a series of photographs, in color, of the scene where they planned to commit the crime.

Two men hung a sheet on a dark spot on the wall, and the briefing of the operation got underway.

First picture was of a train, a streamliner.

"That's the Bluebird," the yellow-haired man said. "She is the only blue, streamlined train that time of the day. She has a Diesel engine, and a whistle that sounds like a horn."

He rigged up an electric phonograph and played a recording which was nothing but train sound—noise of the train, of the whistle.

"That's what the Bluebird sounds like," he said, switching off the phonograph.

Next picture was an aerial view.

The yellow-haired man walked forward and pointed out different features in the picture. "Here is the railroad and highway layout. The railroad is this line, and the Bluebird will come from this direction. Here is where the train will be flagged, and here is where the track will be blocked. Automobiles one and two will be here, number three will be here"—he was indicating the spots on the two highways, one on either side of the railway— "and four will be here."

The next picture was a bush.

"Car one will park here behind this bush."

Next a picture of a farm.

"The farm is abandoned. Car two will drive into the barn and wait there. Better back into the barn. Drivers will stay with all cars."

To a photograph of another bush, he said, "This is where three will be," and to a stretch of open highway, "Car four will cruise here. The spot commands the scene where the train will stop, and you can cover it with machine guns. The crew of car four will not leave the machine. They will not shoot unless they get a signal from me, or from one of the others. The signal will be a bright yellow cloth which somebody will wave. All of you will have yellow cloths to wave in case you get in a jam."

There was a lot more of the detail that went with a job as thoroughly planned as this one was, following which the lecturer asked for any questions.

A practical soul immediately asked, "How much are we going to make out of this?"

"They've been moving about four million in gold at a shipment," the yellow-haired man told him. "There is no reason to think it will be less, and it probably will be more, because they're going to increase the shipments."

"Suppose a shipment isn't on the train?"

"It will be. A shipment is being made every day this week."

"That's a heck of a lot of gold to be moving around, isn't it?"

"Not when the government is doing it. This gold is being shipped to New York, in preparation for a deal with a foreign country whereby currency over there will be stabilized. As a matter of fact, it's only a small part of what will be eventually shipped."

The doubter scratched his head and asked, "How do we know this is straight?"

The yellow-haired man said positively, "It's straight. My brother is a clerk at the Fort and he knows what is going on. I got this from him. He gets a cut."

The other snorted. "He'll get a nice big cut of jail, that's what. The police have identified you, Davis. They'll snap your brother up the minute we pull this thing."

"That's his hard luck," the yellow-haired man said without much feeling.

Now there was some talk about timing. The operation, it seemed, was to take place tomorrow evening.

During this discussion, Charles Mayland stood in the background making sounds with his asthma —he had made the asthma noises throughout, but softly—and throwing ill, miserable glances at his sister.

The yellow-haired man was saying, "Now, here is how we will divide up until time for the caper," when Monk and Ham and Renny swapped their interest in what was to happen tomorrow for concern about what was going to happen to them right now.

It hit hard and heavy in the pits of their stomachs when a voice behind them said, "Listening, eh? That's not a nice thing to do."

THEY turned over—they had been on their stomachs—to stare at a hard-eyed man with a machine gun. The gun was locked on continuous fire; the man had his finger on the trigger, had his body braced for the recoil.

"One move makes you dead," he assured them.

It was true. Ham and Renny froze. Monk's chest got as big as a barrel with rage, but he didn't move either.

"Hey, come see the visitors!" called the man with the gun.

There was no stampede, but in the other room every man got out at least one gun. Three of them came in and helped escort Monk, Ham and Renny in to confront the others.

A short fat man's remarks set the tone for what everybody had to say. "Well, well, we got Doc Savage, and now we've got the rest of them," he said. "A very sweet situation."

Monk, Ham and Renny were lined up on the left side of the room, the side where the girl had been standing and still stood. Monk was nearest the girl, it happened.

Monk glanced at the girl, then blinked, looked again more closely, and his mouth became round with surprise. Lee Mayland's wrists were tied, something they hadn't noticed before.

She was—unless her tied wrists had some other significance, which wasn't likely—a prisoner like themselves.

While Monk was in the middle of his surprise, the girl said, low-voiced, "Pick me up and carry me through the door behind us and slam the door."

Monk and half the men in the room heard her. Monk lunged, scooped up the girl, came around with the same motion to the door, got it open, followed it through, and slammed the door. It had a spring lock which he tripped.

Bullets began coming through the door without much trouble, so it wouldn't keep anyone out for long. There was plenty of cursing on the other side, together with men assuring other men that Monk was a dead duck, that they'd get him, that there were no windows, so how could he get away? Which, Monk saw upon looking around, was true.

"Get my wrists loose," the girl told Monk.

Monk, inclined to be sour about his predicament, said, "You ever hear of frying pan into the fire?"

She said violently and with purpose, "Get me loose."

She sounded so urgent, as if they would be safe when she was free, that Monk began having trouble with the knots.

The room was large and rectangular, with scarred plaster walls and floor grooved by storage of heavy articles in the past years. The one electric bulb gave none too much light, which spread over a pair of tables and a number of boxes, cases, packages, and some cots covered with soiled bedclothes. On one of the tables was a neat array of four small glass phials containing a very dark red fluid and a larger bottle which was empty. Nothing else was on this table.

Monk got the cord off the girl's wrists and watched her run to the table, pick up one of the phials, race back to Monk, extend the phial, say, "Here, drink it!"

Backing away, Monk said, "Huh, drink it?"

"Yes, quick!" She shook the phial of red stuff.

"What is it? I don't—"

"Oh, you dumb ape!" the girl said wildly. "Why couldn't I have picked some of the others who had some sense—"

That fixed it. Monk didn't care about being called dumb, and he was curious, anyway, so he drank the red stuff, taking the whole phial contents at one gulp.

At first, he only thought he had swallowed a red-hot coal.

THEN the stuff, whatever it was, began to operate in his stomach, and the world started coming apart, at least as far as his personal feelings were concerned.

He had fever, then chills, faster than seemed possible. It was like being hit by a sledgehammer made out of flame, then one made of ice, successive blows. Coupled with this was a cat fight in his stomach, with plenty of indiscriminate clawing.

It was slightly funny—although there was no reason for it to be funny—to Monk at first, and he said something about swallowing a circus. Then as the effects grew worse, shooting agonies through his muscles, and a hellish banging in his heart, he grew alarmed. Downright scared.

Enough bullets were coming through the door to make him more alarmed. They had not yet gotten the bright idea of shooting out the lock, however.

The world went around Monk two or three times, and he put out his hands, knowing he was going to fall. But he did not fall, and he began to notice something strange—for he chanced to look down at his wrist watch, which had a sweep second hand, and he discovered that the second hand had slowed until it was hardly turning.

"That stuff even stopped my watch!" he said.

He turned to the girl when she answered, surprised at the sound she was making. It took him a moment to realize the sound was words, but words spoken so slowly that it was like one of those sound films, or a phonograph record, which had almost stopped.

"What's the idea of talking like that?" he demanded.

But she was still speaking, or making the noises, for the words were so slow that he could not make out just what they were.

Monk became tired of listening to her, and went to the door.

The shooting had changed. It had almost stopped, and the shots themselves sounded different. And the men on the other side were now speaking in the unutterably slow fashion that the girl was using.

Monk stood there.

The world continued to slow down around him.

THERE was no feeling of limitless strength inside Monk. Just an impression that the world had slowed down fantastically about him.

Curious about what was happening in the other room—what had changed the sound of voices and shots—he opened the door.

A man was standing inside aiming a submachine gun at the door lock. He lifted his eyes very slowly to look at Monk. The slowness with which his eyeballs moved was weird. And after a while, the muscles in his hands began to tighten and the gun to lift.

Monk thought, "Something sure threw them into slow gear!"

All the other men in the room were just staring at him, not yet moving their guns toward him, although all of them still had guns in their hands.

Monk lunged forward, was astonished at how his feet slipped on the floor before they got traction, and seized the submachine gun which was moving so slowly towards him. He twisted the gun out of the other's hands.

As he took the gun, he noticed that at least three fingers of the man who'd held the gun seemed to break, and the right arm was unjointed or broken. This accident to the fellow rather pleased Monk.

He took the machine gun by the stock and went around knocking guns out of men's hands. He noticed that some arms broke. He noted also that that short barrel of the submachine gun became slightly bent, and that the drum magazine was damaged badly.

A darned poor gun, Monk thought, and took hold of the barrel. He found that he could bend the barrel in his hands without difficulty. He discarded the weapon as unsuitable.

The behavior of the men in the room was peculiar, but satisfactory. They had hardly moved. Some of them were trying to face Monk, but they moved only with the greatest slowness, although the convulsive position of their muscles showed that they were trying very hard.

Monk thought, "Brother, I've always dreamed of a fight like this!"

And he went to work collecting guns. He had more trouble with his feet skidding; the floor didn't seem to offer much traction.

Another fantastic difficulty which Monk had was in gauging his leaps so as not to jump farther than he intended as he went from one man to another. He realized this was a problem when he sprang to kick a gun out of a man's hand, and leaped completely over the fellow's head, and had to come back. He was more careful after that.

When he got his hands too full of guns, he tossed them away, went on collecting more. He discovered, to his disagreeable astonishment, a finger sticking in the trigger guard of one of the guns he had taken. It occurred to him that it must be an artificial finger to have come off so easily, but it looked quite natural. He had jerked it off a man, apparently.

About that time, he observed that the guns which he had tossed were still in the air, falling slowly toward the floor.

Everybody was now disarmed. Three of the men, acting as if they were rather badly injured, were falling toward the floor. But it was in very slow motion.

"Miss Mayland!" Monk called. "Something has thrown all these guys in slow motion. The way they're moving, I can get you out past them before they do anything about it."

He went back to get the girl.

THE girl was still making the rundown-phonograph sounds. Monk beckoned several times, saying, "Come on! Step on it!"

She was, he saw, in slow motion herself, like the men in the other room. So he picked her up. She was very light. He dashed through the whole mob in the next room, out the door, and put her down.

"Run for the roof!" he said.

Monk then went back for Ham and Renny, both of whom were still in the room with the slow-motion men.

"Get the lead out of your shirts!" Monk shouted. "Come on! These guys are liable to snap out of it and massacre us!"

To his horror, he saw that Ham and Renny were likewise incapable of anything but the slowest of motion.

Monk went over and picked Renny up with an arm around the middle. Renny seemed to have no more weight than a cat. So Monk picked up Ham also.

Making for the door, Monk asked, "What the heck's happened to everybody, anyhow?"

Out in the hall, the girl was taking the slowest of paces going away, but looking and acting as if she was running as hard as she could.

Monk managed to pick her up in passing. He reached the window by which he had entered, and tossed everybody through. He tossed them a little too hard, and they traveled about thirty feet before they landed, nearly going over the edge of the adjoining roof into the alley below, before they stopped.

That, Monk reflected, was a funny thing to happen.

Since the fight had gone so well, he thought that he might as well go back and take another pass at the men. He liked a fight, and while he couldn't lick all sixteen of them probably, he wanted to see what the chances were. He might find a gun, preferably a submachine gun with a barrel that he couldn't bend around in his hands, and hold them all at bay until the police could be summoned.

As an incidental thought, he grabbed up Marvin Western and pitched him out on the roof where Ham, Renny and the girl had landed.

It was when he was heading back for the fight that Monk happened to observe an opening in the ceiling. Just an aperture into the attic. But there was a head withdrawing from view up there.

Monk leaped for the hole. Normally, he would have to make a terrific jump to reach the edge of the opening, since the ceiling was high. So Monk put all he had into the upward leap.

Results were more than he anticipated by a great deal. He miscalculated—he was running when he jumped—and hit the ceiling before he reached the opening. And he hit it with great force, driving his head and shoulders through plaster and lath, then through a layer of boards which formed a floor above.

He was aware, as he hit, of the smashing of lath and boards about his head and ears.

Then all faded to blackness.

Chapter XI
THEFT TONIGHT

THERE were ropes around his legs, his body, his arms, binding his legs together and his arms to his body, and all of him in turn was tied to a stout plank about a foot wide and four inches thick. Under the ropes everywhere, so that they would not cut into him, there were folded blankets and sheets.

In his body was an awful sickness. In every muscle a furious aching.

Ham Brooks, leaning over him, was saying, "Here he comes out of it. The stuff didn't shorten the time that he was knocked out."

Renny Renwick rumbled, "You're sure his skull isn't fractured?"

"I don't think so. There isn't too much scalp left on his head, or much hide on his face and shoulders, but I don't think any bones are broken."

Monk tried to form words, and couldn't. He could groan, though, and did.

Ham looked at him and said, "Don't ever tell me again that your head isn't made out of granite. You jumped from one floor of that building up to the next, making a hole for yourself with your head."

Monk felt too bad to make an insulting answer. He looked about.

The girl stood nearby. Also Marvin Western.

The room, Monk decided from the shabby appearance, was in the same building where the late—and strange—fight had occurred. The blankets and sheets were evidently off the cots in the room where the fight had taken place.

Johnny Littlejohn was standing on the other side, beside Doc Savage, who was sitting on the floor. There was a nasty gash in Doc Savage's scalp, and he was carefully bandaging the wound.

"What's the matter with Doc?" Monk asked.

"Don't you remember bumping him and knocking him unconscious when you jumped through the ceiling?" Renny asked.

"No, I—" Understanding hit Monk. "He's alive. *Doc's alive!*"

"And somewhat disgusted," Renny agreed.

"How—what—" For the moment, Monk was feeling fine.

Ham came over and told Monk, "You were going great, but you messed everything with that ending. Doc and Johnny weren't on that houseboat when it blew up. They were on the cliff, but down about a hundred yards. They were close—and that was just luck—to where the yellow-haired man and the others walked out of the water with their diving lungs. Doc saw them watching the boat, watching for him, so he made his voice sound a little distant and muffled, and called out, and they blew up the cliff and the boat."

"But," Monk said, "we saw them go on the houseboat—Doc and Johnny—and not come off."

"We just didn't see them leave. They suspected something was wrong, and when they left the houseboat, they pulled a sneak in case somebody was watching."

"Then what?"

"They trailed the gang here. They were hiding in the attic when we showed up. They were all set to pull a rescue when you threw your act. They climbed back in the attic, because Doc wanted the gang to think he and Johnny were dead—that would make it easier for Doc to work against

them, he figured. Then you jumped through the ceiling and knocked Doc out, and yourself."

"What about the sixteen guys?"

Ham spread his hands. "With the breeze."

"They got away?"

"You bet they did. They picked up their guns and walked out. Or maybe they ran. They didn't know but what you were still running loose, and they wanted to get away. They carried off the casualties with them. We didn't catch a one. They even got the guy we kayoed in the outer room, and took him along."

"Then," Monk said, "they must have gotten over moving slow."

"Slow? They never were moving slow."

"Eh?"

"It was you."

"Me?"

"You," Ham told him, "took a taste of that Whisker of Hercules. Or didn't you have gumption enough to know that?"

MONK thought it over. It was becoming difficult to think. Everything in his body ached, twitched or throbbed, making a red-shot fog of pain through which he had to push his thoughts with the utmost willpower.

"They didn't slow up?"

"No."

"It was me?"

"Yes."

"Whisker of Hercules?"

"Yes."

It didn't make sense, and so Monk moved his attention to the ropes, asking, "Why am I all tied up?"

"Doc's suggestion," Ham explained. "You might injure yourself badly when you regained consciousness, he said, if you were not tied. He said the strain on your muscles and bones was terrific, to say nothing of your possibly jumping through another ceiling, or something."

Monk squinted doubtfully. "I really did that? I mean, I really took the guns away from those sixteen guys, and tossed people around, and jumped through the ceiling?"

"You sure did."

Monk closed his eyes, said, "That's great. That makes it all perfectly sensible."

"I'll admit it's a little skippy," Ham confessed. "But there is sense to it, or Doc says there is."

"You say all the sixteen got away?"

"Yes."

"That makes sense anyway. What are we going to do about it?"

Doc Savage now got to his feet. He came over and looked down at Monk and asked, "How do you feel?"

"Like cat meat," Monk said. "Doc, I'm sorry about—"

"Nothing to be sorry about," the bronze man told him. "You were going great guns. You did a fine job. You saved Ham, Renny, Miss Mayland and Marvin Western. If you had not done what you did, there would have been about one chance in a thousand of everyone getting out alive."

Monk grinned wryly. "Those are kind words. But I messed up your plan of keeping watch on the gang until you had them corner—cornered." Monk frowned. "Hey, they were all here. You had them cornered. Why hadn't you called the police and closed in on them?"

"They were not all here," Doc corrected.

"No?"

"Someone who is the mastermind, the brain behind the thing, was not here. Without whoever that is, the roundup wouldn't have been complete."

Monk nodded. He was thinking of himself, and growing alarmed. "Doc," he said hoarsely. "Doc, how do I look?"

"What do you mean?"

"Old?"

"Somewhat older," the bronze man admitted. And then, observing the alarmed expression on Monk's face, Doc went away and came back with a broken fragment of a mirror.

Monk was more pleased with what he saw in the mirror; it was a better picture than had been in his frightened mind.

"I feel a lot worse than I look," he said. He closed his eyes and lay back and began to really realize how he hurt and stung in every bone and muscle.

He'd been scared. He realized now how he'd been scared. In his thoughts like a bony black monster had been the memory of how the man in the woods had aged and died within a couple of hours.

"The phial which Miss Mayland gave you to drink," Doc explained, "contained a light dose of the stuff. The same dosage they are going to use when they pull the robbery."

THE sound must have been downstairs for some time, without their noticing.

Ham said, "Listen!" but Doc Savage was already headed for the door and the stairs.

Halfway down the stairs, they could hear the noise, enough to know that it was man-made. A man was trying to cry out when he had no voice for crying, only breath and not much of that.

Leaving the stairs and running across the floor, they saw the crumpled figure. A man. Doc Savage turned him over.

The man looked up at them with a face upon which blows had rained to change most of its recognizable features. The bullet hole in his chest was high up, but touched the lung or the lung cavity, because it bubbled.

Ham asked, sinking to a knee. "What happened, Mayland?"

Through vocal cords which had just about quit, Mayland said, "Quarreled—I—washed—up. Got—away—shot."

"What they were going to do to your sister changed your ideas, eh?" Ham said.

Charles Mayland looked sickly. His eyes closed and his lips parted. He was passing out.

Doc Savage gripped the young man's shoulders. "Mayland! Mayland! Who is behind this? Who developed it—the Whisker of Hercules?"

Mayland pried his eyes open with desperate willpower, moved them, looked at Marvin Western.

"He—Western—caused it—found—found—this evening—robbery—time—changed," he said, and fainted.

MARVIN WESTERN looked at all of them as they stood up and faced him. Western's face lost color, and his shoulders drooped, his mouth looked ill, all his splendid muscles seemed to sag.

"I don't deny it," he said. "It was my fault—my foolish carelessness."

Renny went around warily behind Western, ran his hands over the athlete searching for weapons and finding none.

"Brother, you're my prisoner," Renny said. "If you're stronger than I am, you may get away. But otherwise I'll break every bone in your body."

There was no fight in Western's sagging marvelous muscles.

Doc Savage went up the stairs with long leaps, and came back in a moment carrying Monk. Appalled at not being able to walk, Monk was swearing in a small polite voice, swearing polite oaths that sounded remarkably prissy coming from Monk. Behind came Lee Mayland, to scream when she saw her brother.

"He only has a bullet in the chest and some lacerations," Doc told her. "Not enough to keep him from getting well."

They went outside, Ham and Johnny carrying young Mayland, Renny walking behind the ill-looking Western with big fists blocked out. They loaded into a car and drove to a hospital.

Lee Mayland was perfectly willing to remain behind at the hospital with her brother and Monk. And Monk was pleased, too, having for once had all the physical action he wished.

The girl talked to them in a corridor before they left.

"I want to explain," she said.

Doc nodded. "Make it brief. They are going to pull that weird robbery this evening. We haven't long, if we intend to stop them."

She twisted her hands together and talked. "I don't know how I first knew Charles was in something bad. I guess it wasn't one thing, but many. You know how it is—you know a brother so well you can almost read his mind. And then he came home tight—he never drank much as a rule—and talked some. It was the foolish talk of a drunk. But he said things about Hercules, which didn't make sense. And about Taft Davis, enough that I knew Taft Davis had gotten him into it."

She talked faster and told them how she had gone to see Taft Davis about it. The interview had been satisfactory in only one point, or maybe the word was unsatisfactory, because she had gone away from the talk convinced that her brother was in something pretty bad. She had thought of talking to Doc Savage, and then she had done a foolish thing—she had told Charles she was going to get Doc to straighten him out.

"Charles must have told Taft Davis, so they seized me at the airport. But just before that, Charles gave me a paper with writing on it that said he was guilty, and he would be tried, possibly for murder, if I didn't keep my mouth shut. The paper was mostly lies, but I didn't know it. So I was very scared, and I refused to talk when you rescued me from the cabin. Incidentally, they were torturing me in the cabin to see if I had told you anything more than I had admitted telling you."

Doc asked, "This paper your brother gave you—was that what you burned in the cabin? It was what was in the brown paper parcel?"

"Yes."

"Why did you go to Marvin Western?"

"I got the idea he was mixed up in it—from Charles' drunken talk—I forgot to tell you that."

Renny said, "Don't worry about Western. We'll take care of him."

DOC SAVAGE left the hospital room. Western trailed along, looking wildly concerned.

"Mr. Savage!" Western said. "I want to tell you the truth. I insist on telling you—"

"Later," Doc said. "We have some fast moving to do."

Downstairs, Doc Savage got hold of the hospital manager.

"Call the police," Doc told the hospital head. "Get them here as quickly as possible. Have them watch that girl, Lee Mayland, and her brother. Tell the police they had better throw at least twenty officers into the building. Have them patrol the corridors, and outside of the building."

The hospital manager said, "That sounds rather alarming!"

"It is alarming," Doc assured him. "About the most alarming thing that could happen to this world—if any strangers get in to see that girl, or her brother, without being caught."

"I'll get the police immediately."

"In the meantime, have all your strong-bodied interns guard the girl and her brother. If you have any guns, arm the guards."

"I certainly will."

Marvin Western had listened to this, and he looked considerably less worried. He clutched Doc's arm in gratitude.

"Thank you, Mr. Savage, oh thank you!" he blurted. "I was horribly, most horribly, frightened for a while. I thought things had happened so that you no longer realized how clever she is."

Doc said, "Come on. You can tell your story while we drive."

"We must stop that robbery!" Western said excitedly. "With the capital they get from the crime, they can do anything they want. They can rescue the girl. She will lead them on to—who can imagine what terrible things!"

WHEN they were in the car headed for the robbery spot, there was a little discussion about whether or not to call in the police.

There was not much time. In fact there wasn't any spare time at all. The spot was thirty miles away, the Bluebird was due in fifty minutes, which didn't leave any time for explaining anything to anyone.

"Also," Doc pointed out, "it's over in the next state, across the state line about ten miles. The police are efficient, but there would be some delay, and they might not make it in time."

Doc was also of the opinion that the police, not knowing with what they had to cope—they doubtless wouldn't believe it, either, if they were told—might not accomplish too much. They wouldn't be helpless, but some officers would probably get killed.

The decision was that Doc, Renny, Ham and Johnny should drive like the devil to the spot and see what they could do.

So they drove.

Renny, in the back seat, reached out suddenly and slapped Marvin Western. "Tell it! Tell it all!" he said.

Western took the slap with no offer to fight back, then began talking, trying to make his voice oratorical and convincing, saying, "You gentlemen have me in the same pen with the goats, which is where I don't belong. Although on second thought, I have been made a terrible goat of."

"Stick to the truth minus the platform delivery," ordered Renny.

Talking the same way, or more oratorically, Western continued, "Body-building, you know, is my business. It has been my hobby, my interest, my livelihood, my special field. I study it as a good engineer studies engineering. I have studied the lives of the great strong men of history. Their lives and deeds fascinate me. That is how I came to study Hercules, and to learn—you will not find this information in the usual books—that Hercules got his strength, his legendary strength, by making and drinking a brew in which the principal ingredient was one hair from the whiskers of a legendary deity."

Renny said impatiently, "Cut out the legends and hocus-pocus."

"But you don't understand—that is the secret," said Western.

"Yeah? Secret of what?"

"These whiskers, I found, were not whiskers at all, but the name of a plant common to the regions where Hercules lived. You know of the common fern called maidenhair? Well, this was a plant called a beard. The Arab nickname for it today is *sharah baqq*. I won't go into the scientific background of it. But I studied it closely. This studying began several years ago, when—"

He stopped and covered his eyes with his hands in fright as Doc Savage took a curve. They were on the open highway now, and the car flew. Ham muttered something about hoping they weren't war tires.

MORE confident now, hence more oratorical, Western resumed, "I began studying, as I say, several years ago, when I began to get the suspicion that magical properties might be latent in this little-known Arab plant."

He smiled at them. "If this is boring you—"

"Just the way you tell it bores me," Renny snapped. "Get on with it!"

"My beginning experiments were entirely barren of results. I obtained the root, the stem, the leaves, the seed, the flowers of the plant. I made stews, teas, brews of all kinds. Nothing happened. I gave up for a year. But the thing fascinated me, and I went back to the Mediterranean, and I gathered many specimens of the plant from many spots. I brought the stuff back, and experimented for another year before—well, that day, I fed it to one of the guinea pigs which I was using for tests."

He rolled up a sleeve. "You see this?"

The marks of a past injury on his arm were impressive.

"The guinea pig did this," he said. "You know how helpless guinea pigs are? You have heard of the rabbit that turned and chased the dog? Well, that is what the guinea pig did to me. It became an incredible little monster of fury and strength. It actually disabled me, indeed it did. And then, within an hour, it died of old age."

Doc Savage entered the conversation to ask, "You are sure that the aging effect does not persist beyond the interval in which the drug affects the strength and agility of the taker? I have Monk's future welfare in mind."

"No danger."

Doc said, "You developed this stuff. We haven't time to listen to the exact details about how. How did it get in this mess?"

Western stopped being bombastic, or couldn't be. He was getting onto ground which scared him.

It was all the fault of Davis, Taft Davis. Western confessed that he always had known Taft Davis was no account, but he had underestimated the depth of the man's rascality. Davis had proven to be an unutterable villain. He had, in short, stolen the secret of Hercules' whisker-soup, and perverted it to ways of crime.

"And then I was a fool," Western admitted. They could tell that he was getting frightened as he went into this part of his story. "I was afraid I would be blamed. I pretended to know nothing about it. I pretended to you. I was afraid. That is the truth. I am ashamed."

"What else?" Renny asked.

"Taft Davis," said Western, "had to have a brain telling him what to do. Not his own brains. He didn't have that many. And I am sure now that it was that girl, Lee Mayland, who directed him."

"You have proof that Lee is behind it all?"

Western groaned. "Only my—my feeling—and the holes in her story. You noticed she didn't explain how she left my house? She didn't explain it satisfactorily. Didn't you notice how she avoided that?"

Renny said, "Her story, what she said, hung together fairly well."

"Yes, yes indeed. It was a story designed to keep her safe, and her brother safe, until her minions could use that—that horrible Hercules stuff—to rescue her."

Renny looked at Doc. "So that's why you wanted so many police around the hospital."

Doc was silent.

Western moaned, "I am ashamed of my part in this. So ashamed. I should have been more careful."

Ten minutes later, Doc Savage turned the car off the road. It bumped over a grader ditch, pushed through some bushes, and went down a hill dodging trees. It was completely hidden from the road, and in tree growth thick enough to hide it from just about everything else when it stopped.

"This it?" Ham asked.

Chapter XII
A BIT OF SMOKE

AGREEING, "This is it," Doc Savage swung out of the car and dragged out an equipment case. He began stuffing things in his pockets.

"Get what you'll need," he told Ham and Renny and Johnny.

Johnny was looking at his watch. "I'll be superamalgamated! Doc, we're not going to make it. It's train time already."

"The Bluebird may be running late," Doc said. "We might make it."

Then he knew they were going to be too late. He could hear the train coming out of the distance.

"Renny, stay with Western," Doc said. "Do what you can. No plan. Just do what you can—but use your heads."

Doc left them then, running through the woods. He ran with straining haste, listening to the train coming. It was coming fast, the way streamliners come at you, like airplanes.

He heard the train begin whistling. That meant the engineer had seen the attempt to flag him down. The excited continuing of the whistling told that.

Doc came to a car, a parked sedan. It was parked by the bush which had been shown in the colored slide in the old warehouse, when the robbery was being briefed.

There was no one in the car, and Doc swung to it, paused long enough to lift the back seat and chuck a small black-cased box under it. He put the seat back, then went on.

They were too late, all right.

The train had stopped by the time he came out on a bare ridge from which he could see what happened.

Not a shot was fired. No shots were needed.

Two men—thieves moving with speed which no men were supposed to have—leaped into the streamliner engine cab and threw engineer and oiler out bodily.

Others tore open the doors of express coaches. Evidently they didn't know which coach contained the bullion shipment, because they ripped open four.

When they found the right car, they signaled, and the others quickly converged on that one. There was evidently a fight with guards inside, but Doc was too far away to hear any of it but the screaming of one man.

The man who did the screaming, probably badly hurt, began yelling at the top of his voice screeches of awful agony which seemed certain to at least take the lining out of his throat, and kept it up. Each shriek—and he kept it up until the whole thing was over and they were out of earshot—seemed fully as loud as the cry which it succeeded.

Doc Savage looked on, astonished in spite of himself at the unbelievable speed of it. The whole affair was something like a motion picture with some of the characters in normal motion, and some of the others in the comic ultra-high speed sometimes used for a gag shot.

The men all gathered around the express car door, bouncing up and down in their excitement. Possibly they were bouncing because they were elated with their new strength. They were bouncing about a yard.

The gold began to fly out of the express car. Doc knew what gold bars that size weighed, and they were being handled as if they were confetti.

One man would catch the bars and pile them in the arms of another until the fellow had all he could carry. The burdened man would then dash off. Another would take his place.

Before they got all the gold, two or three were loading at once.

When they had three million dollars or four million dollars—whatever it was—in their arms, they all left the scene. Some of them staggered under their burdens in spite of the unearthly strength they had gotten from the Whisker of Hercules brew.

They went out of sight.

The porters and conductors were just beginning to step off the rear coaches to see what had stopped the train.

DOC SAVAGE wheeled and went back to intercept Ham and Johnny and Renny.

As he ran, he yelled loudly, "Get back to the car. Do not try to mix with them." He shouted it in Mayan.*

Swinging to the south, Doc avoided passing the empty car which he had found earlier. The machine, he could tell, wasn't empty now. The men burdened with their bullion had already reached it. He heard the motor start.

Renny came charging through the trees with Marvin Western. Then Ham and Johnny were there.

"See any of it?" Doc asked.

"Some. Holy cow!" Renny was discouraged. "We certainly got nowhere fast, didn't we?"

Doc said, "Come on. We will try to follow their car. They must plan to rendezvous somewhere."

---

*Mayan, as Doc Savage and his aides speak it, is the tongue of ancient Maya in his heyday, not the contaminated tongue which the natives of Central America speak to some extent today. No so-called civilized person speaks or understands the tongue, other then Doc and his assistants, as far as he knows. He learned the language in the course of the first great adventure in which he was associated with his men—published in *Doc Savage* [Volume #14] under the title *The Man of Bronze*. —AUTHOR.

Legging it back toward their car, Ham asked, "What about your yelling in Mayan for us to come back here? Won't they have heard that, and be suspicious?"

Doc got the motor started, trusting that the noise the other car was making would keep their own from being heard.

He suggested, "That stuff they drink causes some kind of mad speed-up. If you noticed Monk when he was under the influence, he did not seem to understand anything that was said to him. Presumably the voices sound so slow that it is hard to understand them."

Ham shook his head, baffled. "What a crazy thing!"

Doc said, guiding their car back to the road, "Such things are bound to fall on us now and then, with the amount of scientific knowledge we are accumulating. Usually they come slowly, as a result of years of scientific development about which everyone knows. But it just happens this one arrived suddenly."

Marvin Western groaned miserably where he sat in the back seat. "This doesn't seem sudden—not to me. I spent years on it, as I have told you. But my mistake was in not letting the world know what I was doing."

"Why didn't you?" Renny rumbled.

"Let the world know? Why, the world would have laughed at me."

Renny said he guessed Western was right, and hung to the car as Doc got up speed.

THE chase led only about five miles. It was not in a true sense a chase, for at no time did they see the car ahead, but they were in its dust some of the time. And then Doc took a precaution.

The bronze man got out and rode on the running-board, letting Ham drive. The running-board position put Doc's head higher than the car, and he had Ham drive very slowly as they topped each hill.

They came up a long ridge, and Doc said, "Stop!" and added, "They are down there. All together. A truck, too."

They scrambled out and put their heads over the ridge and watched the swag being changed from cars to the truck.

None of the thieves were moving very fast now, and some of them seemed to be getting sick.

Western said, "Small doses, such as they took, wear off very quickly. The stuff isn't nearly perfected, you know."

"It's perfect enough to get this mess stirred up," Renny told him sourly.

"Well, it is far from practical. I hadn't nearly finished my experiments with it."

Ham said, "Well, well, there goes the truck up a side road."

One car also went up the side road.

"I think that was Taft Davis and one man in the car that followed the truck. Am I right?" Ham asked.

"You are right," said Doc.

The other cars—three—remained at the crossroads. The men stumbled around, taking their seats. But the machines remained at a standstill. One man, still under the effects of the brew, stood looking at a car for a while, then jumped from a flat-footed stand, completely over the car.

"Showing off," Renny said.

Ham nodded. "Think what those guys, doped up that way, could have done to us back there at the train—if we had been suckers enough to close with them."

Doc was thoughtful. "We might as well go down now. They have slowed up enough for us to have a chance. And probably they are feeling pretty tough."

Western, blanching, wailed, "They'll kill us! The police—"

"Shut up," Renny told him. "And let's see you put that set of muscles you've got to some useful purpose when we get down there."

They climbed in their machine and drove over the hill. Western began shaking and got down on the floorboards.

Seven other automobiles—Renny pointed at them excitedly—had come into view, approaching from the north.

Doc's machine reached the three cars filled with crooks standing at the road intersection. The crooks, disturbed by the seven machines approaching from the other direction, did nothing at all about it. Probably because the other seven cars were filled with police—state police, sheriff's men, city police.

The police alighted with plenty of guns.

They included Doc Savage and his party under the general waving of gun muzzles.

Calvin Stout, the sheriff of Cedar County, pushed out his lips and whistled as he examined Doc Savage.

"So you finally turned into a crook," he said. "All right, you're under arrest. You started out in a big way, I must say."

Renny roared, "We're not one of that gang!"

"Now, now, let's save the fairy stories," Stout said.

Chapter XIII
Hill Flight

THE police force, with enough guns to take a Jap stronghold, got around Doc Savage and his three men in a way that meant business. Because at least a dozen of the guns pointing at them were cocked, Doc and the others did not resist when they were ordered to submit to being searched. Their pockets were relieved of a remarkable quantity of gadgets.

"Hey, they've got more mysterious-looking things in their pockets," a policeman called.

"Get them out of those bulletproof vests," said Cedar County Sheriff Calvin Stout.

Doc, letting them relieve him of his alloy mesh shirt, which would stop almost anything under a .50-caliber pellet, said, "We are innocent."

"Oh sure." Stout grinned skeptically.

Doc Savage blanketed his indignation with patience. "Do you want to hear our story?"

"Sure, sure, I'll bet it's a wonderful story," said Cedar County Sheriff Stout. "I'll bet it's a wonderful story, yes indeed!"

Ham said, "He believes us like we believe Hitler's solemn oaths."

The three carloads of crooks, getting the general idea of what was happening, became helpful.

Pointing at Doc Savage, they shouted accusations.

"It was all Savage's idea! He made us do it! He fooled us with drugs. He's got some mysterious kind of drug!" This was a fair sample of what they were all saying.

The police, pleased with themselves, went through the cars searching for the bullion from the train. When they didn't find it, their pleasure evaporated.

"Where's the yellow stuff?" Sheriff Stout asked Doc in a nasty tone.

"How did you police happen to show up here?" Doc countered.

"We got a telephone call to be here. A tip," said Stout.

"A call from who?"

"A friend."

"Somebody who didn't give his name?"

"Did you get the call personally?" Doc asked.

"Sure."

Doc Savage, imitating Taft Davis' voice with a fidelity to tone and speech mannerism that was hair-raising, said, "This is level stuff, Sheriff, and you had better get to this place at just the time I say." Then Doc asked, "That sound like the voice?"

Sheriff Stout gave Doc a pop-eyed look. "So that's going to be your alibi—that you made the tip-off call yourself?"

"Not being guilty, we do not need an alibi."

"Oh, sure. Apples have fleas."

The police were organizing the prisoners for a trip to jail.

A cop, looking into Doc's car said, "Here's some metal cases, but they're just full of some kind of gadgets."

"Don't waste time looking at the stuff now," Stout told him. "Time for that later. Load them aboard and let's go."

"Get in the car," Stout told Doc, Johnny, Ham and Renny.

Doc got in the front seat. Ham and Renny and Johnny climbed in the back, planting their feet on the equipment boxes.

They were—since a moment ago—as pleased as cats with paws in the goldfish bowl.

"They handed it to us," Renny said. But he said it in Mayan.

"On a silver platter," Ham agreed in English.

Sheriff Stout was getting in the front seat. "What's that you say?"

"In a silver frame," Ham said. "I was just saying we were framed."

"You said platter."

"Platter of what?" Ham sighed. "I hope we feed well in your jail. And the beds—brother, we haven't slept a wink in umpteen hours."

"Oh, go to blazes!" said Stout.

Ham found the catch on a metal case for which he had been fishing. He kicked it. The case began to hiss like a big snake.

Ham said, "Okay, watch us go."

THE lid jumped off the chest from the *whump!* of an explosion within, and from the pressure of an astonishing amount of smoke that was the color of the blackest of blacks.

When the smoke had filled the car and blinded the driver, Doc Savage reached across the driver and seized the wheel. There was a cliff on one side going down and one on the other side going up. Doc turned the car into the up-cliff.

The police automobile jarred its front wheels into a grader ditch and rooted against the cliff with a mild crash. The shock tangled everybody up inside, and they got busy undoing themselves.

Doc felt to make sure the doors had burst open. That was so the smoke would get out.

"Stay in here until the stuff spreads over the road and covers the other cars," he said.

"What equipment case do we take?" Renny asked.

"Better take seven. We may have to run for it, and more than one case would be too much to carry."

"I've got number seven," Renny said.

Using a voice almost inarticulate with anger, Sheriff Stout advised, "And I got a gun, and I got the intention of blowing holes if you fellows move."

They laughed at him, and got out of the car in the smoke. Stout swore, fired his gun and hit nothing.

Other guns now went off. There was some threatening yelling.

Sheriff Stout got excited and bellowed demands if the prisoners—the other prisoners, not Doc Savage and his aides—were escaping. It seemed they were not. The yelling and shooting was just for effect. Just to scare them back, one man put it.

Stout said profanely that they were not scaring anybody, and they were making fools of themselves.

Covered by all this, Doc Savage and his three men reached the end of the line of cars. They towed Western along.

Doc Savage used Sheriff Stout's voice and said, "Get out of the cars. Hold everybody against the cliff, out of the way if anybody tries to escape in a car. We don't want anyone run over."

The police and their prisoners in the car obediently unloaded. They couldn't see a thing in the smoke.

Doc and his men got in as they got out.

"Set?" Doc asked.

"Set," said his men.

They got going slowly backward, not leaving, but turning the car.

"What're you doing?" a policeman demanded.

"Turning the car across the road to block it," Doc said in Sheriff Stout's voice.

He turned the car clear around, and they took out, very slowly for the time they were in the smoke, then making all the speed the car would make.

A FEW bullets chased them after they were more than half a mile on their way. When these had missed them, Doc said, "Get a grenade out of the case, and we will try to block the road."

The case—number seven—was a sort of specialized setup which had been worked out by Monk Mayfair for what he termed occasions when they would need a lot of luck. The case contained among other things a radio direction-finder which could be converted into a weak but efficient radio transmitter-receiver—a tiny set that was, in fact, one of the most versatile pieces of apparatus Doc Savage, Monk Mayfair and Long Tom Roberts, the three mechanical scientists of the organization, had developed. Besides this, the case contained explosive grenades, smoke grenades, gas grenades. Not many of them, but enough. There were chemicals for specific purposes, such as quick destruction of metal such as a handcuff link or a prison cell bar. And odds and ends of useful nature.

While they were following the road around the face of a cliff, they came to a small bridge over a stream which foamed down the mountainside.

"Allah is good," Ham said, and put the grenade on the bridge after they had crossed.

The explosion threw parts of the bridge in the air, the noise jumping down the valley in a succession of boisterous echoes.

Renny rumbled, "Now we can have something like peace."

Marvin Western spoke for the first time. From the time the police had taken them prisoner, until now, he had behaved in a human fashion. He had looked as scared as the rest of them.

But now the athlete got organized with his chest-puffing again.

"It was a sad day when I got involved with you fellows," he said, sounding like an orator denouncing the demon rum from the platform.

"Goes for us, too," Renny told him.

Western said, "Now you have the police mad at us. What you did was idiotic, unnecessary, foolish, impulsive, dangerous and chaotic."

"Ultraindubitably," said Johnny.

"Eh?"

Renny told Western, "Holy cow! I didn't see you holding back none when we were escaping from the police."

"That," said Western, "is because I was accepting your judgment."

"Well, what you squawking about now?"

"I think your judgment was bad."

Renny and Ham and Johnny all looked at Western grimly, and Ham spoke for all of them, asking, "Have any of us embarrassed you with an opinion of what we think of *your* judgment—and behavior—in this business of Hercules' Whisker?"

When they reached the road intersection where the police had captured them, Doc Savage took the side road taken by the truck and the automobile containing Taft Davis.

"Get the radio finder going, Renny," Doc said.

Renny gaped at him. "What—what do I find with it?"

"One of our little radio transmitters which we developed to mark cars and planes and any other vehicles we wish to trail or locate with a direction-finder," Doc said.

"Holy cow!" said Renny. "I don't—"

Doc Savage told them about finding the car parked empty in the woods while they were trying to get a look at the train robbery, and told them of the pause he had made at the machine, and what he had put under the rear seat.

"I chucked one of our radio transmitters under the seat," he said. "We have a break. The car turned out to be the one which Davis took."

Marvin Western did too much wailing about their troubles as they traveled the winding mountain road.

"Running away made us look guilty. If the police catch us, we will be hung," he howled.

"No, no." Renny gave a realistic imitation of an electric spark popping. "They use an electric chair. Sounds like that."

Chapter XIV
Mountain Madness

THE night settled in the mountain valleys as black as darkness from a bat pit.

When the radio direction finder signal got louder in a way that indicated they were getting near the transmitter, Doc said, "Wait here," and walked a quarter of a mile through the forest and took a cross bearing, after which he came back to report, "They have stopped not far ahead. About a mile."

The night was silent with a stillness that would carry sound, so they decided to walk. Doc carried the equipment case.

Marvin Western kept mumbling about hanging and lifetimes in the penitentiary.

They tried to ignore him.

When they were still half a mile from their destination—whatever it was—Doc Savage called a halt with, "You fellows wait here while I go ahead and see what we are up against."

Renny followed Doc a few yards from the others. "Doc."

"Yes?"

"I've been thinking this over and we *are* in a tight corner," said Renny. "This Whisker of Hercules stuff is just wild enough to sound like something we would develop ourselves. And every now and then, over a period of time, there are rumors that we have turned crooks. Probably an enemy starts the talk, and other enemies do all they can to keep the ball rolling. Anyway, if they stand us up in court, we might have some trouble."

When Doc did not say anything, Renny went on, "With that three or four dollars—I mean, million dollars—that they got off the train, with that missing, nobody is going to be of a mind to listen to reason. Three or four million! Whew! That alone is about the size crime people would expect us to tackle if we went wrong. That won't be good, either."

"Any ideas?" Doc asked.

"No," Renny confessed. "I guess I just wanted to talk."

"Keep together."

"Sure."

Doc Savage moved off into the darkness. He wished they had brought along other equipment cases. In one of them was a scanner using so-called "black" light, or light invisible to the unaided eye because it was outside the visible spectrum, with

which it was possible to "see" with fair efficiency in pitch darkness.

As it was, the night was utterly dark, and Doc could not come much nearer seeing in the darkness than any other man. He felt his way along.

It was common sense to expect a lookout, if there was one, to be keeping a particular eye on the road, and possibly have a string stretched across it. So Doc left the road.

He found himself moving through underbrush that was thick and composed mostly of thorn blackberry bushes.

After he had collected all the bramble thorns his skin apparently would hold, a large dog jumped on him unexpectedly and sank its teeth into his leg.

The dog made quite a racket taking hold, and kept growling after he had hold.

Nearby a man shouted.

"Rover's got somebody!" the man yelled. "Get your guns and a light!"

MORE than one man, and lights, began running toward the spot, apparently from a house.

Doc began to squall and snarl and spit. His squalling, snarling and spitting was louder than the growling of the dog.

He felt for the dog's throat, got it, did some throttling until the dog's main idea became getting away. The animal became easier to hold.

With the tongue of his belt buckle, Doc made enough gouges and scratches on the man-eating dog to give the appearance that the animal had been in a fight with something pretty tough.

When he released the dog, it went away. It was not a courageous dog.

Doc took the opposite direction, found a tree, and climbed it.

The men found their dog. A voice—the yellow-haired man's voice—fell to cursing the dog for a so-and-so coward.

Another voice burst out laughing.

"What's so blamed funny?" demanded Taft Davis.

"Old Rover and his wildcat."

"Wildcat?"

"Didn't you hear the cat yowling and spitting? Sounded like an old tom. Boy, I bet Rover thought he had hold of something. Look at these scratches."

"You figure it was a wildcat?" said Taft Davis suspiciously.

Doc Savage, deciding they were fooled, and that the dog had all it wanted for the time being, got carefully down out of his tree. The ground was less thickly matted with underbrush—no blackberries now—and he was able to get to the house.

He was almost at the point of entering the front door when the odor of tobacco from the clothes of a heavy smoker warned him that a man was standing inside. He drew back.

Taft Davis and two other men returned.

"Old Rover tied into a wildcat," said the man who seemed to own the dog.

"Where's the dog now?"

"Left him with Nick, on lookout," Taft Davis said. "I guess the pooch will be all right after he gets over his scare."

"Damn a dog that scares that easy," said the man who had been waiting inside the door.

The dog owner asked indignantly, "Did you ever have hold of an old tom wildcat? Rover's a good dog."

"Oh, shut up about the dog." Taft Davis' temper was short.

After they were inside, Davis said, "Let's have a light," and another man shortly complained, "Where's the matches? Who's got a match?" Then there was a yellow glow from a kerosene lamp.

Doc Savage found himself standing outside a screened window. Inside there was a table, on the table two hats, a coat, a pack of cigarettes, and more than half a dozen of the phials containing the drug—if it was a drug—which everyone was calling the Whisker of Hercules.

Doc looked at the phials.

IN the house, they were fooling around with the gold. But the fooling had a purpose.

They had a table, three carpenter's planes and a canvas spread on the floor. They were industriously planing the edges of the gold bars, and catching the shavings on the canvas.

One man got busy sharpening a plane which had been dulled.

"This is a hell of a slow chiseling job," a man complained.

"Slow!" Taft Davis said. "We're planing about five hundred dollars a minute off these bars."

"Yeah, but as long as we're chiseling, why not just hide out a few of the bars."

"Sure, and have the boss catch us," Davis said contemptuously. "There will be a check on how many bars were taken. My brother will know the exact number, and when the cops get him, he is going to sing, and the boss will find out how many there were. If he don't find out that way, he'll find out another."

A man examined one of the bars which had been planed.

"Well," he said, "they look all right. You can't tell but what the planed edges are part of the way the bars were cast."

Davis chuckled. "Sure, there you are. We chisel fifty or a hundred thousand extra for ourselves, and nobody knows it."

"It's a dirty trick."

Davis straightened indignantly. "What's dirty about it? Didn't the boss think up that idea of double-crossing the others—of having the police pick them up so they couldn't get their split?"

"Why couldn't we do the same, turn him in?"

Taft Davis considered the suggestion seriously. "The way I see it, that wouldn't be profitable. This is only the first job. Just the beginning. And we haven't got the formula, so we don't know how to mix that stuff that speeds you up." He chuckled heartily. "But you've got an idea there. Later we might do something about it."

They fell silent, working the planes industriously, the gold chips curling off the soft, pure golden bars and rattling noisily as they fell on the canvas.

By that time Doc had the corner of the screen wire pried up.

He reached in and got the phials full of stuff that looked like red ink.

There was something at the corner of the house that could be a rain barrel. He investigated, finding it was a rain barrel.

After he emptied the little bottles and refilled them with water, there was enough red ink in his fountain pen—he had the habit of carrying two, one red, one black—to color the water satisfactorily.

Getting the phials back on the table was not much trouble.

RENNY RENWICK jumped a foot when Doc appeared beside him, and got his big hands around Doc's throat. "Oops, sorry," he muttered.

"There is one lookout and a scared dog," Doc said. "Three of them in the house. Apparently that is all."

"Four. That's one apiece." Renny sounded happy.

"You aren't counting me," Marvin Western whispered. "I want to help."

"All right," Doc agreed. "But there are half a dozen phials of that stuff on a table by the window. Do not let them get to it, or we may have more than we can take care of on our hands."

"I'll watch the phials." Western's voice was hoarse. "This horrible thing is all my fault. I'll see they don't get the stuff."

"Good," said Doc. "I will go ahead, because the dog is probably afraid of me now."

Renny said, "The dog will bark."

"Probably. We will have to do the best we can about that. You two follow about fifty feet behind me."

But the dog didn't bark.

The lookout was holding to the animal's collar saying, "Nice Rover, nice dog," and, "I ought to beat you to death, you cowardly whelp."

Doc landed on the lookout. He landed with a fist, which put the man on the ground.

The dog yowled and ran away before he could be caught.

Falling on the lookout, who was dazed, Doc hit him again, making him thoroughly unconscious. And Renny, Ham and Johnny arrived, excitement in their breathing.

"Doc!" Ham blurted. "That fool Western—"

From the house, a voice, Taft Davis' voice, bellowed, "What goes on out there now?"

Doc stood up. He imitated the lookout's voice as best he could, calling, "That blasted dog. I gave him a boot in the ribs."

"Why'd you do that?"

"Whelp bit me when I tried to find out how bad the wildcat clawed him."

The owner of the dog cursed and complained, "You got no right treating Rover that way."

But Taft Davis and the others were silent enough to indicate they had accepted the explanation of why the dog had howled and ran.

Ham whispered excitedly, "Doc—I was trying to tell you—Western made for the house. Broke away from us."

"What is the matter with him?"

"The fool has gone nuts. Said this thing was his fault, and said he wasn't going to see us get killed, maybe, because of something that was his doing. Said he was going in there and kill or be killed."

Shots came from the house. Five shots, the whole contents of one revolver.

"That's probably the end of Western," Ham said. They ran into the house.

Western was in a fight in a corner with the owner of the dog. The dog owner, a much smaller and weaker man, was doing a job on the athlete. He had his teeth fastened in Western's left ear, was choking Western with both hands, kicking him with both feet.

Two men—Taft Davis and the other—were dead on the floor. Davis had been shot twice in the forehead. But the last muscular convulsions of death were driving quite a bit of red fluid through three holes in the other man's chest.

Renny, Ham and Johnny got the dog-owner loose from Western and clubbed the man with their fists as long as he was conscious.

Western staggered to his feet.

"Now I can live with myself"—his voice was wild—"because I took all the risk of ending it."

Doc was looking at the five phials standing on the table. He said to Western, "So you shot two of them, and tackled the other bare-handed?"

"Yes, yes, I—"

"Where did you get the gun?"

"The gun? I grabbed it from one of them."

Doc Savage, in a voice so quiet that it meant he was very angry, said, "You mean you asked him for the gun, and he handed it to you, don't you?"

WESTERN, speaking rapidly, wildly, said, "Then when I got the gun, I—" He stopped, staring at Doc. The muscles started loosening on his face. "What did you say? I asked—"

"You did not come in here and grab any gun from anybody," Doc said grimly. "You walked in and asked for it, and it was handed to you."

"No, I—" Western's face had come completely to pieces. It was sagging everywhere. "What insane talk!"

Doc said wearily, "I made a mistake letting you tag along. I thought it would do no harm, because you were not armed. I only let you come along because I thought, at some time or another, you would do something that would show you were guilty. Proof was what we needed. You have been pretty smooth. We did not have any exact proof that you were the one."

Western began shaking. "You're mad!"

Renny rumbled, "So he's the plan maker!" as he pointed at Western. "It wasn't Lee Mayland after all!"

"It was Western," Doc said. "Lee Mayland is just what she said she was—a frightened, confused girl trying to save her brother. A brother who got into something and then became scared of it."

"Holy cow!"

"Watch him!" Doc warned. "He may have another gun—"

Marvin Western had the second gun up his right sleeve, and tried to get it by shaking it out of the sleeve. He hadn't practiced the trick enough. He had a little trouble catching the gun. Renny and Ham were on him with their fists, had him out on his feet, before he could accomplish anything.

Doc pointed at the phials on the table.

"There were six phials. Five there now," Doc said. "I filled them with water and red ink."

Johnny pried Marvin Western's mouth open with a revolver barrel.

"An ultracoquelicot embouchure," Johnny said.

"If you're trying to say he has an ink-stained mouth," Renny said, "you could have used smaller words."

THE next morning at the hospital, when they told Monk Mayfair the story, Monk was somewhat indignant.

"A fine thing, leaving me out at the end," Monk complained. "So you knew Western was behind it."

"Doc apparently did," Ham said. "We found

out later—after Western came to his senses and we threatened him with truth serum and he talked—that Western got crooked ideas right after he developed the stuff. Taft Davis was working with Western and Davis knew about the stuff. Davis got the gang together, but it was Western's idea. Western stayed in the background. Nobody—and this is surprising, considering everything—but Taft Davis actually knew Western was the main wheel."

"Then Western, right at the end, was trying to kill off Davis—"

"He did kill him."

"—so that Davis wouldn't give him, Western, away? That the plan?"

Ham nodded. "That was it. Western drank some of the ink-stained water, thinking it was the stuff, to turn himself into a superman and get rid of us, if it was necessary. Only that didn't work, of course."

"Everybody in jail?"

"Yes. Except the girl's brother, Charles Mayland. He's still in the hospital here, but will recover."

"What do you think they'll do to him?"

"Oh, turn him loose with a good scare and a lecture from the judge, probably."

"His sister will be glad to hear that."

"Uh-huh."

Monk frowned. "Where's Doc? He rushed in here early this morning, found out I was all right, and rushed right out again."

Ham grinned. "Doc has dashed off to our New York laboratory with samples of that speed-up stuff. It isn't practical in its present form—too rough on the guy who takes it. But Doc hopes he can develop a milder form, which our soldiers can use in this war."

"I had thought of that, too," Monk admitted.

Ham adjusted his hat. He brushed a bit of lint off his impeccable coat sleeve.

"Well, I think I'll drop around and see Miss Lee Mayland," Ham said.

Monk mumbled something violent. He reached under the covers and brought out a small phial filled with a reddish fluid.

Ham stared at the phial. "What's that?"

"A shot of the stuff I saved," said Monk ominously. "You leave the Mayland gal to me, see! Or I'll take a sip of this wow-juice and do what I've been threatening to do to you for years—take an arm and a leg off you!"

THE END

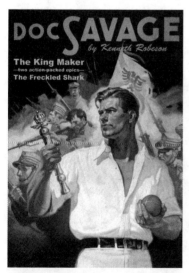

DOC SAVAGE in FOUR COLORS

by *Will Murray*

It was inevitable that the mighty Street & Smith publishing company would one day launch a line of comic books. Historically, S&S had been at the forefront of popular fiction—a giant in the pulp magazine field and in dime novels before that. Back at the turn of the century, the publishing house had issued reprints of the seminal newspaper strip, "The Yellow Kid," which many historians recognize as a prototype for the comic book.

When the modern comic book—a package virtually identical to the nickel weeklies S&S had ground out a generation before—began proliferating in the late 1930s, S&S had to respond in kind.

These colorful comic books—especially those featuring superheroes like Superman and Batman—were outselling its formidable pulps by gigantic margins. All while brazenly pilfering novels like *The Monsters, Partners of Peril* and many more.

Naturally, Street & Smith threw their mightiest heroes against these costumed interlopers. The Shadow's Walter B. Gibson had been lobbying his publishers to move into comics as early as 1937. But Street & Smith wasn't yet ready.

By the spring of 1940, they had no choice. With their pulps fast becoming buried under a flood of newsstand superheroes, S&S president Allan L. Grammer authorized a retaliatory strike. And The Shadow would lead the charge.

Already dominating radio, with a movie serial starring Victor Jory in theaters, he was a natural. And he had most of the standard superhero ingredients—a catchy name, a secret identity and a cape.

The first issue of *Shadow Comics* featured other Street & Smith heroes as well, chief among them Doc Savage. For that, S&S supplied an old Doc radio script written by Lester Dent. Artist Maurice Gutwirth executed the six-page story.

Doc and Monk are in Africa to head off a native revolt against the government of an unnamed nation and to capture the gunrunner who's been supplying the Africans, "knowing that the natives would be slaughtered by the government troops if they revolted," the scriptwriter assures us. For six pages, they rescue explorer Mary Fuller, sabotage the natives' rifles and fall into the gunrunner's trap.

Left to die in a flaming hut, Doc escapes his bonds through a variety of gadgets, including a flame-throwing belt buckle and a smoke bomb.

Art and story were crude, even by the standards of 1940. Gutwirth gave us a fair-skinned, blond Doc and a burly Monk Mayfair. In his torn shirt and riding boots, Doc did not cut the most impressive figure in four colors. And it was impossible to squeeze his colorful crew into the brief tale.

Still, the Man of Bronze was the company's second most popular hero. The following issue of *Shadow Comics* featured a compressed but atmospheric version of the 1939 Doc novel, *The Crimson Serpent,* wherein murderous conquistadors prowl the swamps of Louisiana. More reasonable editorial thinking soon decreed that an 80-page pulp novel needed more room to breathe than eight pages.

With the third issue, pioneering black artist Elmer C. Stoner began a three-part serialization of the second Doc novel *The Land of Terror,* titled "The Smoke of Eternity." It had everything. Kar the Destroyer, a masked mystery villain wielding a a death ray, and a lost land teeming with dinosaurs. Unfortunately, script and art remain dull, and Doc is almost indistinguishable from the apelike Monk in most panels.

Sales on the earliest issues of *Shadow Comics* exceeded expectations, so the first installment ended with a full-page illustration announcing that Doc had been promoted to his own comic, on sale April 16, 1940. With part two, Stoner's adaptation moved over to the first issue of *Doc Savage Comics.*

The move to his own title opened Doc up to longer adventures. Other adaptations followed. "The Polar Treasure," drawn by Jack Alderman, was one of Doc's most swashbuckling exploits. But it was cramped in the confines of eight pages.

"The Terror in the Navy" came in at a respectable 17 pages. The story was well-realized, and exciting. The script was much improved, as was the art.

This was the high point for Doc Savage adaptations. Had S&S continued in this vein, *Doc Savage Comics* might have amounted to something. But Doc Savage still lacked the flair of The Shadow, not to mention the stupendous sales of Superman.

Something had to be done.

Enter the unlikely duo of writer Carl Formes and artist Jack Binder. Formes was a retired opera singer who had somehow fallen from artistic grace to script crude comics. Binder was an artist-turned-entrepreneur whose assembly line "shop" produced the early S&S comics. The Doc Savage feature showed his distinctive style—although it's certain that every page featured contributions from a wide variety of assistants and inkers separately doing backgrounds, foregrounds and figures.

Someone at Street & Smith, possibly recognizing the derivative nature of the costumed superheroes, decided to transform the character they called the "greatest of all Supermen" into a superhero. This happened in a 16-page story entitled "Doc Savage and the Angry Ghost" published in the fifth issue of *Doc Savage Comics.* While the story bore the same title as an earlier Doc novel, it was no adaptation.

When Ellen Dare is kidnapped via submarine off Long Island, Doc, Monk (who is now bald!) and Ham Brooks investigate. They learn that Ellen's explorer grandfather once displeased the mythical Ghost of Thibar in China, and that the still angry ghost is seeking revenge. Through Chinatown contacts (whom they pummel into giving information), Doc and his men learn the whereabouts of the sub and Doc boards it mid-ocean. He's captured after a busy fight, but later escapes.

Leaving Monk and Ham behind, Doc flies to China in his personal plane *Lightning Bolt.* But a storm over the Himalayas forces him to crash-land. "Looks like curtains for the great and fearless Doc Savage," scriptwriter Formes observes.

Not really, for after passing out in a blizzard, Doc wakes up in the home of the "kindly Hermit of Thibar." The hermit tells Doc that the gods have indicated he is to undergo a test. Producing an open-faced hood with a square-cut ruby set in the forehead, the hermit proclaims: "Oh son, hearken to me! Only one absolutely fearless and just can wear the Sacred Hood and live. A lesser one dies. Dare you try the Sacred Hood?"

"I know no fear," Doc staunchly replies. "Nor have I ever wronged man or beast... Give me the hood." Doc dons the Sacred Ruby Hood and, with the Hermit's blessings, sallies forth to rescue Ellen from the Priest of the Ghost of Thibar, who has conveniently kept her alive while Doc convalesced. Doc comes upon the scene just as Ellen is about to have her throat slit. "Give me, oh ruby, the power to eliminate them." Like Samson, Doc rips into them, hurling priests about, dropping great weights onto them and bringing their temple crashing down.

In later stories, it is established that the Sacred Ruby gives Doc super-strength, invincibility, and the power to control people's minds—especially if they are evil. "No other mortal can wear the ruby hood and live," we are told. In addition to the blue hood, Doc wears blue pants and brown boots. His chest is bare. This will be his official "costume" for as long as he wears the Sacred Ruby.

In the next issue, Doc battles the Peace Clan—really Nazi Fifth Columnists attempting to keep the U.S. out of World War II. Imprisoned, Doc becomes The Invincible, saying "Grant me, oh Sacred Ruby, the strength to break out of this cell. And lead me to the fountainhead of this baneful, subversive movement, which hides its ugly serpent head under the wings of the dove of peace."

Thereafter, Doc bowls through scores of robed KKK-style-clad clansmen, and uproots a gigantic flaming sword from a mountaintop, hurling it down upon them. Superman couldn't have done it better.

Nazis and Japanese became Doc's chief comic book enemies—especially after Pearl Harbor. But he fought more traditional foes like the Beggar of Hate and the Black Knight.

One of the perils of relying on shops to produce comic features would seem to be a lack of continuity. Doc Savage never seemed to have a steady artist for very long. No sooner did Binder and Formes establish the strip's new direction than other hands became involved. A new scriptwriter named Edward Gruskin took over the writing in 1942. For a while, William A. Smith—later a *Saturday Evening Post* artist—handled the art chores.

Gruskin was also tapped to script a new *Doc Savage* radio series, which aired only in New York City for seven months, beginning in January 1943. This show was adapted from the comic book, not the pulp magazine. It was a horror series, patterned after *The Shadow,* in which Doc and Monk (played respectively by Bernard Lenrow and Earl George) battled hordes of mad scientists, monsters, and resurrected corpses. At every climax, Doc put on the Sacred Ruby, and exposed the seemingly supernatural for what it really was.

Gruskin adapted some of his radio scripts for the comic—or perhaps it was the other way around. It's difficult to be certain when they were both coming out at the same time. The radio show shared the same core cast, consisting of Doc, Monk, his gum-cracking secretary Myrtle Rose, and friendly Inspector Rankler of Homicide.

Gruskin also concocted a recurring villain for Doc to fight. He was the Skull, a criminal with a death's-head face, who first appeared in the November 1942 issue of *Doc Savage Comics.*

Monk and Ham are drawn into the murder of a cab driver whose sister, Myrtle Rose, is the bait in a trap for Doc. Responding to a message signed "The Skull," Doc goes to a cemetery at midnight and up from a fresh grave pops a skull-headed fiend. Doc recognizes his voice. It's his former assistant, Zashu Mittory, who had been horribly burned in a laboratory accident. Now, as The Skull, he's out to exterminate the entire population of the planet with a lethal gas called Formula X.

Of course Doc foils him, using a combination of brawn and the Sacred Ruby which, among other tricks, creates confusing multiple images of the Man of Bronze. The Skull soon returns—and even deeper and darker secrets are revealed in the May 1943 issue.

Street & Smith never told Doc's origin in *Doc Savage Comics,* so readers may not have known that Doc had been raised by scientists to be a superman. In "A Toast to Blood!" that background is briefly sketched in—but with revisions. According to this version, Doc's father tried his superman experiment on someone else at the same time as Doc. That

was Zashu Mittory, a childhood friend of Doc's.

After he became The Skull, he turned evil and joined forces with Hitler. Doc and the Skull battled it out over three consecutive issues. In "Death Traps of Hidden Valley," backed by his Nazi Blood Raiders, The Skull invades the Valley of the Vanished, bent on capturing Doc's Mayan gold. But Doc defeats this plan. An attempt to blow up the strategic Panama Canal is foiled in "The Skull Strikes." Presumed dead, he vanishes from the series for years—although a variation appeared in Gruskin's final *Doc Savage* radio script, "The Skull Man."

Doc made a couple of appearances in *Supersnipe Comics* around this time. In the January 1943 issue, Ed Gruskin's kid hero tangled with a Doc Savage impersonator—fake Sacred Ruby and all. In June, Doc himself met Supersnipe, "the boy with the most comic books in America."

The wartime paper shortage forced Street & Smith to cancel numerous pulps and comics. *Doc Savage Comics* was among the casualties. The final issue of *Doc Savage Comics,* dated October 1943, featured "The Pharaoh's Wisdom," adapted from radio. Doc was shoved to the back of the book, with Huckleberry Finn taking over the cover and lead spot. A final Ed Gruskin story, "The Glacier Peril," although drawn, was shelved.

Beginning with the January 1944 issue, the strip returned to *Shadow Comics* with another radio adaptation, "Murder Is a Business," illustrated by Charles Boland. Here, Doc utilizes a "helicopter car" capable of operating on roads and in the air. Although the Man of Bronze wears the Ruby Hood, he doesn't employ its powers once. By the next issue, the feature had been revamped. The Sacred Ruby is gone and Doc is now a scientist-detective in a business suit. The new artist is Alphonse Bare, whose art had the blandness of most of the Penn Art stable, which was the new producer of Street & Smith comics.

In the August 1944 issue, Monk pays a visit to the Street & Smith offices to "pulverize the artist that draws our stories! You'd think I looked like

an ape!" Cartoonist Al Bare assures Monk, "I'll make you better looking—but it'll be a lie!" In one of the first comic book stories to depict a member of the creative team, the cartoonist escorts Monk to the offices of *Pic* magazine where they interrupt burglars ransacking the office.

Bare had the honor of drawing the first and only Doc Savage/Shadow crossover story to appear during the Golden Age of Comics. The untitled story appeared in the October 1944 issue.

The story opens as The Shadow boards a plane. Doc, Monk and Ham are there to see him off. "I'll be back in two months—if I come back from Japan…" The Shadow explains. "Keep an eye on things in the meanwhile, Doc." They've obviously known one another for a while. After this, we see no more of The Shadow while Doc and the boys do battle with a criminal who possesses The Shadow's powers of invisibility, thanks to a bizarre black paint he developed.

Continuity wasn't a strong point in the Doc strip. In "The Man Who Wasn't There" (March 1945), the story of how Doc first met Ham is told (they were neighbors and Doc cleared Ham of a murder charge) and two issues later, in "The Touch of Death," the story of Doc's first meeting with Monk is related, in which Monk accidentally gets involved with criminals. The problem is that in the Ham story, Monk is already involved with Doc, and in the Monk story, Ham is present!

The stories in this period were short, about ten pages as a rule. They often hinged on obscure scientific facts, with Doc solving fairly minor mysteries via his arcane knowledge. Beyond one Mayan story, little of Doc's vast empire is ever mentioned. His Arctic Fortress of Solitude is never seen, but in "The Man Who Hated Miami!" a brief glimpse is given of his Crime College, here called his "Rehabilitation Clinic." But it's been relocated from upstate New York to the North Pole!

The writer experimented with some continued stories, such as the four-part 1946 sequence in which Doc battled an evil woman named Sinistari and the Elders of Evil, who are responsible for all the wars mankind has fought over the centuries. The action starts in an Aztec pyramid, jumps to Egypt, and winds up in Atlantis, where the Elders are planning to nuke all life on earth.

In the "Black Room Society" trilogy later that year, the series inexplicably leaps ahead to 1950. The U.S. runs on atomic energy, and Doc heads the Doc Savage Atomic Research Foundation and flies around in his personal rooftop-launched rocket ship.

"The Skull Returns" in part two, declaring, "It is five years since the war ended. Industrial utilization of atomic energy is now practicable. One person controls the secret.... Doc Savage!" As leader of the Black Room Society—a shadowy group that secretly funded Hitler—The Skull is after those secrets.

Bruce Elliott

During the battle that extends into the following issue's "Pursuit of The Skull," Doc again dons the Sacred Ruby Hood. No explanation is given for this, and he never employs its mystic powers. It's possible that this serial was scripted during the war and suppressed due to wartime censorship issues. It would not be the first time Street & Smith ran afoul of the War Department's sensitivity to mention of atomic weapons or power.*

In the end The Skull drowns in his mountain lair, his death engineered by Doc, who has no compunctions about killing in these adventures. Back in '42, Doc had vowed, "I will not stop until either I have killed him … or he has killed me." This time the Skull is gone for good. After that, Doc Savage had a brief hiatus from *Shadow Comics* and when he returns, the Sacred Ruby does not.

For the rest of the strip's life, the art is signed by various names— Charles Coll, Zangerle and Bob

Bob Powell

Powell, who was running a shop of his own. The scriptwriter during much of this period was Bruce Elliott, a magician who specialized in tricky little stories and later took over The Shadow's pulp novels.

A typical Powell/Elliott story is "The Puzzling Puzzle Box," in the December 1947 issue. It starts off in a violent rush and never lets up. Doc races to overtake a Chicago-bound bus before a bomb aboard it explodes. He drops onto the roof from

a plane piloted by Monk Mayfair and saves everyone in the nick of time. Flashback to Doc's discovery of a plot to blow up the bus to obtain a jewel shipment and a nest of Chinese boxes which are supposed to contain exact information—but prove to be empty. Doc, we learn, deduced that if the boxes were empty, they were meant to be. By piling the boxes atop each other, he makes a stepladder, which brings him within reach of a secret message in a chandelier. Make sense? Not really, but the Powell art carries the story nicely.

Bob Powell continued to draw the Doc strip to the bitter end. His pleasantly chunky art made the feature bearable. Toward the end, Elliott began recycling ideas. "Blind Flight," in the April 1949 issue, uses the same plot and gimmick (Doc is tricked into flying to a strange land by an ingenious if implausible television illusion) as well as the same title as a story first published in 1944. Powell did the art for the second version.

The final issue of *Shadow Comics,* August 1949, featured Doc and Ham in "Flying Serpent," an adventure in the land of the Incas which is noteworthy because it is the only time Monk Mayfair didn't take part in the comic adventure. A telegram asks him to come to the bedside of his sick uncle. So Ham goes in his stead. Since Doc's roots lie in pre-Columbian cultures, this was a fitting conclusion to the four-color adventures of the Man of Bronze. The story ends with Monk's discovery that the telegram was a fake. Ham finally got the best of him.

Street & Smith killed its entire pulp and comic book lines in 1949 to concentrate on its fashion magazines. So ended what could have been a great comic book house.

That it never was great, despite S&S owning such iconic characters as Doc Savage and The Shadow, was because the firm felt comics were beneath it. None of its regular editors wanted to handle the comic line, so they farmed the work out. In doing so, none of their features was handled with any of the thought and care that they put into their pulp fiction heroes. It's ironic, because the company had a tradition of creating great heroes which today are household names—heroes like Doc Savage, The Shadow, Nick Carter, Frank Merriwell and Buffalo Bill. Just imagine if the same creativity that went into those characters had been poured into Street & Smith's comics. •

---

*A 1942 atomic bomb story concocted by John W. Campbell and Walter Gibson for *Bill Barnes, America's Air Ace Comics* had resulted in a visit from G-men and a stern warning against publication of similar stories.